REDEMPTION

AN ASH PARK NOVEL

MEGHAN O'FLYNN

REDEMPTION

Copyright 2017

Distributed by Pygmalion Publishing, LLC

IBSN (paperback): 978-1-947748-00-2

For those who knocked me down.
Looks like I got back up, motherfuckers.

"You must be ready to burn yourself
in your own flame;
how could you rise anew if you have
not first become ashes?"

~*Friedrich Nietzsche,*
Thus Spoke Zarathustra

PROLOGUE

Focus, or she's dead.

Petrosky ground his teeth together, but it didn't stop the panic from swelling hot and frantic within him. After the arrest last week, this crime should have been fucking impossible.

He wished it were a copycat. He knew it wasn't.

Anger knotted his chest as he examined the corpse that lay in the middle of the cavernous living room. Dominic Harwick's intestines spilled onto the white marble floor as though someone had tried to run off with them. His eyes were wide, milky at the edges already, so it had been a while since someone gutted his sorry ass and turned him into a rag doll in a three-thousand-dollar suit.

That rich prick should have been able to protect her.

Petrosky looked at the couch: luxurious, empty, cold. Last week Hannah had sat on that couch, staring at him with wide green eyes that made her seem older than her twenty-three years. She had been happy like Julie had been before she was stolen from him. He pictured Hannah as she might have been at eight years old, skirt twirling, dark hair flying, face flushed with sun, like one of the photos of Julie he kept tucked in his wallet.

They all started so innocent, so pure, so...*vulnerable*.

The idea that Hannah was the catalyst in the deaths of eight others, the cornerstone of some serial killer's plan, had not occurred to him when they first met. But it had later. It did now.

Petrosky resisted the urge to kick the body and refocused on the couch. Crimson congealed along the white leather as if marking Hannah's departure.

He wondered if the blood was hers.

The click of a doorknob caught Petrosky's attention. He turned to see Bryant Graves, the lead FBI agent, entering the room from the garage door, followed by four other agents. Petrosky tried not to think about what might be in the garage. Instead, he watched the four men survey the living room from different angles, their movements practically choreographed.

"Damn, does everyone that girl knows get whacked?" one of the agents asked.

"Pretty much," said another.

A plain-clothed agent stooped to inspect a chunk of scalp on the floor. Whitish-blond hair waved, tentacle-like, from the dead skin, beckoning Petrosky to touch it.

"You know this guy?" one of Graves's cronies asked from the doorway.

"Dominic Harwick." Petrosky nearly spat out the bastard's name.

"No signs of forced entry, so one of them knew the killer," Graves said.

"*She* knew the killer," Petrosky said. "Obsession builds over time. This level of obsession indicates it was probably someone she knew well."

But who?

Petrosky turned back to the floor in front of him, where

words scrawled in blood had dried sickly brown in the morning light.

Ever drifting down the stream—
Lingering in the golden gleam—
Life, what is it but a dream?

Petrosky's gut clenched. He forced himself to look at Graves. "And, Han—" *Hannah.* Her name caught in his throat, sharp like a razor blade. "The girl?"

"There are bloody drag marks heading out to the back shower and a pile of bloody clothes," Graves said. "He must have cleaned her up before taking her. We've got the techs on it now, but they're working the perimeter first." Graves bent and used a pencil to lift the edge of the scalp, but it was suctioned to the floor with dried blood.

"Hair? That's new," said another voice. Petrosky didn't bother to find out who had spoken. He stared at the coppery stains on the floor, his muscles twitching with anticipation. Someone could be tearing her apart as the agents roped off the room. How long did she have? He wanted to run, to find her, but he had no idea where to look.

"Bag it," Graves said to the agent examining the scalp, then turned to Petrosky. "It's all been connected from the beginning. Either Hannah Montgomery was his target all along, or she's just another random victim. I think the fact that she isn't filleted on the floor like the others points to her being the goal, not an extra."

"He's got something special planned for her," Petrosky whispered. He hung his head, hoping it wasn't already too late.

If it was, it was all his fault.

1

FIVE YEARS LATER

"Come with us, Petrosky. It'll be a fresh start. For all of us."

He'd known this was coming; for weeks she'd been hinting about how nice it was in Atlanta, how great the weather was. But Shannon didn't really want his company. She probably thought that if she left, he'd finally have the guts to stick his gun in his mouth.

Not yet. Had Edward Petrosky believed in the afterlife, he would have killed himself a long time ago. Even now, the mere thought of a reunion with his daughter Julie made Petrosky's heart ache with such sudden ferocity that he would have splattered his brains all over the wall in an instant if he thought it would bring such a wish to fruition. As it was, the void of nothingness wasn't much better than his current situation. Here, there were at least cookies on the counter that Shannon had brought from home. Not that they really filled him up. And now, looking into Shannon's agitated eyes…he really wished she'd brought more cookies.

He squared his shoulders. "You don't need to do this just because your ex-husband is a fuckweasel."

Shannon shook her head. "I got a great offer in Atlanta."

She rocked back and forth to keep baby Henry from waking up.

"But if Roger wasn't here in Ash Park—"

"I'd still be leaving," she said, her voice as cool and measured as if she were giving closing arguments in a court case. "Everything reminds me of him, Petrosky. Every place I go. It's like being hit in the stomach over and over again. I thought it might get better with time, but…"

Petrosky gritted his teeth, determined not to let the sorrow in her eyes creep into his chest, where it would surely hurt worse than the hollowness that gutted him now. Shannon's big blond hippie of a husband had been Petrosky's partner, his friend, almost his son, or that's what it had started to feel like just before he was killed. It was six months since he'd discovered Morrison's body in a back alley, blood still wet on his lips. Six months since he'd lost his boy.

His boy.

Back and forth, Shannon rocked. Henry stirred, then stilled. "In Atlanta, we'll be with my niece. With Alex."

With Alex, her brother-in-law, but not with her brother. How could Atlanta feel any less empty than Ash Park? Here they'd literally burned Shannon's brother to ash after cancer took him. Ash Park was a sinkhole, sucking all the goodness out of the world and smothering it beneath metric tons of shit, but it was *their* sinkhole. And it would go from empty to utterly unbearable if she left. "You have friends here."

"Not the same." Shannon blew a blond curl out of her face. "You of all people should understand."

"You want me to move to Atlanta? What am I supposed to do in—"

"Work. Get a detective position. Retire for all I care—just come with us. Evie and Henry love their Papa Ed. And maybe with a change of scenery, you'll be able to get out of this"— she gestured to the room—"funk." She swallowed hard and appraised him, eyes narrowed in question, or maybe she was pissed at him again. She probably had a reason to be angry, not that he could recall why right now when he was still half-drunk, or he must be from the way her face was wavering in and out of focus.

"You criticizing my man cave?" He followed her fingers. The apartment was tiny, one room, with electrical wiring that, had he been a luckier man, would have caught fire and burned up the place with him in it. A toilet that only flushed half the time. Nothing sentimental or vaguely homey on display; even Morrison's laptop had been relegated to the closet because it hurt too much to look at. Some days the cobwebs were the only thing he could look upon with some semblance of affection—Julie'd hated it when he killed spiders.

"A cave has better amenities," Shannon said. "You don't even have a comforter." She nodded to his single mattress that lay on the floor next to the cardboard box he used as a nightstand. The box that held everything he had left of his daughter: a poster of her favorite music group, a Mason jar she'd used to catch fireflies, a few hair ties. Sometimes he pulled out Julie's night-light and thought about sticking it into the wall, but he was scared the faulty wiring might cause it to explode, shattering a piece of his heart along with the frosted rosy glass. And he had no pieces to spare.

"I'm fine here, Shannon." Or as fine as he'd ever be.

"I can't even bring Evie over for fear she'll hurt herself," she huffed. "This place is... I know it's only a few miles from the precinct, but Jesus, Petrosky."

The location mattered as much as IQ in a boy band member. He'd come here to die. Sold his house, all his shit —the cash was in an account waiting for Shannon and Henry and Evie. Waiting for him to finally be done with this life. Until then... He glanced at the tiny kitchen sink, the single, scarred cupboard, the brand-new coffeepot Shannon had given him that he just couldn't bring himself to use. Until he died, he'd suffer in this hellhole. He deserved that.

He deserved worse.

Morrison had died because Petrosky hadn't caught their suspect in time. He'd failed his boy, just like he'd failed his daughter a decade before. Ten years since Julie had been murdered, raped, and left in a field with her throat slit, and though he'd done his best to work the case, he'd hidden the pictures of her body behind the written case notes as if he could make it less real by avoiding images of her mutilated corpse. Nor had he been able to bring himself to read parts of the written file, sections about the brutality she'd endured while still alive. Yet Julie's last moments found their way into his nightmares, dreams where he was always a ghost, misty and powerless, forced to watch as someone yanked Julie from the walking path. He always woke up, gasping and slick with sweat, before he could bear witness to the rest. Petrosky had searched for her killer, even found other connected crimes, but every lead had died. No arrests. Eventually, he'd given up.

Some father he was.

"I belong here, Shannon," he said, his voice as low and tired as he felt. He belonged here because Julie was here. Everywhere he went brought a whisper of suffering, the old park calling "Daddy, Daddy" in Julie's voice so clearly he could almost believe he'd turn and see her there. Sometimes he'd be driving and suddenly find himself wandering through a field, and he'd realize he was searching for her, expecting her to suddenly spring from behind a tree, eyes wide and laughing. But he'd have no memory of pulling his car to the side of the road.

I've failed everyone I ever really loved. Petrosky inhaled deeply, suppressed a sneeze as the dust motes tickled the inside of his nose, and then blew the air out through his nostrils like an agitated crackhead. "I'm not going anywhere."

"I was afraid you'd say that." Shannon looked at her shoes, her index finger tugging at a loose string on the infant carrier as if she was trying to gather her thoughts. "Just think about it, okay? We love you. I just can't...stay. Not here, not where he..." When she looked back up at Petrosky, her eyes were brimming with tears. "I think you need a change of scenery as much as we do. I don't want you alone here, just thinking about him,"—she held up a hand when Petrosky balked—"and don't try to tell me you don't. You were the closest thing to a father he had. He loved you." She lowered her hand and swayed side to side as Henry stirred. "Listen, I'll get the house in Atlanta set up, and we'll have an extra bedroom. You can stay with us if you want to visit, or even for the long haul while you're looking for a job—"

"I don't need your pity."

"And you won't get it." But the look in her eyes said she pitied him all the same.

His phone rang, and he squinted around the room, trying to figure out where the sound was coming from. Just a standard ringtone, not "Hail to the Chief," the song Morrison had programmed into it for when Chief Carroll called from the station. And he'd never again hear Morrison's "Surfin' U.S.A." ringtone, though he sometimes imagined the jingle tinkling through the air late at night when the rest of the world was hushed and still. Sometimes he heard Morrison's laugh. Even his car still smelled like the coffee Morrison used to make every morning. Thank god Chief Carroll hadn't assigned him another partner—he'd probably punch the new asshole in the jaw for not offering him hippie shit like granola. And he hated granola.

The phone rang again...from near the window. Petrosky stepped around Shannon and headed for the windowsill behind the mattress. "Petrosky."

"Need you out here, Detective Beefcake." The voice was female, with a demanding edge that made the hairs on the back of Petrosky's neck stand up. "Shooting vic," the voice continued, "suspect on the loose. Gas station at Eleventh and Stone." In the background, tires squealed, and a male voice yelled something Petrosky couldn't discern.

Was the caller from dispatch? He peered at the screen but didn't recognize the number.

"Whoo, son, this shit is crazy. Gotta be a white boy."

"What the—" But the line had already gone dead, taking the voice and the squeal of traffic with it.

Petrosky stuck his phone in his jeans, wanting to slap the shit out of dispatch or whoever'd told that crazy woman to call him. Why weren't they doing their own jobs? But at least he had a reason to get away from Shannon's third degree.

And she was watching him, of course, with the measured wariness of an attorney appraising a guilty client. He wanted to tell himself that he was letting her go to save her the grief of having to deal with his broken promises, of which there would be many; Jack Daniels didn't help him to be very reliable. But he wasn't doing it for her. Even seeing her was a knife in his chest. He'd lost Shannon her husband, and she'd be far better off without him now, just as Morrison would have been. Just like Julie would have been—her mother would have taken her far away from Ash Park if he hadn't been there to hold them back.

And Julie'd be alive.

Shannon kissed Henry's hair, as blond as Morrison's, and the thought made Petrosky's heart ache behind the pacemaker tucked against his breastbone. "Well, if you decide you want to go, just bring your stuff when you come help me load up the moving truck."

"What makes you think I'm loading up the moving truck?"

Shannon stepped over to him and kissed his cheek, her lips soft but cold. "You promised Evie after you missed her dance recital last week. So you'd better be there." She headed for the door. "See you next Tuesday."

Petrosky watched her go, his face hard. There was no place he'd rather be than with Shannon and Evie and Henry next week, loading up the truck, watching them pull down the drive on their way to a new city, a new life. Shannon would assume it was because he loved them, and she wasn't wrong. But she didn't know it would probably be the last time he'd see them. Maybe once the car full of his family—his last lifeline—sped away in a spray of gravel, he'd finally have the guts to put himself out of his misery.

2

———

THE SUN WAS high in the eastern sky as Petrosky left the crumbling lot of his apartment building and headed north toward Stone. Summer was a bitch this year, like living in the devil's asshole, with air so muggy and thick it had a taste—damp grass and sulfur. Every ray of sunshine wanted to melt your skin off and leave your guts boiling on the sidewalk.

Another killing, another victim. Sweat beaded on Petrosky's brow, though it might have been his body trying to purge the Jack from his blood. He shoved another stick of gum in his mouth to hide the stench of liquor on his breath.

Why the hell was he being called out on a shooting anyway? Sex crimes didn't go after drive-by perps or even standard homicides. Maybe someone had stuck the gun up their buddy's ass and pulled the trigger. But more likely, they'd just shot a rape victim like she wouldn't have suffered enough.

He really hated people.

The Ash Park playground came up on his right, with the old bench where he used to sit and watch Julie play. Now it was cracked and graffitied with wooden splinters as big as his pinky that were just waiting to stab him if he got close enough.

Watch me, Daddy! And there she was, running across the grass, eyes alight with what he could only describe as the magic of youth, of knowing the world was safe and you were safe in it. Lies, all of it. A bird fluttered past him and landed on the now barren dirtscape, and Julie disappeared from his peripheral vision as quickly as she'd materialized.

He hadn't watched her closely enough—he should have tried harder. Not that she would have let him watch her that closely by the end; what fourteen-year-old would? But he was a cop, surely capable of protecting his own flesh and blood. The tattoo of Julie's face on his shoulder—half obliterated after a gunshot wound—burned like she was feverish with the urge to speak to him.

Petrosky shifted in his seat and forced his attention to the other side of the road, absentmindedly rubbing at the nodule in his chest, a scar from the pacemaker that was probably the only reason his heart was beating at all. Maybe he should rip it out this time...but that was too messy. Not as messy as life, or as sticking a pistol up your buddy's ass, or whatever was waiting for him at the gas station, but still. Turning the wheel hard to the left, he swung the car into a fast-food drive-through. God knows he'd tried to force the pacemaker to falter enough times—maybe a double fake-egg and not-really-cheese muffin would finally push it over the edge. Make it give up like the rest of him had.

His fingers were slick with grease when he pulled into the gas station at Eleventh and Stone. Four gas pumps, three with the numbers worn away, hulked at measured intervals in the center of the lot. Two other cop cars were parked haphazardly in front of the nearest pump, their flashing blue and red lights reflecting off the white gutters. A blue Escalade was tucked neatly between the white parking lines in front of the shattered window. *Feds?* Then why the hell was he there?

Petrosky parked around the side of the building in one of three spaces facing a dirty door marked with a unisex bathroom symbol. Dumpster to the right. No bullet holes on this side, no footprints apparent either, though he stepped carefully to avoid marring potential evidence before the forensic team arrived. Hopefully, they'd get Katrina. She was three thousand times more efficient than the rest of the techs combined, and she hated dealing with him enough to get the job done fast.

The sidewalk was fractured but not entirely broken—falling apart but present—and he followed it around to the front of the building where the window was blown out, but the door was intact. One neat bullet hole punctured the green and yellow striped awning. *Bad aim.* No tire marks out front, though they could be hidden beneath one of the officers' cars. *Asshole flatfoots.*

Petrosky raised his arm to grab the door handle when it suddenly launched toward him, and he stepped back to avoid getting nailed in the face. "Hey, watch where—"

"Out of the way." She was shorter than he was—five-three tops—with hair buzzed close to her scalp, and skin darker than the deep, determined gleam in her irises. She wore no jewelry except a badge on a cord around her neck like a necklace, and it was this she flashed him when he tried to stand in her way. She skirted him when he didn't budge, his arm still outstretched as if seeking the door, and then she was hightailing it around the side of the building without a backward glance.

Good riddance. He frowned at the now-empty walk then entered the building, scanning the rows of candy, chips, magazines. Nothing unusual there. Behind the chest-high counter, an officer in street blues stared at him, his face the same sickly green as the walls.

"If you're going to puke, you better get out of there," Petrosky said, heading around the counter to the rear of the store and snapping on latex gloves as he walked. Whatever he was after was back there, next to the guy ready to retch all over the Formica.

The officer straightened. "But Jackson told me to—"

"I don't care what anyone told you to do. If you hurl on my crime scene"—and it was his scene until he heard otherwise—"you're going to answer to me." *Jackson*. Who the hell was Jackson?

The officer backed off, his eyes on the floor as Petrosky came around the counter. They squeezed past one another in an awkward dance.

As soon as the guy got out of the way, Petrosky saw the victims. A woman—dark hair fanned around her head, her face against the linoleum. Entrance wound to the back of the skull. He didn't want to look at her face. No pants, underwear intact but yanked to the side, crimson staining one torn cotton panel by her upper thigh. Blood pooled around her head, still wet and shiny but already darkening at the edges. It hadn't been long since she'd died, but long enough—the killer was probably halfway to Toledo by now.

Another vic lay beside her, face up, his pants intact, the front of his "Gas-Co" collared shirt stained scarlet. On the wall behind the man's body, where the vic had probably collapsed after being hit, chunks of meaty gore clung wetly to the paint as if alive. His glassy eyes stared blankly at nothing, his mouth open like he'd been screaming for help when his body finally gave out. His fingers were tucked into the woman's palm as if they'd been holding hands, one final squeeze while blood poured from their broken bodies. Who said romance was dead?

"Rape, double homicide," the officer said from the other side of the counter-wall.

"Genius," Petrosky said. "Trained by Sherlock himself?"

"Um…well, I don't know, sir. But, uh…the perp maybe came in to rape the owner, but he didn't know her husband was around the side of the building, cleaning the bathrooms. When the husband showed up, the guy blew them both away."

Chatty bastard. "Thanks, Officer. Now do me a favor and go watch the lot."

"The lot?"

Petrosky stared at the bodies as though looking away might make them reanimate, bloody and dead and vengeful against the living. "Make sure the pavement doesn't run away," he said, eyes on the mess.

The officer snorted, his footsteps pausing at the door, but then Petrosky heard the jingle of the front bell.

He was alone—alone with death.

At least the dead were quiet.

He knelt at the edge of the cooling pool of gore and examined a smudge on the tile near the feet of the corpses. Not mud, probably oil, but forensics would be more conclusive. He peered at the woman's ruined underwear. No fluids visible—just the smear of blood, probably hers. But maybe they'd get something from the medical examiner.

The walls and cubbies beneath the register were speckled with a fine red mist. The register itself was still closed. The killer might have slammed it shut after cleaning it out, but Petrosky doubted it: a small hand-held safe sat just below the register, in plain sight. A gun? Cash? If robbery was the objective, the killer would have taken the safe to be sure, along with whatever was in the register.

The front door bell jangled, and Petrosky's back tensed. The incompetent street cop was back. "I told you to—"

"You didn't tell me anything." Not the officer. Brian Thompson, the Ash Park medical examiner, started around the counter, his watery gray eyes fixed on the bodies at

Petrosky's feet. Thompson wasn't a friend by any stretch, but he sure as shit commanded respect—and got it. If nothing else, the guy was thorough.

Thompson pursed his thin lips. The gray in his brown hair caught the purple neon from a cigarette sign above the counter, turning his temple into a bruise. "Double homicide and rape, huh? Guess I could have waited for this one at the office."

Petrosky stood slowly, bracing one gloved hand against the countertop to hoist his own fat ass. He grunted anyway, moderately relieved that Officer Pukes-a-lot wasn't there to hear it, but annoyed that Thompson was. "Why didn't you wait at the office?" he snapped.

"Chief called me. Said you were out here and that I should head over before you got your panties in a twist." His barely concealed scowl said he appreciated the errand as much as if someone had shit in his cereal.

Chief Carroll knew Petrosky liked Thompson more than he liked most people, always had. Maybe she already knew about the feds at the scene and didn't want Petrosky more on edge—he wasn't above telling them all to fuck off. Or maybe she was tired of fielding complaints about him from Dr. Woolverton, the other on-call ME. Petrosky'd worked with the man for ten years, and to this day, Woolverton's mere presence made Petrosky unreasonably pissed. *Snitches get stitches, my ass.* Maybe he'd move to Atlanta after all.

Petrosky left Thompson with the bodies and headed outside to make sure the woman who'd tried to smash him with the door wasn't screwing shit up. She was probably out checking the bathroom, but she wasn't going to find anything there—not like the perp would wash his hands before he took off when anyone might drive by and bust him.

But she wasn't on the walk out front, and the only things around the side of the building were his Caprice and a huge blue dumpster. The bathroom—*might as well make sure*—was empty and scuffed, rank with some bleach-y cleaning fluid that made his eyes water. He'd turned to head to the front of the building again when a scratching sound from inside the dumpster made him jerk back around, hand on his gun.

"Whoa there, slick." She leapt like a gymnast from the top of the dumpster to the walk, her teeth bright white as she held up one gloved hand, pinching a plastic bag between two latexed fingers. Inside the bag—a used condom.

"Were you in the dumpster?" Why was he asking that? He knew she'd been in the dumpster; he'd just seen her escape from it.

She cocked her head. "Damn right, smarty pants. Sometimes criminals are dumb as rocks, and that's good for us—guess he decided not to stick this nastiness in his pocket like a pack of chewing gum."

Like he didn't know about idiot criminals, he'd been a detective when she was just a twinkle in her father's eye. "I just meant we could have waited for the crime techs."

She lowered her hand and started up the walk toward him. Petrosky repressed the impulse to block her way and demand she tell him who she was. Instead, he fell into step beside her as she headed back around the building to the front lot.

"It's not even dry," she said, grimacing at the bag and its contents. "If he's in the system, we've got him."

"It'll take a few days." Lately, everyone down in the forensics department seemed hell-bent on giving Petrosky shit. *Bastards.* It was like they were purposefully trying to push him over the edge—and he didn't need much encouragement.

"I got someone down there who owes me a favor. He'll do it fast, too, unless he wants to risk me telling everyone about his tiny pecker." She shrugged. "Or maybe he'll do it because

I'll ask nicely. Unlike you." Her eyes remained steadfastly on the walk ahead as they turned the corner, and for some reason, her refusal to meet his gaze pissed him off more than her words.

She'd probably been talking to Valentine or Decantor, Morrison's annoying buddies at the Ash Park precinct. He was opening his mouth to ask which of them he needed to punch in the dick when she yelled: "Hands off the car!"

One of the flatfoots jerked his palm off the Escalade's hood and retreated, hands in the air—an "Okay, my bad" gesture. *Fucking twat.*

Petrosky nodded to the car. "That's your ride?"

"I can drive whatever I want, you old sonofabitch."

She was the one with the feds. This had to be Jackson.

"And I know about you," she continued, "so don't try anything funny."

She didn't know him. She didn't know anything about him. "Funny? What—"

"I know, I know. You've got no sense of humor. But let me assure you, I do, so if you can't smile, you're gonna be scowling half the day at least." Her eyes narrowed. "Kinda like you are now." She snorted like his attitude was the least important thing in her life, and maybe it was, but this woman and her smug face were already giving him a goddamn headache.

Her gaze darkened as a shriek came from inside the building.

They both ran for the door, but she was faster, flinging it open and rushing for the counter before he was even over the threshold. He found her standing beside Thompson, the man gloveless now, his arms around a slight woman—no, a girl—in a collared uniform shirt who was sobbing into Thompson's shoulder. That would have been Morrison's role if he hadn't died. The kid had been such a softie. Petrosky rubbed at the pacemaker scar on his chest and listened to the medical examiner murmuring into the girl's hair in his calm, measured tone, but that wasn't going to fix this. A mere voice couldn't bring anyone down from the horror of seeing a couple of bloody corpses.

Jackson turned on Petrosky. "Where's Officer Elliot?" she hissed.

"I sent him—"

"Need some help in here!" Jackson called outside, and the officer, now less green and more worried, entered with some other burly bastard at his heels.

"Take her to the station," Jackson said.

The sobbing girl raised her eyes, and Thompson released his grip on her and stepped back. "I'm so sorry for your loss," he said. "We'll find who did this."

After one final squeeze of the shoulder from the ME, the girl let the pukey cop and his buddy lead her to their squad car.

Thompson stared after them, his mouth drawn, his eyes tight. "Excuse me," he said quietly and headed out the back door. For a fleeting moment, Petrosky saw Morrison standing outside the doorway, eyes tight with sorrow. The air thinned. He turned away as the door clicked closed behind Thompson.

Out front, the squad car doors slammed, and Jackson made the sign of the cross. Petrosky wondered again why the hell they'd sent the feds, though he didn't have time to dwell on it because she was glaring at him. "That's the daughter," she said. "They live a few miles up, and she always walks here through the field behind the store. Comes in through the back."

"How do you—"

"Officer Elliot gets gas here every morning before his shift." She turned toward the lot. "Techs will be here in a minute. Might as well follow the daughter down to the station."

"You're coming down to Ash Park?" She sure as hell wasn't from any local station. He looked again at her car. "Why is this a federal case?"

"I'm not with the feds, you idiot." She rolled her eyes and started for the Escalade. "I'm your new partner."

3

───────

"Jackson's a lunatic."

Chief Carroll's suit jacket rustled as she crossed her arms, but the twinkle in her deep, dark eyes suggested she was way more amused than he appreciated. "More of a lunatic than you are?"

"She's impossible to work with."

"She just ran down a rapist and a killer in three hours. Her solve rate is nearly twice that of anyone in the department—we would have been stupid not to hire her. "Plus," she said, dropping her arms and leaning toward him over her desk, "you need a new partner." Her black braid slipped to the desktop like a snake slinking from a tree, ready to strike. And he'd rather drop dead of a snakebite than work with Jackson.

"I don't need a new partner."

"You've got one anyway. It's been six months. Valentine and his partner are kicking ass, Decantor's taking names, and you're doing okay, but—"

"I'm doing more than okay. I solved three in the last month, two that got passed over from homicide when they realized they were dealing with sexual predators."

"Really? I haven't seen paperwork. It's almost like they didn't happen at all." Her wry tone made the muscles in his neck go rigid.

"Donuts in the conference room always helped me concentrate. You should bring that back." When Carroll crossed her arms again and glared, Petrosky sat back in the chair, grinding his teeth together so hard his jaw ached. "I'll get the damn paperwork done. But I don't need a partner following me around, bullshitting me."

"You want Morrison back. You can't have him. You want to be alone, grieving, whatever. But I read your return evaluation from Dr. McCallum."

Petrosky had read it too. The department shrink had said he was stable enough to return to duty but had recommended Petrosky be paired with someone who was familiar with grief. In private, McCallum had also said he hoped Petrosky'd be paired with someone who knew about alcohol abuse and would be "well-suited to intervene if it became necessary." Petrosky had taken that to mean McCallum wanted him stuck with a narc.

Apparently, the bastard had gotten his wish. "I don't need a babysitter."

"She isn't a babysitter. She's a detective and a damn good one. Which you should have realized after today."

"I was at the scene too."

"And what did you do besides send an officer to the street, depress the hell out of Thompson, and unnecessarily traumatize an eighteen-year-old girl?"

I knew it. She tattled on me like a four-year-old.

Carroll's eyes grew serious, and he realized he'd spoken aloud. "You're in trouble, Petrosky. I don't know if you're depressed, disenchanted, what, but you were on a downward spiral even before you lost your partner. And last year, you were called up twice for using excessive force."

One claim was erroneous—some privileged little Mitt-

Romney-looking prick who'd raped his girlfriend had accidentally tripped over Petrosky's foot. So maybe Petrosky had *accidentally* let his arm go, then *accidentally* watched the bastard fall to the pavement with his hands cuffed behind him. *Oops.* The other was a coke dealer who spent his time prostituting little girls. He'd had information about Morrison's killer, and Petrosky had beaten the ever-loving shit out of him until he coughed up those details—and maybe a little blood. Petrosky wasn't sorry then, and he wasn't sorry now.

"That's been taken care of." He chewed his gum more aggressively, the sound making his skin crawl as it smacked against his eardrums. Hopefully it was annoying Carroll too.

"You can't slap people around for doing things you don't like. You're one step from being fired for good."

So fire me. The bloody floor from that morning smeared itself across his brain—he could still see the victims' hands, clasped in the sticky pool. They'd refused to give up hope... but there was no hope for them. He clenched his jaw again to keep from saying that one out loud.

"I know it's been hard for you since—"

He held up a hand before she could say it. *Morrison.* Even thinking the words burned like it had happened yesterday. *Time heals all wounds? Bullshit.* Julie's death only seemed to hurt more as the years went by; ten years later, the agony of grief was still so vibrant it made the rest of the world fade.

Carroll sat back, her face solemn. "Listen, just get your reports to me this week. All of them. Show me you're okay." She raised a brow, and he nodded. A smirk played at the corner of her mouth. "And have fun with your new partner."

<hr>

DECANTOR'S chatty ass was already at Jackson's desk—*Morrison's desk*—grinning at her in that idiotic way he used to do with Morrison. Probably telling her some lame joke or discussing the Kardashians or maybe J-Lo's newest hit. *Asshole.* When the desk had been empty, Petrosky'd still seen Morrison there some days, and it had ripped his guts out every time. But he'd never felt Morrison's presence when someone else was sitting there instead. It was as if Morrison had no choice but to take a back seat to the living.

Decantor laughed, his teeth a slash of white in his mahogany face, and Petrosky's fists clenched. Decantor had been there the day Petrosky'd found Morrison's body. He could still see the defensive wounds, the gashes across Morrison's chest and forearms, the skin split to the white bone beneath. The crimson on his gaping mouth—and the glassy stare of his unseeing eyes. If Decantor hadn't been there to knock the gun from his hand, Petrosky would have blasted the back of his own skull all over that alley.

Decantor was a bastard—he'd had no right to interfere. When Petrosky finally managed to die, he was going to haunt Decantor's sorry ass out of spite.

Petrosky slumped into his chair, trying to ignore the chatter by glaring at the stack of files on his desk. Did he really want this job? He could do the reports to avoid Carroll's mouth…or he could just walk out, go to Atlanta, keep screwing up Shannon's life. He sat motionless, hand poised over the keyboard as if he was waiting for someone else to make the decision for him.

He was pathetic.

Petrosky was reaching for the first file when Jackson showed up at the side of his desk, a fast-food sack in her hand. Maybe she was there to make nice. Already the air was filled with salt and grilled almost-meat. Petrosky's mouth watered. Sausage sandwich? Hash browns? Maybe even those breakfast burritos with cheese and—

"Your boy just told me to steer clear of some flatfoot named Mitch, who hits on new hires." She pulled up a chair and sat across from him, plopping the sack on the desk.

"Then he asked if I knew some other jerk who works upstairs, who's out with the flu. I thought he had a card to sign, maybe, but...nope."

She dumped the bag. One burger, which she unwrapped, every crinkle of the paper sending greasy deliciousness wafting toward his nostrils. "So, what's shakin', bacon?" she asked, taking a huge bite of the sandwich.

Petrosky frowned. What was with the stupid nickname? "I should ask you the same thing, the way you're getting all buddy-buddy with Decantor." *Stupid motherfucking Decantor.*

"I've got no time for that boy's nonsense. I'm getting mine."

Getting your...what? What the hell was she babbling about? "You go thank your buddy in forensics yet?" He scowled at her and then at the last bit of her meal.

She saw him looking, met his gaze, and popped the bite into her mouth. Chewed slowly. "Nothing from forensics. Finished up with your friend Thompson, though—one of the best medical examiners I've ever worked with." She wiped her lips on a napkin. "Forensics said they're backed up. Should be ready later on."

"You said someone in forensics owed you over their tiny—"

"I was kidding." She crumpled the bag and tossed it into the can beneath his desk, where he'd have to smell the salty, fatty goodness for the next four hours. No burger for him. She was probably torturing him on purpose.

"Your funny bone must be broken." She shook her head. "You'll have to fix that if we're going to work together."

His funny bone wasn't broken; he couldn't remember ever having a funny bone at all. And he had no intention of working with her. But if she didn't have time for chatty Decantor either, or tiny-peckered forensics dudes... Nah, she was still a jerk. He pushed the thought away.

She gestured to his desk. "Get the forms done?"

"What forms?"

"On the bust earlier," she said. "I offered Decantor five-to-one odds you hadn't done it yet, but he refused—apparently he knows you. Bummer—I'd have gotten us both breakfast with that." She winked. "Anyway, I did my half, but we need to have them turned in in a few hours."

Petrosky reached for the top folder on the desk and flipped it open. Sure enough, Jackson's neat, square print lined the first half of the page—only the first half. Morrison would have gotten it done. "What if you just finish it since you're such a good writer?"

"Forgive me if I don't jump on that after spending my morning dumpster diving. Maybe next time, you can get knee-deep in trash and then complete all the paperwork on it." She shoved her chair back. "I got the evidence that brought the perp in, you finish writing it up. Fair is fair."

"I—"

"You want someone else to do your work, you've got the wrong woman. I'm too old for that shit."

He studied her unlined face. She couldn't be a day over thirty-five, and he highly doubted she'd ever been the age to take anyone's nonsense. "You're too old for this shit?" Petrosky muttered. "What are we, a goddamn *Lethal Weapon* movie?"

Jackson cut her eyes at him. "I wish. But you ain't no Mel Gibson. Not that I'd screw that bigot anyway." She smiled. "Anyway, I hear he has a tiny penis."

SEVEN DAYS PASSED, every one of them shittier than the one before. Jackson was unflappable when going after perps—serious as a heroin addict coming off their high. The rest of the time she'd spent harassing the shit out of Petrosky with her stupid food. If you don't want to share, eat it in the car and don't make everyone else smell it. Every selfish gesture had reminded him he'd never again have a partner like Morrison. The kid had always brought him something, even if it was hippie shit.

Their second day together, they were called out to track down a seventeen-year-old boy who had attacked a classmate during *drama* camp, as if teens needed more drama in their lives. Jackson pursed her lips when he called the kid a "fucking jackoff," but Petrosky was only disappointed he couldn't ram his foot into the kid's balls. On the way back to the precinct, Jackson bought herself a sack of muffins from some bakery and then ate a fat blueberry one at his desk, giving him a sly look like she knew something he didn't. It made him want to stick a fork in his temple.

Day three, she ate two bagels—one for breakfast, one for lunch, none for him—while his fingers cramped from completing his half of the mountain of paperwork. That day, they caught a child molester and drove the guy back to the precinct, Jackson's presence pushing all ghosts from the car —and the smell of Morrison's coffee. This time, Jackson said nothing when he called the DA a dickhead—*two years for rape?*—but she probably told Carroll about it. Jackson left at four o'clock that day, not a word about where she was going. Not. One. Word.

Days four and five were more of the same. On day six, the slightly smaller stack of files was little consolation when she brought two paper bags to his desk. The one she passed him contained a rape kit. The one in front of her held a bear claw which she ate in front of him, unceremoniously licking sugar from her fingers like an asshole while his stomach grumbled. Jackson somewhat redeemed herself that evening when some idiot was caught flashing people at the park, pretending his dick was avant-garde art. When she told the guy her cuffs carried a lot more weight than his childlike willy, it'd almost made Petrosky not hate her so much.

But this morning was shaping up to be exceptionally shitty. His wrist was already sore though he hadn't even picked up a pen. If he thought Shannon wouldn't find out, he'd tell the whole lot of them to kiss his huge, pasty ass, maybe even show them a full moon on the way out. But then he'd have to come up with a reason to stay in Ash Park when he had literally nothing left. He wasn't ready for that. He didn't want to explain to Shannon that he was trying to screw up his courage to take that final step into oblivion.

"For you." A paper bag dropped in front of him with a *thunk*.

"What's this?" Petrosky eyed the bag warily.

Jackson pulled a chair up to his desk. "Breakfast. What does it look like?"

"For me?"

She shrugged. "They were buy one, get one free. But hey, if you don't want it—" She reached for the bag, but he snatched it from the desktop before she could take it away.

"I'll eat it, I guess," he muttered, peeking inside. "What is it?"

"Like you care. You'd eat the sack itself if they salted it right."

Petrosky put his hand on his belly—bigger now than a year ago. If she wanted to give him shit about his gut, he was going to give her shit about her annoyingly fast metabolism, though that might not actually be an insult. Either way, if she kept bringing him food, he'd probably keep his mouth shut. "What are you trying to say?"

"It ain't my job to keep you healthy." She smiled. "I'll get a few weeks paid time off if you kick it, partner."

He opened the package—sausage muffin—and took a bite. *Eat this, Boss, it'll make you feel better.* He could almost pretend it was one of Morrison's granola bars, but the moment passed as the smell of salt and oil invaded his sinuses, and peppery meat slid from his tongue down his gullet. His stomach clenched, then accepted the grease. Morrison would never have brought him something so unwholesome—or so delicious.

He glanced at Jackson, whose gaze flicked to his shirt and away. He shoved the last bite in his mouth and looked down, expecting to see a grease stain. Nothing but his hand. He hadn't realized he was rubbing that sore spot on his chest, but now he felt the ache there, not just from the old, healed stitches, but from deep inside his heart—the kind of pain that would never heal.

He was getting ready to ask Jackson what she was leering at when she stood abruptly, whipped her phone from her pocket, and stalked toward the stairs with her phone to her ear. Probably Chief Carroll calling her. Maybe today was the day for his report card, and Carroll'd finally fire him. He'd have to get creative with his excuses about Atlanta. Fear of spiders? Hatred of peaches? From the side, the Georgia state fruit *did* look like an ass.

His own phone rang as Jackson disappeared down the stairs. Petrosky pulled out his cell, expecting to see a number from the precinct, maybe even the chief; though the phone wasn't playing her special jingle, Carroll had been known to call him from another line just to get him to pick up. But it wasn't her. It was Shannon like she'd read his mind.

"I was just thinking about you," he said.

"Thinking you'd like to pack up that crappy apartment and come with us instead?" Her voice had the lilt of teasing, but she wasn't joking. He knew her better than that.

"I was thinking we might want to hire another guy or two. To help us pack."

"I've got Decantor and Valentine coming."

"Oh." She really didn't need him at all. And the thought of dealing with Decantor outside the office made him want to punch someone in the nose. No, not just someone—Decantor. He had a stupid nose anyway. And suddenly he heard Morrison's laugh behind him, a low, hearty chuckle, the sound of it sending an icy shiver sliding up his back and into the roots of his hair. He whipped around so fast he almost dropped the phone. But his old partner's chair was empty.

"Just wanted to make sure you were going to be here tomorrow because I have something for you. Nine o'clock."

Petrosky cleared his throat, the ice in his veins liquefying again. The door to the stairwell shrieked like an angry bird, and then Jackson was back in the bullpen, phone still pressed against her head, her eyes drawn, mouth tight. Her suit jacket was wet. Must be raining. *What the hell is her deal?*

"Petrosky?" Shannon said.

Petrosky swiveled in his chair, leaving Jackson and her worried gaze at his back. "I'll be there."

"See you tomorrow."

Tomorrow. One more day visiting anytime he wanted, though he'd visited a whole seven times in the past year. He'd failed Shannon and the kids before they'd even left. But he'd fail them if he went, too.

Jackson rushed past him to her desk, shoving the phone into her pocket, her eyes hollow and tight. He wondered who she was failing.

$$4$$

THE EVENING WAS thick with the sultry aroma of sweat and grass, the raucousness of children, the dog panting at his side. The killer turned his face toward the sun, the light from the red orb weakening as twilight approached, so low and red near the horizon that it might have been a welling drop of blood. He squinted, and the drop smeared—he could almost hear it, a wet squelch, over the keening of a lone dove. At his heel, the dog whined. He reached into his pants pocket and fiddled with his lighter, wishing he could light a cigarette, but respectable people didn't do that, not at a kids' soccer game, and that's what they all thought he was: respectable. Even funny.

Flick. Flick. Flick.

"Long time no see!" The sun disappeared completely as another man blocked his view: a behemoth as tall and broad and sturdy as a bear. Hairy too, and with a snaggletooth that made him seem more animal than human.

The killer dropped the lighter and put his hand out, as expected, watching his fingers disappear into the bear's grasp. The tendons in his fingers ached, not that this was anything new. Age came for everyone eventually.

Not everyone.

"Evening, Jay."

"Always so formal." Jay laughed in a way that sounded as if it could shake his belly, but Jay had less fat than a filet mignon and more muscle than an entire bull. "Enjoying the game? The girls are looking good out there. Gotta love soccer."

"Sock her? I just met her!"

Jay chuckled and clapped him on the shoulder. "Ultimate dad joke. You're the master."

He smiled, as was expected of him.

When Jay finally sauntered off, the sun was lower than it had been just moments ago but still bright, the brilliant red drip congealing to the deep purple and blue of pulsing veins, and then to a lifeless black at the corners of the horizon. He flicked the lighter again, relishing the coolness of the metal against the heat of his hand. The lighter was death itself, bringing forth a raging inferno that would engulf his quarry in flames. But when the smoke cleared, he always felt cold, like the metal of the lighter. Hot to cold—it was duplicitous, hypocritical. A conundrum. Like him.

No one would believe how much cold existed within a person so outwardly warm.

Which one?

Number eighteen? Her legs pumped as she chased the ball, her dark skin glowing beneath a sheen of sweat, tight curls bouncing. Then she leaped for the ball and grimaced, and her irises glinted red in the fading twilight like the eyes of a vampire. He turned away. Number...four? Her blond tresses were stuck to the side of her head with sweat. She was too far for him to see her face properly. Jay's daughter streaked by him, as rough and hairy and imposing as her father.

Number twenty. A waif of a girl with thick, dark hair, but that wasn't what drew him. Nor was it her age. The papers had once speculated that it was the variety itself he sought as if changing the color of her hair could make one girl stand out more than another. Narrow-minded Neanderthals. They couldn't see the fire inside these girls, begging to be set free. But he could see it. He was perceptive, intuitive, unlike Jay and all the other men around here.

He doubted they'd catch on—to any of it. He sometimes thought he might want to be found out, simply to see the looks on his neighbors' faces. Just to have an excuse to burn his Ugg-wearing, Starbucks-drinking cliché of a housewife alive. The thought of their shock was enough to quell his boredom some nights. But not all nights. And not today.

Number twenty approached him and then passed by as if he wasn't even there. No one saw him, really saw him, and the longer he lived here, the more invisible he became. But not completely so. Just as the girl came even with him, she looked up and smiled at him, and the setting sun glinted on her braces—the slightest hint of orange like a spark of flame was burgeoning inside her. There it was, that fire, that smile. So polite. He wanted to fuck her mouth but figured she'd probably bite off his cock before he came. And he never came before he could smell their flesh burning.

He smiled back, keeping it friendly, almost fatherly. That was, after all, how people saw him.

Respectable. Decent. *Trustworthy.*

Before he stared too long, he looked down and rested a hand on the dog's ears. His daughter had named the animal Buddy, which was the stupidest thing he'd ever heard. The beast was an ugly thing, with a square black head, constantly pricked-up ears, and jowls that could tear off his entire arm. Not that the dog had ever shown signs of viciousness—but every creature had it in them.

When he glanced back up, the girl was headed down the path toward the park bathrooms, the building's thick outer door open to the night air to keep the interior from stinking of shit. The light from inside haloed her silhouette as she walked closer, closer to the glow, and the significance of that was not lost on him. If this were a dark road in another city, another state... Even here, the doors on the stalls were useless at keeping anyone out, and the dark behind the building was thick. He could do it quickly enough that no one would notice, so long as he kept the spray from her jugular off his shirt. But he wouldn't have time for the best part, and it was no fun without that. He flicked the lighter again, enjoying the pleasant ripple of electricity that traveled from his arm to his groin.

Not here. Location-wise, he'd made enough mistakes already.

Back on the field, the girls were still running, kicking, jumping. He watched intently, waiting for another one to look his way.

Flick, flick, flick.

To think he used to be content with lighting up abandoned buildings, satiated by the sensual curves of the smoke as it wafted skyward. But the acrid stench of burning wood didn't compare to the seductive scent of human skin sizzling like bacon in a pan.

He might never have discovered the richness of burning human flesh if it hadn't been for that one night. The night that bastard of a cop had happened by a house on the outskirts of the city just after he'd lit it ablaze. He'd spent weeks looking for the perfect target—isolated, abandoned, quiet—and hadn't even gotten to watch the place go up in flames. The rest of the night had been the most intolerable kind of boring, the kind that tries to swallow you up from the inside, and no matter how long he touched himself, how hard he fucked his passionless vanilla wife, he couldn't find release in any of it. The next week he'd punished the cop who had denied him the pleasure of watching the inferno. And once he'd smelled the girl's burning flesh, he knew there was no going back. There'd been something intimate about it, something lascivious, watching the flames cast shadows on her face while her lower half burned.

If only he'd dragged it out a little more. But it had taken so much time to follow that cop home and locate his daughter, and even more time to choose the correct spot to take her. And it had to be perfect—he had known she'd be special the moment he saw her.

Julie'd had an exceptionally lovely smile.

5

———

THE PHONE JOLTED Petrosky awake like someone slamming a spiked heel into his forehead. He groped for it, sending the empty bottle of Jack Daniels tumbling to the floor with a metallic clang that didn't sound like glass on wood. He squinted at the bottle, and at the gun poking from beneath it, the red warning of its disengaged safety magnified through the empty glass in the light from the streetlamp outside. He could have shot his mattress and killed it. He did not want to buy a new one.

Wait…no, it was just a mattress. He could shoot it all he wanted. And then he'd go back to the precinct and shoot up the last three guys he'd arrested—perverts, all of them.

He was drunk as shit.

The world undulated around him in fuzzy waves as he scrambled again for the phone to silence that infernal racket. He finally found it beside the bed, still in the pocket of yesterday's pants.

"'Lo?" He'd tried to form the entire word, but it hadn't come out. His tongue felt thick and bristly like it was covered in hair.

"Detective Petrosky?" The bastard on the other end of the

line sounded as perky as Petrosky was wasted, and it made him wonder briefly what the guy was smoking and how he could get some. He shook his head, trying to clear the liquor from his vision, from his brain.

"Yeah. This is him." He was pleased his voice sounded moderately sober, or at least not as trashed as a reality star after their show was canceled.

"This is Detective Scott with the Willowshire Police Department, and—"

"The where?"

"Just outside of East Burke, Vermont, if you know that area, sir? I wondered if I might have a few moments of your time."

Vermont? What the hell? "I'm not familiar with that area at all." Petrosky collapsed back against his pillow. "Can you call back in the morning?"

"Detective? It is morning."

Petrosky squinted at the window, at the thin film of dawn barely graying the edges of the sky. Vermont mountain people probably had to get up early to catch moose for breakfast or some shit. *Goddammit.*

"Do you need me to call back at a more convenient time? I'd be happy to—"

"Shit, just hang on, okay?" The sheer politeness of this jerkoff was going to give Petrosky an aneurysm.

The guy on the other end of the line went silent, and Petrosky hauled himself to seated once more, again trying to shake off the vestiges of the Jack and crappy sleep. The police were on the line. The Vermont police. What did the Vermont police want from him?

He grabbed the pack of cigarettes off the box and shook one between his lips, listening to the asshole's quick breathing from the cell. Nervous, maybe. "What can I do for you?" Petrosky finally said through a cloud of smoke.

Scott inhaled sharply. "Might have a case here, connected

to one of yours." The sentence fell from his lips rapid-fire, each syllable running into the next until the words were almost unintelligible. *Nervous as all hell.*

No doubt some rapist listed on the sex offender database here in Michigan had moved out to the mountains to escape the prying eyes of his neighbors. But the database was national—those bastards couldn't hide. And if they had a crime out there, it meant one of Petrosky's criminals was reoffending. Another system failure. Put away the bad guys all you wanted, but there were always more, and even the ones who got caught had some defense attorney arguing for their freedom, or the DA agreeing to ridiculous plea deals. Maybe the lawyers would feel differently if it was their own children who'd been abused. *Hypocrites.* Petrosky pulled more bitter smoke deep into his lungs, blew it out, and watched it disappear into the blackness of the room, reaching the corners the dawn couldn't. He waited for the kid to go on.

Scott stayed silent, so Petrosky said, "I don't have all day." Which was a goddamn lie—he had all the time in the world. He just wasn't going to waste it on this breathless fuckstick.

"Sorry, Detective. This is just… It's wicked bad."

Wicked bad, eh? Maybe the mounties didn't see as much nasty shit as he did in the city; though those picturesque towns, with the sun-kissed autumn leaves, were often as brutal behind those trees as any inner-city crackhouse. The kid was probably just new, but Petrosky'd be damned if he'd be the one to train him. "Get to the point, rook."

"Yes, sir, okay. I do apologize. It seems I have a case that has…similarities to a string of crimes in your jurisdiction around five years ago."

Five years ago. A string of crimes. A rapist or…

No.

Five years ago, a serial killer had terrorized Ash Park, disemboweling prostitutes and anyone else who got in his way. He'd left macabre poems at each crime scene, written in the victim's blood, all from Lewis Carroll's prequel to *Alice in Wonderland*. The *Looking Glass* killer, they'd called him. The killer had disappeared after murdering prominent businessman Dominic Harwick and kidnapping Harwick's girlfriend, Hannah Montgomery, a girl thought to be the target all along since she'd had some connection to every victim. Hannah'd had Julie's hair and Julie's eyes and Julie's...innocence. Petrosky had wanted nothing more than to save her. But he hadn't.

He still sometimes dreamed about Hannah, the way he did about Julie. In both dreams, he was impotent to help. In both, he stood watching the girls get carved into bloody pieces.

Scott cleared his throat. "Three and a half years ago, we found the body of Hannah Montgomery's father, Theodore Montgomery, in the home he shared with his wife and thirteen-year-old daughter. He'd been stabbed in the gut. The wife and kid were out that night, thank god."

"What does some guy getting stabbed in the gut have to do with the *Looking Glass* killer?" That maniac had liked to take his time with the vics. He hadn't murdered them in their dining rooms and raced away before family showed up.

"Well, the crime itself. Stabbed...disemboweled, kinda."

Disemboweled. That was a little close for comfort, but not close enough; the *Looking Glass* killer had tied his victims up, tortured them, slowly dissected their innards. He'd wanted them alive. He'd wanted them to suffer. Except for Dominic Harwick, the last victim: Harwick had been stabbed, then gutted after the fact. But they'd assumed the killer was busy kidnapping Hannah Montgomery. Maybe that wasn't it; maybe it was a change in MO.

"Any words written in blood?"

"Nothing like that. No poems at all."

Petrosky wondered how well they'd checked. At one of

the Ash Park crime scenes, he'd had to bring in a dolly just to find the bloody words. Any copycat worth his salt would have held onto the most newsworthy feature of the killings.

Petrosky took one final inhale, crushed the cigarette butt under his heel into the wood floor, and lit another. The asshole on the other end of the line remained quiet, and for a second, Petrosky thought he heard birdsong through the cell.

"Listen, I think the fact that Hannah's father was the victim makes this worth looking into."

And as Petrosky filled his lungs with ash again, the dread in his belly awoke and squirmed and swelled up his esophagus until it was trying to choke him. The *Looking Glass* killer'd had a vendetta against Hannah Montgomery, stalking her, murdering prostitutes from the shelter where she volunteered, and killing her abusive ex-boyfriend as well as her then-current love interest, Dominic Harwick. And the crime techs had found her blood all over the Harwick murder scene, which meant the killer had hurt her badly before taking her. Now…her father was dead. That was awfully bad luck. And Petrosky didn't believe in luck.

"But why kill Hannah's father over a year after the girl was kidnapped?" he said. A copycat could pop up anytime— and surely that was what they were seeing here, even if it was a shitty reproduction. But a spark of hope lit in Petrosky's gut. If the real *Looking Glass* killer had murdered Theodore Montgomery to terrorize Hannah as he had terrorized her in Ash Park—by hurting those close to her—she had to be alive. Or at least still alive when her father was killed. Illogical, a stretch, maybe, but they'd never found her remains, and the *Looking Glass* killer had never hidden a body; the crime scenes were always close enough to civilization to ensure that someone would stumble upon the victims. The killer had wanted the public to witness the bloody remains of the women he'd tortured to death, had wanted them to discover the gory scrawls he left behind. He'd wanted the notoriety.

Maybe the killer had dragged Hannah up to Vermont and made her watch her father die, a new escalation for his sadistic game.

"I don't really know why your killer would come after Theodore Montgomery, Detective," Scott said quietly. "Or even *if* he did. But I'm certain there's some connection here."

The room spun. "You think the killer took Hannah up there?"

"Wait...what?" The squeak in Scott's voice said the thought hadn't even occurred to him. "She's not up here. I've seen her photo, and it's a real small town."

Why did the size of the town matter? Petrosky's stomach soured from last night's booze and old disappointment. He grabbed the bottle from the floor and frowned at how light it was.

"We'd know if she was here. I'm sure of that," Scott said. "Half the residents don't even have numbers on their houses because everyone knows everybody else."

Petrosky hacked soot from his lungs, then sighed. He was being ridiculous. He'd looked for Hannah. He'd stopped sleeping. He'd told himself she was surely alive, but still, the guilt tightened around his neck like a hangman's noose; every time he lost one of these girls, every time he had to close a case with a body in the morgue, every time he looked into a body bag and saw another girl he'd failed, he saw his daughter's face staring back at him from the depths of the coroner's drawer. And Hannah had looked so much like Julie. He knew Hannah was dead, but the thought of finding her body... It would be like he'd killed Julie all over again. It would be as if he'd murdered her with his own hands.

But if she was alive...

Irrational. Illogical. Petrosky could almost hear the department shrink, Dr. McCallum, talking to him in that measured tone he'd always used so as not to piss off unstable patients. After Hannah's case went cold, McCallum had lectured him even more: "Don't you recall the guilty women you've presumed innocent because they bore a passing resemblance to Julie? The patterns you see when none really exist? The disastrous decisions you've made based on those irrational hopes?" Petrosky puffed on the cigarette, fast, hard, and kicked the near-empty Jack bottle.

Stop it, asshole, you know she's gone. Of course she was; her clothes were probably rotting in a ditch off some highway, her bones carted off by wild animals. He'd find Hannah's body, decayed and crumbling, and then he'd do what he did when they found Julie: close his eyes, take off in his car, and get shit-faced in some liquor store parking lot.

But as long as he wasn't looking at her dead body, he hadn't killed her yet.

"Detective?" he heard Scott say, but his voice sounded far away as if Petrosky were listening through a cloth.

Petrosky stood, relishing the sudden electricity in his muscles. Waking up. He had to go to Vermont. He owed it to...someone. "They really don't have addresses on the houses?"

"Don't need 'em. People know where—"

"I don't care about your backward hick town. Where'd you get Hannah's picture from?" She'd changed her hair the week before she disappeared. What photo was this kid looking at?

"Newspaper articles."

Newspaper articles. Not the database. Not the FBI. That was why this guy had called Petrosky: Petrosky's name had been all over the papers at the time, discussing the case and how he'd finally caught the killer. Until he realized he'd been wrong. The bastard Petrosky had put away for the crimes had killed himself in prison before they could release him.

Now, this kid was going after a serial killer with just a photo from the newspaper. Petrosky snorted. Too new to know better, or did the kid have something to prove?

"When did you start, Scott?"

The silence on the other end stretched. "Last month."

Figures. A kid that green couldn't do this on his own, but at least Scott wasn't going to get in his way. Petrosky yanked open the closet and rummaged around for a duffel bag. First, he had to determine whether the person who had kidnapped Hannah Montgomery—the *Looking Glass* killer—really was the same person who'd murdered Hannah's father. Then— was there any way the killer had taken Hannah out of Harwick's house that night five years ago and brought her to Vermont? If he could find her body, maybe he could find her killer.

And maybe he couldn't, but hell, finding Hannah's body might be the final push he needed to leap into the abyss. And this time, Decantor wouldn't be there to save him.

6

─────────

Petrosky shoved the cell phone underneath the duffel on the seat next to him. It wasn't even noon, and Jackson had already called him twenty times. Maybe she was at his goddamn apartment by now, trying to decide whether to go to Chief Carroll and get his ass officially fired. She would, today or tomorrow. Sometime this week, surely—because he wasn't going back until he found out who had killed Hannah's father. Maybe he'd even find out what had happened to Hannah. Outside, in the light of day, he knew she was dead, but at least he'd give her a proper burial.

He owed the girl that much.

The radiant sun loomed over the highway, the tops of the trees glittering with the remnants of last evening's rain—or he assumed it was rain from the damp ground on either side of the road. Could have been Jackson's God pissing on everything, though. Below the canopies of leaves, sharp boulders jutted from the earth like the knuckles of some ravenous beast trying to haul itself from the depths of hell. From the crevices between the stones, water trickled from some hidden place, each exposed droplet like tears, as if the earth itself were crying.

And his eyes burned too, his head throbbing after last night's binge. He almost wished for Jackson's presence; annoying as she was, she was real, and when she was with him, the ghosts took a back seat. But now, his car felt haunted. His brain felt haunted.

Everywhere he looked, he saw them. Above him, there was no sky, only the brilliant blue of Morrison's eyes like he was trying to remind Petrosky of something just out of his reach. Had he missed a clue from the *Looking Glass* case? Clearly, he had—but what? When he passed a dark-haired girl driving a Sebring convertible, he slowed, peering into the car, willing her to turn her face toward him. She turned to him suddenly—brown eyes, not green—and he nodded. Forced a smile. The girl in the car frowned and switched lanes.

Of course. Because she wasn't Hannah. He ran a hand over his face, the stubble catching on his calloused fingers. Even if this girl had been Hannah, she'd be none too thrilled to see him five years after the fact. But back then, they'd had nothing to go on.

The scene at Dominic Harwick's home had been a massacre. Smashed glass sculptures, a lake of blood, and Harwick's rag-doll body, the intestines torn from his gut and unrolled like a spool of yarn. A chunk of Hannah's scalp, hair attached. But not a single trace of DNA, no evidence of any other person besides Hannah and Dominic. Harwick had a number of defensive wounds, so he'd tried to fight off their attacker, but he hadn't managed to get a piece of the killer's skin under his nails. And someone had bleached half the place, including the path to the garage. Any trace of the killer was long gone by the time Petrosky had arrived.

He took his foot off the gas to let the girl in the car next to him accelerate and disappear over the next sloping hill. Probably still freaked about the way he'd grinned at her.

Though he wouldn't have hurt her, she'd have done well to run from him nonetheless.

As he crested over the next swell in the road, a tinkling laugh rang out behind him—*Julie's laugh*—and his nostrils were at once filled with the scent of her shampoo. *It's a dragon in the clouds, Daddy! There's a bear! And a goldfish!* He swerved, pumping the brakes as he turned to peer into the back seat. Petrosky's jaw dropped, and for a fleeting moment, he was utterly shocked that the car was empty. Then he turned back to the road, the grief running anew through his chest and tightening around the pacemaker like it might finally let him die of a broken heart. He maneuvered the car around the next bend, the cliff to his left, a drop-off to his right so steep he could see the tops of trees below the road. *Look at the trees, Daddy!* His knuckles went white on the wheel. It wasn't fair.

Julie was not the last in that string of rape-homicides either: there were two others after Julie that he knew of. Three dead girls. Every time a new victim popped up, he'd gotten involved, pounded the pavement looking for any lead, any clue, but there was never anything to go on. No DNA—the asshole wore a condom and latex gloves. No set pattern for location, either—Julie was first, in Ash Park, but the bastard struck all over the state from the upper peninsula to this side of Toledo. Not a single witness. And the things done to them…

Petrosky couldn't even let it come near his mind, couldn't picture his daughter, lying there, being—

The phone. He yanked it from under the duffel and slapped it against his head hard enough that he winced. "Petrosky."

"You coming?"

Shannon. Where was he supposed to… *Oh shit.* "I… Listen, I had to take a trip, go out to Vermont on a case."

Shannon was silent on the other end of the line.

"This wasn't intentional, Shannon, I—"

"Is it really a case, or is it like that time you said you had a case, and then you spent the night getting hammered?"

"No, it's a real case and—"

"You don't have jurisdiction in Vermont," she snapped.

Lawyers. But she wasn't wrong. "It's about the—"

"I don't care what it's on. You were supposed to be here. You said you'd be here. I told Evie you were coming, and she made a card for you and everything."

The sky, once the same blue as Morrison's eyes, went dark—thunderheads rolling in from the east. "I'll be back—"

"Forget it. I don't need your help."

"I can talk to Evie, Shannon, maybe—"

"The kids need stability. All they get from you is broken promises."

Julie was dead because he hadn't been there to protect her. Morrison was dead because Petrosky hadn't killed Adam Norton first. Hannah was dead because while he'd been fixated on the wrong guy, Hannah'd been taken to some abandoned school or a warehouse or a barn where the killer could watch the life bleed out of her.

"I'll call you when we get to Atlanta," Shannon said. "I'm sure the kids will want to say goodbye to their Papa Ed."

Not hello. Goodbye. He had fared as terribly on his second chance at being a family man as he had on his first.

"Shannon," he began, but the line was already dead. Out the side window, water ran from the stone, darkening a path toward the earth. He shoved the silent phone back under the duffel as the first drops of rain splattered against the windshield.

7

———

HE STOPPED at a grocery store a dozen miles outside of Willowshire and loaded up on snack cakes, Doritos, a fifth of Jack, four packs of gum, and a bottle of mouthwash. He consumed all the food and one shot out of the bottle on his way to the station house. Used the mouthwash too.

The town was so adorable and quaint that he wanted to punch the shit out of everyone in it before he even got to the precinct. Cops' headquarters was encased in red brick and tucked away in a strip mall between a used bookstore and some type of health food place that looked like it sold products made from syrup or honey—some sticky shit in a bottle. The precinct had bright yellow shutters on either side of the front window, and no bars and no signs, save the sheriff's star in the lower corner. Beyond the window, an officer in street blues turned from his desk, smiled, and waved. The glass was thin; it didn't even look bulletproof. What the hell kind of operation were they running here?

Petrosky hauled open the front door, and a bell rang like the one inside the Gas-Co. gas station, where he'd recently spent half a day staring at a pair of bloody corpses. But this place was free of dust, of mud, of gore. The waiting area was small—a few hundred feet square—with a newer-looking cherrywood desk in the front window and a water cooler in the back next to a table holding a single-serve coffee maker and a basket of muffins and scones, probably from the sticky shop next door. The whole place smelled like wildflowers and sunshine and rainbows. Respectable precincts were supposed to stink of broken dreams, filthy perps, and unsolved cases. He didn't trust cops who smelled like they'd just fucked a garden.

"Afternoon, sir. How can I help?" The officer behind the desk stood, thick and heavy as the stone mountain Petrosky'd just driven through. "Crowley" glinted from a pinned badge on his shirt; his smile stretched across his too-square jaw.

Was this some twisted *Mary Poppins* remake? "Detective Petrosky, Ash Park PD. I'm here to see Detective Scott."

The officer's brows drew together on his wide forehead, possibly in response to Petrosky's brusqueness, and his stance remained so rigid and still that Petrosky almost expected him to salute. Crowley finally nodded and gestured to the padded chairs along the far wall. "Have a seat. I'll find him for you."

I bet you will.

The officer marched through the door at the back of the room, and Petrosky hit up the snack bar. The scones were triangles, dense, and he took a bite expecting some kind of muffin-ish goodness but ended up with a mouthful of cardboard. He tossed the rest in the trash. Seriously, what was with these people? He was reaching for the coffeepot when the door opened, and a tall kid strode into the room, all limbs and umber skin and enormous dorky glasses. Like Steve Urkel had grown up to be a cop. In a suit. Behind him, Crowley leaned against the doorframe, smirking, his arms crossed over his barrel chest. But his eyes had darkened. Angry. At Petrosky's presence or at the kid?

"Detective Petrosky?" Urkel extended a hand. "Detective Scott."

Scott's hand was cool and firmer than Petrosky'd expected though it did little to quell the certainty that Scott wasn't old enough to drive, let alone solve crime. How the hell had a rookie one month into the job gotten this case anyway? Petrosky should have considered that before he left the house, but he was drunker then.

"Grab whatever you want, and we can order dinner in a bit if you're hungry."

"You're wasting his time too," Crowley said to Scott, then headed back to his post at the front desk. Scott didn't look his way, but he frowned at his own shoes.

Mary Poppins was gone, replaced by some depressing movie Petrosky would rather not watch.

"Come on back, Detective. I'll show you what I've got."

Petrosky bypassed the scones, grabbed a muffin instead, and contemplated throwing it at Crowley, wondering if it would explode against his head in a shower of crumbs or stay intact. If Petrosky was going to die, it might as well be defending himself against an angry ex-military man wounded by shrapnel from an overcooked baked good. It would make a hell of an obituary. He glanced at the pastry and back at Crowley, then followed the kid.

The hallway was carpeted—but not a single stain. Maybe this was a fake precinct where no one actually worked, and they'd called him in under false pretenses just to mess with him. He dropped a single raisin on the carpet, half because it was unfathomable that anyone would think it was a good idea to put raisins in muffins, and half because it might end up serving as a breadcrumb trail if he needed to find his way out of this alternate reality.

Scott led him though a bright white door with his name on the doorjamb. Inside, a large wraparound desk had been pushed into the corner and outfitted with two chairs. The desk was stacked with files: messy and fat with notes and paper. The walls above the desk were paneled with corkboards, thumbtacked with notebook pages and overlapping pictures and crisscrossed string. One of the pictures was...

Julie.

His heart stopped. But the dark hair, the light eyes, those features belonged to a grown woman—not Julie at all. Hannah Montgomery. *Petrosky, you idiot.* His stomach clenched, and he shoved the muffin into his mouth, hoping that would force everything—the chips and the booze and the bile—to stay in his belly instead of creeping back up his throat.

Scott gestured to one of the chairs, then positioned the other so they could sit side by side in front of the desk. *Cozy.*

"I'm glad you came, Detective."

Petrosky said nothing, just collapsed into the chair, trying not to grunt with the effort. He scanned the desktop. How had this kid managed to make such a mess in a month? Almost gave the impression he was a real cop in a real precinct. The only neat element was Scott's academy certificate, framed on the wall...no, it was from a university. *Masters in Forensic Science?*

"Little young for that, aren't you?"

Scott followed Petrosky's eyes. "I started young." He lifted his chin. "I'm halfway through my MD too. So I can be a medical examiner."

"Show-off."

The kid's face fell until Petrosky raised an eyebrow. "Kidding, Scott." The other fuckheads in this precinct must be working him over. Was it because they thought he was wasting his time, like Captain Cockblock out front seemed to think? Nah, that jerkoff was probably just pissed he couldn't manage a master's in anything, let alone forensics. "Let's do this, Scott."

"Oh. Right." Scott grabbed a folder from the desk behind him and passed it to Petrosky: crime scene photos. The pictures showed a man on his side in the fetal position like he'd been trying to force his organs back into his gut. Blood pooled around a gaping wound in his abdomen. No cuffs or restraints like the ones used in the *Looking Glass* cases, but if the intestines peeking out like corkscrews of flesh between the man's fingers were any indication, he'd been eviscerated. No other stab wounds visible.

"Theodore Montgomery, three-and-a-half years ago," Scott was saying. "Looks like he was stabbed once in the belly while he was sleeping, and then someone drew the blade across his gut. When he stood, his insides came through the abdominal wall—it didn't take him long to bleed out."

Petrosky studied Scott's face. He had an earnest look about him like his eyes were lit from within. A smirk played at one corner of his mouth. This kid knew more than he was saying.

Scott turned back to the desk and pointed at another photo on the corkboard with "Theodore Montgomery" written across the top. Hannah's father. Hard jaw, crooked nose, and the cold, agitated eyes of a predator. Or not—Theodore Montgomery was the victim here, not the aggressor. Petrosky'd been working the beat too long.

"He was murdered over a year after the last crime in Ash Park," Scott said. "Plenty of time for another killer to research your cases, or for the real *Looking Glass* killer to go underground and emerge here. But I think the MO is too similar to be coincidence. Call it a *gut* feeling."

No wonder the other cops hate you. The kid was smiling like a psycho. Petrosky turned his attention back to the board, carefully avoiding—*Julie's*—Hannah's picture. Her father's death had been faster than the torturous killings of the female prostitutes five years ago, but Dominic Harwick had been murdered in almost the same way as Theodore Montgomery. Petrosky scooted his chair to the desk, passing his gaze from one crime scene photo to another.

"There are inconsistencies, though," he said finally. "No words were written anywhere, nothing printed in blood, and nothing from a poem or from *Through the Looking Glass*. That's an issue. In Ash Park, the killer used cuffs or shackles and committed the murders in abandoned warehouses and old barns—out-of-the-way places where he could take his time torturing his victims. He didn't do that here—just one wound to the belly." Consistent with Dominic Harwick to be sure: no drawn-out torture, no cuffs, just evisceration and left to bleed out. But most killers escalated. They didn't become less brutal. Though maybe the killer had liked how Harwick's murder had turned out, the frantic, grisly messiness of it. The killings prior to that had been almost... clinical.

The kid opened his mouth to interject. Petrosky put a hand up, then lowered his finger to the image of Theodore Montgomery's body, the close-ups of the wound: rough, jagged at one edge. "And here...this isn't the same weapon as in Ash Park either." They'd never found the weapon at the Harwick crime scene, but the medical examiner was certain it had been a scalpel, consistent with the other cases.

"This was done with a knife," Scott said. "Probably a paring knife or a pocket knife, and it was a lot more dull than a scalpel would be: the skin tore in a few places where the blade didn't cut cleanly." Scott wrinkled his nose but didn't show any other signs of distress. Put him a head above half the rookies out there; some of those newbies threw up the moment they saw a paper cut. "And there were imperfections in the blade itself," Scott continued. "There was a secondary scrape on the wound, starting two inches from the tip of the incision, and running along the bottom edge of the cut to the other side, probably from a snag or divot in the weapon two inches from the tip of the blade. Traces of the same metal in that scrape as in the main wound, so it wasn't from the handle or something else—the knife was at least that long." He cleared his throat. "I need to get my hands on your case files, so I can compare. One of the reasons I called you."

"That's not the only reason you called me."

Scott drew himself taller. "I'm a book geek, Detective. Got the degrees, the forensics background, but…" He shrugged. "I'm new. Young. So instead of giving me something serious to do, they gave me a stack of cold cases from the last ten years."

"You solve any?"

"Not yet. But I think I can solve this one, even though all the other cops think I'm crazy." His skin got darker, redder, and he rolled his chair back a touch and averted his gaze. "Crowley out there actually laughed at me, said there was no way what happened to Montgomery was related to the cases in Ash Park. They didn't even want to send someone with me to ask a few questions. The chief doesn't want me to ask about Montgomery either—he was a family man, a blue-collar worker, well-respected in the community. No reports from anyone that indicate he had enemies. He even paid his taxes on time. No reports of any sick…stuff."

Petrosky narrowed his eyes. "You can say shit, kid."

"Nah, it's okay." Scott shrugged. "Anyway, the original detective might have overlooked a few things. Montgomery seemed like a great guy on paper."

But a killer, especially the *Looking Glass* killer, wouldn't have cared if Montgomery was a great guy or a total dick. How many of the Ash Park victims had met the *Looking Glass* killer before the night he ripped them open? And though the guy out front seemed like an egocentric asshole, that didn't mean he or his counterparts were incompetent—maybe they just didn't like to be challenged by a rookie who was smarter than they'd ever be. Petrosky pictured Crowley's smug features, his crossed arms. "Was Crowley the original detective?"

Scott nodded. Petrosky sighed.

Crowley probably loved the fact that Scott was second-guessing his work. And if Crowley'd had no leads since Montgomery's murder, it made sense he'd want to put it behind the community altogether. No one liked to think about senseless crimes or serial killers any more than they had to. But someone had to.

"Were people around here starting to freak out?"

Scott swallowed hard, his Adam's apple bobbing. "Montgomery's wife, mostly. At first, she was scared, jumpy all the time. Had to have people at church bring her food for a few weeks there. She even told Crowley himself to drop the case because dragging it out was making her more anxious. Said it reminded her that it was a senseless crime, which made her lose faith in humanity or something strange like that. But this wasn't random." Scott glanced to the door and back to Petrosky, his lips tight and determined.

Petrosky still wasn't sold that the crime wasn't random. And he was starting to suspect that Scott's motives for pursuing this case weren't just that the kid thought he was right—if they could prove there was a connection, whoever had told Scott to drop it wouldn't have a leg to stand on when something bigger came up. The kid was smart, and not just the kind of smart that came from books. Wily. Ballsy.

"So what do you think the reason was, Scott? Why did Montgomery die?"

"I'm not buying that good guy stuff." Scott's brows furrowed. "I know no one reported anything, but I have a...

hunch, I guess, that Montgomery maybe did something he shouldn't have. And his wife's always been kinda weird."

"Hannah's mother?"

"No, his second wife, the one trying to get us to drop it. Melinda Charles."

Huh. As far as Petrosky knew, Hannah didn't even know the woman existed, so he hadn't investigated Charles during the *Looking Glass* case. "Define 'weird.'"

Scott rifled through a stack of folders behind him, came up with a thin file, and flipped it open to the image of a fine-boned woman, thin as a meth head, with mouse-brown hair curled around her face. "After a few weeks, she didn't seem too worried about herself or her daughter—even refused officer presence at the house—but she had no issue telling other folks that they might be in danger, telling anyone who'd listen that Montgomery's death was 'senseless' and 'random' and the like. I talked to Hannah's mother, too, and her sister. Both estranged, haven't seen or heard from Hannah or Theodore for almost nine years now. And both have alibis. Polite enough people, but cold."

That meshed with Petrosky's experience: he'd contacted Hannah's family a few times over the years for follow-up, and they'd been distant with him too. Her mother had asked if he had new information and then thanked him and hung up when he said no. Hannah's sister had told him she'd call him back but hadn't. And Hannah's father... Petrosky thought back to the way Montgomery had answered the phone: friendly until he'd heard why Petrosky was calling. Then he'd snapped and demanded to know where she was. Montgomery had called every week for months, asking if they'd located Hannah, and his manner had irked Petrosky— less grief, less depression, just nervous. He'd chalked it up to the man being desperate to find his daughter, but maybe he'd misinterpreted at the time. If Montgomery had been killed for a reason, if he'd had a secret—a secret Hannah knew

about—and if all that was related to the *Looking Glass* case…
That was a lot of *ifs*.

"Theodore's wife has always been kinda standoffish," Scott
said. "And her last husband had a laundry list of charges for
domestic abuse. I thought Theodore maybe…hurt her too."

It wasn't uncommon for victims of domestic violence to
end up with another abuser, but sometimes they escaped that
cycle. "You have to have more than—"

"She had a hospitalization a few months before Theo
died: broken arm, some bruises. She denied abuse to hospital
personnel, said she fell climbing a tree." Scott raised an
eyebrow like he didn't believe the story any more than
Petrosky did. A grown person didn't climb a tree unless they
were trying to escape a bear.

Maybe domestic abuse was the dirty little secret Montgomery hadn't wanted Hannah to share. Though the most
likely person to kill him for that would have been his wife,
which would mean these cases weren't connected at all.
Surely the Vermont PD had looked at the wife already. He'd
check again, but if it wasn't the ex or the widow…who else
might have had it in for Montgomery? If he was a domestic
abuser, he might have had enemies in his wife's family, but…

Scott's feet were jittering against the floor, frantic like
he'd smoked too much crank. And Scott was staring at him,
his eyes even brighter, and biting his lip like he was trying to
keep his words inside his mouth.

I come all the way from Michigan, and he's still holding back.
"What aren't you telling me, Scott?"

Scott shuffled his feet some more, and Petrosky thought
he was going to roll the chair backward again, but this time,
he exploded up from the seat so fast Petrosky jumped.

"What the hell, kid, you—"

"The day Montgomery was killed…"

Petrosky blinked. *Why is he messing around?*

Finally, Scott pointed at the corkboard. "July twenty-third, the day Theodore Montgomery died, is Hannah Montgomery's birthday." He dropped his voice on the last line and darted his gaze at the closed door.

"You…" He'd been dragging Petrosky along this whole time.

"Sorry, I just…wanted to know what you thought about the rest. Before I told you." He averted his eyes like a chastised puppy.

Petrosky's gut roiled with chips and booze and that lame-ass raisin muffin. *Hannah's birthday.* That was far too much coincidence. "You tell your superiors this?"

"They didn't believe me before…" He shrugged, like "Screw them." The kid really was ballsy.

"You hiding other shit from me, Scott?"

"No, sir, I swear."

Petrosky stared at the corkboard, at Montgomery's picture as if searching his cold eyes might bring forth an answer. A three hundred and sixty-five to one chance—Theodore Montgomery's killer had chosen the date for a reason. But did that mean they had a copycat? The *Looking Glass* killer had never murdered a victim on a significant date before—that they knew of. Yet all the crimes had revolved around Hannah Montgomery, and it might make sense for the *Looking Glass* killer to vary his pattern with her, especially for a date so vital: the day Hannah had come into the world and the day he took her father out. She was the original killer's target. His goal. Petrosky thought of Hannah—cold and dead and decomposing—and dragged his eyes from the corkboard to the ceiling.

"You think we're dealing with the original killer, Scott?" The *Looking Glass* killer wouldn't just murder one person over the five years since he'd left Ash Park—unless he'd started burying his victims to avoid detection. With the change in location and in the crimes, it was more likely they had a copycat. And yet...

"I... It's hard to say." Scott tapped his index finger against the corkboard, and Hannah's picture shuddered as if she was trembling. Petrosky winced, suddenly as hot with fury as if Scott had struck the girl herself. He breathed deeply through his nose to slow his heart.

"Someone targeted Montgomery for a reason, Detective Petrosky. They killed him on his daughter's birthday. If it wasn't the *Looking Glass* killer, it had to be someone who knew the circumstances surrounding the *Looking Glass* case. Someone who knew about Hannah." Scott finally drew his gaze to Petrosky's. "Do you think it's a harebrained idea? That this is connected to your case? Because I'm okay freaking my chief out if there's even the tiniest chance—"

"I'd have done the same as you did, Scott." The pounding-the-pavement part, not the calling-in-another-detective part. Once you called in other people, you risked them taking over your investigation: Graves, the lead FBI agent in the *Looking Glass* case, had yanked it from Petrosky and hadn't had any better luck solving it. But the kid clearly knew he had a better shot at getting credit with Petrosky than with the FBI. Petrosky's eyes lit on the degree on the wall again. Scott was smart, and this place was tiny; probably saw less crime in a year than Ash Park did in a week. A snooze fest for a driven forensics guy.

"Why are you sticking around here anyway?" Petrosky asked. "With a forensics degree and all. A lot more opportunities to hone those skills outside this town."

"I don't want to leave my family." Scott shrugged, but Petrosky recognized that deeper undercurrent in the boy's voice; he'd worked hard to disguise that tremor in his own. Stress. Maybe grief. But if someone in Scott's family needed him to stay here, at least they were still alive—for now.

He shook the thoughts from his head. "So who else would

have wanted to hurt Theodore Montgomery? What are we missing?" *Think, goddammit.* He'd always suspected that the *Looking Glass* killer was obsessed with Hannah, someone who loved her, maybe, who wanted to make her his own. If the killer were just picking off people who were related to her, Hannah's mother and sister would have been brutalized. Instead, he'd gone after those Hannah was involved with on a regular basis—mostly women from the shelter where she volunteered. Dominic Harwick was probably collateral damage, murdered so the *Looking Glass* killer could kidnap Hannah. But Hannah's ex-boyfriend Jake had been an anomaly: the only man tortured. He was found brutally murdered after he'd dared raise his fist to Hannah. Had Jake been targeted *because* he'd hurt Hannah?

Petrosky stepped toward the board and squinted at Theodore Montgomery's photo. That ludicrous tree-climbing story—seemed like Montgomery had hurt his wife. Had he hurt Hannah too?

"Detective?" Scott said.

Petrosky ignored him. If Montgomery had abused Hannah, maybe he'd been murdered by the *Looking Glass* killer for the same reason the guy had killed Hannah's ex-boyfriend: for harming the object of the killer's obsession.

"Detective Petrosky?"

If the cases weren't connected, Montgomery had most likely been killed by someone close to him—possibly someone he'd wronged privately because Montgomery didn't get a stellar reputation by publicly being a dick. The tree-climbing thing was nonsense—and there was nothing like marriage to bring out murderous rage.

The air was almost too thick to breathe, weighing on Petrosky's lungs like a damp cloth. He needed a cigarette. And another shot—his brain was all over the place. But whether the man had hurt Hannah or his current family, the answer would be at Theodore Montgomery's house.

He heaved himself out of the chair. "I'm off."

Scott gave him a delighted grin. Jesus, this kid was starved for support. But if Scott was looking for flowery bullshit, he'd called the wrong guy; even if Petrosky did let Scott come, the kid'd be doomed before they got out the door.

Scott stood, and Petrosky waved him back down. "I'm going alone."

Always alone. It was better that way.

       8
  ———————

MONTGOMERY'S WIFE and stepdaughter still lived in the same
house where Theodore Montgomery had been brutally
murdered. Hopefully, they'd at least changed the carpet,
though Petrosky knew that whatever blood had soaked into
the subfloor was never coming out. Montgomery's gore
would stay in that house until they tore the bitch down.

The street was normal enough: road paved in asphalt, no
sidewalks, small houses with bigger porches wrapped around
the lower levels. But the homes were widely spaced, with
several acres of land apiece—too far for neighbors to hear
someone screaming, let alone witness a crime. Maybe the
isolated location fits better with the *Looking Glass* case than
he'd originally thought.

Though there was no house number, just as Scott had
said, the enormous maple tree full of shrilling birds in the
front yard was the same as the one in the crime scene photos.
Now it obscured the house from the street as if the property
itself was hiding.

Petrosky didn't see the girl until he pulled up to the top of
the limestone drive. She looked about sixteen, except that she
was sitting on the ground in the shade, drawing with her

finger in the soil, which made her seem far younger. She had dark hair, like Hannah's, like Julie's, with thick bangs framing a heart-shaped face. Tight mouth. Blank expression. She glanced up as the crunching of stone under his tires silenced the birds' cawing. Had to be Stacey Charles, Theodore Montgomery's stepdaughter.

Petrosky waved to the girl, who stared at him, eyebrows furrowed, and waved back, the tips of her fingers still brown with earth. But when he got out of the car and stepped off the walk to approach her, she jumped up and took off around the back of the house, fast as a junkie trying to escape the police. He froze with one foot on the lawn. What was that about? Scared of the cops? Of strangers? She might just have been shy, but the twitchiness didn't bode well for everything in this house being as hunky-dory as a *Brady Bunch* vignette. And that didn't bode well for Montgomery's innocence when it came to harming his wife...or his children.

He tucked Scott's case file under his arm and picked his way through a few runaway weeds and up the path to the screened front porch. Inside the screening, on the far wall, a blue couch and a wooden stool topped with a potted plant had been shoved against the aluminum siding. To his right was a metal door painted the color of blood.

The knocker rang with the clatter of hail on tin when he dropped it. Behind him, the birds resumed their shrieking as the door to the main house opened, and a woman with curly brown hair appraised him with eyes as wary as her daughter's. Petrosky flashed his badge, hoping she wouldn't look closely enough to realize he wasn't with the Willowshire PD. She barely glanced at it. "Yes?"

"I'm here about the death of your husband, Mrs. Montgomery." Petrosky waited for the sadness, the hurt, but the woman just watched him, ready for him to get on with it. Apathy? Over Montgomery's death already? Perhaps three years was long enough to grieve a husband. If only there were a finite period for grieving a child.

"Ma'am?" Nothing. Petrosky raised an eyebrow.

"It's been a while," she said. "I thought the case was closed."

Apparently, Scott hadn't come to speak with her since he'd started a month ago. That was odd. If Scott thought she'd been abused, he should have come here to determine whether she was a suspect.

She crossed her arms. "And you don't look familiar."

"I'm consulting from the Ash Park PD." Petrosky kept his face expressionless, unreadable—like hers. "We may have some new information on your husband's murder. May I come in?"

She glanced at the front yard as if looking for Stacey, then nodded. He followed her through the foyer to a kitchen laid with hardwoods. The wood flooring extended through the living room now, a far cry from the dingy, gore-soaked carpet that had covered the floor in the crime scene photos. Why had they stayed here? Family home? Or were they stuck? It was hard to get rid of a murder house; people were superstitious fools.

"How long have you lived here, Mrs. Montgomery?"

She blew a curl out of her face. "Stacey was seven when we moved in, so about nine years now. And please, Detective, Melinda. Melinda Charles."

Not Melinda Montgomery. Earlier, he'd assumed Scott was using her given name, but… "You get remarried?"

She shook her head but offered no other explanation and gestured to the living room couch. Petrosky eyed the floor, picturing Montgomery's body, almost smelling the iron and the literal shit from his perforated intestines. He frowned. "So you moved in around the time you married Theodore Montgomery?"

She sat across from him and nodded. "He'd had this home

for nearly thirty years. Couldn't bear to part with it, even though it was a little small for the three of us."

Thirty years. One of these rooms had been Hannah's. If Montgomery hadn't died, would the man have kept Hannah's things, leaving what was left of his daughter in boxes to be taken out on holidays or her birthday? Petrosky kept Julie's things in a box beside his bed, but he refused to open it.

Petrosky ran a hand over his face, and it was like touching sandpaper. What was he after, anyway? Hannah was dead.

Dead. Like Julie.

It wasn't Hannah he was looking for, not now; he needed to know if Charles or someone she knew was a suspect in Theodore Montgomery's death. And if not...he was here to find a serial killer. Either the *Looking Glass* killer or a copycat would've had to stake the place out to see when Montgomery's family came and went. No way he would have risked showing up when the house was full, especially after the bloodbath at the home of Dominic Harwick.

"Before the murder, did you notice anyone out front? Looking at the house? Or maybe your daughter mentioned seeing someone wandering around?"

"I never saw anyone—I already told them that. Stacey didn't either. She usually keeps to herself, so if she'd met a new friend, she surely would have said." She shrugged noncommittally like she didn't have a care in the world.

What the hell did she think this was? He was looking for a killer, a kidnapper, not a playmate. *Connections. Look for connections.* And so far, there was only one.

Something sharp tugged at his gut. *Let's get it over with.* He cleared his throat. "When was the last time you saw Hannah?"

"Who?"

The sharpness in his gut twisted, hot and painful. Who? *By all means, let's drag this out and beat it like a dead horse.* "Your husband's daughter, ma'am."

"Never met his ex or his daughter, but he was so good with Stacey…" She sniffed, but not like she was holding back tears—irritated. "This Hannah really missed out."

Missed out? On what? Hannah had been kidnapped. Attacked. Maybe there was something weird here he should have known about. Maybe he'd fucked up here just like he fucked up everything else he tried to fix.

Get it together, asshole. Petrosky straightened as he pulled a picture of Hannah from the folder and showed it to Charles, keeping his eyes on Charles's face and not on the image in his hand.

"Doesn't look familiar," Charles said.

He balked. "This was your husband's *daughter*. You've never even seen a picture of her?" It was insane to think that this woman had no idea what Hannah looked like, and yet Charles was shaking her head.

"It brought up bad memories for Theo."

"It?"

"She. Hannah. Whatever. Theo's ex-wife…she turned Hannah against him. Not that he needed all that nonsense once he had us. His ex and her family were probably jealous of what we had." Her deadpan expression made gooseflesh tingle on Petrosky's arms.

Hannah's mother had been a little standoffish—he'd had to keep on her just to get basic information, like her last date of contact with Hannah. But Hannah's mother had been alibied during the *Looking Glass* crimes—ditto on Montgomery's murder—and her inability to fill in the blanks had felt more like estrangement than vindictiveness. Theodore Montgomery, though…he'd erased Hannah as if she'd never existed.

"Ma'am, did you know Hannah was kidnapped?"

Her mouth dropped open, but she recovered just as quickly. "I remember something about her being gone, yes," she said slowly, "from the lawyer after Theo died. But the lawyer said Theo left everything to me. That I didn't have to find her." She met his eyes, shook her head. "I didn't know she'd been taken. Theo never...talked about her."

But that didn't mesh with the man who had called the precinct constantly after Hannah disappeared. The hairs on the back of Petrosky's neck rose. What if...Montgomery hadn't been calling to find out if they'd rescued his beloved daughter? What if he'd been trying to locate her for other reasons? Montgomery had always sounded tense, more nervous than depressed. More...guilty.

In his hand, the photograph shook, and Hannah's smile quivered, her eyes filled, and they were back in the interrogation room where he'd asked her questions during the Ash Park killing spree. At the time, he'd thought her tearful responses, her trembling, were due to the fear of being discovered—that she'd been involved with the murders herself. But maybe she hadn't been terrified of getting in trouble. Maybe she'd been worried because she knew who was after her. Maybe Montgomery used to read his daughter bedtime stories as a child. Stories like *Through the Looking Glass*.

"Did your husband like *Alice in Wonderland? Through the Looking Glass*, maybe?"

She squinted at him and shook her head.

Was he actually entertaining this? *I have to be crazy.* He was here trying to find out who had killed Theodore Montgomery. It wasn't as if Montgomery had murdered a bunch of people, killed himself, and hidden the murder weapon. But Petrosky could almost feel the sick, wet squish as the ideas burrowed deeper into his brain. Theodore Montgomery, a psychopath. And psychos were dicks—someone else could have offed him for that, or because they'd found out Montgomery had murdered their loved one.

Charles's gaze had sharpened like a hawk's. Did she know more than she was letting on? If he was right, and that was a huge if, she might not have been aware her husband was a killer—but she'd have known he was a twisted fuck.

The more Petrosky considered the *Looking Glass* killer's profile, the more the theory fit. Psychopaths were often married; they were good at faking affection even if they didn't feel it. And they were master manipulators, so Montgomery could have hurt his daughter, hurt his wife, hurt his stepdaughter, and found a way to keep them all quiet. Later, Montgomery could have hurt those around Hannah just to frighten her or to punish her for leaving.

Or to punish those who hurt his offspring, like the boyfriend—not out of adoration or a sense of justice, but because Hannah had been *his*. And Theodore Montgomery had wanted her back. He'd found her and tortured her by killing people closer and closer to her until he'd finally taken her. Maybe that was why the killings had stopped: he'd gotten his target. And then he'd killed her.

But Montgomery had been living here in Vermont then, and it was half a day's drive from Ash Park, twelve hours with traffic. His wife would have noticed those absences. Unless…

"Did your husband travel out of town much?"

"He used to go hunting."

Hunting. Maybe for more than deer. And hunting happened in the winter when the *Looking Glass* murders had taken place. Petrosky slouched back in the seat, trying to appear nonchalant, but his muscles were so tight they felt ready to snap. "Do you remember the dates he was gone about five years back?"

She looked at him like he'd lost his mind. "No, I don't remember the precise dates of my husband's hunting trips from years ago. Wasn't like he had a schedule." She crossed her arms. Was she purposefully trying to make this hard?

"What about a planner? An old calendar?"

"He was retired for six years before he died. He didn't need any of that."

Montgomery could have left any morning, been in Ash Park by the evening. Once a month, that's all it would have taken.

Petrosky pulled the photo back from her and returned it to the folder, noting her crossed arms, her tight lips. That, and the dark glittering in her irises as her gaze darted from him to the wall at his back—she was hiding something. Knowledge of her husband's crimes, or knowledge about his death? Maybe both. But if Petrosky was right about Montgomery being a monster, a child in a house like this wouldn't emerge without physical or emotional scars. He didn't have to guess why a sixteen-year-old girl might sit under a tree dragging her fingers through the dirt, unable to connect with other kids her own age. *Trauma.* He'd seen it in seconds. No way Mommy'd missed it.

"So Stacey was seven when you moved in with Mr. Montgomery?"

Charles nodded, the hard look in her eyes brightening—anxiety? Rage? And why couldn't he tell?

No more liquor before an interrogation. Montgomery might have abused the girl physically, or used psychological warfare, breaking her down in other ways. If Montgomery was the *Looking Glass* killer, he was the most dangerous kind of predator: smart. Sadistic. If he wanted to abuse Stacey, he'd have taken the time to groom her, so she didn't out him. He might even have faked normalcy for a time, something psychopaths often did. But kids usually picked up on that crazy, demented energy. "Did Stacey ever seem…upset when your husband was around?"

"Upset? Why would she be upset?" Her gaze was as blank and emotionless as her daughter's had been out front like she couldn't understand "upset" at all.

But Stacey had sure as hell been upset in the front yard

just moments before, racing around the house to avoid him. "Try to think back, Ms. Charles. Maybe some regression after you moved in with Mr. Montgomery? Bed-wetting?"

"She was just starting a new year at school. A few changes of sheets, and it passed." Charles waved a hand, dismissive. "All kids go through that."

No, all kids absolutely did not go through that. But some trauma victims did. "What about nightmares? Changes in sleeping or eating habits?"

She shook her head, her glare so sharp he almost touched his throat to check that she hadn't slashed it open with her eyes.

"What about angry outbursts? Tantrums?"

"Nothing like that," she huffed. "Just what are you trying to ask me, Detective?"

Whether your husband was a serial killer. Whether you...knew about it. The *Looking Glass* crimes were brutal, the mark of a man who caused pain for the fun of it. The ones closest to the killer would not have escaped unscathed. "Is it possible that your husband hurt your daughter?"

Charles reared back like Petrosky'd hit her, her hand covering her mouth as if trying to hold her aggression back. But the anger won out as she snapped: "I—that—that's absurd. Theo would never have hurt Stacey."

As if summoned by their conversation, the back door slammed, and the girl appeared in the archway from the kitchen, staring at him and then her mother in turn.

"If he never touched her, that should be easy to verify with your daughter," Petrosky said, low enough that the girl couldn't hear him. "Then I can be on my way." But Charles's jaw went rigid.

"I'm just covering all the bases, ma'am."

Charles's posture softened only slightly as she waved the girl over. "Stacey, come meet Mr. Petrosky."

Detective. But Petrosky didn't correct her. The girl was

looking at him now: eyes wide, lower lip trembling almost imperceptibly. Stacey sat next to her mother on the couch, then crossed her arms and sighed at her own knuckles. Agitated, like her mother.

"Say hello, sweetheart. Don't be ugly."

Ugly. As if not talking to a stranger made you unattractive. No wonder little girls smiled when they were uncomfortable. No wonder they kept their mouths shut when someone raped them.

"I'm Detective Petrosky. I'm trying to find the man who hurt your stepdad."

Stacey looked up from her hands, her eyes narrowed. "Hi." He had to strain to hear her, but there was no mistaking the tremor in her voice. Afraid? She definitely didn't trust him.

And she shouldn't—trust needed to be earned. *All they get from you is broken promises.*

"Do you like the Backstreet Boys?" he asked.

She finally met his eyes and winced. "They're…old."

Boy bands weren't like the classics. The Doors, Jimi Hendrix, The Rolling Stones—those guys stuck. "Maybe they are," he said. "My daughter…she liked them. Had a poster in her room." Just mentioning Julie made his throat tighten like someone was trying to strangle him—he forced air into his lungs. "Who do you listen to?"

Stacey turned to her mother, eyebrows raised, and Charles nudged her with her elbow. The girl faced forward again. Not very compassionate, but were they responding to more than tension at the situation?

"Um…I guess there are a few people," Stacey said. "But I don't really know their names. I just listen on the radio."

Morrison used to tell him that no one listened to the radio anymore, that you could create your own radio kinda thing—*playlist?*—on your phone. *Looks like you were wrong, Surfer Boy.* Bile rose into the back of his throat, and he swallowed it back down. "Listen, I know this is difficult to talk about. You've been through a terrible ordeal."

Stacey sniffed and huddled closer to her mother, her eyes glassy and distant. Surely more than just a response to her stepfather's death, but he couldn't make her trust him in ten minutes. And he sure as shit couldn't make her admit to being hurt by her stepfather, something she hadn't even told her own mother if Charles was to be believed.

Though maybe the tingle at the base of his neck had nothing to do with Stacey at all. Maybe Montgomery had died because of what he'd done to Melinda Charles. When Stacey turned to her mother again, he followed her gaze—Charles's eyes had hardened to steel. She pulled the girl closer to her, her knuckles white on Stacey's shoulder.

If Charles thought Montgomery had harmed Stacey, she wouldn't have remained here, in a house that would re-traumatize her child. She wouldn't cover her husband's gore with wood laminate and pretend he was a saint. Unless she had no empathy—and psychopaths sometimes had partners who acted "strange" the way Scott had described Charles. Or maybe Charles wasn't protecting Montgomery at all. Maybe she was trying to cover her own sins.

Petrosky put his elbows on his knees and leaned toward the girl. "I'm on your side. I just want to figure out who hurt your stepfather." *Maybe it was your mother.*

Stacey looked at her shoes. Head shakes all around. These people weren't giving him shit, but perhaps he could shock them into letting something slip.

"Montgomery's daughter, Hannah, was assaulted, sliced up, hair ripped from her scalp. And taken. Her boyfriend ended up gutted, just like your husband." He stared at Charles with the same ferocity she was giving him.

"Are you implying we're in danger?" Charles scoffed.

"Right after he died, you were pretty hung up on telling the world it could happen to anyone."

Charles reddened. "It was senseless—unprovoked. It could have happened to anyone, but dragging it out wasn't helping." Stacey winced as Charles's fingers tightened around her shoulder, forcing the girl against her. "But it's been years since that happened. *Years.* If someone was after us, they'd have shown up by now. I want to put this all behind us." She released Stacey and shoved her hands into her lap, her knuckles white around balled fists. But from the agitated gleam in her eyes, Petrosky could tell Melinda Charles knew she had nothing to fear. Whether Montgomery was the *Looking Glass* killer or not, this woman knew more than she should about her husband's death. If Montgomery had hurt Charles or Stacey, maybe Charles wasn't sorry he was dead. Maybe Charles had known exactly what Montgomery'd done, had known what had happened to Hannah. Maybe she'd ripped him open like Harwick to throw everyone off. Or for fun.

Maybe Melinda Charles was just as sick as her husband.

9

____

THE KILLER'S feet crunched along over the dirt, pebbles catching in the soles of his shoes and releasing onto the path over and over. She'd passed him when she came in, the girl with hair the color of smoke. Dyed, not natural—she was only a little older than his daughter.

And she was as stupid as his daughter, too. She hadn't thought anything of it when she'd passed him, sneakers already pounding the dirt, earbuds firmly in place. But then, why would she suspect him? He surely didn't look like someone who could be dangerous.

Aside from his latex gloves—which she wouldn't have noticed—he looked like a bird watcher. A sightseer. He definitely didn't look like a runner, because he wasn't; chasing her would have been a fool's errand. Instead, he'd parked his car well into the woods in a worn dirt lot covered in last season's leaves.

Though the state park was enormous, with miles of thickets and trees and fields, there was only one popular running trail this side of the park—but that wasn't the one she'd preferred two days ago. It was this overgrown trail, thick with briar and pine, where he waited now, camera at the eye of the enormous glasses he didn't actually need, cigarette in his hand. It was a rarity to see others in this section of the park, but it wasn't unheard of—she'd see his back and not be alarmed. Not at first. Stupid girl. She should know better than to run alone in a place so remote. Hopefully she didn't suddenly smarten up. If she didn't show today, he'd have to look for another girl and another place, and his time here was limited—another hour, and he'd be gone.

Then he heard her. He felt the smoke from the cigarette eat into the soft tissue of his lungs, released it, and watched the mist rise into the canopy of trees.

She drew closer, the steady *thump thump thump* of her shoes faster than the beat of his heart, for the hard part was already done: stalking was always more difficult than pouncing.

Closer. *Closer.*

He tossed the cigarette on the dirt path behind him, toward the sound of her thudding sneakers.

"Hey!" She dodged the lit cigarette, and when she did, he turned and lunged at her, throwing all his weight into her chest, clamping his hand over her mouth as they hit the brush, her on her back, him on top. "Don't scream," he whispered, his mouth at her ear. The fall had knocked the breath out of her, rendering her unable to scream for a moment, and it was statistically unlikely that anyone else would be by —not in this thicket of brambles, not when clear paths existed another mile up the main drag. But it didn't pay to take the chance. He peered around and listened to her breath wheezing through her nostrils.

She nodded, her eyes wide and blue as the cloudless sky, a barely audible whimper escaping from beneath his fingers. This part was always interesting. Sometimes they screamed anyway, one futile cry for help, but some remained quiet as if they obeyed thinking he'd let them live.

This one didn't scream when he removed his hand; she was a trusting one, though he could have guessed that from her choice of trail. Her chin trembled like she wanted to cry out, but she kept her lips pressed together so hard the fluids were forced from those pillows of flesh, leaving only a thin, bloodless line. He straightened his glasses, then hooked his fingers under the waistband of her workout pants and yanked them down, just to the knee, but enough for his purposes. He never bothered with the shirt. You'd seen one pair of tits, you'd seen them all.

And then it happened.

A fox, a coyote, something scrabbled beyond the trees, and she screamed, maybe mistaking the first sound for someone who might save her. She yelled again, opening her mouth so wide he could see her tonsils. He sighed and drew the knife from the back of his pants, and ran it over her throat.

Blood spurted from the wound, staining his shirt; air gurgled through the gaping hole in her neck. He unzipped his pants, the condom already on—he'd been hard since he lit the cigarette—and rammed himself into her. Rape was always a little cliché, but it provided an explanation for the attack; the cops would look for suspects with a history of sexual assault arrests and assume this crime was merely an escalation of that pattern.

She gurgled, struggling, but weakly, her hands at her mangled throat as he thrust, five times, six times, and again, until her head finally dropped to the dirt, eyes closed. He pulled himself from her and stood, jerking his underwear up to cover himself. Sex was boring—one of those things he was supposed to do, even here, and so he did it. He was still shocked he'd managed to help his bride conceive their daughter. That night had been cliché too: on a rug in some cabin, in front of a roaring fire. His wife had said it was romantic. If she knew he'd been picturing her flesh burning in the fire from the hearth, she might have reconsidered.

To think that he used to ignore those fantasies. That he'd embraced those thoughts only as he grilled meat on football Sundays. But now…well, when you'd done it once, there really was no going back. Nothing compared to watching human flesh sizzle—smelling the fat burn.

He smiled as he retreated to the tree line and grabbed the lighter fluid: a small bottle, easy to carry and conceal, and he didn't need much. His heart rate increased, sending electricity zinging through his veins as he inserted the tip into her vagina, squeezing the bottle until the fluid began to leak out of her. Then he pulled it out and squeezed more over the tops of her legs, from her knees up, and emptied the rest onto her groin. To the naked eye, the rivulets of clear liquid were as innocent as water. But since when did the eyes see all?

He scanned the ground for his cigarette and found it about ten feet from her shoes, still lit as if it knew it had a job to do here as well. Fire never disappointed. He inhaled deeply, savoring the caustic burn in his throat. Then he pulled out the lighter and bent, relishing the scrape of the flint and the heady kerosene perfume that jacked his heart into hyperdrive.

His hand heated for an instant as she went up, the tendrils of flame licking her flesh, and his cock grew hard, far harder than it had been when he was inside her. He peeled off his gloves, catching the persistent reek that clung to him from work, now mingling with the scent of accelerant and flesh. He shoved his hand into his pants. The flames crept outward from her thighs, igniting her knees, singeing her pubic region, and though around him the wind was thick with the stench of burning hair, he could still catch the butane tinge on the breeze. Then the skin of her thighs blackened, and his breath caught. The cells were transforming in front of his eyes, living the last of their otherwise boring lives in one blistering moment of glory. Relishing that final second when they were, at last, utterly captivating. He'd created that excitement.

A tiny piece of something—fabric or skin—was released from the body and fluttered toward the ground, still aflame, as if the spark itself was dancing. The flicker went out as it hit the earth, and he drew his eyes from the fire to her face. Her eyes were closed, her essence gone, but her body was aroused with the excitement of the flame, just as his was—for one perfect moment they were in sync. The sun kissed her cheek, but it was the subtler glow of orange dancing on her chin that he adored, the reflections of fire that caressed her skin, a new and merciless lover preparing to fuck her all over again. He touched the reflected glow on her cheek—hot, but not hot enough. At least the flames *inside* her body had seared her flesh even if the fire had extinguished itself. In his mind's eye, he could see the swaths of bloody meat surrounded by the black of char, all the charred tissue so tender, so thin. And as the scent of her searing flesh invaded his nostrils, he came, one hand stuffed inside his underwear, the other propped on his knee to keep him upright as the violent contractions ripped through him. The air was ripe with salt and cooking meat, the smoke from her burning body in his hair, on his bloody face, the essence of her enshrouding him.

He righted himself and kicked dirt over her, but the flames were dissipating now that the accelerant had been used up. It depended on the material, how long the blaze lasted. Some companies added flame retardants to their fabrics. Sometimes the sweat dampened the clothing enough to extinguish the fire.

But it didn't matter. The lighter fluid always managed to keep the flame going over their cunts: so much more interesting to burn than to touch.

He zipped his pants and considered the rest of the afternoon. He'd have to go home eventually if he was going to remain *respectable*—he had a job to get back to. It would be interesting to see if Petrosky noticed this one; it seemed the man had stopped paying attention, though maybe one day the detective would decide to open his eyes and ears again—and by then, it'd be too late. It was too late already. It was bad enough that the detective had extinguished his last house fire before it had a chance to taste the night air, but talking down to him…that would prove to be a more grievous error.

Petrosky was out of the office today. Interesting, but not unusual. The detective had a tendency to go on benders, yet this seemed different—his drinking binges were usually triggered by a case, another loss of some bitch he'd connected with. Petrosky was the worst kind of asshole: cliché. The kind who thought he was a savior. One day the detective would surely drink himself to death on the heels of yet another funeral, some dead girl who'd never mattered to anyone until Petrosky made it his mission to care.

The killer smiled. One day he'd push Petrosky all the way over the edge. One day he'd get to go to Petrosky's funeral and peer into the casket at the detective's bloated corpse.

He'd surely be invited.

10

THE STREET WAS hotter than it should have been, the black pavement soaking up the sun's oppressive rays and firing them back at Petrosky as if trying to roast him from the bottom up. The Jack he'd nipped before parking his car in the drugstore lot was dulling his irritation, or at least his shakes. Already he'd almost gotten hit by someone on a bicycle—a grown-ass man with a Kermit-green helmet and matching bike shorts that looked like they would crush the dude's nuts if the guy actually had any.

On either side of the street, little shops that one might call quaint—he called them bullshit—hosted the occasional customer. Few vehicles in the parking spaces. Did all these assholes ride bikes? In front of him, the hot-as-hell road crested over a hill, and when he reached the top, he could see that the shops petered out just after the Willowshire precinct, making way for farms, and in the distance, a mountain: blue-purple and dotted with green vegetation.

He wiped his face and stalked into the hardware store. A far cry from Home Depot, it was just one room the size of a 7-Eleven, with an old paint mixer on the back wall and a few aisles of tools. The place reeked of oil like an auto mechanic's shop—though that might have been coming from the actual auto body place next door.

The wiry man behind the counter looked up and picked at his white afro. Despite the button-down shirt, Petrosky got the distinct impression the guy'd be wearing bell-bottoms behind the tall counter. Maybe they were in some alternate universe where time had reversed direction.

If only.

"Help you?"

Petrosky flashed his badge. "Detective Petrosky. In town from the Ash Park PD," he added when the man raised a bushy white eyebrow. "And you are?"

"Perkins."

"Mr. Perkins." Petrosky opened the folder with Montgomery's picture, more for ceremony than out of necessity: if the guy knew Montgomery, he didn't need the image, and if he didn't know Montgomery, he wouldn't be able to help. Petrosky needed answers of a personal nature. "Did you know Theodore Montgomery?"

The guy smiled, but it was tinged with regret, even sorrow, unlike the reaction of Montgomery's wife and step-daughter. Then again, it wasn't like Montgomery would've ever made this guy "fall out of a tree."

"Everybody knew Theo. Went hunting with him a few times."

Montgomery had actually been hunting? But that didn't mean anything; if Montgomery went hunting regularly, it wouldn't have appeared suspicious had he disappeared for twenty-four hours on his own. Montgomery could have gone to Michigan, gutted a victim, and then headed right back to the woods to hunt furrier prey, claiming he'd been out in the forest the whole time. Cold. Calculating. Manipulative. Like a guy who would keep his daughter's kidnapping from his new family even as he called the precinct to make sure they weren't on his tail.

Whoa, now. He could still be wrong about all of this. Montgomery could have been a normal guy, a family man, a hunter, and not the *Looking Glass* killer or even an abuser. But the memory of Stacey's glassy eyes spurred him on. "He have any enemies?"

"Theo?" Perkins chuckled and shook his head. "No way. He was a great guy. Even let his younger daughter stay with him after his wife left."

And the elder daughter had gone with mom. Not the most common arrangement, splitting children up like that, but playing favorites wasn't unusual, especially in sexual abuse cases. Had Hannah wanted to stay with him, or had Montgomery fought to keep the child he'd groomed? But he couldn't ask Montgomery's friend that, at least not directly. "Tell me more about the kids."

"Stacey doesn't get out much, but Hannah was always well-behaved when they came into town."

Well-behaved. Code for compliant? That was a predator's wet dream.

"I was a little surprised that Hannah was the one who went off to study abroad," Perkins was saying. "She was always so quiet—not like her older sister. Spitfire, Emily was."

If Hannah's sister was a spitfire, that would explain why Montgomery wouldn't want Emily around—pedophiles didn't like a challenge. But that wasn't what sent Petrosky's heart ramming into his breastbone. He'd looked through Hannah's history before: she had come straight from Vermont to Ash Park with no lag time, and she'd stayed there for five years. She hadn't taken off for parts unknown. No suggestion of wanderlust. She hadn't even left the country. So why did this man think she had?

Because that's what Montgomery had told him. For a child to run away, that was a big deal. So instead of fielding uncomfortable questions about why his girl had run off from her obviously loving parent, Montgomery had made up a story to tell his friends until he could find Hannah himself. And bring her home again.

Hannah'd had a reason for leaving Willowshire. And Stacey had a reason for her twitchy demeanor; for the symptoms of trauma her mother insisted weren't symptoms at all. Maybe other girls had fallen victim to Montgomery there in Willowshire. His prime suspect for Montgomery's murder was still Melinda Charles, but if there were more molestation victims or rape victims—whatever it was Montgomery had done to these girls—then Petrosky had a larger pool of potential suspects. He sighed. Even then, he couldn't rule out the connection to the *Looking Glass* case. Without a viable suspect, he had to consider that the *Looking Glass* killer or some sick copycat had strolled into town, offed Montgomery for hurting Hannah, and disappeared into thin air. Again. "You ever see Theo with anyone else?" he asked.

"Like who?" But Perkins narrowed his eyes.

"Other women? Other kids?"

Perkins was staring as if he'd smelled something bad. "You sound just like that kid. Detective whatever-his-name-was. Trying to make a big stink over nothing." He shook his head. "Don't trust that kid, not at all."

Petrosky sighed again, trying to disguise his frustration, though it made sense that Perkins was unaware of any wrongdoing on the part of his buddy; people were often blind to what they didn't expect. "Did Theo ever take vacations?" Maybe he could at least pin him to the *Looking Glass* killer's timeline. "Disappear for a couple days when he was supposed to be hunting with you?"

"Can't say I recall that."

The bell behind Petrosky dinged, and Perkins's expression soured. Petrosky turned to see Scott coming through the door, beads of sweat along his hairline, a case file clasped firmly against his chest. His gaze danced nervously from Petrosky to Perkins and back again.

Petrosky cleared his throat. "What are you doing here, Scott?"

"Around here, people call when they see a strange guy walking up the road. Besides, I already talked to Mr. Perkins here."

Perkins snorted, sat back down behind the counter, and picked up his magazine again. The guy wasn't going to be any help, and from the look in Scott's eyes, he was well aware of that fact. Petrosky pushed aside the sinking sensation in his gut. He had hijacked Scott's investigation and was probably doing the same shit the kid had already done, even though Scott clearly hadn't considered that Montgomery himself might be the *Looking Glass* killer. And though Scott had missed interviewing Montgomery's widow, he might not have even picked up on the subtle signs of distress that Petrosky'd seen in the stepdaughter. Kid was smart, but he was still a rookie. Petrosky glanced once more at Perkins—nose still in the magazine—and headed for the door. Scott followed close behind.

"Who the hell you calling strange anyway?" Petrosky said as they turned onto the road.

Scott's eyes widened. "No, I mean...these people don't know you."

"I'm kidding, Scott. Your funny bone broken?" He sounded like Jackson. She'd probably have busted into Perkins's shop or Melinda's house, gotten their perp, and been en route back to Michigan already.

Why the hell was he thinking about Jackson? Like he missed her or some bullshit, which he definitely did not—he was just anticipating her lip when he got back to work. If he got back to work. He might already be fired, but he had no way to tell; he'd conveniently left his phone in the car with his bottle of Jack Daniels. He didn't need to be reminded of how badly he'd messed up with Shannon—or that he should probably call her and apologize again.

The sun beat against the back of his neck as he followed Scott up the street. "Where we going anyway?"

"There's a girl I want you to meet."

A girl? He rubbed his neck with his hand as if his palm could keep the sun from burning him. It only made him feel more feverish. But it wasn't cooking skin that he smelled—it was salt. Grease. *Pizza.* Two doors down, he saw a thick orange awning with white bubble letters that looked like a finger painting. Scott inclined his head toward the door.

Inside, four pies lined the front counter behind sneeze-guard glass, and on the back wall, an enormous pizza oven rotated, filling the air with the scent of oil and cheese and oregano. His mouth watered.

Scott held up two fingers to the woman behind the counter, and she grinned. She had dark hair, dark irises, and painfully pink skin with rings of white around her eyes like she'd been wearing sunglasses when she passed out on a lounge chair. Petrosky touched the back of his neck. His skin was still hot.

"Hey, Ophelia," Scott said.

She nodded and smiled again, but her eyes clouded. "Man, you guys really know how to welcome a girl. You were just here yesterday, and you're the third random person in here today trying to check me out." Her face went an even deeper shade of maroon when Scott raised an eyebrow. "No, not check me out, but like…you know. See who I am."

Before Petrosky could ask why anyone would care who she was, Scott said, "Ophelia just moved here from Canada."

Petrosky nodded, though he couldn't give a shit less where she came from. His stomach was growling, as persistent as the headache taking root in his brain. *Enough screwing around, Scott.* But then the kid was passing him a pepperoni slice, which tempered Petrosky's agitation as Scott asked

Ophelia who'd been in to see her and whether she'd made any friends yet. Petrosky would have thought the kid was hitting on her if it hadn't been for the standoffish position he'd taken—stiff and professional—at the head of the counter. Petrosky shoved a bite of pizza into his mouth and chewed. Delicious.

"There was that one guy I told you about who comes in almost every day. From the bookstore?" She shook her head. "He's creepy."

"Yeah, about that," Scott said, leaning his weight on the countertop. "What's he order?"

Cool it, rookie—can't be too eager. He glowered at Scott, but the kid ignored him.

She paused and licked her sunburned lips. "Large meat lover's and a veggie deluxe, usually. Sometimes pepperoni and double cheese."

Scott was staring at Petrosky like he was supposed to know why this order was significant. It wasn't like the mystery guy had asked for pineapple; that would have been a dead giveaway. Only a psychopath ruined a pizza with pineapple.

"What else?" Scott said, and Petrosky narrowed his eyes at the girl as she replied: "And sometimes he winks. It's gross."

Maybe this bookstore guy was a creepy dickface. But Scott couldn't possibly think the pizza parlor girl was another of Montgomery's abuse victims—she'd just gotten into town.

Scott said, "He say who the pizza was for?"

Uh...for himself? Petrosky could put away a whole pie in ten minutes.

"Nope." She shrugged.

Scott had his own slice of pizza boxed for later, though the kid looked like he could eat three pizzas a day and still need a little extra padding on his bones.

"Want to tell me what's so amazing?" Petrosky asked as they left the building.

"I was in here last night, and after you left this afternoon, things just clicked, about the bookstore owner, like in the movies."

Jesus Tap-dancing Christ. "More details, less bullshit, Scott."

"Right, okay, so you asked who else might want to hurt Montgomery."

"You got a bookstore owner with a motive?"

"I… Maybe." He frowned. "Crandall, the bookstore owner, lives alone. No reason he needs two large pizzas."

"So what? Maybe he's got employees. Maybe he's bringing it to a girlfriend or—"

"He's probably throwing it out."

Blasphemous. "Arrest his ass for wasting pizza, then. And steal his leftovers."

Scott raised an eyebrow. "No, listen, Crandall has a record: a sex offender conviction. I think he's showing up here to talk to Ophelia."

The kid was giving him a fucking headache. There could be a hundred sex offenders in this town who had jack shit to do with their case. "Still not following, Scott. Ophelia isn't a child. And Crandall might be a creep, but if Montgomery was hurting those around him, they're more likely—"

"I know, it's usually someone close to the victim. Look at the family. Melinda and Stacey alibied one another—said they were out walking. Nothing that I can verify. But I can't imagine that a thirteen-year-old would have held it together like that if she'd watched her mother kill her stepfather. Plus, neither of them knew it was Hannah's birthday."

"So they said, but—"

"They had never spoken to her. Never met her. Had no idea what she even looked like. Even Hannah's flesh and blood—her mother and her sister—haven't spoken to her in ten years. And the stories from both Melinda and Stacey have been consistent from the day it happened through last week when I interviewed them again."

So Scott *had* been at the Montgomery house recently. Had Petrosky misunderstood Charles? He racked his brain, trying to recall exactly what she'd said, but came up blank. *Stupid Jack.*

"I think we should go talk to Crandall," Scott said.

Because he had a sex offender rap? Montgomery hadn't been sexually assaulted, nor had the victims in Ash Park. "Explain to me why Crandall has dick to do with this. Explain it like I'm an idiot, Scott." A history of sex offenses didn't make one a murderer. And Crandall wouldn't have known Hannah's birthday—everyone in this town thought she was off studying abroad. Not like Montgomery was going to celebrate her birthday on his own.

"Crandall has a history of being rather...aggressive about his record. Five years back, he coldcocked a guy from out of town just for bringing it up."

Petrosky stared into the distance as if an answer might be hiding in the sinister purple hills. It made sense for a sex offender to get defensive about someone outing him. But—

"Crandall didn't even register as an offender, there or here," Scott said. "The guy who outed him found out through the grapevine. And at the root of the vine..."

"Theodore Montgomery." No wonder Scott's eyes were lit up like a five-year-old's on Christmas morning. "Then why the hell didn't they investigate Crandall before?" *And why didn't you tell me about this earlier?*

His smile fell. "They did investigate him."

"Then why—"

"They looked at Crandall in a different context. There were rumors he'd been having an affair with Melinda Charles, and when those rumors couldn't be substantiated, they dropped it."

Petrosky sucked his teeth, considering. If there'd been

truth to the rumors, he could see Montgomery telling the world about Crandall's sex offender conviction—hell, he could see *anyone* who found out telling the town, either for safety reasons or because the gossip was just too juicy. It would especially make sense for Montgomery to out Crandall if he thought the man had a thing for his wife. He could also see Crandall killing Montgomery in a jealous rage, or because good old Theo had hurt Charles. But… "There's a big problem, though, Scott."

"Yeah, I know. Hannah's birthday." Scott hung his head. Rookie or no, he'd need to grow a thicker skin.

"It's not a coincidence. Montgomery's killer had to be someone who knew about Hannah." *Someone who wanted to make Hannah suffer.* Petrosky didn't want to say that out loud; that was the insanity McCallum was always warning about, illogical thoughts masquerading as logical so he didn't have to deal with the shit he didn't want to. "Fine," he said, heading for the car. "Let's go talk to Crandall."

It didn't hurt to be thorough.

CLOSED. How do you close a bookstore early in the middle of the week? Petrosky wanted to talk to that bastard, wanted to prod him. Analyze Crandall before the guy caught on to why he was being examined. Watch his face to see if he'd slip. Petrosky'd have to wait until tomorrow to catch the guy by surprise. He wasn't about to stake out the bookstore—by all accounts, Crandall was unlikely to return to the shop tonight, and the place was right next to the precinct. How much trouble could he get into?

Scott headed home while Petrosky settled into his room for the night. The bed-and-breakfast he was staying at was not a real motel: no minibar, and at the bottom of the stairs, someone had set out a plate of berries, a bowl of apples, and a jar of some kind of butter made out of almonds. Morrison would have loved it. A sign on the sideboard promised smoked salmon in the morning, the accompanying image cringe-worthy: a slab of meat, raw and pink like someone had just killed it. Some jackass, bike helmet tucked under his arm, nodded to Petrosky. Petrosky grimaced at him until he looked away, then made his way up the stairs.

Bicycles. It was like everyone here wanted to be ten years old. He finished half the bottle of Jack in his tiny room, but the liquor didn't stop the throbbing in his temples. Was Theodore Montgomery himself the *Looking Glass* killer? Or did they have a copycat, some random stranger obsessed with the *Looking Glass* case, who'd killed Montgomery because he was related to Hannah? The other theory was that the *Looking Glass* killer had murdered Montgomery a year after the Ash Park rampage.

Something had shifted in the air, making the hair rise on his arms, though he couldn't place the source of his sudden disquiet. Things were never clear until it was too late. And then answers were of no consolation, not when the ones you cared about were beyond saving.

SHE WAS THERE, standing at the edge of his bed, watching him sleep, her smile wide. But her eyes were tinged with a sorrow beyond reckoning as if somewhere in her too-short life she'd felt the anguish of her coming demise. *Julie.* Petrosky opened his mouth to cry out to her, to tell her he was sorry, but instead of sound escaping his lips, smoke billowed from his insides as if his guts were on fire. The walls faded into nothingness, revealing the dusky gray of the field, a swarm of newly hatched fireflies...and *him*. Creeping up behind her, a dark shadow, but Petrosky knew who he was—what he was. Closer. Fireflies skittered around the killer as if in warning, and the air filled with the stench of a corpse left out in the sun: rotting fruit mixed with something meaty and putrid and horrible. Closer. But Julie didn't see the shadow—didn't move—just stood there smiling at her father. Petrosky's limbs were weighted, thick, immobile. A firefly lit on the tip of his ring finger. He willed his hand to clench around the bug, but he could not even flick it away.

And he could not get to his daughter. He was going to watch her die.

A single tear leaked from Julie's eye, and she reached out, brushed Petrosky's fingers, and captured the bug from his skin. Then the shadow attacked, a fog as thick as oil, engulfing his baby girl in an impenetrable void of blackness. The last thing to vanish was her lithe fingers as they released the firefly into the air.

"Fly away, fly," she whispered as she disappeared into nothingness.

Petrosky jolted upright, heart hammering in his temples, his shirt soaked through with sweat. He reached for Julie's box but found only air, and then he was falling, his shoulder hitting the wood like he'd just tried to bulldoze his way through someone's front door. Should have at least had a rug to break his fall.

Shitty B&B. Cocksucking, moose-humping jerks.

He heaved his way back onto the bed, groping for a bottle in the sheets.

Just weeks before she was taken, Julie'd caught him a firefly. He'd kept it in a jar on his desk, dead and dry, for months after her death until his wife had found it and thrown it in the trash. He'd rescued the jar, but he'd never forgiven Linda for that.

He refocused on the bottle and thought of nothing but the crisp clack of the cap, and soon the liquor was burning down his gullet and smothering the remnants of the dream.

The rotting flesh stink of Julie's attacker was still cloying at the back of his throat.

Through the window, the sky was black. Empty. Cold. Far too early for the raw fish breakfast this place had promised him. Far too early for much of anything. But when Petrosky peered into the back corner, he could almost make out a revolving black mist still encroaching on the room. He could almost smell it. And as he tipped the bottle to his lips again, he was certain he heard Julie's voice, whispering from the darkness for him to save her.

11

———

THE BOOKSTORE WOULD BE empty this time of morning, but it wasn't like Petrosky could sleep now—might as well stake the place out. From the passenger seat, Scott rubbed his hands over his arms, and Petrosky cranked the heat to ward off the chill that had set in the moment the sun had dropped behind the mountain the night before. The hillside was masked in gloom as black and soft as a rotten tooth. Not even a mosquito buzzed by the windshield as though the frost in the air had frightened even the insects away. In those fuzzy woods in the distance, though, surely warmer predators lurked, unfazed by the cold.

The bookstore was dark inside, not a single security light. As he drove closer to the building, Petrosky squinted at the precinct lot next door, where one lone cruiser was parked—probably belonging to Crowley. No doubt that asshole was sitting in his chair by the window and glowering into the murky dawn, just waiting for someone to show up, so he could put on his fake-ass smile and act like he was making a difference in the world. Hopefully, Crowley would at least keep that shit inside the building instead of coming out to harass them. With no inconspicuous place to park on the deserted road, Petrosky slid his car into the spot beside the empty police cruiser and glanced at the rookie.

Scott's eyes were closed, the side of his head against the passenger window. He must have been up late, probably investigating more pizza-related hunches. Or maybe not; when Petrosky had arrived at Scott's house at four-thirty that morning, the kid was already awake, holding what looked like an empty IV bag in his hand. Scott had only hesitated a moment before nodding at Petrosky and disappearing into the back bedroom. Sick family member? Hidden illness? Petrosky'd waited outside while the rookie finished his business, and didn't ask about it when the kid emerged.

In the light of the single streetlamp, Petrosky opened Scott's file on Crandall to memorize the photo: round face, clean-shaven, and hair as white as the snow that probably covered this entire town from September through May. This old geezer had been chatting up the girl at the pizza joint? What a prick. Maybe more of a prick than anyone realized if he'd been a part of Montgomery's death. If Montgomery had told the town about Crandall's sex offender conviction, that was motive. And it was his job to trap Crandall into admitting it.

But even if Crandall did admit that Montgomery had outed him, would Montgomery's case lead them to the *Looking Glass* killer? To Hannah's killer? That was why he'd come here, wasn't it? And if Crandall had killed Montgomery out of anger, he was no closer to finding Hannah's body, or to wrapping up the *Looking Glass* case.

Hannah. He could still see her dark hair crusted with snow, swirling in the breeze from the frozen lake. He could see her green eyes too, wide and hurt and glassy—upset that he'd accused her of murdering her boyfriend. And he'd been wrong. She'd probably died believing he thought her guilty. That sat like a rock in his gut as he watched the sky lighten behind the mountain, changing the peaks from black, to dusty gray to midnight blue to purple. The rock in his belly would grow heavier when he finally found Hannah's bones, for no matter how often he wished for her to be alive, she had been the *Looking Glass* killer's *target*. And the killer had already hurt everything around her.

He'd always hoped for irrational things. That the body they'd found wasn't really Julie's. That he'd find Morrison alive. He'd even hoped beyond hope that he and his ex-wife could manage to find one another in the bleak days after Julie's death, but Julie'd had Linda's eyes, her chin, her hair, and Petrosky's ears, the only part of him he would ever wish on another person. After they'd buried Julie, those physical similarities were no longer pleasant or comforting—they were painful reminders of the daughter they had lost. And to think he'd hoped—even briefly—that he could get his shit together and be a solid part of Shannon's family after Morrison died—he should have known better.

Every time, he'd hoped. Every time, he'd been wrong.

The sound of Scott's soft snores permeated the inside of the car like the subtle growling of a moderately irritated beast. Like his ex-mother-in-law, though the muted din of Scott's restless sleep was nowhere near as unpleasant as any sound that came out of that wench of a woman. Petrosky lit a cigarette, exhaled a plume of smoke through the crack in the window, and for a moment, the cloud morphed into the shadowy figure from his dream before dissipating into the mountain air. He swallowed hard, leaning back against the seat until the gun strapped against his back pressed into his ribs. Still there. Maybe once he found Hannah's body, he could put it all to rest with her, and then he'd go home... alone. With his ghosts and his gun.

Isolation. That was what he always did, and he was too damn old to change it now. Shannon could surely feel it, the way he'd been pushing her away. He'd done the same to his wife after Julie's death when their love had been replaced by something aching and awful. Alone, he didn't have to see the agony of grief mirrored back to him. Alone, he could subdue the pain into a blunt, persistent ache instead of the all-encompassing pressure that threatened to make his chest implode. Petrosky tossed the cigarette from the window, glanced at Scott's closed eyelids, and slid the bottle from the sleeve of his jacket. The liquor burned its way down his gullet and eased some of the tightness in his chest, though it still felt like an invisible rope was winding its way around his rib cage.

He readjusted his hips in the seat and drew his gaze back to the quiet bookstore, its red brick dusky in the tempered glow of morning. He stared down the road. Empty. No sign of Crandall. Petrosky turned back to the file in his hand, the liquor already softening the sharp edges around his heart as he tried to review what he knew—which was jack shit outside of the fact that *someone* had killed Theodore Montgomery and that the killing had something to do with Hannah because he'd been murdered on her birthday.

But as Petrosky read Crandall's file, the quiet discontent that had followed him all morning swelled, tightening his chest again, despite the liquor. Crandall had been busted forty years ago at age eighteen for the statutory rape of a fifteen-year-old. Crandall had married his victim the month she turned eighteen. They'd never had any children but remained married for almost thirty years until she died in an automobile accident ten years ago.

On paper, Crandall seemed to have been convicted on a technicality. That had to chap Crandall's ass, especially if Montgomery was spouting off about him being a pedophile.

Petrosky scrunched his eyes shut and rubbed at his pace-maker scar. If Crandall had motive, fine. But the birthday. Why her birthday?

Crandall could have come upon Hannah's birthday by researching the man; maybe Crandall had hoped to find dirt on Montgomery after Theo had spilled Crandall's sex offender conviction to the entire town. But that was far-fetched, even for him.

Movement down the street caught his attention, and he set the folder aside. *There he is.* The dark obscured Crandall's features, but the hair seemed right. And he was walking up the road from the direction of his house, less than a mile away.

Petrosky frowned as Crandall approached, more slowly than seemed normal, his gait...unsteady. The bookstore owner was hunched, one hand holding a bat— no, a *cane*— and he leaned on it every so often as he made his way up the walk and past the precinct. He came close enough to spot Petrosky sitting in the car if he'd been looking, but Crandall kept his eyes on the walk as if working to keep himself upright. *What the hell?* As Crandall approached the book-store, he raised a Styrofoam coffee cup to his lips and tried to take a sip, but a tremor in his wrist caused the drink to splash through the hole in the lid.

Petrosky leaned over Scott in the passenger seat, squinting at Crandall's back as the man set the cane against the brick wall of the bookstore and fumbled for his keys. It took him four tries to unlock the door.

Palsy? Some type of degenerative muscular disease? Or just old as dirt?

Petrosky glanced at his sleeping comrade, balling his fists to avoid slapping the kid awake. They'd gotten up at the ass crack of dawn and wasted good drinking time on a guy who couldn't physically have murdered anyone. It was possible that Montgomery had been napping, and Crandall had managed to run a blade over his belly, but that wasn't likely. Unless Crandall *used* to be steadier. It had been three-and-a-half years since Montgomery's death, but two years before that, Crandall had gotten into a fistfight in another town over his sex offender conviction—and he'd been stable enough to slug someone then.

Crandall disappeared inside the building, and soon the interior brightened with yellow lamplight. No movement on the street. No customers. Petrosky waited until tendrils of sunlight had crept over the mountain and onto the pavement before he shoved a piece of gum in his mouth and elbowed Scott awake. Might as well have the kid play lookout while he went inside to talk to Crandall.

Without the acrid cloud of cigarette smoke to precede him, the morning air assaulted Petrosky with the sickly sweet aroma of fresh-cut grass and cow shit, and whatever was growing up in those mountains. But inside, the bookstore was cool and paper-dry and smelled of dust mites and something almost like leather. Bookbindings? Every available surface was covered with novel upon novel. Even the purchasing counter, no bigger than an average desk, was more than half-hidden by paperbacks. An older-model cash register—with buttons like a typewriter and a pop-out drawer—nestled in the empty space between the stacks.

Petrosky stepped to the front window and peered through the glass to the road outside where the sidewalk was practically glowing with the rise of dawn. Birds twittered at one another, a poor man's alarm clock. He ignored the giddy bastards and turned his attention to the tables on either side of the front window, one of them already drenched in sun. Poetry books. That was interesting, wasn't it? Or perhaps not; this was a bookstore. The shaded table was stacked with novels. One with a rain-washed woman on the cover, fingernails clawing her own hip, caught his eye. *Beyond the Break?* He flipped through it, squinting at the words. Girl-on-girl. Shit, with all the assholes out there, women'd probably be better off going with other women, especially here in the land of bicycle shorts—he couldn't imagine a more appropriate place for women to shun the moose-riding idiots altogether.

A grunt behind him turned Petrosky around. Crandall had appeared behind the counter, bushy white eyebrows raised in greeting, or maybe suspicion. His white hair was long enough on the sides to cover the tops of his ears, but thin enough that Petrosky could clearly see the wires from a hearing aid. He remembered Ophelia from the pizza place, and his stomach soured.

Crandall didn't seem to notice Petrosky's disdain: the guy smiled, revealing teeth as yellowed as the books in his dusty store. His toffee eyes crinkled at the corners. "Wicked hot out there, eh?"

"It is, sir, it is." Petrosky tucked the girl-on-girl book under his arm and approached the counter. He would give it to Jackson, and she'd either think he was funny and decide not to tell on him for skipping town this week, or she'd report him for sexual harassment. Either way, the look on her face would be worth it.

"Find what you were looking for?" Crandall's smile remained, but he searched Petrosky's face as if he was trying to decide what Petrosky was really doing there.

Petrosky shook his head. "Not sure. Just poking around, seeing if anything jumps out at me." Petrosky watched Crandall carefully and leaned one elbow against the counter. Crandall sat back in his chair at Petrosky's nearness, but that didn't mean much—he'd been raised in a generation where men did not like their personal space invaded by other men. Petrosky couldn't remember his own father ever so much as hugging him. "Maybe you can help me, though," he said. "I'm on the way out to Presque Isle for the week. To see a woman I met online if you can believe that. It's been a long time since I dated, I'll tell you what." If he was just passing through, maybe Crandall would be more loose-lipped.

Though Petrosky still wasn't sure what he expected the man to say.

A corner of Crandall's mouth turned up, and his gaze lost a little of its suspicious edge.

"Thing is, she's younger than I am, and I'm scared I'll get her the wrong thing—never dated anyone so much younger."

"I understand that, sir." Crandall smiled with his entire face, eyes gleaming as brightly as the sun on the floor.

"Do you now?" *Or do you just wish you had a piece like Ophelia?*

"A real man never kisses and tells. You and I are of a generation that knows that." The friendly twitch at the corners of his lips faded.

Petrosky leaned toward him, close enough to detect the faint hint of tobacco on the guy's breath. "True, true. My kids drag it out of me, tell me they worry about me being alone. Maybe they wonder what I'm up to in my spare time." He forced a smile, but even the liquor couldn't quell the erratic pounding in his temples. *My kids.* He'd never get to say that and mean it.

Crandall sniffed and leveled a glare at Petrosky. "I'm too old to care what anyone thinks."

Well, that escalated quickly. Petrosky eased off the counter. "I don't have to kiss and tell to know my girl loves books. Said she wants to be an author someday."

"That's no trouble," Crandall said, his eyes softening a touch but not enough to suggest he trusted Petrosky. "What kind of novels does she fancy herself writing?"

"Poetry."

Crandall's gaze darkened for only a moment—had Petrosky imagined it?—but the man nodded knowingly and said, "I've got just the thing."

He heaved himself from his chair—stool, rather—every step requiring far more determination than seemed fair for simply moving through a room. No cane now, but still shaky. He ran one gnarled paw along the shelves until he reached a bookcase at the back. "I have everything here from Edgar Allan Poe to Emily Dickinson to Robert Frost." He waved at the shelf, the tremor in his wrist turning his hand into a leaf shuddering on a breeze.

"Got anything a little more unique?" Like *Through the Looking Glass*? If Crandall brought that out first, Petrosky would slam him against the wall and haul him in. His fingers twitched with anticipation.

"Hmm. I can order you whatever you're looking for. I have a little William Wordsworth, and I had a collection by Rabindranath Tagore, but I gave that one to my girlfriend."

His…girlfriend? If he had a girlfriend, the nosy assholes in this town would have known, even with his don't-kiss-and-tell policy. Did he mean Ophelia? That woman sure as shit wasn't his girlfriend. Unless he was a stalker who fancied himself her boyfriend—he was enough of a creepy dickhead for Petrosky to believe that, too.

Crandall leaned against the back bookcase with his elbow on the shelf. Petrosky nodded, every muscle in his face taut with the effort of not scowling. "Your girlfriend likes poetry, too?" he said, impressed that his voice remained even.

"She does." Crandall glanced at the front door as if hoping someone would walk in and save him from the conversation. He turned back to Petrosky. "If you're just passing through, I can send something to your final destination. Do you have an address in Presque Isle?"

"Actually, I think I'll come back by on my way home. Fingers crossed she'll be leaving Maine with me." Crandall would find out soon enough that he wasn't going to Maine, and that the only girls he was concerned about were Hannah and the others who'd lost their lives to the *Looking Glass* killer. But he wasn't going to find a killer by tiptoeing around everything.

"One last question, sir. I had a friend here once—Montgomery. Theo Montgomery. We lost touch a few years back, but I'd love to catch up before heading out. You know him?"

The helpful twinkle disappeared completely from Crandall's gaze, which hardened to stone as the air around them fell into silence. "He's dead now. Murdered." Crandall averted his eyes to rest on the bookshelves along the far wall. Even the birds outside seemed to be holding their breath.

"Well, shit." Petrosky shook his head. "That's a damn shame."

By the time Crandall turned back, he'd arranged his face into a neutral mask, but Petrosky caught the subtle flare of his nostrils. Crandall most definitely did not think it was a shame that Theodore Montgomery had been sliced open in his living room.

"His daughter must have been devastated," Petrosky said slowly.

Now the planes of Crandall's face softened. "Yeah, Stacey was a little shook up."

"Stacey? He have another daughter since I knew him? I was talking about Hannah."

Crandall shook his head. "Never heard of her." Petrosky waited for the hairs on the back of his neck to stand at attention as he watched for a shift in the man's face, a telltale twitch of the eye suggesting he knew about Hannah—and her death. But Crandall, who had thus far been terrible at hiding his feelings, showed no sign of recognition at all. Crandall'd had a reason to off Montgomery, but without knowledge of Hannah or her birthday...

Time for a different tactic. Throw him off balance, see if something slipped. "Can't say I'm shocked Theo's dead," Petrosky began. "He could be kind of a bastard, you know. Guess it isn't a surprise he finally pissed off the wrong fellow."

Crandall's eyes narrowed. "Thought you said you were friends."

"You know how it is. Since I was here, I guess curiosity got the better of me." Petrosky shrugged, trying to appear nonchalant, but the dark glitter in Crandall's eyes was enough to tighten his shoulders. The man had something else to say about Montgomery, but he wasn't going to spill it now. Maybe he'd give it up at the station.

"You want to buy that?" Crandall gestured to the book in Petrosky's hand.

"I do."

Crandall trembled his way back to his perch behind the counter, Petrosky following. He would come back to the bookstore tonight and poke around, see if he could find anything to lend credence to Scott's hunch. Scott had said Crandall didn't have a security system at the store or his house. Guess you didn't need an alarm in a place where everybody knew everybody else. For now... No matter how fast Crandall walked, he'd never make it to his house before Petrosky could search it. It was a long shot and a half, but no one else openly hated Montgomery as much as Crandall did. Hopefully, he would find something they could use, some tiny bit of previously hidden information about the town or someone in it, to put away Montgomery's killer—and maybe close the *Looking Glass* case, too.

Close the case—but there'd be no closure. Not until he buried Hannah's bones.

12

———————

"THIS IS A TERRIBLE IDEA, Detective Petrosky. We can go to jail for this."

Petrosky jammed his Swiss Army knife into the space between the knob and the doorjamb. "Wait in the car if you're that worried about it," he said through clenched teeth. "Otherwise, shut the fuck up."

Scott closed his mouth. Petrosky glanced back over his shoulder at the road, then went back to wiggling the blade. Crandall's place was on a piece of land that might have once been a horse farm, though Petrosky had seen nothing about horses or livestock in Crandall's file. The house itself sat at the top of one of the rolling hills that surrounded the mountain, perched as if watching the entire town. The grazing land below the crest of the hill was green and dotted with bright orange wildflowers—zits on an iguana. The wind was crisper up here than it was in town, hissing down the mountains and through the blades of grass like an avalanche of chilled breath that still bore the earthy tinge of ice and snow. Down in the valley behind the house, a creek meandered through the hills, stretching past other farmhouses in the distance. Petrosky could see what looked like barns and

III

electric fences, and maybe a few horses or cows wandering the grounds. But Crandall had no animals. Just the flowers in clusters of orange or blue or yellow as if the field were a graveyard, each burst of color an otherwise unmarked tomb.

The click of the lock seemed to echo through the quiet air, and though it was surely his imagination, he stilled, listening to a distant tractor, the breath of the ghostly wind on his back.

"Detective, really—"

"I told you to wait in the car."

But Scott followed him into the dark kitchen and closed the door behind them. No windows in this part of the house, though dusty morning light whispered through an archway from what was probably the living room. Petrosky held his flashlight in his teeth—dim, but good enough. There was no point in risking the overheads. Anyone in the field below wouldn't catch a downward-facing flashlight beam, and he couldn't bear to use the flashlight on his phone any longer, the same app he'd used the day he discovered the scene of Morrison's murder. Now, every time he turned the cell light on, blood burned across his memory and tinted whatever he was looking at a vibrant crimson.

The flashlight showed him nothing of importance in the first kitchen drawer: sharpened pencils, a pad of paper, keys. In another drawer, silverware glinted dully in neat rows, every fork nestled inside the one beneath.

"Oh no." Scott's whisper was so faint that Petrosky thought he was imagining it for a moment. He turned to the kid and trained the flashlight in Scott's direction, hoping his little prodigy-sidekick for the week had found a clue that might make the morning's exercise in futility mean some-goddamn-thing. But the kid's gaze was not riveted to a drawer or a book or scouring the lines of some message on the fridge; he stared behind Petrosky with a look of unbridled horror. Scott's neck was corded—shoulders tensed. The kid was ready to bolt.

What the—

Petrosky heard the growl then, a low rumbling like a vehicle trying to decide whether it would start. Then a sneeze-like snarl. He turned slowly to see a Great Dane, black and sleek, its monstrous head as high as Petrosky's belly, its teeth bared, cropped ears trained on them—less than ten feet away from where he stood. The dust motes in the air halted their fevered dance, and the wind outside suddenly hushed and stilled, all the world seeming to bow to the beast in the doorway.

Petrosky flicked his gaze to the counter, the floor, but saw nothing that might shield him from the dog's wicked bite. If the animal leapt at him, Petrosky would be on his back, unable to get at his weapon before the dog ripped his throat out. He kept the light in his teeth and reached slowly, carefully, for his gun.

The silence was shattered by the barking of the animal, deep and throaty and vicious. "No, no, no, down boy," Scott moaned behind him. The edges of Petrosky's vision tunneled so that he no longer saw anything but the dog. But he could hear the shuffling of Scott's feet, *shh, shh, shh*, almost as loud as his own labored breathing.

"Stay still," Petrosky whispered. "You run, it'll attack." *Shh, shh, shh.* The kid was going to lose it. No matter how smart he was, he was still a kid. Impulsive. And it might get them killed.

Petrosky took one step back, sliding his feet as slowly as he could, until he could see both Scott and the animal, hoping his presence would convince Scott to stop moving. But the kid wasn't moving at all. He wasn't shuffling. And still, the sound came, slowly, quietly: *shh, shh, shh.*

Not from them. Not from the kitchen at all.

Someone else was there, in the living room behind the

dog. Had Crandall come hobbling home, scooted around some back way to ambush them?

Then he saw the glint of the gun in his flashlight beam, the smooth, metal cylinder pointed at his head, the barrel itself like a black hole ready to suck them all into oblivion. But it was not Crandall who held the weapon.

His heart stopped. She was at least fifty pounds heavier than she'd been the last time he'd seen her—he wouldn't have recognized her if it hadn't been for those eyes, still sparkling green in the beam of the flashlight. Her hair was dark again, but stringy, held back in a messy bun, and her face had grown rounder and was now marred by acne. But still…

Hannah?

The flashlight dropped and shattered, casting the room into darkness. From the north-facing living room at Hannah's back, a hint of graying dawn peeked through the mist, turning her into a fuzzy silhouette.

For a moment, no one moved. No one spoke. No one breathed. There was no sound save for the snarling beast still shrouded in the dusky light from the doorway. Petrosky strained his ears trying to hear the telltale clack of claws on linoleum, but the animal held his position by the entry to the kitchen.

"Ma'am?" Scott said, but Hannah's outline remained motionless. "We're with the police, ma'am."

Now she moved, her silhouetted shoulders dropping like she was lowering the weapon though he couldn't be entirely sure.

"Detective?" she said.

A sound from Scott, as if he were pushing himself from the counter. He took a step closer to Hannah, and his arm bumped Petrosky's. The dog crept toward them, snarling. "Yes ma'am, I'm a—"

"Detective Petrosky," she said, so quiet it seemed he should not have been able to hear her with the dog's incessant chesty rumble permeating the air between them. But every syllable she spoke screamed at him, louder than the animal, louder than his shuddering lungs, louder than the noise of his own heartbeat keeping a frantic tempo in his brain.

He hadn't lost her. He hadn't killed her.

He hadn't failed.

Scott was frozen at Petrosky's side, perhaps trying to work out who she was and how they knew one another. But he was a smart kid—he'd figure it out soon enough.

"Hannah…" Petrosky began, but he didn't know what else to say.

Her silhouette got shorter as she bent down next to the great beast of a dog. It stopped snarling at once. Beside him, Scott sighed, one long, shaky exhale.

Hannah stood, fingers still on the dog's massive head. "I think I've been expecting you," she said.

13

———

IF SOMEONE HAD TOLD me years ago that I'd be there—*"Hannah, just imagine hiding in your hometown with your dead boyfriend's dog for company!"*—I would have told them they were insane, and there was only room for one crazy-ass person in our relationship. I was different then. That Hannah wouldn't have been standing in front of two cops in the kitchen, shivering with the nervous energy of a Chihuahua about to go into battle. That Hannah wouldn't have been covered in blood.

But no... I wasn't covered in anything. Not anymore. Though the walls did seem closer than they'd been moments before as if each breath I took shrank the room by some incremental degree. Even the yellow wash from the overhead lights I'd flicked on felt threatening, casting black shadows from the dome fixture against the paint as if the wall had been caught in the knife-like claws of some unseen predator. Like a tiger, but not the Barnum and Bailey kind. The asshole kind. The rip-your-throat-out kind.

"Hannah? What are you doing here?" Detective Petrosky looked pensive, worried, but mostly confused, and even more so when his gaze ran to the picture of Crandall and his late wife, pinned to the wall next to the fridge. I could pretty much read his thoughts: *From Dominic to this?* Maybe even: *That's a big step down.* But he would be giving me too much credit. Dominic had wanted me for many reasons, none of which were my personal merits. He'd wanted to watch me die.

"Neil had a room for rent in the paper," I said. "Things just kind of…clicked." The day I met Neil Crandall at the bookstore, I had picked out an old book of poems, the same one Dominic had read to me back when I thought we were in love. Seeing the book again had made me feel connected to Dominic like he was watching out for me from beyond the grave, though I didn't tell Neil any of that; we'd talked about the weather and dogs and, weirdly enough, the best paninis. He was stable and safe and boring. Not that stability was a bad thing—and once you'd fucked a psychotic millionaire, all bets were off when it came to excitement.

"That's not what I meant," Petrosky said.

"What did you mean?" My voice shook. Petrosky's eyebrows furrowed. He thought I was a killer, just as he had back when we were in Ash Park.

Back then, he'd been wrong.

I could smell Dominic's blood on my hands, feel it soaking through my jeans and staining my shirt. I wanted to run, but the idea of heading out into broad daylight sent daggers of fear tearing through my insides so violently that I could hardly breathe. Here, with Neil, I was safe. Here, no one would hurt me. No one knew where, or even who, I was —except Petrosky.

"Hannah, the entire police force, the FBI, everyone's been looking for you for the last five years since you disappeared from Ash Park. We assumed you'd been kidnapped, and that you were dead. How did you end up out here after Harwick's murder?"

He had to have known I wasn't kidnapped. What

kidnapper would bring me here? Yet the look in his eyes and the timbre of his voice were that of a father whose daughter had returned after running away from home: terrified for my well-being and so relieved to have me safely back that every ounce of anger had dissipated. That didn't make sense. Then again, I didn't really know what a father was supposed to do, now did I? *Focus, Hannah.*

He was a detective. I was a suspect.

Which meant that he knew—or he would. Something twisted deep in my gut, and my chest throbbed like a thousand rabid horses were racing over my rib cage.

You'll go to jail, Hannah.

I can't go to jail.

The air thinned. The world spun.

Then someone had their hand on my head, guiding it down between my knees.

"It's okay, just breathe." Petrosky's voice was kind, soft.

Wasn't he supposed to keep hammering until I cracked like an egg? And I would crack. Of course I would. Even if I said nothing, Petrosky would know I was guilty. But if I told him…would he let me off lighter? Dominic *had* tried to kill me. I had the scars to prove it.

I panted until the tile floor at my feet appeared solid again and then raised my gaze to Petrosky's solemn face. "He tried to kill me."

His shoulders slumped, bulldog face drawn, the messy smattering of stubble on his cheeks shining gray in the light and making him look ten years older. "I'm sure he did." His voice was so steeped in compassion that it made my eyes burn with tears though I couldn't be sure if I was crying for him or for myself.

"I…" *I killed him.* "I didn't want to die."

"I know you didn't. And I'm sure you were scared."

Just say it, Hannah.

"It was an accident," I blurted before he could ask me anything else.

Petrosky's shoulders stiffened, but his face did not change. "Scott." The detective kept his gaze locked on mine, but the spindly guy behind him stepped forward—I'd forgotten he was there.

"Yeah?"

"Secure the house."

"But—"

"Outside."

Why did he want to be alone with me? The young guy's eyes narrowed, and he bit his lip. I watched him walk out, feeling Petrosky's gaze drilling holes in my skull. Was he going to smash things like they did in old cop shows? Throw me over a table and slap me until I told him the truth?

I can't tell him the truth.

The door clicked shut.

Then: "Let's go sit in the living room, and you can tell me what happened, from the beginning."

It's happening. I'm in so much trouble. I led him to the living room couches, and he sat across from me, the same way we'd sat in Dominic's living room, but here the arms of the burgundy sofas were threadbare, and there was no marble floor, no modern art, no psychopath watching us and silently plotting how to murder me.

He's going to find out.

Keep your mouth shut, Hannah.

Petrosky cleared his throat. "Tell me what happened."

I shook my head, but he just sat there waiting for me. My heart stopped. And I told him. I told him that Dominic had murdered those women, had murdered my ex-boyfriend. I told him that I hadn't known and that I'd found the drugs Dominic had used to keep me sleeping on the nights he sneaked out to do it. And how I'd found the book: *Through the Looking Glass.*

"We didn't find the book in the house," Petrosky said. He sounded like he didn't want to believe me.

"I…" I swallowed hard. I was admitting to the worst thing I'd ever done, and he was…unsure whether I was lying? "I burned it. I was so…scared." I hadn't been scared. I had been distraught. I rubbed at the scar on my arm, the place that had never quite healed after Dominic stabbed me, just under the shoulder, a little triangle-shaped divot that kinda felt like someone had carved out a snack-sized portion of me—and he had. He'd taken a piece of me with him. Left something, too: nerve damage, by the way my fingers tingled on that side like I was holding fire ants if I moved the wrong way. That bizarre feeling was still this weird, cathartic keepsake I had to remember Dominic by. Not that I needed much help remembering—the dreams wouldn't let me forget.

Blood, so much blood. And then there were the memories that came to me when I was alone: The sound of glass shattering on the floor, the way his eyes looked when I shoved the fractured piece of sculpture into his belly, and the pool of gore that poured from his abdomen—some days I saw my whole body covered in it. Half the time, my skin still felt slick like some huge animal had slobbered all over me.

This was all my fault. Maybe if I hadn't told Dominic I knew he was a killer, we'd still be together. Maybe everything would have been fine.

Yeah, on the days your lover wasn't out torturing people to death. Seems legit, Hannah.

Petrosky nodded to Duke. "That Harwick's dog?"

I glanced down at the animal's mammoth black head and nodded. *My sweet boy.*

"We thought it had run off during the murder. Why's it here?"

I swallowed hard, but the lump in my throat remained.

"Hannah? Why's it here with you?"

Maybe Duke was here for the same reason I'd covered up

Dominic's crimes: love. I hadn't wanted anyone to know Dominic was a killer, because if the man I adored was a monster, what did that make me for loving him so completely? I was just as sick as he was. Sick for ripping his insides out and writing on the floor in his blood so they wouldn't think he was the killer. Sick for sobbing over his corpse, not tears of relief but of a grief so deep and poignant that I felt it even now, swelling and pulsing like a raw, gaping wound in my chest. The dog was part of a man I'd truly loved, psychopath or not. I watched Petrosky's fingers drumming on his knee—his eyes stayed on my face. "The dog made me feel…safe. And I felt sorry for him. I couldn't leave him alone there."

"You couldn't leave him." Petrosky's fingers stopped moving, and he sat back against the couch. "But…if no one was coercing you, why'd you come back here?"

"It's where I grew up." This place was all I'd known before Ash Park—and we both knew how that had turned out.

"You're trying to tell me that you hacked apart a serial killer in self-defense, stole his dog, and then drove to the mountains without telling a soul?"

I opened my mouth to reply, but he cut me off.

"You seem like a smart woman, Hannah. You had to have known you'd get in more trouble if you ran than if you just called the police. And your blood was all over the house. How did you manage to drive all the way here without passing out?"

I hadn't. "I pulled over a few times, trying to keep from fainting." The adrenaline and the pain, maybe shock—they'd gotten me the rest of the way. But Petrosky was staring at me with narrowed eyes, the crinkles at the corners deeper than I remembered. He didn't believe me.

"How did you feel when your father died?"

"I…" The air was gone again. *He deserved it.* But I couldn't say that.

"I know what he did to you. Why he might have wanted to come after you, to make sure you never told."

No. No one knew what my father had done except Dominic. Because of Dominic, I'd finally let that terrible secret out into the world where it no longer hurt quite so much. Maybe the only reason Dominic hadn't judged me was that he was a psycho and didn't care about anything. But he'd still helped me heal from what my father did to me. Dominic had saved me—and there was no greater love than that, regardless of your reasons.

"Hannah?"

"I… How do you know about my dad?"

Petrosky's face fell as if I'd just told him something terrible, and I had to replay the conversation in my head. Had I said something he wasn't expecting? Or…had he not actually known about the abuse?

Was that a test?

Duh, it was a test. And you failed it with flying colors.

I'm an idiot. I'll never survive a real interrogation.

"He killed those people, Hannah. Killed your boyfriend."

Oh. Not my dad. *Dominic.* But at least Petrosky knew. Dominic had killed many women, and he'd killed Jake, my abusive ex-boyfriend. He'd tried to kill me. I didn't want to have to say that out loud. "Yes."

He's trying to confuse me on purpose.

Don't let him mess with you, Hannah.

"Did you know it was him? Before the end?"

If I'd known…I was an accessory. "I didn't know."

"You sure? You were pretty nervous when I questioned you. Did you ever suspect he might have followed you to Ash Park?"

Followed me to Ash Park? Dominic had lived in the area long before I'd moved there. Why would Petrosky—

"Hannah, it's okay. I'm just trying to figure out why you'd follow him back here."

What the hell was Petrosky talking about? Was he trying to bait me? But his eyes were so sincere, so kind…

"You don't have to cover for him. I know the guilt." He rubbed at his chest, then dropped his hand back to his knee. "I understand. But you can tell the truth."

"The truth about… ?"

"Your father."

"My…father?"

"And his role in the Ash Park murders."

Oh, shit. Petrosky thought…my father had killed those women? That he'd killed Dominic? If I lied and told him it was true, maybe I wouldn't have to go to jail.

"Where were you the night your father was murdered?"

The hope that had begun to flutter in my belly like a thousand happy butterflies fizzled out as though the insects had been sprayed with a harsh pesticide. Petrosky thought my father was the *Looking Glass* killer. He thought my father had followed me to Ash Park, murdered strangers to…to what? Toy with me? But that wasn't right. Dominic was the *Looking Glass* killer. And my father… The world began spinning again, and I studied my feet to keep my bearings. One set of toes was pinned beneath Duke's massive paw like he was trying to trap me, too. "I was…here. The night my father died."

"Alone?"

"Neil's always here with me. I mean, unless he's at the shop."

"Sounds like he has you on a tight leash. Maybe he left to go to your dad's instead?"

Why would Neil go to my dad's? "I can't really…remember. I know…I don't think Neil went anywhere."

Because you weren't really here. The air was trying to disappear again, but I swallowed hard and forced a breath through clenched teeth.

"Maybe the two of you went for a stroll? Walked together over to your dad's place?"

"No, nothing like that."

Because Neil was asleep. If Petrosky asked Neil, Neil would tell him what time he always went to bed, and Petrosky would know I didn't have an alibi. I'd be off the hook for Dominic's murder but on trial for the murder of my father. "I… Please, I came back here on my own, and that night…I can't remember right now. I get stressed and I…I can't think." *No, don't say that.* "I didn't go anywhere." *Liar.* "I'm… agoraphobic."

Petrosky's pug face became all the more wrinkly as he squinted. "Come again?"

"Every time I try to go anywhere, I start to feel like"—*I'm going to get arrested*—"someone's after me."

"You don't feel like that when you're here?"

I shook my head.

"Did you know your boyfriend is a sex offender?"

My mouth dropped open. *That wasn't his fault.* "What he did…it wasn't a crime."

"A jury thought it was."

"They were three years apart. And he married her." I'd been in love when I was far younger than fifteen, and I knew all about living with the fear that someone would come arrest your soul mate.

"Your dad know about that? About your boyfriend?"

"Know about…what?"

"When was the last time you saw your father?"

The day he died. "Before I ran away. Ten years."

Petrosky cocked his head. "And so we're back to that. Because this is the part that I'm stuck on, Hannah. If you ran away in the first place, why come back here if no one was forcing you?"

"Maybe… I wanted closure?" *Oh shit. Did I just tell him I*

killed my dad? "But not like…closure, closure." *What does that even mean?*

Petrosky raised one whiskery eyebrow. "Did you get your closure?"

I frowned. "I never got the guts to go over there."

"You lived here in this town for over a year and never went because…why?"

Because I needed to be okay. Because I needed to forget. Because I needed someone to hold me and tell me they needed me too and that they'd protect me. And because I really didn't have the guts to go there and actually hurt him, no matter how many times I'd fantasized about it. I had loved him as much as I'd hated him.

The apprehension rose, itching beneath my skin where no razor could ever scratch. Since the day I left Willowshire, month after month, year after year, I had obsessed about my father hiding in the shadows, ready to make good on his promise to find me. To kill me. His twisted oath had controlled my entire life. Even now, I couldn't fully shake it.

"Living here, never going to talk to him, never going to talk to anyone…all that seems weird, Ms. Montgomery. And I don't like weird."

"Weird? But—"

"Your father, dying on your birthday, you sitting here in this house, no one knowing you're here at all. That doesn't bode well for you." And yet the sadness stayed on Petrosky's face. In his eyes. He didn't want to arrest me. He was sad that he even had to consider it.

"I didn't come here to kill my father." But that wasn't true, and from the look in Petrosky's eyes, he knew it.

"He forced you to come, kept you prisoner—"

"No, he didn't. Dominic…Dominic was…"

"Dominic was what?"

Dominic would have wanted me to save myself. *You're*

stronger than you think, Hannah. I could almost hear him whispering it now.

"I killed Dominic."

Petrosky stilled. I wasn't sure he was breathing.

"You stabbed Dominic Harwick? Sliced him open? Wrote on the floor with his blood?"

"Dominic was the *Looking Glass* killer, and he tried to kill me. And when I got here…Neil saved me."

"Harwick was…" He shook his head and rubbed a spot in the middle of his chest. "So you just randomly decided to pull his intestines through his belly button? Never seen self-defense like that before."

"I—"

"And you don't need this old dickwad, either. He didn't save you." Now his eyes had an edge, an anger strong enough that I flinched.

"What?"

"You heard me."

I heard him, but I didn't understand.

He wants to protect you.

Like a dad should.

The notion struck me as oddly romantic.

But I'd just admitted to killing Dominic. He had to take me in—had to arrest me. The thought of spending my life behind bars made the panic well so hot and furious in my chest that I thought my heart might explode—I was certain my lungs were smaller than they'd been just moments before.

No...no. I'd been planning for this. My heart slowed. All this time, I'd been waiting for Petrosky to show up to take me away. All this time, I'd been protecting the secrets I had until I could use them. And now, I knew what I needed to say. No one but Petrosky would be as motivated to help me escape the consequences of my crimes because no one else would want the information I had more than him.

"Detective Petrosky," I said, in a voice that sounded too confident to be mine. This was it; my last card to play: "I know who killed your daughter."

14

SHE'S ALIVE.

But Hannah was a liar. Petrosky could see it in her posture, in the quiver of her mouth, in the way her eyes darted everywhere but at him. The way the hairs on the back of his neck were standing, bristly and rough.

But...which part was she lying about? All of it? Pieces? Her story was all over the place, though she seemed rather certain that she had killed Dominic Harwick and that he was the *Looking Glass* killer. Petrosky could accept Harwick as the *Looking Glass* killer—he had seemed like a cold bastard. He could even accept that Hannah had killed him in self-defense. But he could not accept that she had brutally sliced open her boyfriend, torn his intestines out, written a poem on the floor in his blood, and then driven to Vermont while bleeding like a stuck pig. Had she suddenly snapped? And if she had snapped and murdered Harwick, she was surely capable of murdering her father as well, especially if she'd run away from Vermont because he was abusing her.

Not Hannah. Hannah was a survivor, not a killer. There was an alternate explanation, and he was going to find it.

The room was stone-cold silent save for the creak of the couch and the snoring of the great dog at Hannah's feet, his every breath magnified until Petrosky was sure he could feel the animal's lungs shuddering. It was as if the beige room itself were breathing, heaving great gasps of air and sucking every coherent thought from his head as her words whispered through his brain like the final release of air from a dying man: *I know who killed your daughter.*

She was still staring at him, waiting for him to respond to this news that she'd somehow solved Julie's murder from this little house seven hundred miles from Ash Park. Solved it when he and a dozen other cops could not. The shock of seeing Hannah alive had sent adrenaline trickling into his veins, but now the trickle had swelled to a raging gush. How could she be so certain? How could he be sure she wasn't lying? Yet, if he could find the man who'd killed his daughter... *You can't bring Julie back.* His chest tightened. He couldn't, but he might be able to breathe again.

That pesky hope bubbled up, and he tried to beat it down, back into his chest, willing it to submit. If she was wrong, the heartbreak might destroy him. "Who do you think killed Julie, Hannah?"

She paused, and the room shrank around them until there was nothing but her face and the rapid wheeze of her breath. She shook her head. "It's not that easy."

"Make it easy." Earlier, as she told him about the night she'd disappeared, her words had rung false, but this... She was sincere. She might be wrong, but her eyes, the set of her jaw—she believed, at least, that it was true.

But she's a murderer. The logical side of his brain was practically screaming at him that she'd admitted to killing Dominic Harwick. That she might have killed her own father. Sure explained Montgomery dying on Hannah's birthday. Freedom from fear: what a gift to give oneself.

But his gut refused to believe it. It didn't *feel* right. This girl in front of him wasn't a cold-blooded killer; she was vulnerable, damaged. She needed his help.

And he couldn't help her if she screwed him around.

"Start talking," he snapped, and her eyes widened. "Tell me what you know about my daughter." From the back of his mind came a physical sensation, tingling up his spine and swelling like an idea struggling toward realization, but then the dog raised its head and glared at him, and the feeling disappeared.

"I…" She stared at her hands, but he could hear the tears in her voice—this was the Ash Park interrogation all over again. She'd been through something horrible. Scaring her would make her shut down. *Easy, Petrosky.*

"Why don't you just start at the beginning," he said, and for some reason, this made Hannah nod as if starting from the beginning had not occurred to her. But when he looked into her eyes, he felt no anger. Just sadness, and the urge to take her in his arms and tell her everything would be okay like he had with Julie when he'd accidentally run over a squirrel with his car or when she would tell him about a mean classmate or a strict teacher—on the rare occasions that he was home. Julie'd died with far more memories of him being absent, of him taking a call and leaving her sitting at the kitchen table, alone.

Get it together, asshole. He hunched forward, elbows on his knees, the weight of his own body suddenly too heavy to remain upright. "Whenever you're ready, Hannah."

She sniffed. "Um…so, I met this girl, Robin, soon after I got here. I was…having a hard time. Still am, I guess."

"I thought you said you were agoraphobic." He kept his voice soft but adjusted his gaze, hoping his eyes radiated gentle accusation as if he'd already caught her in a lie but was going to let her explain. Scary, but not too scary. "How'd you come to meet her if you're afraid to go out?"

"I didn't meet her in person. Online. In one of those survivors groups for women. After Dominic…" She swallowed hard. "I needed to talk to someone. And over the next year, I found out what happened to her. To Robin, I mean. And it was just like what happened to Julie."

Just like Julie. He tried to force the images from his mind, but they kept blinking back at him like a stubborn television ad you couldn't turn off: the angry slash across Julie's neck, her blue lips, her eyes, closed forever. *Stop.* He gripped his knees and pushed himself up taller. "Go on."

"He…raped her. Left her in a field."

But lots of women went down that way. Rapists liked fields and abandoned parking lots and old warehouses—anywhere there was little chance of discovery.

"Her vocal cords are damaged because he…slit her throat."

Petrosky's heart seized at the look of determination in Hannah's eyes. Was it possible? Did she actually know who'd killed Julie? This rape victim wasn't enough to tie the cases together, but Hannah was so sure…or maybe he just wanted her to be sure. "What else?"

She averted her eyes, whispering now. "He burned her."

Fuck. Petrosky could feel the flames licking at his own bare skin, crawling across his abdomen and turning his guts to ash. He clutched at his roiling belly, but when she squinted at him, he moved his hand to his chest and tapped the skin over the pacemaker. Julie had still been alive when her killer had doused her with lighter fluid and lit her up. McCallum thought he didn't know about that. He did. Brian Thompson was too good a guy to let him believe a lie. But every day, Petrosky focused on the lie McCallum had told him: the tests had been inconclusive. He needed to believe that Julie had already stopped breathing by the time her attacker had covered her pelvis with accelerant and set her on fire. He needed to believe that the last thing she'd smelled hadn't been her own skin burning.

Hannah opened her mouth to continue, but Petrosky put up his hand to stop her. He'd gone the last ten years without knowing what had really happened to his little girl, and he refused to think about it now. Some days it took all his energy to keep from picturing Julie that way, to replace the images of her writhing in pain with ones of her as a child, doing the things she'd loved. And every day, Petrosky hated himself for not being there to save her. For letting Julie die in so much pain.

Hannah was staring at him, her face drawn with worry.

This might not be connected at all. If the killer had wanted Robin dead, he would have made it happen. "How is Robin still alive?"

"She was a paramedic. She…kept her chin down over the slash in her throat to staunch the bleeding. And she pretended to be dead."

If Robin had passed out, she would have bled to death. So she'd been awake. Lucid. Gritting her teeth, trying not to scream while a maniac lit her on fire. Had Julie pretended to be dead, hoping to survive? Had she screamed? He swallowed hard to avoid gagging.

But there was more, niggling at the back of his brain, and as the dog lowered his massive head, the thought emerged fully formed: *How does she know about Julie at all?* His daughter's murder happened years before the *Looking Glass* case—years before Hannah lived in Ash Park. Was she messing with him? Stalking him? Was this just an elaborate game? Maybe she was buying time so she could run away again. Maybe *she* was the *Looking Glass* killer.

No. Now *he* was delusional. She had alibis for those killings, and some of the murders would have been physically impossible—she wasn't strong enough to lift a body. But something had happened in Ash Park, something terrible. And if she was lying about Julie to cover up her own crimes, so help him, he'd lock her up himself.

"Hannah? How do you know about Julie?"

"I was…worried. After what happened with Dominic. I thought I'd get in trouble."

Worry didn't explain why she knew…unless Harwick had something to do with Julie's death. *You're grasping at straws, old man.* "You didn't answer my question."

"It wasn't on purpose. I called the precinct and told them I was a student and that I needed the file on Dominic's case. I was afraid you guys would be after me." Tears rolled down her cheeks. "The police wouldn't send me much. I know it was dumb, okay? I just… I was scared, freaked all the time. And I kept having these dreams…" She inhaled sharply, but her voice did not waver as she said: "I needed information. I looked at a few other things online, and I saw her. Julie. There were some articles. And when Robin told me what happened to her, it sounded so close to what happened to Julie that I thought…you know. They had to be connected." She drew herself up taller—confident.

Julie. Julie. Petrosky ground his teeth. Using a loved one's name was the oldest trick in the book if you wanted to connect with someone quickly—and get them to do what you wanted. He'd made so many mistakes over these last ten years, mistakes born of grief, of alcohol abuse, of the overwhelming ache of incompetence, the unbearable knowledge that he, a detective, couldn't find his own daughter's killer. Hannah was hitting him right in the gut. And she had only brought up his daughter when he'd questioned her about Montgomery's death, about Harwick's death. She'd deflected, purposefully, and he had fallen for it.

Focus, asshole. He'd be an idiot for believing this shit straight out. He needed a truth he could prove before he went off chasing ghosts.

"Let's go back to why you ran, Hannah." His words were

sharp. "You had to know you weren't in trouble. If it was self-defense—"

"It was, oh, please, believe me, it was. I tried to…here." She grabbed her T-shirt from the bottom and pulled it to her shoulder, freeing one arm. Petrosky reared back, not sure what she was doing, but then he saw: her shoulder was covered with flattened scars and several tiny raised welts that could have come from a set of jagged stitches.

"My head is messed up, too…under my hair." She lowered the shirt and touched her temple, and Petrosky remembered the piece of scalp left on the floor of Harwick's mansion, how the bloody blond tendrils had curled toward him as if beckoning him closer. He'd known that hair was Hannah's, even then.

"He tried to kill me," she said. "He stabbed me in the arm, came after me, and I ran, but I wasn't fast enough, and then the sculpture broke, and I"—she took a deep, shuddering inhale—"I stabbed him with a piece of glass."

That part was probably true—Harwick's abdominal wound from the fractured sculpture had indeed been fatal. But someone had come back postmortem and sliced him from end to end with a scalpel just like the one used in the other crimes. Someone had yanked out his intestines. Not someone—the *Looking Glass* killer. He'd pulled out Harwick's insides and written a poem in his blood.

He watched her finger as it wrapped itself in a strand of hair, vibrating slightly, twitching in a way that wasn't quite anxiety. Permanent damage from Harwick? Which meant… "How's your penmanship?"

She frowned.

"Your writing. With the injury on your—"

"I type now. Because of the…nerve damage."

I knew it. There was no way she'd killed Harwick—that she'd killed him in self-defense and decided to pull his guts out, then miraculously regenerated the still bleeding nerves in her arm so she could paint the floor with his blood. She hadn't driven twelve hours—in shock and while bleeding profusely—to Vermont. And she hadn't waited to heal first— she had been long gone by the next morning when they'd had every cop in Michigan and the surrounding states out looking for her and her car.

She's hiding something. He couldn't shake the thought. "Tell me again what happened the night Dominic Harwick was murdered."

She licked her lips, her eyes dull and glassy, her entire body shaking. "I killed him. I killed Dominic," she wheezed. "Oh god, I'm so *sorry.*"

"But who cut him open, Hannah?"

"I don't *know.*" She could barely get the words out over her labored breathing.

The hairs on his neck danced. She knew who had done it. But who would she be protecting? Maybe she just didn't want to tell him that her father had slit Harwick's belly open and pulled his guts out. That her father had hurt her, his own little girl, then brought her back here. That she'd waited... then murdered him. But if her father had brought her back to Vermont, she wouldn't have been living with Crandall when he died, and she wouldn't be lying about murdering Harwick now. Why *was* she lying about murdering Harwick? Or was she? It was possible Petrosky was looking for someone else entirely, someone she'd managed to escape from while they were murdering Harwick. But she'd have no reason to hide that killer's identity by admitting to a crime she hadn't committed. And none of this explained why her father had died on her birthday.

You just don't want her to be a killer. In the back of his brain, he heard Dr. McCallum chastising him, saying that Petrosky was letting his emotions get in the way of doing his job. And he was, he knew it, but he couldn't seem to help himself. This was too far outside the realm of logical.

Hannah wrapped her arms around her body, and watching her fold in on herself made Petrosky's gut clench like someone had punched him because another scenario had taken root in his head. Maybe Hannah had managed to escape her *dad* the night Harwick died. She had escaped him and run home because this place, the only other place she knew, was somehow better, less risky than taking another chance on the outside world. Maybe her father hadn't known she was here until she—or Crandall—went to kill him. Maybe she felt responsible for Harwick's death the way Petrosky felt responsible for Julie's death. Perhaps she felt guilty enough to confess to something she hadn't done—the murder of Dominic Harwick—because she was atoning for murdering her father. Unlikely, but...

"Your dad...some asshole, right?"

Her breath slowed. She stilled, but when she brought her gaze to his, her eyes were cold as ice. The dog raised its head, and together they listened to the wheeze of air through Hannah's nostrils—measured, but too heavy, too hard.

"Did your father hurt you, Hannah?"

"I loved my father," she whispered.

The lack of a "no" told him more than any words ever could have. Her father had hurt her terribly. She'd run from Vermont to Michigan to escape him, and he'd followed her. He had terrorized Ash Park, trying to teach her a lesson. He had killed women she worked with, then one boyfriend, and then another. And even now, after his death, her fear was keeping her locked up at Crandall's like a prisoner.

Petrosky's chest burned with rage. He wasn't one ounce of sorry that Theodore Montgomery was dead. "Your father tried to kill you. In Ash Park."

Tears dripped from her chin onto the head of the dog, and for a moment, Petrosky worried the beast might come after him for causing the flood. She squeezed her rib cage tighter. Back and forth, she moved back and forth, like

Shannon rocking Henry, but Hannah had probably never had a real parent to comfort her. "No, it was all an accident! All a big mistake!"

Frustration heated his face. Why the hell was she still protecting him? Had she developed Stockholm Syndrome before she'd run away from Vermont, such an intense connection with her father that she was unable to see the monster for what he really was? Abusers looked for vulnerability, both to abuse and to cover up their crimes—and it was vulnerability Petrosky saw every damn time he looked at her. "Did you really kill Dominic Harwick, Hannah? Or was it your father?"

She bit her lip and said nothing.

There had been no trace of Theodore Montgomery at Harwick's murder scene, consistent with Hannah's version of events. Maybe Hannah was ambidextrous and had managed to write the bloody words. Maybe she had—against all odds—driven herself to Vermont. But was that…plausible? Or was it his half-drunk, half-insane mind that could not accept the possibility that she'd murdered anyone?

"Hannah? Did you kill Dominic Harwick?"

The dog whined, and Hannah stopped rocking, her eyes darting around the living room like she was watching an invasion of insects no one else could see. Hannah gasped. Choked. "Please, stop. Please. I can't…I can't…"

Petrosky reached for her, waiting for her to reel back. When she didn't, he put his hand on the sofa beside her and said, "You know you'll have to come with me to Ash—"

"No!" She clenched her fists, eyes wide. "I…I can't. Please, I can't."

But Petrosky couldn't leave her here—Hannah had just said she'd killed a man. Whether he believed her or not, they needed to sort it all out. In Michigan.

He startled when she leapt up and bolted out of the living room. *Shit, what now?* He heaved himself from the couch and gave chase, but skidded to a halt outside the kitchen when she threw herself against the counter and vomited into the sink.

Agoraphobia. His heart felt like it would give out every time she retched. No matter what else she had done, she was still a victim. And she was scared.

"I know you don't want to leave." He kept his voice soft, calm. "But you need to remember why you went into hiding to begin with."

She hacked again, wiped her mouth on her sleeve, and straightened. "I had to do it."

"Do what, Hannah?"

"Dominic. I had to—"

"Let's not worry about that now." He already knew what she wanted him to believe, and he could have her sign a confession about the *Looking Glass* killings anytime—and he would. But at least he'd wrap up the Montgomery murder before he left Vermont. Maybe he felt he owed it to Hannah. Maybe he wanted to get closure on *something*. He'd come here thinking he had a chance to finally nail the *Looking Glass* killer, and now his brain was jumping all over the place, from Ash Park to Theodore Montgomery to Julie, each topic tumbling into his line of sight and then slipping away before he could firmly grasp it. If he could just find a viable suspect, he could prove Hannah was innocent of her father's murder. Then maybe the rest would fall into place.

"Do you know who killed your father, Hannah?"

Her lower lip trembled, and her nostrils flared. She rested her forehead against the upper cabinet. "No," she whispered.

She was lying—he could feel it in every cell of his body just as he'd felt it when she'd first opened her mouth. Whether or not she'd done it herself, Hannah knew who'd killed that child-abusing prick. Though no one had a reason to hate the man more.

The hairs on the back of his neck returned to their latent

state, and his chest had, at some point, settled. Did it matter who had killed Montgomery as long as he was dead? If Julie's killer met his end, Petrosky wouldn't care who had done it—he'd buy them a donut before he'd arrest them. But he still needed to get to the bottom of this—he had to know.

"You need to come back to Michigan with me." Petrosky held up a hand when she opened her mouth to protest. "I can take you in right now, Hannah, cuffs and all."

Determination glittered behind her tears, and he thought she was going to deny him again. Her reaction at the mere suggestion of leaving the house had been a touch too good to be an act—her fear was real. Whether it was because of the agoraphobia, or because she feared retaliation from the person who had actually murdered Harwick and her father, or because she'd killed them all herself, he had no idea, and he didn't care. Hannah was his connection to Julie. He had to find a way to get what he needed without traumatizing her further.

But she only said, "Duke has to come."

"Who?"

She pointed to the beast still waiting at the side of the couch, his head now raised, ears pricked toward his master. "I need to take care of him."

"You don't trust your boyfriend to take care of—"

"I won't leave without him."

He sighed. The dog would probably eat his face off while he slept. But it didn't matter. Petrosky needed to find the man who'd killed his baby girl, and this time, when the hope in his chest bubbled up, he did not try to dampen it. Against all odds, he had found Hannah. Maybe he could find Julie's killer, too.

"Fine. I'll give you a day or so to get ready. In the meantime, either Scott or I will be here." The rookie would do fine in a squad car out front, though Petrosky didn't want to leave Hannah at all. Something about her had always drawn him, like an insect to the brilliant blue of a bug zapper, optimistic until the very end. But Petrosky was more aware than a witless insect—his inevitable destruction burned within him as real as the breath in his lungs.

He'd find the man who murdered his daughter, or he'd die trying.

15

———

So it's true. Petrosky squinted at the computer propped on the Caprice's console—Julie's killer had never stopped. He'd just stopped raping and killing in Michigan. How many more victims had been claimed by that sadistic prick?

Scott had gone to the precinct on foot to do research on Robin's case, leaving Petrosky to park in Hannah's—*Crandall's*—driveway, intent on watching the house. He'd be damned if she ran on him again.

"We need to take her in for questioning," Scott had said before he headed off. But they didn't need to. It wasn't like she was a murderer...was she? Petrosky didn't know yet, and he sure hadn't mentioned that little tidbit to Scott. Maybe Petrosky was trying to rationalize it away. Even if he thought she had done it, he wouldn't have taken Hannah in. If Hannah wound up in jail, he might miss some vital information he needed to catch Julie's killer. Had she counted on that? Was that the only reason she'd told him at all? If she was telling the truth about his daughter's case—another thing he wasn't sold on—she'd sure waited to spill it, waited until she needed something from him. All this could be an elaborate scheme to get him off her back while she tried to run.

Petrosky sighed. McCallum would have a field day with him when he returned to Ash Park.

From his computer screen, Robin blinked at him—waiting for him. Would she lie for Hannah? To keep up some ruse? But no one could fake the wounds on Robin's neck or the hollow look in her eyes. Death might have been kinder than what had been done to this girl.

Pink gouges scored her throat from just under her jawline to her clavicle—smooth, healed vertical sutures and one ragged horizontal scowl, thick as lips, as if she might at any moment tip her head back and snarl through the angry break in the skin. Had that wound become infected? None of the other victims had lived long enough for infection to set in. Julie's body had been worm food before they'd even—

He shoved the thought aside so violently he felt it in the muscles of his arms. *Stop.* He pictured Julie running after him in the backyard on the rare occasions he played soccer with her. Back before his gut had become more swollen than the ball. Before his heart threatened to stop beating each time he walked up the stairs.

Focus, old man.

From his computer screen, Robin blinked again. She'd been attacked in Boston six years before, but now lived in some little town in upstate New York. As Hannah had said, she couldn't speak on the phone—couldn't speak at all—but Hannah had been able to get her online through some social media bullshit.

Petrosky glanced at the dashboard, at his pack of cigarettes, and then back to the girl on her leather couch. She was clutching a throw pillow bearing a picture of a cat, but he saw no actual cat anywhere in the frame. There was no shuffling either, or sound of any presence in the house besides Robin's—just her breathing, louder than normal, though that might have been from her damaged neck. He nodded to her. She set the pillow aside and leaned toward the computer, and Petrosky's car filled with the sounds of the clacking keyboard, louder even than her breath, louder than the hum of insects outside.

The message pinged:

"I won't testify."

Didn't she want to catch the person who'd done this to her? Or was she just Hannah's friend, a friend who'd had something terrible happen to her and was using her scars to get Hannah out of a tight spot by telling him what he wanted to hear? By distracting him. By making him believe.

"Why don't you want to testify?" Brutalized victims weren't generally psyched to come face-to-face with their attackers, but he needed to assure himself it wasn't because she was lying.

"I moved away to escape this. He doesn't know where I am.
Or that I'm alive. I don't think."

Had the police been able to keep the attack that quiet? He'd find out soon enough; Scott would be back within the hour with the case files from the Boston detectives. Probably better for her sake that it had happened in the city. In a town like this, she wouldn't have been able to keep her miraculous recovery under wraps, and whoever had tried to kill her could come try again.

"Why did you leave Boston?" Petrosky asked over the sinking sensation in his gut. No one else in the Vermont PD knew Hannah Montgomery was here, but they couldn't keep that secret for long in this town either; even now, Crandall's neighbors were probably peering at Petrosky's car from the bottom of the hill, wondering who in the flying hell he was.

And if they called the precinct about him... *I'm running out of time.* He didn't want to deal with Crowley.

Robin's breath shuddered through her as if all the pain she had experienced had concentrated in her trachea and was now fighting to escape. She typed, and the movements of her arms as she leaned over the keyboard threw her neck into sharper focus—the jagged scar seemed to gape at him. The image twisted a knife in Petrosky's chest. He could almost see Morrison's face, the gore, his boy's lolling head, the once strong neck severed nearly to the spine, and suddenly he missed Morrison so horribly it was like the air had turned to stone and was crushing his lungs. He kept his eyes glued to the screen, certain that if he glanced to his right, he'd see Morrison in the passenger seat, smiling at him through lips red with blood.

Bing.

"I moved because I worried I would see him. Didn't even want to leave the house."

Sounded a lot like...Hannah. Lots of trauma victims, really, fearful of leaving their houses, convinced they might be attacked again. Sometimes they feared the panic attacks that were all too common with PTSD. Hannah's reaction—running from Harwick's home after he was dead, coming up here—wasn't so far out of line, but Robin had called the police. Robin wasn't protecting her attacker.

"Tell me what you remember."

She did, the clacking of the keyboard steady, insistent. Petrosky scanned the room behind her for vestiges of who she'd been before the attack. On the bookcase beyond her left shoulder sat a photo of a three-story house, pastel blue, the balconies and eaves adorned with elaborate moldings. In another picture, Robin stood with a tall, dark-haired man, his arm wrapped around her waist. Husband? No other photos or trinkets, but on the bottom shelf lay three books: *The Bazaar of Bad Dreams, You, Innocence.* He didn't want to know what those were about, though *Innocence* felt oddly out of place. There was no innocence in this girl's world, not if her haunted eyes told the truth. The *Bazaar of Bad Dreams* was her reality now.

When she finally hit send, she looked up, tears glistening on her lashes, lip trembling, but she inhaled briskly and swiped at her face as though she was agitated about the crying and not the reason for it. He pulled his eyes away from her and read.

She'd been walking home through an under-construction Boston suburb after a twelve-hour shift as a paramedic. Her attacker had grabbed her and dragged her into an over-grown, abandoned yard, probably as close to a field as he could get in the middle of the city. Holding a blade to her neck, he'd yanked off her pants and raped her right there on the cold, hard ground. When she cried out, he had slit her throat.

Robin gasped. Petrosky glanced up and saw her shaking, sobbing in the hiccuping way of a small child.

But he couldn't stop reading. He needed to know whether she had been awake—lucid—for the next part. Julie had been burned alive, the ME had told him. McCallum had said it was inconclusive. Mere moments on either side of death—but moments mattered. And Robin hadn't written about the blaze except to say: "he burned me."

"Tell me about the fire."

"He pulled something out of his pocket, a bottle of something, and squirted me with it. I couldn't see, had my eyes closed playing dead, but I felt the wetness. He shot it inside me too."

Petrosky swallowed back bile. Lighter fluid. He had covered all his victims in it.

"I knew if I moved, he'd know I was still alive, and he'd make sure he killed me. But when he lit it, I wished I was dead."

He could almost smell the flesh burning. He wanted to bark questions at her, get all he could to find this man, this sorry motherfucker who had hurt his baby, but if he did that, he risked scaring her silent. Instead, Petrosky reread the conversation, trying to glean additional meaning. She'd already given the Boston PD a composite, and she put that fact in capitals, probably to make it clear that she wasn't about to do it again. She didn't want to talk to him, either. She just wanted the ordeal to be over so she could move on, even if she'd never be the same.

On the second read-through, Petrosky's eyes jumped back to one line as if of their own accord: "He had soft hands." But the other girls—*don't think about Julie*—had latex residue on their skin. The killer had worn gloves, so how... "How do you about his hands?"

"He took his gloves off and touched my face. After he was done. Then I heard him walking away, and I...peeked. And I saw the bracelet."

The bracelet? Was his jewelry unique? Traceable? *Like I'd get that lucky.* "Can you tell me more about his bracelet?"

She sighed, no doubt frustrated at his questions; she'd surely gone over this before, numerous times. But he had to be sure. He had to hear it from her.

"Black or brown hair."

Hair? *Human* hair? Was the killer taking souvenirs from

his victims? A hair bracelet might make sense; after all, this asshole did seem obsessed with burning the pubic hair off the women he murdered.

But there'd be no way for Robin to know whether the bracelet was human hair, and suddenly Petrosky didn't want to know either. The thought of some maniac running around with even one lock of Julie's hair on his soft, pansy wrist soured Petrosky's stomach and made his insides feel as if he were on a roller coaster: weightless for one moment in time, just waiting to crash down to earth.

"Did he take your hair, Robin?"

She shook her head but winced as if it hurt. Probably did; muscle damage, nerve damage…those would never heal, much like his busted heart.

But Petrosky's stomach settled back into his gut. If the MO held, the killer hadn't taken Julie's hair either. At least the bastard wasn't walking around with a piece of Petrosky's daughter.

The thought was of little comfort.

WHEN SCOTT RETURNED to Crandall's house, Petrosky drove to town—or rather to the parking lot of a convenience store just outside the city limits. He didn't need the Willowshire jerkoffs accusing him of being a lush or some shit; not that they'd have been wrong, but he wanted to finish up in this hellhole and head out without getting popped for DUI.

By the time he got back to Crandall's house, the trees were casting long shadows over the lawn. Petrosky listened as his car whined up the hill, practically feeling the gravel tearing away under his tires. He patted the steering wheel of his Caprice like it was an old dog as he parked next to Scott.

Scott's Toyota was conspicuous, not just because it was a damn foreign ride, but because of its brilliant red that stuck out like a beacon on top of the hill. They were in plain view out here; when Crandall showed up, he'd be worried or pissed or both. Hopefully, he would be unnerved enough to screw up if he knew anything—if he'd done anything. But Crandall was looking more and more like a bystander. Just Hannah's old-ass boyfriend. And even if he wasn't…Petrosky couldn't seem to care about the *Looking Glass* case or Montgomery's murder the way he needed to; whether Montgomery was guilty or Harwick was guilty, they were both dead. Maybe Charles had killed Montgomery, or maybe Hannah had, but it wasn't like either of them was chomping at the bit to kill again. And Julie's killer was still out there. Other men were losing their daughters. Other girls were losing their lives.

I'm so sorry, honey.

Julie. His baby girl.

Scott grinned as Petrosky heaved himself into the Toyota's passenger seat. "Been doing rounds every hour, Detective, but I can see her in the living room now. She's just been reading."

Stressed and reading. Must be a coping skill, right? Julie had done that sometimes, like the night before a big test, when she couldn't sleep. He should have brought her warm milk or something. Petrosky's heart squeezed and then settled, and he rubbed at the spot over the stitches near his heart, the place that ached anew each time he considered how much he had hurt Julie, and how much he was hurting Hannah now. How hard it would be for Hannah to go with him when she was terrified.

But she had to. *She's lucky I haven't arrested her ass already.* She was. He was sure being nicer than any other officer would have been—Jackson would surely have dragged her in already.

"Boston PD says Robin Lowenstein's case is cold. No DNA, no leads." Scott had pulled out a file folder and was rifling through it, though he had surely read it while Petrosky was in the parking lot with Jack Daniels. "Not much here that will help us, though we do have a composite now."

But Scott was not looking at the composite photo; his gaze was glued to the laptop computer on the dashboard, where a single line blinked green, like a heart monitor flatlining on a dead guy.

"What's that?"

Scott clicked a button, and a low buzz filled the car.

"The hell are you doing?"

Still nothing. Then a slight whisper like the hiss of a snake.

"She might be turning a page in her book," Scott said.

Petrosky's eyes widened as realization dawned. *Holy shit.* He'd bugged the house.

Scott smiled. "Said I had to use the bathroom."

Wily. Petrosky almost nodded his approval but tamped it back down and ground his teeth. Scott could have gotten hurt if she'd actually been dangerous. And it would have been Petrosky's fault—one more lost on his watch. "No more of that. You need to be careful." Scott's face fell as if his entire supply of self-esteem had rested on Petrosky's validation. *What the hell, Scott. Suck it up.* "Tell me more about Robin's case."

Scott stared at the folder, avoiding Petrosky's eyes. "Well, most of what I read is on Robin herself. The details..." He shook his head. "I don't know how she stayed still while she was burned alive, but she did. And because she was a para-medic, she knew to tuck her chin down to stop the flow of blood from her neck wound. If he'd waited just a few more minutes to leave the scene, or if he'd cut *just* a touch deeper, she'd be dead."

Petrosky blinked hard, picturing Robin's ruined neck, the vicious, angry scars, and her eyes—open, shimmering, *alive.*

It could have been Julie who had come so close to death. Julie who'd survived.

But it wasn't. *Julie's dead.* His chest burned as painfully as if he'd just identified her body at the morgue.

"No other attacks in the Boston area," Scott said, looking up. "Or even in Massachusetts as a whole. And Boston isn't integrated with Ash Park reporting systems, so they were unaware of the crimes you mentioned and didn't see the pattern then, though you and I can see it now."

You and I.

Scott shifted in his seat like he was uncomfortable. "Boston PD believes there's a connection, and they're willing to revive their efforts after coordinating with you. I didn't tell anyone here about it yet."

Good. They didn't need the feds crawling all over this, and he sure as shit wasn't going to step aside, not this time. Not when they were looking for the bastard who'd murdered his daughter.

Petrosky peered through the windshield at the house, yellow now with the waning sun. Hannah sat near the front window in the living room, the back of her dark hair barely visible beyond the curtain. Why would she sit right there? Was she watching them as much as they were watching her? Trying to discern when she might sneak away and disappear?

A subtle *thup, thup, thup* covered the hiss of Hannah turning another book page as Scott flipped through his file, but Petrosky kept his eyes on the front window of the house, on Hannah's head—suddenly so still. Like she'd passed out sitting up. From here, it was impossible to tell if she was even breathing, and the thought of losing her a second time made his own lungs seize.

"The other weird thing they found in Boston was dog hair." Scott tapped the folder. "Not too many—two hairs, I think—but there were no tracks or other evidence of an animal at the scene." He shrugged. "The cops in Boston didn't think much of it."

Why would they? The hair could have been on Robin from one of her numerous EMS calls that night, or even left in the field earlier, only clinging to her when she was forced to the earth.

But...there had been dog hair at Julie's scene too, something they'd written off at the time as strays or scavengers. Petrosky rubbed his chest, feeling the tiny nodule where his pacemaker sat forcing his heart to work. It still might be a bust. If the hairs were from the killer, from a family pet, they'd yield nothing across cases—Julie's case was ten years old, Robin's six, and dogs didn't live forever. But their killer had been *wearing* hair. On his wrist. On the hand he used to touch these women after they died. Animal hair? It seemed unlikely now that the bracelet was made from the hair of his victims; he hadn't taken any strands from Robin's head. They could possibly verify that the hairs came from the same bracelet, but it could be made from the hairs of a dozen dogs for all he knew. They already knew they were looking for the same guy. And unless they found the animals or the bracelet itself...

Inside the house, Hannah sat still as a mannequin. The dog was probably at her side, ears pricked, ready to attack at the merest hint of intrusion. Maybe it was Duke's hair they'd found at the scene.

He brushed the thought away.

Scott closed the folder. "Do you think it's possible that someone in the online group targeted Theodore Montgomery? They'd know Hannah's birthday, maybe. It's a therapy group, so they'd surely have heard what Montgomery did to her." Petrosky opened his mouth, but Scott was faster. "I know she's in there because of her old boyfriends and that Dominic guy and whatever, but it's worth a shot."

They could walk in there now and ask Hannah whether she'd disclosed her abuse to the group, but it was insane to think that yet another random person near her was murdering folks. Petrosky sure as shit didn't believe in some prophetic notion like karma or the idea that evil followed Hannah around like a dark cloud. "There was no trace of Hannah at the Theodore Montgomery crime scene, right, Scott?"

"There was no trace of *anyone* else at the scene besides those who lived there. Just like in the Ash Park murders." He raised a brow.

"She isn't the *Looking Glass* killer, genius. She isn't physically capable—can't move bodies, for one. And Hannah sustained a nerve injury during the attack at Harwick's. She can't print legibly." Though he had never seen her handwriting. He'd never asked. "Someone else wrote those words in blood at the Harwick crime scene, and I'm betting it was Theodore Montgomery."

"But Hannah… I mean, if that's true, wouldn't it be extra weird that she's here? That her dad goes to Ash Park to kill her, and she comes back here, and then he dies and no one—"

"Find me someone else," Petrosky barked.

Scott averted his eyes and spoke to the driver's side window. "Even if Hannah did nothing wrong, you know we need to take her in."

Despite what he'd told Scott, Petrosky wasn't sure what he believed. She might be completely innocent. She might be guilty of something else—or guilt-ridden enough to confess to things she hadn't done. Yet he couldn't shake the images of Hannah holding a bloody knife over the body of her father or driving the blade into Harwick's gut. The muscles in his back screamed with tension. If they took her in for questioning, she might magically forget whatever she knew about his daughter, a risk he wasn't willing to take. Meanwhile, Scott was probably trying to keep her off the radar of the rest of the force lest they steal another case from under him. Some team they were.

"There are other possibilities, Scott, including Melinda Charles. Lots of ways for Theodore Montgomery to end up dead. Lots of scenarios that don't involve Hannah."

Scott turned back to Petrosky and met his gaze earnestly. "But Detective, this online group *is* a solution that doesn't involve Hannah being Montgomery's killer."

The kid was right; Petrosky wasn't thinking clearly anymore. "Fine." He wanted Scott out of the car, out of the driveway, out of the way. Already the shakes were creeping up on him, and the bag with the rest of the Jack was practically howling at him across time and space from under the front seat of his own car. "Who runs the group?" Petrosky asked, trying to keep his voice from trembling like his muscles.

"That's just it—no one."

"No therapist?"

"Nope. Just the survivors—peer support, they call it. And it's on a site where anyone can go in and start a private group. Most of them use pseudonyms, but I should be able to track them down, see the IP addresses, and what state they're signing in from and when. Might as well weed out the people who can't possibly be suspects because they were online and too far away to commit the crimes."

It was a waste of time, but it would give Petrosky a chance to consider what he needed to do here. He nodded. *Go on then, rookie. Get out of here.*

"I can even join up, maybe. Sprinkle a few questions in there, see if anyone bites."

"Sprinkle? Geez, kid, you sound like you're baking cookies."

Scott actually smiled.

That wouldn't last long. Sooner or later, the job would break him too.

16

———

"It's okay, sweetheart. We gave him a good life. You gave him a good life." But no good deed went unpunished. Buddy was the third dog to go on them in as many years.

The big dog's head rested on his lap, filling the room with its labored breath, as thick and hot as jungle air. The killer wrapped his arm around his daughter's shoulder. This morning, her shrieks of "You'll never understand" had almost forced him to believe that he was the dictator she made him out to be. But in times of sorrow, she showed her age, her insecurity. And he was glad of it.

Teenagers. Sometimes Layla had to be reminded that she still needed her daddy.

"We got Buddy from the pound, sweetheart. He was old when we got him." His voice stayed soft, practiced, measured, though his heart was racing as the animal grunted and vomited a thin stream of what looked like bile and blood onto the towel under its head.

The dog's harsh, thick breath mingled now with his daughter's high-pitched whine, then a choked sob from the girl as if she, too, were about to vomit. Never boring, this part. He never could predict the course death would take, just as he could not predict how the fire would consume the body of the animal afterward. No matter where you lit the hair, the oils in the fur spurred tendrils of flame like a web, stunning and unpredictable and utterly captivating. It was as if fire, by its very nature, was as alive as any of them before it collapsed into ash, a life lived to the fullest in mere moments then extinguished for good.

Layla sniffed again and made a snotty noise as though she'd inhaled something slimy.

He tried to suppress a grimace but failed. "Get a tissue for that, dear."

The moment she disappeared beyond the doorway, he bent toward the animal's face and lifted one frothy jowl to peer into the dog's mouth. Its gums were already discolored, the edges almost black and more rotten looking than the slick brown surrounding Buddy's teeth as if the old boy had eaten mud. But he hadn't.

The killer knew exactly what the dog had eaten. And when.

Dogs got boring fast, just like Layla's soccer games. She and her teammates bounded around the field day after day after day, kicking the same stupid ball into the same stupid goals as if any of it mattered. None of it did. At work, only a few insistently friendly assholes knew he had a family at all. Competition thrived, even in the land of cops, and he had no interest in fielding questions about weekends or what lame shit his kids wanted for Christmas. In a place like this, where your car was your calling card, your occupation your worth, your relevance dictated by the number of activities your children were involved in...

The unknowable was glorious. And once you got past appearances, right or wrong became irrelevant too.

He cocked his head, relishing the heat burgeoning inside his chest. The dog's breath hitched, stopped, and started again. *Ahh, release.* He needed it—needed it more here than anywhere else. He didn't give a shit about soccer, or football, or the goddamn PTA, though he attended the meetings as was expected. Sometimes he participated vocally. The rest of the time, he imagined the PTA president bent over her desk, fucked bloody, engulfed in flames from the inside out. But even that got boring after a while.

He put his hand on the dog's head and scratched behind the animal's ears. The dog struggled a great breath into its lungs and whined, practically shrieking for help. Its eyes were a darker, deeper yellow than they'd been earlier, marking the dog's progress toward doom: from bright white to off-white to a creamy beige that wasn't any more visible to the rest of his family than the lethargy that plagued the animal. Then the upset stomach, as if the dog had eaten something bad, but no one had been around to see that. Work and school made an animal's illness less visible—by day, the forgotten family member—and by the time dinner rolled around, the progression was too far for anything to be done. The dog's yellow corneas had darkened to ochre while Layla sat in class, chatting with her idiot friends. What color would those eyes become before the animal panted its last?

Death was interesting. Every single time.

Layla returned, her dark hair disheveled like she was homeless. She wasn't attractive in the conventional sense: nose too wide, eyes too close, too many freckles, though his wife had once had pageant aspirations. Thank god she'd given up on that. If he'd had to sit through another year of people judging ball gowns, he'd have lit his daughter's face on fire while she slept just to avoid the monotony of one more talent competition. The only thing that had ever kept him occupied during the pageants was imagining the blaze that would turn her skin into a blistered ruin. Then the surgeries —the grafts. The sympathy. The roadmap of scars emerging from patchwork flesh as she healed, a constant reminder of what flames could create from a living person. *That* would have been interesting too.

"Maybe next time we can get a puppy," Layla said, snuggling close against him. "Then they wouldn't die so soon. It wouldn't be so sad."

"These animals need us more, darling. They're old, so no one else will take them in. Don't you think they deserve a little love before they pass?" And no one thought twice about an old dog dying. These animals were socially acceptable casualties.

He ran his hand over the dog's fur, soon to be enshrined in the bracelet in his closet. It wasn't critical to him, this little piece of nostalgia, but it felt like good luck as if he had the ghosts of all the animals with him while he watched each new body burn.

Clearly illogical. But interesting too, the chance to leave even the tiniest piece of his conquests behind while anything that was a part of him went up in flames. It surely made for a fascinating case file: animal fur, no roots, no conclusive DNA. Even if they came upon him and the bracelet tomorrow, they could prove nothing. They'd suspect—there had been many suspects over the years. Never him. No one suspected a man like him.

He pulled Layla closer, wishing she'd just suck it up already, but knowing that this, too, was expected. This was life. This was living. This was hiding.

In plain sight.

No victim had ever figured it out either, not until it was too late. At first, he was just another unassuming pedestrian out for a stroll around the block. By the time she realized, her blood was already running over his fingers, warm and wet and sticky, hot as the flames he'd soon reduce her body to. Parts of it anyway. Sometimes the fire went out too fast, burned through the clothes, and left the skin behind. But the hair always went. Still, he felt no need to risk an inferno or tempt the surrounding area to catch and alert someone with flickering orange ash against the night sky. He didn't need the fire to be big—just very hot. No need to make a fuss. Making a fuss was how you got caught.

That was why they'd never find him until the day he torched the home around him.

He kissed Layla's head. If it finally came down to it, he'd light her room on fire first. He would let her watch the tendrils of flame creep closer, seductive: her very first lover. He'd let Petrosky think there was actually a chance to save her, but there wouldn't be. She'd choke on the ashes. Petrosky would get there just in time to see her die.

And maybe that would finally plunge the detective into insanity. After all, Petrosky was the one who had pushed him over the edge—it was poetic, really. Life coming full circle.

He hoped he'd get to see that. If nothing else, it would be interesting.

17

As Scott's stupid, foreign taillights disappeared down the drive and up the road, Petrosky moved his car to the corner of the property where he could see the front and side doors and keep track of the cleared land around the house. *Nowhere to hide.* Unless Hannah had a hidden tunnel under the mountain, she wasn't walking out of there unseen, and he'd be damned if he lost her twice.

Scott had left his laptop for Petrosky and headed home to hack into the survivor's group and do more research. He also planned to check out any veterinarians with a record—if the killer liked animal hair so much, maybe he had a job that focused on animals. Hopefully, Scott would get some rest, too. One of them needed to be on his game.

Petrosky passed the time searching for bracelets made of hair. A dozen websites advertised jewelry made from the hair of dead pets, and one used the hair of dead people. *Gross.* He took a slug of Jack to steady his hands and typed in search after search, narrowing the businesses to those that had been around at least ten years since hair had been found at Julie's scene as well.

He copied his list of dog hair jewelry websites into the file and glared at the computer, wishing that everything he needed would just pop up. But it didn't. He still had jack shit. *Think, Petrosky.* The killer had some connection to Michigan, maybe; he'd killed there three times. If they could find that connection, they could find him, and Petrosky could put a bullet between the eyes of Julie's murderer.

For now...though they had Robin's composite sketch, most of the other information they'd gleaned didn't mean a whole hell of a lot. Latex gloves were easy to come by. Having soft hands cut out laborers and several other professions, but the man who had attacked Robin Lowenstein and murdered Julie could be anyone: a computer geek, a surgeon, a manicurist. A vet like the ones Scott was probably checking out as Petrosky typed.

He lit a cigarette and looked over the mountains to the west, at the brilliant blue sky, the sun itself a white-hot eyeball above the horizon. They'd surely find more murders with this pattern elsewhere, maybe outside Michigan and Massachusetts, and if they could combine the evidence from those cases with the information from Robin Lowenstein, they might have a chance. Just because there hadn't been more victims in Michigan didn't mean the killer had stopped. This killer hadn't stopped—no way in hell.

But Petrosky had. He'd just...given up. The pain had been too great, and the leads nonexistent. Dr. McCallum had said he was torturing himself, that he needed to let it go. And so he had.

How many other girls had died because of it? He should have kept torturing himself. He could have prevented this. And the thing that sat heaviest in his chest, crushing his heart: he'd allowed himself give up on his daughter.

He frowned and grabbed his cell.

"Jackson, got a job for you," he said before she could say hello.

Wet sounds, chewing maybe, came through the phone,

and he glanced at the clock—almost six. Dinnertime. "The chief's pissed. I told her you were taking a few days off, but—"

"Did you give her a reason?"

"Nope."

Well, that's just great. He was going to get fired because his partner couldn't cover for him for two goddamn days. It wasn't so much that he cared about the job, but getting the boot because of that bullshit made him madder than a motherfucker on bath salts.

A wet slurping came through the line—she was drinking now—and it made him want to punch someone in the kidney. "I didn't tell Decantor jack either," she said.

"Come again?"

"He's been after you like a stalker. He in love with you or what?" Jackson said, and Petrosky pulled the phone from his ear, stared at it like he didn't recognize the cell, and then replaced it in time to hear Jackson say: "I don't care if you're gay, but I'm not playing interference for—"

"Jackson, what the—"

"I'm messing with you. He is after something, though. I told him to piss off. This ain't his business."

She'd told Decantor to piss off? On his behalf? "Not his business," Petrosky echoed, his brain suddenly fuzzy. Why was Decantor on his ass?

"Darn right. He's not your partner."

Petrosky lit another cigarette and watched the lighter's flame dance, the heat of it singeing his nostril hair. *Decantor.* "Listen, Jackson, this isn't a fucking vacation." Plastic crinkled over the line like she was unwrapping something. Jesus Christ, couldn't she stop eating for three minutes? He hit his cigarette again. "I'm following up on a lead out in Vermont, and the info I need isn't in the database here. But there might be more in Ash Park."

He filled Jackson in on the specifics of the case, conveniently leaving out the part about Julie being one of the victims. Saying Julie's name out loud, reminding himself that soon he'd have to reopen her file, was more than he could consider right now if he wanted to keep his shit together. He stared at the blinding sun through a haze of cigarette smoke —it looked like the mountains were burning. And then he caught movement in the rearview mirror: Crandall himself, walking up the street—steadier, maybe, but still slow.

"Jackson? You still at the office? I emailed you a composite." Or rather he'd asked Scott to do it. Scott had smiled like being given the task was some great honor. If he'd asked Jackson, she'd have slapped the shit out of him.

At the foot of the drive, Crandall stopped briefly—he'd noticed Petrosky's car. Did he think Hannah had a guest? That she was cheating on him? But his face in the waning sun didn't appear angry or even concerned. Just curious.

"Yeah, I'm at the office finishing up some paperwork," Jackson said, bringing him back to the conversation. "You at the precinct out there?"

"I'm in front of the house." He followed Crandall with his eyes as the man drew even with the back bumper.

"The house? What house?"

Oops. "Can you just take care of this, Jackson? And call me back when you've got something."

He waited for her to protest, to invite him to kiss her ass, but she said nothing. Through the receiver, he thought he heard the telltale scratch of pen on paper. Crandall approached the passenger window.

"I'll call you back," she said and hung up on him just as Crandall bent and peered into the car.

Petrosky reached over and rolled down the window. "Evening, sir."

"Ah." The bookstore owner cocked his head. "You change your mind about that book?"

Only in the boonies could someone think that a man

outside his house was just a patron wanting to buy books after hours.

Petrosky flashed his badge, and Crandall's jaw dropped. "Nope. Working on a case. Missing persons." Saying that was a calculated risk, but Crandall's reaction might give him a clue about the man's state of mind—he didn't want to put Hannah at risk if this asshole was an undercover abuser like her last two boyfriends.

"What kind of case?" Crandall was saying.

"Just routine, sir. Someone spotted in the area who matches a description."

Crandall narrowed his eyes, finally looking worried, and grabbed the window with one gnarled hand. "Were you looking for this person at the bookstore earlier?"

Petrosky let the mountain breeze be his response. Crandall glanced at the house, then back at Petrosky. "You work for the Willowshire department?"

Petrosky nodded. If this guy called the station, hopefully, Scott would be there to intervene. The tenacious bastard was probably still working, drinking burnt coffee and eating those godawful cardboard scones instead of going home to IV bags and whatever else was waiting for him there.

Finally, Crandall nodded. "You let me know if I can be of assistance." He straightened and sauntered to the house without another word, leaning heavily on his cane.

Petrosky rolled the window up and clicked on the volume for the bug inside the house. Through the bay window beside the front door, he watched Hannah get up from the couch and disappear beyond his line of sight.

"You know there's a cop outside?" Crandall's voice.

"That's… Yeah." Hannah's voice was shaking. Petrosky put his hand on the door, ready to rush in at the first sign of trouble.

"You know who they're looking for?"

When Hannah stayed silent, he said: "You think he's

keeping an eye on the Leibowitzes down in the valley? You can see the house real good from up here. I never did trust them much."

From the computer came a shuffling—footsteps. "I think they're looking for someone in this…online group I belong to. I might even have to go with them, help locate her."

She was making plans to go to Michigan with him. Lying her ass off, but she wasn't going to run. He lit a third cigarette and exhaled, watching the smoke flutter against the windshield and disperse.

"Group? What group?" Crandall asked.

"Oh…um, it's for…you know. My anxiety."

Anxiety. Crandall must not know about her traumatic history with her father or anyone else. Still, spreading rumors was enough for him to kill Montgomery over, Hannah's birthday aside, and—

Stop it, goddammit. He really wanted to believe Crandall was a psycho just so he could get the asshole away from Hannah, but Crandall wasn't anything more than a creep— not like he was forcing Hannah to be with him. And Petrosky could hardly write off Hannah for Harwick's murder because of a physical injury and then accuse Crandall despite his tremors. He was looking for any reason for Hannah to be innocent.

"I was getting ready to make dinner." Hannah's disembodied voice floated around him in the car, and the vibration in her words made him reach for the bottle again. "Vegetable penne sound good?"

"Sounds perfect."

Petrosky imagined Crandall grinning with those yellowed horse teeth of his, and his insides clenched. The bastard was taking advantage of a traumatized girl—*no, woman*—who clearly needed help and not some old, wrinkled dick.

No sound from Hannah. Footsteps, then: "I'm going to

get cleaned up before dinner. But careful you don't overcook the noodles like last time, Noelle." Water running, the clank of a pot, the clatter of silverware.

Petrosky stared at the screen. *Noelle?* What the hell was that? Noelle had been Hannah's best friend at the time of the *Looking Glass* killings, and she'd disappeared not long after Hannah did. Though Noelle hadn't left a forwarding address, there hadn't been anything suspicious about her disappearance, and she had never been a suspect in the murders. Did Hannah know where Noelle was? Why would Hannah assume her identity?

But he could guess. Hannah'd lied about her name because she didn't want Daddy to know she'd come home—and if she never showed her face in public, there'd have been no reason to connect "Theo's daughter" to "Crandall's girlfriend." But even after Montgomery was dead, she'd kept the other woman's name. In too deep? Or trying to hide terrible crimes behind a fake name, a fake life, with a kindly old man? Maybe Crandall wasn't the one being shady. Could be Hannah using the old bastard and not the other way around.

Petrosky watched the sun set over the mountain as he tried to imagine a way to keep Hannah from prison. But the image of her tear-filled eyes as he led her away made his heart seize. Arresting the victim—he might as well have been arresting Robin.

Or Julie.

18

I HAD, at some point, grabbed mushrooms from the refrigerator drawer. I had, at some point, managed to get out a frying pan. But every action I took was being done outside of me—the only real thing was Petrosky's worried eyes in my mind. I could still see his jowly face. The way he'd looked sorry like he was concerned about me. The way he'd narrowed his eyes when we first met like we had known one another forever.

From the butcher block in front of me, the handles glinted dully, and I paused for a moment and traced the cool steel before yanking out a paring knife, the sharpest blade we had. That woke me up. Pretty sure even my subconscious recognized that operating a blade while being a zombie was a bonehead idea, especially with my track record. I set to work slicing the mushrooms into haphazard chunks, trying not to compare the way the skin split to the way Dominic's flesh had ripped under the scalpel. Tears stung my eyes, and I blinked them back and tossed butter into the pan.

The knife sliced cleanly through the onions too, the aroma burning my eyes and blurring my vision. Onions were by far the jerkiest of vegetables. "Assholes," I muttered, trying to put my focus there instead, on my anger at the food, knowing it would give me an out if Neil came back from the bathroom and saw my red eyes and damp face. "I'm not crying," I'd say. "Just cutting onions." *Those smelly punks.*

I choked back a sob and dumped them into the pan to kill their stink.

What am I doing?

Murdering vegetables.

Why am I here in Willowshire?

Because I'm a moron.

I brought the knife down again, harder than necessary, and it was therapeutic somehow, the way the zucchini cracked open, baring its insides for all to see. My forearm shuddered and shook from the frayed nerves.

I should have gotten that wound checked. Then my hand would still work.

Like it worked the night you killed your boyfriend.

I grabbed the counter, dizziness pulling at me, and gnawing my vision out of focus like a deranged beaver had taken up residence behind my eye sockets. This wasn't a nerve thing—it was probably the lack of oxygen in my blood. Or maybe I just needed to leave. Pack up my things and go.

You'll be running forever, Hannah.

I'd be running until I was dead. Or eventually, they'd catch me. I needed a solution—a chance to clear up the mess I had gotten myself into. A chance to stop running and settle down and actually live a life instead of hiding from one.

I need to call Petrosky.

Like he can protect you.

So far, he hadn't handcuffed me. *Maybe he won't.* But Petrosky's eyes flashed in my brain. There was no statute of limitations on murder. And one day, they'd find Julie's killer —Petrosky would have no problem taking me in then.

"Smells good."

The knife clattered to the counter, and I stared at my hand, at the narrow strip of skin I'd filleted from my palm. Blood welled in the wound and dripped down my arm.

"Noelle, my god, here." Neil grabbed a paper towel and pressed it against my hand, and I kept my eyes lowered, worried he'd see my guilt, though he had never noticed, not once, in the years I'd been here. "Are you okay?"

"Fine. It's… I'm not feeling great." *Think about something else. Talk about something else.* "I got a lot done today." I didn't recognize my own voice, throat clogged as it was with tears and the wild panic encircling my throat like a mink stole that had come back to life. "The articles I've been writing are doing pretty well on that website, so I think they might give me a raise."

"Congratulations, Darlin'. You want a back rub to celebrate?"

I shook my head. I wanted a lot of things more than his hands on my body. Skunk oil perfume. A fork to the eye. A cobra in my bed. More than anything, I wanted to run.

Dominic wouldn't have run.

Dominic was brave and sensual and brutal and terrifying. And he was the only one who'd ever really made me feel whole.

"Here, have a seat." Neil touched my back, and my skin crawled, just for a moment, and then settled as I stepped from the counter. He set to work finishing the vegetables, probably doing an even more haphazard job than me, slicing with his palsied fingers. He kept his eyes on the cutting board. I kept my eyes on his back.

I couldn't tell if Neil believed me about why Petrosky was there, but eventually, he'd learn the truth. Then what? Up until now, I'd stayed hidden in more ways than one. My hair might have been the same color, my eyes the same too, but all resemblance to Hannah Montgomery was hidden beneath a fifty-pound layer of blubber. Once, I might have worried about that part—the attractive thing, the skinny thing—but then I'd realized that cake was delicious.

Maybe my true identity wouldn't matter. Neil didn't know my father was a child rapist, so it wasn't like he'd know how messed up I really was. But hiding the fact that I was Theodore Montgomery's daughter...would Neil see that as betrayal? The look on my face had stopped him from discussing my father's murder when it happened, but he'd probably thought I was worried because a killer was running around. If he only knew.

I sat at the kitchen table, listening to the *chop, chop, chop* of Neil's knife, and I could almost feel the sharpness of my father's name in my head, even sharper than the blade. *Theodore Montgomery.* The room went cold and I with it, every muscle in my body freezing as if someone had injected ice into my veins.

My father had been crazy, and no one had known.

No one but me.

Time was supposed to heal everything, but how could I forget the night my father died? How could I forget the blood, the screaming, the raw shame that slit me open and gutted me right along with him? The blade. His eyes. My tears.

They're coming for you, Hannah.

How much do they know?

They knew enough. Petrosky knew. I swallowed hard to keep from retching.

"You need anything over there?" Neil called over his shoulder. He was still focused on the food, so he didn't look at me, but his tone was as steady and sure as it had been the first day I'd met him. It was something about his demeanor, maybe; a protective, almost...fatherly kindness.

Daddy issues. I know I've got 'em.

"I'm okay." But I was a rabbit frozen at the scent of a

predator. The cops outside—that wasn't a hallucination or some frightening thought I could just brush away. It was real. They *were* here for me.

Chop, chop, chop went the knife.

Run, Hannah, run. But that was silly; they were watching, and if I left now, I'd never make it far. They'd know I was gone and why I ran.

None of this would have happened if I'd just let Dominic kill me.

Chop, chop, chop went the knife.

The night I realized Dominic was the *Looking Glass* killer—the night he'd come after me, the night I'd shoved the dagger of glass into his gut—was a blur. I still couldn't remember the drive to Vermont, and I still wasn't sure why I had come back here, to the one place I'd spent years trying to escape. I guess I'd been feeling…brave. Powerful. Maybe I'd hoped that if my father acknowledged what he'd done to me, I could finally let it all go. But that was stupid.

And I hadn't known I would see *her*.

She had long, dark hair just like mine as if my father had deliberately tried to replace me with a look-alike because he knew I was the only one he had ever loved. Twelve years old or so, the same age I was when he was telling me I wasn't smart enough to play with the other kids at school, that no one else would like me, that I only needed him. And he squeezed her arm just so, possessing her like he'd possessed me, and I could almost feel it, the way his hand had always sent tremors down my spine, the way I'd felt needed, wanted. Loved. And she smiled at him with her whole face like she knew that kind of love too.

Chop, chop, chop.

I hadn't been able to leave her. Couldn't let her just stay there with…him. I'd lain awake that entire first night wondering if he'd started fucking her yet.

You were jealous.

I was protective.

Protective of his penis.

When I was her age, I hadn't known better—I'd gone to him willingly, sure we were meant to be. I had fantasized every night about a world where the two of us could be together. But when I saw Stacey, even with the irrational pang of jealousy slicing through my gut, I'd known better than to dwell on that feeling. Maybe if Melinda had listened when I called her, anonymously, of course, I wouldn't have stayed here in Willowshire. But she'd hung up on me. Melinda Charles had either been in denial about what a freak my father was, or she hadn't cared—but neither would have helped Stacey. Stacey had needed me.

This is all my fault.

Had the police gone through Melinda's phone records? Was that how they'd known I was here? My mouth felt like it had been sucked dry by a Hoover.

Oh god, I'm an idiot.

Finished with the vegetables, Neil tossed everything into the pan, but he didn't flick on the stove. Instead, he turned to me. "Are you sure you're okay?" His mouth was drawn up in concern. "I can get you something. Aspirin, Pepto, if you need it."

No, I'm not okay. And I couldn't sit here, every muscle vibrating like I was inside a dryer set on high.

Get it out. Make it stop.

"You can help."

Neil cocked his head and smiled when I hooked my fingers under the hem of my shirt and peeled it over my head.

Get the crazy out, Hannah.

I wish I was at Dominic's.

Why did you kill him?

I knew the answer: he'd tried to kill me. But it was far more than that and even now, gasping at the too-thin air, watching Neil's flabby back as I followed him into the bedroom, even as I pictured Dominic's face, his bloody gash of an abdomen...I wanted to be the person Dominic had made me. Stronger. Fiercer.

Worthy.

But I wasn't that girl anymore. I was a nobody. A ghost, hidden in some tiny house in a tiny town, right back where I'd started.

You need to run, Hannah.

Can't get out of this shit.

I blew the hair off my face. And lay on the bed.

Neil smiled down at me, the yellow of his front teeth almost endearing. He'd smoked since twenty years before I was born, and when it made me cough, he'd gotten some drug from the pharmacy to help him stop. For me. Something about that made me feel more cherished than anything he could say.

He adores me. He adores me. I forced a smile.

He doesn't. He's lonely.

But the why didn't really matter. He was a step up from Jake, who'd punched me so hard I'd seen stars. A step up from my father, though part of my brain still wanted to argue with me about that.

Neil's body on top of mine was dead weight, but I inhaled around his gut and let him do his thing. The ceiling danced with shadows from the tree beside the house, the setting sun splattering the walls with an eerie kaleidoscope of orange and red and gray. From outside the door, Duke whined, and I could almost see his massive black head turning this way and that at the sounds Neil was making—the man was like an out-of-shape orangutan grunting at a beetle. The headboard creaked, the lamp jiggled. The ceiling kept dancing.

"You're so lovely, Noelle."

The name always made me pause, but *Hannah Montgomery* —that was a name for another girl. A girl who'd been kidnapped. A girl who was dead and, therefore, innocent of any crime. A girl who couldn't be walking around town, alive and well. But even with Noelle's name, even with a life where I could stay indoors at all times, even though my father was dead, I was still half convinced that any day might be the one when he finally fulfilled his promise to make me pay.

Neil grunted and rolled off me, but he wasn't done. It was always like this—he got tired. He was old.

He might be old, but he's gentle and warm and kind.

And safe. Really safe.

I rolled on top of him, his fish-belly almost glowing against the green sheets, and he sighed when I reached down and pulled him inside me.

I closed my eyes, trying to pretend I wasn't there, because as much as this man claimed to care for me, my body didn't want him. He was kind and warm, but I couldn't make that matter to my vagina. In my mind's eye, Dominic swam into my field of vision, and then it was his touch on my ass, his hands squeezing my thighs. I rotated my hips and raised my own thumbs to my breasts, but it was Dominic, biting me, pinching me, his perfect teeth clamping down on my nipple until my body began to pulse with desire.

I ran my hands through his hair and—*hey, baby*—he smiled, square jaw, chiseled chest, perfect arms, ice-blue eyes —god, he was beautiful. He trailed his fingers along my rib cage, and then he was bucking against me, deeper, deeper, until I moaned, feeling the heat of the afternoon sun on my bare back, his fingers digging into the flesh of my hips.

But then—and this was how it always was—Dominic's smile changed. His gaze darkened, and his soft lips pulled back from his bright white teeth, turning his grin into a predatory snarl. My heart rate increased, every beat sending blood searing deep into my abdomen where it raged, hot and thick. In his fist, the scalpel glistened. And as we moved faster together, he reached out for me, the blade flying toward my chest as he captured my shoulder in his other hand, scratching his fingernails against the damaged part of my arm and sending bolts of pain tingling into my hand and fingers.

I moaned and grabbed his wrist, trying to wrest the blade from him, and when I blinked, I was gripping the frigid steel in my palm instead. He smiled. *You're stronger than you think, Hannah.*

I *was* strong. He'd made me this way. And when he reached for me again, I rammed the weapon into his abdomen, blood pouring from the wound like a fountain, and at my most powerful, when his blood covered my hands and soaked my legs, the waves of orgasm ripped through my body like a current of brilliant lightning, and I arched my back as if I were truly being electrocuted. Maybe he'd killed me this time. But the waves of pleasure stayed, and the blood poured down around me like rain spitting on my arms, flowing over my back as someplace deep inside me the muscles released, clenched, released again.

I bit my tongue lest I cry out for Dominic and squeezed my eyes tighter, trying to clear the bloody images, though I could still feel the gore on my flesh. It happened every time; when the last shudders of pleasure left my body, the visions of blood would pass too. Dominic would have been so pissed at me for fucking Neil, but he wouldn't have been upset watching my father bleed. He would rather have liked that, though not for any moral reasons, or because it meant justice had been done.

He just liked the blood. Maybe I did too.

You're insane, Hannah. Sick.

As if there were ever any hope I'd turn out normal.

Electric panic writhed in my gut like a thousand worms with nowhere to go. Trapped. I didn't want to run anymore. All I wanted was to make Dominic proud.

So insane. More than usual. An "anniversary reaction" was what my shrink in Michigan had once called it.

It was almost July twenty-third. Again. The first day he'd raped me and called it a birthday present. And though I hadn't resisted, though I hadn't been sure it was wrong, it was the day my father had turned me into a killer.

19

PETROSKY STILL FELT sick to his stomach from listening to the sounds of their...goddammit, he wasn't even going to think about it. He slugged back a finger of Jack as the clank of forks on plates came through the speakers.

"Good pasta." Geezer.

"Mm-hmm." Hannah, AKA Noelle.

Noncommittal replies. Polite platitudes. As dinner wore on, there was no more talking, and that resonated with him even more than conversation—the sound of things unsaid. He'd had many of those nights with his ex-wife after Julie died. He could still see her face too, her gray eyes marred with grief, skin pale, and the way she'd speared bite after bite of chicken or fish like she wished she were stabbing him in the heart.

As if he'd needed her to. He had stopped eating meals at the table and taken to drinking his dinner in the garage, feeling his wife slipping away, but powerless to do anything about it, heavy as he was with his own loss.

In hindsight, her grief had been heavy as well. She'd probably needed him to help pull her up. Carry some of that weight for her. But he'd had no strength to haul himself from the depths of his own despair, let alone reach back for her. He had hoped her new husband would prove more capable of responding to her needs, but last year she divorced the guy who replaced him. Or so he'd heard. He had almost called her, but instead, he'd drunk himself into oblivion staring at their wedding photo, the only one of her he had left.

From inside the house, chairs scraped the floor, and someone turned on the water. Plates clanked. Silverware jangled like it'd been thrown in the sink. Normal sounds, but they clattered around in his head like ricocheting buckshot, trying to obliterate every one of his thoughts.

He shuddered and shut off the sound. Though he could no longer hear them, he could still see the line on the computer jumping and flowing, probably with the sounds of dishes, but what if she was being hurt? What if Crandall was more than some old man taking advantage of a little girl? But no, she wasn't a little girl—she was a grown woman. And she for damn sure wasn't Julie.

He drew his eyes from the computer screen to the mountains, purple as a bruise as if the whole of the landscape had been in a bar fight. Appropriate—god knew he felt beaten. He needed to get out of there and back to Michigan while he still had any resistance left in him.

The vibration of his cell brought him out of his thoughts. Jackson.

"You were right about there being others," she said the second he clicked answer. "Four vics here, then four in other states, all younger women, all left in a field or some type of abandoned lot. Raped, no DNA, throat slit, burned."

"How'd you get that so fast, Jackson?"

"I've got people who owe me favors."

"More tiny dicks?"

"They're all tiny dicks." Over the line came the shuffling of papers and then: "Some more evidence of hair too, but not all of it is dog. We got raccoon on one of 'em. It's possible that none of the hairs are from a bracelet, and we're just finding them because the bodies were left in the open. The hair follicles aren't attached either, so not a whole hell of a lot to be done in terms of positive ID. Can't match DNA even if we find the bracelet itself."

"Fuck." Petrosky pulled his cigarettes from the console and shook one into his mouth, squeezing it so tight between his teeth that his jaw hurt. He released it long enough to ask, "Any leads on the rest of the cases?"

"Nothin'. The burning destroyed any DNA evidence in the pubic area and no other DNA at the scene. We do have the same latex residue on all the bodies— gloves, obviously. The guy knew what he was doing."

On the computer screen, the sound line from Scott's monitoring device had gone mostly still. *Flatlined*. Petrosky's heart jolted, and he jabbed the button for the sound. Hushed buzzing filled the car. Then a noise like a snore, and maybe the rustle of someone settling on the couch, though he could see no one through the front window—nothing to indicate distress.

Petrosky lit the cigarette with a shaking hand and blew the smoke through his nostrils.

"Petrosky, did you hear me?"

Jackson's voice had an edge: stress, irritation maybe. He puffed hungrily on the smoke. "What'd you say?"

"Get it together. I got no time for this."

"I got it, I—"

"The states where the murders took place. We've got one in California a few months after Julie."

Petrosky froze.

"You didn't think I'd find out? What the hell's wrong with you?"

Petrosky didn't answer. Finally, Jackson sighed.

"So, Julie in Ash Park, then one in Cali, then one near Lansing, and another all the way up in West Branch,

Michigan. Then Robin in Boston. Next, we've got Texas, then Nevada. Then the fourth in Michigan."

"So Julie was his…first." He tried to approach it clinically, but his heart seized. The killer had started with Julie. Why her? What had made her a good first target? *Think, dickhead.* He inhaled sharply, then squinted through the haze of smoke. California and Texas and Boston were new to him this week. Three in Michigan he'd known about. But had Jackson said there was a fourth?

"Did anyone know you were heading out to Vermont?"

Something in her tone chilled Petrosky's blood. "Just you." Right? *Did I tell anyone else?*

"Petrosky, are you sure? It's a little coincidental—"

"When was the last one?" he snapped.

"That's what I've been trying to tell you, you crotchety old bastard. He murdered a girl the day you left. Julie's killer is here."

20

Petrosky needed to get the hell out of Vermont. Screw it, he'd be all-out aggressive, wrap this Theodore Montgomery case ASAP, and if Hannah freaked on him, that was fine. He had Jackson, who had the best solve rate in the department. He didn't need Hannah to find Julie's killer.

But something in his gut told him this wasn't true. While she'd probably already given him what she knew, every time he imagined helping her into his car, loading up her suitcase and that massive dog, he felt something like…relief. What was wrong with him? Maybe he was just happy to get her away from Crandall.

He snatched up his phone and flipped it open, getting ready to call Scott, pausing when he saw a missed text from Shannon. Probably telling his unreliable ass to stay away from her and the kids. It was just as well. He scrambled for the bottle under the seat. He needed that familiar, comfortable warmth to creep through his belly and displace the oppressive emptiness that was trying to devour him. He slugged back a shot, eyes on the house.

Hannah helped shave the edges off that emptiness too. Hannah was *alive*—it was like she'd come back from the dead. Though he wasn't a religious man, it sure as hell felt like a miracle. That's probably all a miracle really was anyway: a feeling born of misunderstanding. He should have known better. He dropped his gaze to the screen.

"Can we talk? I feel awful about what happened. I was just so angry. You need to step it up, but I also know you're actually working a case and not just avoiding me. Just…call, okay? I'm worried about you. The kids miss you."

She was making excuses for him, just like Morrison used to—and he didn't deserve forgiveness. Never had. But he stared at the words a beat longer, trying to pretend that in some other life, maybe he could have done better. And…*shit.* He lowered the phone and stared out into the night.

If Shannon was aware he was working a case, there *was* someone besides Jackson who knew he was out in Vermont. Maybe Shannon had asked Decantor about Petrosky's absence, and that was why that jerkoff was harassing Jackson. His chest heated. Shannon needed to leave Decantor's nosy ass out of it if she expected a call back.

Jesus Christ, Petrosky. Shannon was just trying to make amends—he was being a dick. But what to text in response? His fingers were hovering uncertainly over the letters when Scott rang through.

"You're never going to guess what I found," Scott blurted, then raced on before Petrosky could reply. "That online group shows up on a bunch of social media sites, nothing incriminating, nothing strange. But it's listed as a local group."

Petrosky tried to force his brain back to the Montgomery case, to what Scott was saying, but he kept hearing Jackson: *Julie's killer is here.* He cleared his throat. "Local meaning what? They meet in person?"

"No, not in person. But a higher than usual percentage of

them live in the surrounding area. And it's well promoted as a place to discuss things without divulging your identity—remember, lots of those women have attackers still out there, like Robin, and identification might be an issue for those involved in domestic violence situations, too. But because it isn't run by an actual therapist, the records, IP addresses, and the like are fair game. Unfortunately, there are hundreds of members from Maine to Vermont to New York. Most of them could easily have driven into Willowshire to kill Theodore Montgomery."

"That doesn't sound like a lot to go on, Scott." They needed more. He needed to close this and get out of this town.

"Oh, I'm not done yet, sir."

Petrosky's fingers tightened around the phone.

"We've got one member who had a much higher than usual chance to commit the crime."

Petrosky's heart was throbbing so hard his entire chest hurt. Had the rookie closed it? "For fuck's sake, Scott, who is it?"

"Melinda Charles, Theodore Montgomery's widow."

Sometimes the most logical answer was the correct one. "Any evidence of her talking to Hannah?"

"In the group, not so much, but they might have met in person."

If Charles knew that Theodore Montgomery had abused Hannah, she'd be more likely to accept that he'd hurt Stacey too. If Charles had confronted her husband...maybe Montgomery had ended up dead because of something that had nothing to do with Hannah. Well, birthday aside. Coincidences were bullshit, but...

"Come over here, Scott. Watch the house, and I'll go get Melinda Charles." He didn't want Scott to risk his rookie neck dealing with a murderer. Might as well have the kid watch Hannah—a possible self-defense killer, but at least she seemed sorry about what she'd done.

"No need to get Melinda, sir. She's already here."

<hr>

MELINDA CHARLES SAT in the interrogation room at the station, her arms crossed over her chest, defiant eyes glaring at Petrosky and Officer Crowley in turn. Crowley, the guy who'd made fun of Scott the day Petrosky had shown up. The guy who'd appeared out of nowhere to take over the case the moment they had a viable suspect. Petrosky stood by the door, as far from that moose-fucking asshole as possible. Plus, he was too antsy to sit.

Across from Charles, Crowley shifted his doughy ass in the seat, his big hands resting on a sturdy-looking wooden table that one of these jerkoffs had probably built with their bare hands out of Vermont maple or whatever kind of wood they had out here.

But Melinda Charles did not appear to be worried about tables. She kept her posture rigid, her jaw set, watching Crowley's slab-of-beef hands as if a fist might come flying toward her. She should be afraid or maybe relieved, as some criminals were when they finally got caught. But Charles was agitated like a dog with its hackles up. Either she was innocent and was pissed about being there, or she was hiding something. Petrosky was betting on the latter. She had killed her husband. She thought she'd gotten away with it. And from that resolute glint in her eyes, she was determined to keep that confession to herself.

But eventually, she'd cave.

"Tell us again how you came to join the group," Crowley said.

"I have a rather…checkered past. I wanted a place where I could go and talk about it without being judged."

"You didn't do much talking." Crowley frowned. That much was true—she'd made just a few little comments here and there—"thank you" or "guys are jerks"—but nothing anyone could even respond to in a meaningful way, let alone judge her for.

"I liked reading the stories." She kept her eyes on Crowley's fat hands. "The things those women said made me feel less alone." She did not look up, but her nostrils flared, and her mouth went hard. Defiant.

"Maybe you joined to figure out how to help your daughter," Petrosky said, and Crowley turned and glared at him, eyes beady as a rat's. Petrosky didn't flinch.

"My daughter has nothing to do with this." But her palms were now pressed firmly against the tabletop, her fingertips white from the pressure.

"Your husband was a child abuser," Petrosky snapped, though he couldn't prove that; even Hannah hadn't admitted it outright. Hannah's "How did you know" in response to his words would never stand up in court, and he had a feeling if he put her on the spot she'd deny it. Shame was a powerful motivator.

"Theo never abused Stacey."

Of course she'd claim innocence on that front. If Charles admitted to being aware that Theodore Montgomery had abused her daughter, it would mean she had a motive to murder him.

"My daughter was the same age as yours when she was taken from me, Melinda." Petrosky stepped next to Crowley, ignoring the way the asshole stiffened, and leaned over the table toward Charles. Her eyes widened. "She was raped, murdered, and left in a field." *And burned alive.* A sharp pain ripped through his sternum. He rubbed his chest. "I know what it's like to want vengeance. I know what it's like to have someone hurt your child, terribly— irreparably."

Crowley's posture finally softened, and he turned his bull head back to face their suspect.

"Doesn't mean I did anything about it," she said slowly.

"So you *did* know that Montgomery hurt your daughter," Crowley boomed, and Charles reared back in surprise. *Gotcha.* She shook her head so hard Petrosky was sure it would fall off.

"No, absolutely not. I just said that I didn't know—"

"Oh, but you did." Petrosky straightened. "There was no evidence of anyone else in that house. Just you and your daughter and your daughter's rapist."

Charles's lips were thin and bloodless. "I didn't kill him. Stacey and I were taking a walk—"

"How convenient for you," Crowley said.

If they could keep her off-balance, maybe she'd screw up. A quick confession and he could head back to Michigan. Petrosky waited until she met his eyes, then threw her a curveball: "What about Crandall? I hear you two were rather close, and with the sex offender rumors flying, he had plenty of reason to kill your husband. Maybe he helped you do it."

Her brows furrowed. Genuinely confused. "Neil? I only met him a few times."

"What did those conversations entail?"

"I... Nothing much. The weather." She was faltering, though; her eyes darting from him to Crowley and back.

Hit her again. "Did you know Hannah Montgomery?"

Crowley side-eyed him, probably wondering what he was talking about since no one else knew Hannah was in town. Hell, even Petrosky wasn't entirely sure where he was going with this, only that he needed Charles to slip. He needed her to admit she'd killed her husband. If she did, Hannah was safe. He could get Hannah off on self-defense if she was telling the truth about Harwick; no one would convict the woman who had stabbed the *Looking Glass* killer even if she had run away afterward. He was sure Hannah hadn't killed her father—he could feel by the steady thrumming of his heart, no longer frantic or painful, that it was true. He just wanted Charles to say it.

"I already told you, I've never met—"

"You did." Petrosky shook his head. "In that group of yours. And to kill Theo on his estranged daughter's birthday, a detail you gleaned from her profile…that was a little melodramatic, don't you think?"

Charles's mouth dropped open in shock, her eyes wide. "Her what?"

She didn't know. The liquor sloshed in his belly. Or was she just surprised that he'd figured it out? Maybe Charles wasn't shocked by the connection at all—maybe seeing Hannah alive had messed Petrosky up, made him see things that weren't there. Or maybe Charles was a better liar than he'd given her credit for. Far better than Hannah, who had probably come back here to warn Charles and had ended up getting her father killed. No wonder Hannah was shouldering so much guilt.

But Crowley was already moving on, saying, "Maybe the day wasn't chosen, and it wasn't premeditated; maybe Stacey just told you what he'd done to her, and you killed him because of it." He pushed himself to standing and leaned on his meaty knuckles. "You told the officers you were out taking a walk the night he died, but no one saw you."

"How would anyone see me? The houses are far apart down there and—"

"Listen, we've known one another a long time," Crowley said, his voice softer, but Charles's eyes did not cool—her rage burned hotter than ever. "We've been friends. Our kids go to school together. I just want to know what happened. If you found out that Theo had raped—"

"He did nothing of the kind!" She slammed her fists on the table as if breaking her hand by punching a tree would help calm her down. The wood stayed strong. She winced.

She was behaving the same way Hannah had, defending Theodore Montgomery. This bastard had been good at manipulation. Adept at keeping his victims emotionally close, so he could destroy them.

Crowley put a hand over hers in a tender, familiar way. "Who killed him then, Melinda? Who would do that?"

"I wish I knew." The determined set of her jaw did not change, and Crowley pulled his mitts off her fingers and sighed. *So much for good cop.*

This wasn't working. Time to bring in the big guns. "Stacey is going to end up in foster care," Petrosky said. "If it was self-defense, if you caught him attacking her—"

"I… No, I didn't catch him doing anything."

"Come on, Melinda," Crowley said, his voice low. "No one will blame you. Whether he hurt you or Stacey, your husband was a bad man. I can find a way to make sure Stacey's taken care of, even if you serve a little time. And if it was self-defense, I'll go to bat for you with the prosecutor." He leaned toward her. "But if you keep denying it and we find the evidence on our own, which we will…you'll get no leniency at all."

The determined glint fizzled, and Charles's shoulders slumped. Guilt? Or was she finally cracking? Petrosky backed toward the door, feeling almost like he was intruding on some private moment between lovers.

"Did you do this, Melinda? Did you kill your husband?"

"I can't… I don't know."

"Tell me what happened, Melinda. Let me help you. You know we can't just let this go."

Her lip quivered.

"Give your daughter a chance. Don't turn her life upside down any more than you have to." Crowley's face was still, eyes hooded with sympathy or maybe pity. He wanted her to be innocent. Maybe Crowley had suspected her from the beginning—no wonder he'd been in a hurry to close the case, to keep Scott from trying to reopen it. Hell, maybe Crowley and Charles had been having an affair while Crandall took the rap.

But from the set of Charles's shoulders, she wasn't harboring any unrequited affection now. She just looked sorry. Defeated.

"Melinda?" Crowley practically whispered. "Did you kill your husband?"

When she looked up again, her eyes were glistening with tears. "Yes."

21

HANNAH WAS shaky as he led her to his car, one hand on her back—comforting, not possessive. He was trying to avoid the appearance that he was arresting her, but she had no choice. She could go willingly, or she could fight him, and he'd cuff her, but either way, she was coming back to Michigan with him to close out the *Looking Glass* case. They had Melinda's confession on Theodore Montgomery. Now they'd have the final piece to the *Looking Glass* puzzle, and Hannah would be there to answer questions when Petrosky went after Julie's murderer.

That was the real reason he was doing this, right?

Scott had seemed just as upset about Hannah leaving the state as Hannah had. Petrosky had bulldozed in and taken back the *Looking Glass* killings, knowing full well that solving such a high-profile cold case would have made Scott's career. But if Hannah had anything else, a snippet of memory she hadn't told him, some insight through the eyes of a survivor that might help him locate Julie's killer, then he wanted her there, with him. He promised himself he'd make it up to Scott, somehow, but the rookie's dejected eyes stuck with him.

"Watch your head."

Hannah ducked into the front passenger seat of his car, her breath catching as he opened the back door for the dog. He tried to close her door, but she put her hand on the window. "Wait…please." Her eyes were glassy with unshed tears, and his heart ached, but he turned away before he could give into it. Killer. She was a killer, self-defense or not. He'd do well to remember that.

"Arm in."

"But—"

He shut the door before she could utter another word and headed around to the driver's side. From the back of the car, the dog whined, one long, low howl that stopped abruptly when Petrosky opened his door.

Hannah had her head between her knees.

"Hannah?"

"I…can't…breathe."

Agoraphobia. He'd called Dr. McCallum about that, and the doc had said anyone with the condition would need help keeping calm. Luckily he hadn't asked who the person in question was, and Petrosky hadn't said shit to McCallum about the case. He didn't need the shrink bastard reminding him how his brain stopped being logical around any girl who reminded him of his daughter. McCallum already had enough reason to harangue him for a hundred years to come.

"Want a drink?"

She turned to face him, cheek still on her knee. "What?" She was panting along with the dog.

He peeked at the back seat, where the beast lay on his belly, snout resting on his paws. From under the back floor mat, Petrosky produced a bottle of Jack, one of three hidden somewhere in the vehicle. He might not have any of the good drugs McCallum had told him about, but liquor had never let him down before.

He handed her the bottle and watched her stare at it

before putting it to her lips like she might swing it at him and run—maybe she would as wound up as she was. But she just took a long swallow, winced, and then lowered the bottle, gagging.

He took it before she spilled it. "Okay?"

She nodded and put her head back between her knees. "I don't really drink. And I don't want to talk."

No problem. Petrosky put the car into drive. Julie's killer was in Michigan, and the faster they could get there, the faster they'd find the fucker. And the faster Petrosky could bury him.

The town faded in his rearview as the sun rose behind them, higher and brighter with each mile that passed, the long shadows shortening incrementally with the heat of the day. Petrosky kept his eyes on the road, one ear trained on Hannah's breath.

She was *alive*. That thought had comforted him this morning when he'd awoken from a nightmare. But he would never tell her that, nor would he admit to anyone that each time he looked at her he saw the innocence of youth, the promise of all that Julie could have been. *Self-defense.* If they decided not to file charges, he'd have to let her go home... back to Crandall's bed. Part of him hoped she'd recant, that she'd tell him it was someone else who'd killed Harwick but that she'd stick around to see justice done. Part of him hoped she would stay in Michigan just because.

He was nearing the New Hampshire state line when he realized Hannah was breathing deeply, slowly again. He glanced over. She had curled up against the door, head back on the seat, eyes closed. Asleep.

Poor girl.

But she was more than just a victim. Without her awake to distract him, the concerns rolling around in his brain surfaced, each practically a tangible presence in the car with him. She said she'd killed Dominic Harwick in self-defense.

Fine. Yet they hadn't found a murder weapon at Harwick's home. Or the *Through the Looking Glass* book, though Hannah had explained that away—told him she'd burned the novel. And what of the scalpel? She had refused to talk about that so far. Had she really gutted Harwick and written the bloody words on the floor despite the injury to her arm? Or had Dominic had a partner who'd come in and destroyed evidence after she'd run? Who'd written on the floor instead of her. And if that was the case, if the guy was still out there…was she still in danger?

Stop it, old man. He was grasping at straws, delusional again. Charles had confessed to Montgomery's murder—the birthday thing was a coincidence. And offing Harwick had been justified, so if Hannah was a killer, she was also a hero. He had to stop trying to convince himself she hadn't done it at all.

Her eyes fluttered, and she gasped, murmured something in her sleep, and let out a staccato cry that was filled with so much anguish he was suddenly certain that his heart was made of crystal and the terror in her voice must be vibrating at just the right octave to shatter it. A nightmare? Or just a horrible memory?

He resisted the urge to touch her shoulder, to pull her from whatever horror she was seeing behind her eyelids the way he'd done with Julie so many times. That was why he had bought the night-light—he'd been tired of Julie coming into his room in the middle of the night, wailing about something under her bed or the boogeyman in her dreams. Now he'd give anything to comfort her one last time. To actually be there for her.

This girl isn't my daughter.

And his gut told him that she was a killer, or at least an accessory. He suspected she was protecting someone. He stared hard at the asphalt stretching toward the horizon. Hannah had admitted to killing Dominic Harwick. She'd gutted him too, and written a poem on the floor with his blood. Maybe she'd snap and kill Petrosky in his sleep. Maybe he wouldn't really mind all that much, but hopefully, she would wait until he had Julie's killer by the balls.

He glanced in the rearview at the dog, whose big square face was resting on the back seat, lost in dreamland along with his master. The stillness in the car felt like the quiet before a storm.

His sense of foreboding rose steadily as the hours ticked on. By the time lunch rolled around, they were in New York, but Hannah was still asleep. He pulled into a gas station, turned off the car, and went to fill up, watching her carefully through the window. Would she wake if he took a quick peek through her things? After all, if she had something in her bag —like a stowaway scalpel—he surely ought to know.

After one more glance at her sleeping form, and at the dog—head raised, but still lying down, that lazy animal—he sauntered to the back of the car. The trunk popped with more noise than he would have liked, but he wasted no time pushing his things aside and grabbing her duffel. Pants, bra, shirts. What was he even looking for? If she'd kept the scalpel after killing Harwick, she would have gotten rid of it by now. Unless…she'd used it to murder her father too.

Ridiculous. Melinda Charles had confessed to killing Theodore Montgomery, and the murder weapon wasn't even the same—Montgomery had been stabbed with a paring knife from someone's kitchen. Or a pocket knife. Not a scalpel.

But Charles hadn't known about Hannah's birthday, had she? Or had that been his imagination? And though she had confessed, she'd claimed not to know where the murder weapon was—they'd asked. No matter how many times he went over that in his mind, no matter how he tried to explain it away, he simply could not. How on earth could a person—let alone both Hannah and Charles—forget what they'd done with a weapon they'd used to kill a man?

He dropped the duffel. *Maybe it's in her purse.* He should have searched her before they left. But she'd seemed so… upset.

He really was a stupid asshole.

"Detective?"

She was standing beside the car, staring at him, squinting in the sun. He zipped her bag and shoved it back underneath his before she could come around to see what he was looking at. "Checking if I had more cigarettes."

She didn't even blink, though she slumped against the car as if still recovering from whatever horror had pursued her in her nightmare—a supernatural demon or a real-life monster? "Did you?"

"Did I what?"

"Find your cigarettes."

He nodded and pulled a pack from the case in the trunk. "Sure as hell don't want to buy them here in New York. Taxes and all."

Hannah nodded, but her brows furrowed. Had she seen him going through her things?

He slammed the trunk and walked back to the gas pump on the driver's side. "Let's get something to eat."

Hannah glanced nervously at the gas station, the attached convenience store, and back to him. From inside the car, her dog barked once through the half-open back window. It was cool in the shade here so that lazy punk would be fine for five minutes, but they'd have to take him out to shit before they left again.

"Come on," Petrosky said, nodding to the store.

Hannah stayed by the car, hand on the passenger door,

eyes widening. She bit her lip. The anxiety rolled off her in waves so thick he could practically smell them.

"Hannah?" He stepped around to her side and paused a few feet away, then reached for her, stopping his palm halfway across the divide between them. "Come on. You have to be hungry. We'll get the food and come right back out."

She stared some more. Worried her lip with her teeth. And laid her palm in his.

He squeezed her hand tighter than was probably necessary as he led her inside.

22

———

"Who the hell is she?" Jackson's eyes glittered brighter than the cross-shaped studs in her ears.

"Your God know you swear like that?"

"My God loves everyone the same, even your crotchety butt."

Petrosky glanced over his shoulder at Hannah, who sat at his desk just out of earshot, her head bowed over the laptop he'd dug from the back of his closet this morning. Morrison's old laptop—the one he'd given Petrosky, probably in the hopes that Petrosky would use it to read blogs about forensics. Or tech stuff. Petrosky'd used it for quizzes like "What's your dickhead name?" so he could try out the results on people who pissed him off. Like Morrison. He averted his eyes before his heart started aching.

Jackson was waiting for his answer, arms crossed. But he wasn't sure how to explain Hannah's presence. He sure as hell wasn't telling Jackson he had the kidnapped woman from the *Looking Glass* case staying at his apartment—the woman who'd admitted to killing Dominic Harwick. The woman who claimed Harwick was the *Looking Glass* killer.

But he couldn't leave Hannah at his place alone. She could

just walk out the door. As they'd found out last night, she was no more comfortable in his claustrophobic apartment than she was outside it. She had shaken for hours sitting in his dingy living room, even after his attempt at homey—a new air mattress for her to sleep on, clean and uncontaminated by the lingering stench of cigarettes or dust mites or mold from some piece of food he'd never bothered to pick up from the floor.

At least Jackson was glaring at him and not at Hannah—the less she looked at Hannah, the better. He scanned the bullpen for Decantor's nosy ass, or even Valentine, either of whom might recognize Hannah despite her weight gain, but they were out this morning, chasing down their own cases or seeing a Justin Timberlake concert or whatever those assholes did when they weren't spying for Shannon. Oh, fuck…he still had to call Shannon back.

Later.

"Here. Present for you." He tossed the paper bag containing the book he'd bought from Crandall on Jackson's desk. "To help you forget about the tiny dicks."

Jackson peered inside with her brows furrowed as he plopped into the seat across from her. "You been drinking?" She put the bag with the book into her desk drawer and leaned toward him, too close, all up in his face like she was trying to smell his breath.

"You're welcome," he snapped. "For the book. And it's mouthwash. I'm not chugging that shit, I'm just trying to make my breakfast burrito a little more palatable. Now sit, before you get a face full of Mexican-induced gas."

He belched for effect, and her expression soured. But from the suspicious gleam in her eye, she knew he was lying about being sober. He'd have to watch it—Jackson would be the first to rat him out for being smashed. Not that he'd let it get that far—again. Just a little hair of the dog. He didn't need the shakes distracting him from the most important case of his career. But it was more than that. When he'd awoken this morning, the world had seemed different—more vibrant. Even the green of Hannah's eyes, sad and nervous though they were, was oddly refreshing, and that dog made his apartment feel almost cozy even if it still smelled like ass. He'd been almost twitching with energy to get to the precinct.

Jackson was still glaring at him, though she'd managed to get out of his face and lean back in her chair.

He swallowed the remnants of mouthwash on his tongue and said, "So did you end up telling the chief anything else?"

"Like what?" She crossed her arms.

"Like, did you cover for me, tell her I was on a case?"

"I'm not your errand girl. Tell her that yourself."

So that's how it's going to be. Petrosky snatched the top folder from the desk and flipped it open, avoiding pictures of the victims and their broken, rotting bodies, bloody hips charred from the—

He slapped the folder down when Julie's name caught his eye, but that one scrawled word seemed to have burned its way into his chest, where it sat, fresh and hot and awful.

Jackson's face softened. "You were right, Petrosky. The cases were all cold. But with what you brought back...we can work this."

They would work it. And the fucker who'd hurt his baby girl wasn't going to jail where he'd live out his days watching television and enjoying three hots and a cot—not if Petrosky found him first. Hopefully Jackson wouldn't call in rein-forcements. Petrosky stared hard at her, trying to figure out what she was thinking by examining her grim mouth, but he couldn't tell much outside of the fact that she probably wanted to slap him—not exactly new information. Finesse had never been his thing, but...

"No one is more motivated to find this guy than I am," he began. "He took my..." He couldn't say it. Julie's name stuck in his mouth, more bitter than the liquor still lingering in the back of his throat.

"I understand."

But she didn't. She didn't know what it was like to see your baby on a slab, her essence gone, reduced to meat. His attempt at diplomacy sizzled away in a burst of fiery rage. "Do you, Jackson? Do you really understand what—"

"Don't test me, Petrosky. If I say I understand, I understand. And we'll close it, without involving the FBI. That's what you want, isn't it?"

It was as if she'd read his mind. But…she seemed like the last person on earth who'd ignore protocol. Did she have something against the feds? If so, he liked her better for it.

"And stop looking at me like that," Jackson snapped. "Like you're trying to figure out why. I just want to solve this case." She glanced around the room, at Hannah, and back to him. "Plus, the feds are a bunch of lying dicks."

There it was. And the glint in her eyes was too strong for simple irritation—this was personal. But he could discern nothing from the hardening lines of her mouth. "You get into it with the federal boys, Jackson?"

"I'm pretty sure you mean 'Thanks, Jackson. Now let's go talk to these UP dickheads.'"

As if you ever say thanks yourself. But from her haunted look, she understood more than he'd thought. McCallum had recommended that Petrosky be paired with someone who understood grief—and Chief Carroll wouldn't have ignored the doctor's advice.

Petrosky nodded and turned back to Hannah. He'd gotten what he wanted. So why did his gut feel like it was trying to eat him from the inside out?

"So, you going to tell me who she is or not? Is that the girl?"

He jerked back to Jackson. "The girl?" *Shit. She knows.* Jackson might be willing to solve Julie's case before the feds got their grubby paws on it, but she wasn't going to let Hannah just waltz out of—

"Robin Lowenstein."

His shoulders relaxed. "No, Robin still won't testify. Won't come here, either. But I've got her case file and her number on speed dial in case we figure she hasn't been through enough."

"Then why is *she* here?"

"Niece. School project."

"Petrosky?"

He met her narrowed eyes.

"Who did you think I was asking about?"

He dropped his gaze to the stack of case files. "No one in particular. Why don't you drop it so you can keep your nose clean, Jackson."

"Huh." Jackson's suit jacket rustled as she stood. "I won't let you ruin my career with some shifty bullspit. The only reason we're keeping this case is that everyone else has dropped it. It's cold. And since we're the first to make this connection, I think it's only fair that we get first crack at it."

He considered telling her that it was really Vermont Master Forensics Investigator Scott who'd connected the dots, but she was still talking.

"I spent the last few days submersed in these files." She tapped the stack on her desk and shook her head. "Hard stuff. I went down and met with Thompson, too, tried to get a little insight on the forensic differences I found in the charts. Turned out to be nothing. He was very helpful, though. So was Woolverton."

Petrosky's back stiffened. "Woolverton's a nosy dick."

"Well, yeah, he is, but it made my life easier that he happened to be there on another matter. Our guy Thompson did two of the autopsies—first was Julie's ten years back. Guy named Smith did the one up in the UP. The ones out of state were obviously someone else's jurisdiction, but Woolverton consulted on a couple of them, totally competently, so it was good to get a little more from him, too."

Julie's autopsy. She'd be less than flesh by now. A pile of brittle bones beneath tattered, moldered skin. He pushed the image away, though the gnawing in his belly remained. *Get it together, Petrosky.*

Jackson shrugged. "Woolverton did act weird when I brought up the case in the UP, though. Thompson and I talked it through, and Woolverton just stood there, not saying shit, mouth all tight like he was pissed I was there. He rubs me wrong."

"Woolverton only wishes he could rub—"

"Oh, shut up. Anyway, Thompson said we could go up there together once you got back if you wanted to chat with him. But there wasn't a whole lot more to add."

Petrosky nodded and reached for the file again, but his fingers tingled painfully as if the folder itself were electrified. He yanked his hand back.

Jackson appraised him. "Listen, I'll go over the specifics on Julie's case later this week. We'll split the others, put it all together."

"You don't have to—"

"But you haven't looked yet, am I right? There are only so many reasons a man wouldn't look. Like I said…I understand." She arranged the files into two stacks and pushed one pile toward him. "Don't go thinking I'm picking up the rest of your slack, though. Ain't happening." Jackson didn't look at him as she spoke—his partner was staring daggers at his desk, at Hannah, who had abandoned the laptop and was reading from a paperback novel, hands shaking. Jackson would make sure Hannah ended up in an interrogation room, maybe even a cell. There was no way in hell he was going to let Hannah's insights about Julie get locked away with her.

But Jackson just gestured to the desk and their case files.

"Now, let's see what we have so far because this guy is going to be tricky. He doesn't even have a standard victim profile: all the women were different heights, weights, hair colors, eye colors, ages." Her tone was steady, clinical, like she'd already forgotten the drama of the last fifteen minutes. "And though he might have touched Robin Lowenstein without his glove, we can't tell if it's a signature move—can't pull prints off the skin. The rest of the MO might be more practical, like cutting their throats to ensure the victims stay quiet, and the burning could be about concealing evidence. Hard to tell if he does that for its own sake. Though…" She hesitated, but Petrosky heard what she wasn't saying: this bastard loved every minute of watching his victims burn.

"I do think this is a local guy, too, even if he's killed in other states," she said.

Petrosky nodded, pushing aside a lingering thought about charred flesh. The killer had committed four murders in Michigan, only one in each of the other states, and Michigan was the only place their killer had attacked outside a major metropolis. This was home base. "Probably travels for work, conferences maybe, or a sales job that keeps him close to the major cities." He ran a hand over his shaved chin. Without at least a vague idea of what the killer did for work, it'd be impossible to narrow down a suspect list.

"I checked vet conferences already," Jackson said. "Because of the dog hair. Nothing. I looked at flight information, too, but didn't find any matching manifests for travelers who flew in and out of Detroit Metro. Some matched one or two states, but they look like dead ends. He probably drives, especially if he's traveling with his kill kit: the knife, the lighter fluid, et cetera. I doubt he checks a bag."

Petrosky grumbled agreement. While the killer could buy a knife and gloves and lighter fluid from any local store, the more often he did, the more likely it was that someone would identify him.

"In each case, they canvassed stores for someone buying those items—nothing," Jackson said. "Details are in the files."

She was good. Hopefully, she didn't look deeper into the girl he'd brought to the precinct with him. He couldn't shake the feeling that Hannah had something else pertinent locked in that head of hers, perhaps something she was saving for the prosecutor…but that meant turning her over to the lawyers.

"Afternoon, Detectives. What're you working on?"

Petrosky startled, then grimaced. Decantor. *Like the thing you put mimosas in for brunch. But he spells it differently.* That was how Morrison had introduced Decantor to him the first time, and Petrosky had told Morrison he didn't want to hear any more shit about mimosas or brunch, and Surfer Boy had smiled. Remembering that smile tore open a place in his heart he didn't feel like stitching back up. Petrosky glowered at Decantor as his heart bled out. "Mind your business, Decantor."

Decantor's face fell, and Petrosky almost smiled. He'd make Decantor regret knocking the gun out of his hand the morning they'd found Morrison's body.

"Listen, you talked to Shannon?" Decantor said. "She called here looking for you, and—"

I knew it. "Go get some work done, you nosy cunt." Dammit, he really needed to call Shannon.

"I will, I'm just saying—"

"You heard him," Jackson said. "Hard to concentrate with all this ruckus."

Petrosky looked at her, stunned, but her face was buried in a case file—she hadn't even graced Decantor with a glare. He might have considered a high five, but the muscles behind his breastbone were so taut he doubted he could raise his arm.

Decantor stalked away, and Petrosky waited for the pain in his chest to ease, but another hook snagged inside him and tore his heart a little more. Guilt? He didn't need to feel guilty. Decantor deserved to be treated like shit. Decantor would wish he'd let Petrosky splatter his brains all over that alley.

It wasn't until Decantor was out of earshot that Petrosky remembered Hannah. Thank god Decantor hadn't recognized her—but it was only a matter of time. *It's stupid to have her here.*

"Twenty-to-one odds he'll report you before the year is out," Jackson said. "One day, you'll tell me why we're being jerks to him?"

Petrosky rubbed at the nodule in his chest. "He talks too much."

"You're full of shit, Petrosky." She shook her head, eyes on the file. "But he is a damn chatterbox—you're right about that."

"Jackson?"

She glanced up from the file.

"We have to find this guy. He's gotta be here."

She flipped the folder closed. "Then let's go talk to these UP dicks."

23

———————

THE LANKY UP DETECTIVE WORKING THE most recent rape-torture-homicide had a partner with a flat face that made him appear as dull and dumb as a river rock. They stared at Petrosky and Jackson as Jackson conveyed their suspicions that the rape and murder up here in butt-fuck-Egypt was related to others in the lower part of the state.

The flat-faced one—Officer Newman, according to his badge—shook his head. "Hell, you want it, you can have it." He sat on the corner of his desk and crossed his arms.

Petrosky balked. "Just that easy?" Who gave up their cases like that? What kind of backward hillbilly shit—

"Just that easy," Newman said. "We have no DNA and no leads, and the body was left out near a wildlife preserve. I'd give just about anything not to look at that mess again."

Petrosky winced, trying not to picture the scorched flesh, the bloody gouges, the damage from the animals, the insects.

The tall one glanced his way, then back to Jackson. "Sounds like you've got more than we do," he said. "Your witness going to testify?"

"Not at this time, no." Petrosky folded his arms over his chest.

"Can you convince her?"

Dumbass. Like he hadn't tried that shit twenty times already.

"She's been through enough," Jackson snapped, and her tone left no room for arguments.

"So even if you catch the guy"—Newman was glaring now —"with no DNA and no other forensic evidence, no jury would convict him. You guys got some new information that will actually help us put him away?"

Petrosky sighed. Of course the guy was pissed—they were all pissed. If the perp had left just a little evidence, they'd have caught him before he brutalized another innocent woman. The only one not pissed was the killer, because this wasn't a crime of anger any more than Julie's had been. Their killer knew what he was doing. Knew how to get rid of evidence, how to keep control of the situation. He'd slipped up with Robin, because she'd known, as a medical professional, how to save herself. Maybe he'd slipped up again here.

The phone behind them rang, and Newman's lanky partner reached for the receiver.

"Got animal hair at a few of our scenes," Petrosky said. "Just like yours. Not the same animal and no follicles. But our witness said the guy wore a bracelet made of hair. Might be trace evidence from the perp."

"Without the roots, we've got no proof, and the hair at our scene looks like coyote. Ditto on the tracks and scat nearby—makes sense in the woods. If you think you can find the animals and somehow connect them to this guy, be my guest." Newman's brows furrowed. "How do you weave animal hair anyway? Isn't it short?"

Petrosky opened his mouth to tell him, but the guy was already looking behind them at Hannah. She'd been so quiet, Petrosky had almost forgotten she was there.

"Who's she?"

"Niece," Petrosky barked.

Newman pursed his lips. "She looks familiar."

Hannah backed away, and Jackson stepped in front of her, blocking the officer's view. "Just give us the file and what you've got left of the forensics, will you, slick?"

Newman put up his hands in mock surrender. "It's all yours. I wish we had more time to help you out, but already this morning, we got a kid stabbed to death by a babysitter, and a girl raped in her dorm room by the teenage son of a local politician." He swiped a hand over his face the way Petrosky used to do incessantly before he had a pacemaker scar to fuck around with. Petrosky glanced at his chest, where his fingers were scratching at his breastbone, and lowered his arm.

Newman pulled a file from the desktop. "Have fun with it. I'd love to see this guy put away. What he did to that woman…" He shook his head, grimacing like he wanted to vomit. "If you want a firsthand look at the girl, Camille Urban is still down the street."

"Down the street?"

"Morgue."

The morgue. They still had the…*body*. Petrosky hadn't been able to look at what that bastard had done to Julie. Hadn't been able to lift the sheet, to see the images, even to read the report. Now…just the thought of Julie's face, her eyes closed, peaceful if it weren't for the gaping wound in her throat, a wound so much like Robin's, so much like Morrison's, though his boy had been covered in blood. *Blood.* Garish red against Morrison's pale skin, the gore sticky but cold, staining Petrosky's palms as he'd tried to wake him… but he couldn't wake the dead.

The room around him wavered, and the temperature dropped so suddenly he could practically hear the change like the snap of cracking ice. The walls closed in. From somewhere behind him, a bird squalled, and he could feel the plastic that wrapped his partner, smell the iron, taste the bile in his throat…

Jackson's hand on his elbow brought him back to the precinct, the fluorescent overheads, the gray brick walls. No blood here, and no ice, though the bile taste lingered in his mouth. He gagged, then swallowed, and followed Jackson out.

———

"YOU SURE YOU want to do this?" Though she'd spoken softly, Jackson's words echoed around them, bouncing off the table and walls and floors with a faint metallic ting.

Petrosky stared at the blue sheet and at the doctor standing behind the table, the ME's face solemn, eyes sharp. But that was where the similarities to their own ME ended. Where Thompson was tall and thin, Smith was as short and stocky as a football player, though something in his somber stance said he'd be significantly less of a douche than some quarterback who made millions playing with other people's balls. Unlike Woolverton, who was just an asshole for the fun of it.

He steeled himself. *No, Jackson, I'm not sure about anything.* But he was—he was sure he never wanted to see what was beneath that cloth as long as he lived. Petrosky was convinced that the moment they pulled aside the sheet, he'd see his daughter's accusing eyes staring back at him: *Why didn't you save me, Daddy?* But he had no choice back then— not that he had more of a choice now.

Dr. Smith crossed his hands at his belly and waited, patient, not dickish. Petrosky clenched his teeth then finally nodded. *I'm sorry, honey.*

Her head came first, not dark hair this time, but… gray? She wasn't old, not old enough for her hair to have given up its color. Nor was she a teenager: fine lines around her eyes and mouth said late twenties, thirties, maybe. Skin gray like her hair, eyes closed but for a thin sliver of white under the corner of her lashes. Smith rested the sheet on her upper chest. Not nearly as many scratches on her face as he'd expected from the officer's description at the station—just three thin slices down one cheek, almost uniform, and another slit over one eyebrow. And, of course, the angry slash across her throat.

Just like Julie's.

He hadn't looked at Julie's neck for longer than a heartbeat, though, and he hadn't seen anything else. They'd laid the sheet on her shoulders like they were tucking her into bed, and he was thankful for that at least—he'd needed to avoid seeing whatever brutality lay below the neck. Maybe that was why he didn't feel the tug of remembrance now, why he didn't see Julie in front of him on the table as he'd feared. Or maybe it was that this woman looked nothing like his little girl. For once, he was glad the killer didn't have a type; if he had seen a Julie look-alike on the table, he'd probably have lost his shit.

"What's with the hair?" Jackson asked.

"It's a thing now," Smith said.

Aging was a thing? *Just call me Calvin Klein.*

Smith coughed once, a low, throaty rumble that somehow managed to avoid sounding impatient. "Camille Urban," he began, his voice clinical but compassionate. "She was jogging out near the Hiawatha National Forest. Someone grabbed her a few miles inside the tree line. Kinda stereotypical—girl goes jogging, girl gets snatched. Like we're in a bad horror movie." Veins danced in Smith's temple. His voice was tighter. "Rape took place as she was dying, probably. Presence of bleeding in a few of the internal abrasions, though others were difficult to tell because of the...well..."

"The burning."

"Yes. The burning. Happened after death, at least." He

looked relieved at this, though his mouth stayed hard. He'd probably been the one to tell the girl's family, to tell the girl's…father. Another father. Just like him.

Daddy, it's okay. In his head, Julie was four, wrapping his hand in a bandage, though he hadn't been injured. *It's okay, Daddy, it's okay.*

But it wasn't okay. Smith was taking hold of the sheet again, pulling it down past the woman's shoulders, past the long scratches on her arms, over the Y-shaped incision down the center of her chest, and…

God, no.

Her abdomen had been slashed apart, strips of graying skin clinging to bone, and Petrosky thought he could see a liver there, a stomach, all the bits and pieces torn apart and decaying beneath her ribs. But no, that was surely fat or muscle tissue—Smith would have removed the organs already. Petrosky took a deep breath through his mouth and let it out slowly. *The burns.* The blaze had started just above the knee, the blistered skin wet-looking where it hadn't been ripped up by the coyotes. The skin of her lower abdomen and her pelvis—destroyed by fire.

Had Julie looked like this? Had her legs been destroyed? Her knees? Had she screamed in agony as the flesh was seared from her bones?

Inconclusive. Inconclusive. That's what McCallum had said. Said they didn't know if Julie had been awake—that they never would. *This isn't Julie. This isn't her.*

"How can you be so certain that the burns happened postmortem?"

"Evidence of bleeding is usually a big hint, but with the cauterization, it can be harder to tell." He nodded to the woman's hips. "I did find a few cleaner spots, though, tested for the presence of a chemical called leukotriene B4. The body produces it in response to injury. It was present in some of the tissue in the vagina, but not around the burns."

"Is it a common test?" But Petrosky's chest was lighter already. The killer had burned this victim after she died. He'd tried to burn Robin when he thought she was dead. He burned them when they couldn't feel it.

Inconclusive, inconclusive. He was hit by an almost physical sensation, the presence of his daughter in the room, but that was crazy—he was crazy. All the same, he was convinced he saw a wisp of dark hair fly by him and disappear. And he knew that if he squinted, he'd see Julie in the corner, watching him with her lovely green eyes, waiting for him to take her home for dinner. He slammed his eyes shut.

"Not sure what everyone does down where you are. Lots of ways to test," Smith said.

No way to tell.

"Detective?"

Petrosky looked up and realized he was facing the door—his back was to the table. He turned around to face Smith. "Can we…" He gestured to the body.

"Of course." Smith pulled the sheet back over the woman's head, snuffing her out of existence. Better to be dead than to suffer. Better to have a purpose than to die.

He finally squinted at the corner. Empty, of course. But just because Julie wasn't there didn't mean he couldn't feel her. She was here. And she'd be watching him until he found her killer. *You're delusional,* McCallum whispered in his head.

But maybe being delusional would help him find the bastard. And if he was insane, he had nothing left to lose.

24

"Every day, I wake up angry. And I can't seem to…undo it."

I COULD IMAGINE HER: eyes narrowed to slits from post-cry puffiness, mouth trembling. Maybe clutching a baseball bat in her lap. The other members of the online support group were probably nodding just like I was, sitting alone in their respective houses, watching their own shadows for the one that would prove lethal. Escaping one attack didn't guarantee you'd escape the next one; I knew better than anyone how evil lurked where you least expected it. How pain was never more than a smile away.

"I understand. I sometimes feel like the world hates me."

That response came from someone who went by the name Still Here. The online survivor's group was even more covert than the domestic violence shelter I'd volunteered at in Ash Park—online, people used pseudonyms, and there were no pretty posters advertising the group's existence, no tiny black-and-white ad tucked into the back page of the Sunday paper. But the women were supportive. Open.

Kind. And I had needed to do *something*—I wasn't going back to my therapist anytime soon. I didn't even go to the grocery store. When I'd had to take Duke outside Petrosky's apartment to use the bathroom, I was certain a rabid weasel was flailing around beneath my breastbone. At least Petrosky had gone out with me the first few times. That had helped.

"I hate him."

We'd all been where SugarBaby was, all had that exact same thought, and I was glad that I had introduced her to this place, though I sometimes wondered if I'd caused her more harm than good.

"I think we've all been there. But it gets easier."

Robin this time.

Robin. I swallowed hard and focused on the muscles in my neck, wondering if Robin's neck felt stiff like mine: swollen, but not just from scar tissue. Tight from the sense of impending doom that must follow her, the way it did me. But I'd never had the guts to ask her. She always seemed a little miffed, like a ferret who'd been sprayed with a water pistol. Probably because people acted like she should be grateful to be alive since every other victim of her attacker had died. And she *was* glad...but she wasn't.

It hadn't even clicked until last year when I realized why the details of her case sounded so familiar. And now I was dredging it all back up—for my own benefit. I opened the private message bar and sent:

"How are you doing?"

I tapped my fingers on the desk while I waited for her to

type and leaned toward the screen when her response popped up.

"I feel so…stuck in the badness. I just can't keep doing this."

My heart ached. I wanted to tell her it would get better. That time would help her forget, allow her to get on with her life. But there were no guarantees. I was trapped, just like Robin probably was. I could run again, but there was nowhere to hide from the visions in my head, the bloody scenes I could practically smell every night while I tried to sleep. Would telling the truth free me from my nightmares? Maybe, but it hadn't worked for Robin, had it? And if I ended up in prison, I'd just exchange one nightmare for another. No matter how kind Petrosky had been, he was a cop; my welcome in Ash Park had to be wearing thin. And I had no more bargaining chips to purchase freedom.

"I feel like it won't ever get better."

Poor Robin. Her fiancé had moved out three months after the attack, and she still thought about him the way I thought about Dominic. Though I'd never mentioned Dominic to her —she'd see through me, go straight to the grisly center of that secret. Everyone lies, but I couldn't seem to do it properly. Probably why Neil hadn't called me since I left—my bumbling explanation for leaving with Petrosky sounded ridiculous even to me. "The girl they're looking for doesn't like to talk to anyone else," I'd told Neil. He'd never trust me again.

Not like Petrosky; I had lied to him over and over, and still, he believed me. But Petrosky would find out soon enough that I didn't know anything else about his daughter. Then what?

I typed:

"It's going to be okay."

Trite. Meaningless maybe. So I followed up with:

"How was your appointment?"

I waited while she typed, listening to Duke's snores rumbling through the apartment—it almost made this place feel like home; or as close to home as I ever got. Then her response popped onto the screen:

"Worst day in forever. Horrible panic attacks. I was fine until they were finishing up my root canal and went to paint the fluoride on my other teeth. All of a sudden, I was flashing back to that night. I hit the dental hygienist, knocked the brush out of her hand."

I stared at the words until they went blurry. What she was describing sounded like the night I'd almost punched Neil in the face for dropping a spoon—I guess the tinny clang against the floor had sounded too much like a scalpel. But flashbacks were usually triggered by something.

"What do you think caused it?"

"Not sure. I think the mint smell maybe? I mean, I chew mint gum and stuff, but the fluoride was really strong, and it kinda made me nauseated."

Fluoride.
My heart quickened like I had a hamster on a wheel in my chest, and the creature had been spurred into hyperdrive. My mother had been sleeping with her dentist boss while my father was busy raping me. And the scent that had come off

her every night wasn't the smell of mint gum or mouthwash: it was antiseptic. Medicinal. Distinct.

Like the fluoride they'd put in Robin's mouth today.

WHEN ROBIN FINALLY DISCONNECTED, I pulled up the search bar on the laptop, fingers frozen over the keys. All I really knew was that the killer might be a dentist and that he'd hurt Petrosky's daughter and gone to Boston once. The killer had probably gone other places that would narrow a list of suspects down, but I knew nothing of those other crimes.

I'd have to ask Petrosky for help.

And that was a risk. I'd led him to believe I could help him—and with Julie's case solved, he'd have no reason to keep me out of jail.

From the corner, Duke whined, and I glanced over to see him sitting up in his bed, the bed Petrosky—*"call me Ed"*—had bought for him on our way back here. Next to it on the floor was a stainless steel bowl with a paw print in the bottom, another gift from the detective. Empty now, though. He'd bought dog food, too. "Just a minute, boy."

What does Petrosky want from me?

You need to find something to barter with him.

Okay, so...a dentist. It would be easy to look up those who'd been kicked out of practice, but this guy had still smelled like his office when he'd attacked Robin. Though... Had he been a practicing dentist ten years ago when he'd killed Petrosky's daughter? I scoured licensing databases, trying to do what I could with the little information I had, knowing that, at some point, I'd be backed into a corner. I would have to decide whether to tell Petrosky or hold on to the information as a bargaining chip to save my own ass if Petrosky didn't solve the case himself in the meantime. But the idea of this lunatic out there, doing this to someone else, stealing someone else's voice, or *life*… I couldn't live with that. I couldn't.

But could I live in a jail cell?

You'd do anything to stay out of jail.

I might. It wasn't like Petrosky would pretend I was his niece forever. Too bad. The thought of staying here, pretending to be Petrosky's family…it was better than screwing Neil until the day he died. It was better than being in prison.

How could I get Petrosky to let me stay? Maybe if I was really helpful and cooperative…but I didn't want to go back to the precinct, ever. I didn't just want to *stay* at Petrosky's. I wanted to *hide* here. I wanted him to protect me.

He's using you, Hannah.

Maybe he did have some bigger plan I wasn't seeing. Maybe he was manipulating me, trying to get me to talk. And once I did, he'd take me down so fast I wouldn't know what hit me.

Cuffs. Chains. Bars: my life from now until they found me dead in a cell. Not that I wanted to die, but I understood wanting to just…disappear. Life was enough of a prison already.

I paused, fingers hanging above the keys again, and looked at the door. I could run. I *should* run. But Petrosky didn't seem to blame me for any of this. He almost seemed to…understand. Would the others, though? Maybe the prosecutors would have been kind if I'd stayed after Dominic's death, but I'd run. I'd incriminated myself. They would understand about Dominic, surely—the self-defense part. Not the part where I sliced the guy open, tore out his insides, wrote a poem in his blood, and then burned the evidence and stole the murder weapon he'd used to carve up innocent women. They wouldn't understand that. They wouldn't understand how I could love someone who had hurt so many —who had hurt me too.

And yet…I had loved him. I'd loved my father too. Love wasn't ever rational, but in my case, it was nuttier than squirrel poop. And hearing Petrosky say he was glad my father was dead had made my insides boil even if a part of me agreed. Dominic and my father—these men were everything to me. Their pain was mine. And so was their rage. But I knew how to channel that anger now. Dominic had shown me how to use it. And for that, I'd love him forever.

I wish there had been a way to hide what he'd done. I even wanted to hide what my father had done to me, though if I revealed his fetishes, his sickness…people might actually forgive me for his death. Like Petrosky seemed to. Like I needed him to if I hoped to stay out of prison.

There was only one problem.

I wasn't the one who killed my father.

And despite what everyone was saying back in Willowshire, neither was Melinda Charles.

25

____

"How are things working out with your new partner?" True, Dr. McCallum was a fat fuck in an ugly-as-sin sweater vest, but Petrosky liked him all the same—sometimes. To think McCallum had been Decantor's size when he'd first started here. Ash Park might be depressing as hell, but at least they had more fast food per capita than the neighboring cities.

Petrosky rubbed his own gut and said, "Better than anticipated." Because Jackson was doing what he wanted, for now, anyway. *Odds are one in a million she'll keep cooperating with me.* Her suspicions would get the better of her eventually, and once she found out about his house guest... "Why'd you recommend Jackson for me?"

But he already knew. Jackson had been a Wall Street executive long before she was a cop. Married another finance bigwig, though it had lasted only long enough to spawn two children, both boys. One was now fifteen.

The other was dead. Four years ago, her thirteen-year-old son had been walking home from a friend's house in their upscale suburban neighborhood when he was shot in the back of the head by another resident, an off-duty federal agent who thought the child matched the description of a robbery suspect.

She had more reasons to hate the feds than he did. Far more. And she sure as hell knew about grief.

"You looked her up, didn't you?"

Shrinky mind-reading prick. At least he didn't have to tiptoe around it. Petrosky nodded.

"You'll make a good team if you let her in. She's edgy enough that she won't bore you, and she's strong enough to take your shit and send it right back. She'll keep your sorry ass in line just like Shannon keeps trying to. And speaking of…you should give her a call."

What the hell? "Did she call you too?"

"She did no such thing. Not that I'd tell you if she had." The big man shifted in his seat. "But I know you, Ed. And I know what you're doing. You're allowed to miss Shannon, to miss the kids. To miss Morrison. But don't push away the people who love you."

"Fuck off." But the words were a sigh at best. Because he did miss Shannon and the kids. And Morrison. And Julie. Even his ex-wife, Linda. It was as though every person he cared about reminded him of the life he was supposed to have, a life where, by now, he'd be walking his daughter down the aisle, holding his first grandchild, maybe. He'd almost had a second chance at that with Morrison. Then with Shannon and the kids. Now they were gone too.

Everybody left. And calling her was just going to open them both up to more heartbreak—she'd be better off if she got a fresh start in Atlanta and left him and his nonsense behind. He sighed. The only constant in his life was loss.

McCallum busied himself in a desk drawer, pulled out a stick of gum, and offered one to Petrosky. Too bad it wasn't a donut. Or Jack. Hell, he'd even take a scone. Scott's frown flashed in his mind, and Petrosky's jaw tightened—the rookie was just another person a little worse off for having known him.

"Don't want to talk about how you're screwing up your life, fine." McCallum sat back in his chair. "So tell me what I *can* do for you, Ed."

Petrosky tapped the file folder in his lap. "Trying to hash through some elements of this case."

"You mean Julie's case."

Asshole shrink knew everything—or thought he did. Petrosky gritted his teeth.

"How are you doing with that, Ed?"

"How do you think I'm doing with it, *Steve*?"

"Have you even looked at it?"

Petrosky shook his head. He'd gotten the file back from Jackson and had carried it with him all day, but so far, it had been enough to absorb its contents through osmosis. One day soon, he would have to look, despite Jackson's reassurances that she'd analyzed every possible angle on Julie's case —he owed it to his daughter to explore her file, her murder himself. And when he finally opened it…it would break him.

McCallum's face remained placid—he was doing the shrink thing again. Petrosky's back tightened in anticipation of whatever the doctor was about to suggest. Hot tea to help him cope? Drugs? An electric shock right to the balls would be preferable to opening that file.

"I think you're struggling with it," McCallum finally said. "But I also think it's a great opportunity for closure."

Closure. Like you ever got over losing a child. "It's an opportunity for something."

McCallum studied him, his beady eyes glittering in his fat face. He clasped his hands on the desktop. "An opportunity for…"

"Justice." *Vengeance.* "But I have to find him first. So how about we stop fucking around and get down to what matters."

McCallum removed his hands from the desk and sat back. "As you wish. We've already spoken about the pyromania elements."

They had. Pyromaniacs had an obsessive desire to set things ablaze, and though this guy was probably also a psychopath, the burning was such a large part of the crimes that they couldn't ignore it. Most pyromaniacs experienced intense arousal before the crime, a stress that could only be sated with fire. Some of them even got off sexually watching the flames. Petrosky tried to forget about that part as he filled McCallum in on the case. Though McCallum had reviewed the files earlier this week, it was the bracelet that was bothering Petrosky most now. The dog hairs at the scene.

"Killers take souvenirs," McCallum said. "They often relish the chase, the blood. The pain. And any reminders of the excitement."

Like the scalpel in the *Looking Glass* case? McCallum still didn't know about that. Hannah had to have it somewhere—if she'd done it.

Of course, she did it. She'd killed Harwick and admitted it to him outright. She wouldn't confess to it if she hadn't.

Then why hadn't he officially closed the case? He'd had her sign a confession already, but he had yet to turn it in. He should have made it official, stuck it in the file, maybe even videotaped her statement. Petrosky blinked hard as if he could delete a train of thought as easily as closing a tab on a computer screen. What were they talking about? Oh, right. The dog hair bracelet. "These murders…I'm not sold that he's taking souvenirs. We know he didn't kill any dogs at the crime scenes, and he wasn't taking hairs from animals who were present either. Some of the scenes didn't have a single paw print."

He waited for McCallum to nod agreement before he continued, "So is he doing it on purpose? Leaving a hair here and there as some kind of clue?" The hairs themselves weren't even consistent, or not from the same animal, anyway. It might be nothing. But he'd take any insight he could get.

"If he leaves the hairs on purpose, they could be a peek into his life," McCallum said slowly. "The animals could represent something that gives him pleasure: he could be a vet, or have a farm. Or they might represent the stress he's relieving by burning. Nothing says family like a dog, and if his homelife is crappy..." He shrugged. "But there's no way to be certain which or even whether the shedding was intentional."

A guy who might like or might despise dogs. *Very helpful.* Why was he even here? "Well, in that case, I'll just ask him when I see him next. After he hacks up someone else's daughter." A slow burn blossomed in Petrosky's throat, searing into his brain until he saw nothing but the red haze of flame. "Not like Hannah minds too much now. I failed her as much as I failed every girl he killed after her."

"Hannah?"

"What?"

"You said Hannah. You said 'Not like Hannah minds—'"

"I said Julie."

McCallum's brows furrowed. "What else is going on, Ed? You have other...concerns?"

Petrosky looked down. *Not so fast, asshole.*

"This case, Julie's case...sounds like it's bringing back your feelings about Hannah Montgomery, too, piling hurt on top of hurt. But you didn't fail her then, and you didn't—"

"I *did.*" Petrosky balled his fists. "You convinced me I needed to let the *Looking Glass* case go. Just like you convinced me I needed to let Julie's case go. Why?"

"I consulted with the ME on Julie's case. I knew what was in there. The inconclusive bits would have made you insane, and you were already hanging by a thread."

But McCallum had treated enough people—he knew better than anyone that passion could drive a person to the truth more effectively than puttering around doing your job for the paycheck. And there was nothing inconclusive about Julie's case—she had been burned alive. At least Thompson had been honest with him, even though it hurt like a bitch. And yet, though he knew the truth, though he'd known for a decade, this morning Petrosky had held on to McCallum's "inconclusive" when he'd jolted upright from sleep with the smell of his daughter's burning flesh in his nostrils. Knowing he was lying to himself. Knowing he was trying to stay sane.

"You never told me you consulted with Thompson." Assholes. They were all assholes. What else had they talked about behind his back?

"I didn't talk to Thompson. I spoke to Woolverton."

That fucking piece of shit? He hadn't been on Julie's case, had he? Petrosky tried to think back. Yeah, okay, Woolverton had been around, but he'd been new. Looked like Woolverton had been as much of a nosy jackoff then as he was now—he certainly hadn't helped solve anything. When Petrosky had walked away from the case, all leads were cold. And the detectives who had taken over the investigation had found nothing new. They'd given up not two months later.

They gave up because they didn't love her. They hadn't cared enough.

Neither had he.

But he did now. Self-destruction hadn't helped him find the man who'd killed his daughter. Would love? Would rage?

One way to find out. The truth wouldn't set him free, but it would sure as shit help him kill the correct motherfucker.

"Why did you try so hard to get me off that case, doc?" he asked again.

"There's a difference between holding on to something productive that drives you to do better, and keeping on with something impossible that sucks you down into a suicidal vortex."

I never should have come here after Julie's death. After Hannah's disappearance. He hadn't needed this guy picking away at his brain then, and he sure as hell didn't need his bullshit now.

McCallum had been wrong about whether it was worth it to pursue Julie's murderer before. He'd taken it upon himself to cut Petrosky off from the one thing that might have gotten him some…closure wasn't the word, but there was something. Now all that was keeping him from eating a bullet was the thought of finding Julie's killer and blasting out the back of his head.

"I gave up on my little girl. I just…gave…up. Same with Hannah. And now that she's back, I realize what a huge mistake it was to walk away. I should have kept—"

"Wait." McCallum was staring, agape, eyes wide. "What precisely do you mean that Hannah's back?"

Petrosky swallowed hard. "Shrink's oath, right? Confidentiality?"

McCallum leveled his gaze at Petrosky. "Barring an immediate danger to the self or others. But yes."

"The immediate threat of danger has passed. Hannah Montgomery is alive." Petrosky filled in the doc on the Theodore Montgomery case in Vermont, and with each new revelation, McCallum seemed to breathe more shallowly.

"Sounds like Melinda Charles had a reason to kill him," the doctor finally said. "Whether he hurt her or her daughter."

"That's the thing, doc. She might be a superb actress, but…"

McCallum crossed his arms. "You don't think she did it."

"I…I don't know."

"This Melinda…is she another one of these women who looks like your daughter? Another woman who may very well be guilty? You can't let everyone who looks like Julie off the hook just because you feel sorry for—"

"That's not it. Well, not this time," he said when McCallum raised an eyebrow. "She didn't know it was Hannah's birthday."

"Come again?"

"The murder took place on Hannah's birthday. Melinda Charles had no idea." But his gut roiled. Was he wrong? Again? Like he had been with the young woman who'd shot her fiancé the year after Julie died? Petrosky had been ready to buy her a plane ticket to Athens himself; he was so sure she was innocent. Until she admitted killing "that cheating bastard" when questioned by another detective.

"So the murder taking place on Hannah's birthday…that's too much coincidence for you."

Petrosky nodded, eyes on his hands. *Just let it be Charles.* Then Hannah would be innocent—definitely innocent. But now that his detective brain was kicking back into gear with Julie's case…it didn't feel right.

"Did Melinda say why she did it?"

"Said Montgomery beat her. I thought he hurt the daughter, but the girl denies it."

"She might be protecting him. From what you've told me of Hannah, this guy has a penchant for brainwashing. His victims adored him. Stacey might not even realize she was abused to begin with; she might think they were in love."

"Right." But that wasn't what was eating at him. Hannah Montgomery. He wanted to let her go. Yet he couldn't risk another person's life, and far too many close to her had ended up dead.

"If someone kills in self-defense, how likely would they be to harm someone else in the future?"

McCallum's eyes darkened. "Why are you asking?"

"Just curious. About the state of this Melinda Charles woman."

"She didn't kill him in self-defense." When Petrosky didn't respond, McCallum said, "If it was purely a matter of self-defense, I'd have no issue giving her a clean bill of mental stability. Sure, the trauma could cause residual symptoms, and she'd need assistance working through them, but those who kill in self-defense aren't likely to do it again. Melinda waited until her husband was asleep, and then she attacked him. Temporary insanity, perhaps, but not self-defense. And she had her own issues prior to meeting Theodore Montgomery—abusive exes, right? Yet none of that matters if you don't believe she killed him." McCallum tapped his sausage fingers against the desktop. "But if she didn't kill him, who did? Hannah?"

Petrosky didn't know what he thought anymore, but he was quite sure Melinda Charles wouldn't admit to the crime just to save Hannah's ass.

McCallum lowered his voice and leaned forward as far as his gut would let him. "Hannah Montgomery seems stuck in a self-destructive codependent relationship cycle, probably the result of her unstable, abusive father. But having an unstable parent can trigger all manner of other psychological problems, either through genetics or the home environment that the parents created." *Parents screw everything up.* Petrosky shifted in his seat, but the unease in his belly didn't relent. "And though I don't believe Hannah falls into this category," McCallum continued, "it is well-known that early childhood abuse can trigger conditions like antisocial personality disorder, the closest condition we have to psychopathy in the big book of diagnoses."

"Psychos aren't in your book?"

"Doesn't make them less real." McCallum shrugged. "Listen...you have a suspect, a woman who admitted to killing Theodore Montgomery. Don't go searching for a reason to let this Melinda woman off the hook. You know she has no reason to lie." McCallum furrowed his brows. "But I'm thinking right now, you're also trying to get insight into Hannah Montgomery's state of mind. Is this correct?"

Petrosky scowled and didn't answer.

"I know Julie's case has been at the forefront of your mind. It will bring back some difficult emotions. And Hannah Montgomery, with her resemblance to your daughter...I remember your reaction to her. Your struggle with letting her go. But Ed, she's not Julie now any more than she was then. And though she may have killed Harwick in self-defense, that doesn't mean she is immune to the consequences—"

"I thought she'd be more traumatized if I locked her up. It doesn't seem fair."

"Whether or not she's dangerous, she's a flight risk, Ed. You know it, and I know it. You should take her to the precinct. Maybe have someone else question her. Just to be on the safe side."

That's what was eating him? The fact that he hadn't yet been able to lecture Petrosky on how to handle the Harwick case and Hannah Montgomery? "I'm not taking her in."

"You'll lose your job when they find out."

"So will you if you tell them. It looks like we've got ourselves an old-fashioned standoff."

"Not so much—I'm bound by confidentiality." McCallum rubbed the bare spot on his finger where a ring should have been, but the asshole was too big to wear a wedding band. Was he even married? The psychiatrist had never disclosed anything about his personal life, and here Petrosky was, baring his soul.

McCallum finally cleared his throat. "How's your sleep, Petrosky? Any more negative thoughts? Suicidal thoughts?"

Petrosky knew McCallum had to ask; even though the doc had malpractice insurance, it still looked bad to have a patient blow their head off.

"I'm fine. None of those thoughts."

"Mm-hmm." But McCallum's shrewd gaze said he wasn't remotely convinced. "What about other emotions getting in the way of the case?"

"Like…?"

"I'm worried that your concern for Hannah is making you sloppy on both the *Looking Glass* case and Julie's case." One of McCallum's brows rose. Gauging Petrosky's reaction.

Is he trying to piss me off? "I'm not getting sloppy." But he'd been ready to arrest Crandall. He'd nearly thrown out Hannah's confession about Hawick just so he didn't have to risk getting her in trouble. He'd been convinced the *Looking Glass* case and Montgomery's murder were connected.

"Melinda wouldn't have confessed if she hadn't done it, Ed. Maybe Theodore Montgomery just got a little nostalgic on Hannah's birthday. Maybe he talked about Hannah, or baited Melinda in some other way." McCallum put his palms on the desk and leaned over them. "Would you be convinced if she produced the murder weapon?"

"I… Yeah. But she hasn't told us where it is."

"And there's no DNA evidence to suggest anything besides Melinda's story?"

Petrosky sighed and shook his head.

"Could have buried the murder weapon."

"Could have."

"Or she could have given it to someone else to hide." McCallum folded his fingers over his gut. "Just because you can't see the relationship doesn't mean it isn't there. Melinda might be closer to Hannah Montgomery than either of them are letting on. And Hannah has already confessed to killing one man."

Petrosky balked. "You just said Melinda was the one who—"

"I'm saying I think you need to watch out for these

women, both of them, no matter how vulnerable you think Hannah is. It wouldn't be the first time someone you decided was innocent ended up being a murderer."

"From little spark may burst a mighty flame."
~*Dante Alighieri, The Divine Comedy*

26

———

SHE MIGHT BE A KILLER. Well, she *was* a killer, but she might be more dangerous than he'd thought. In months past, he'd have passed out and slept like a baby, knowing he was tempting fate, maybe even deliberately. There was no better way to take death into his own hands than setting himself up for a passive demise.

But last night, he had remained awake, staring into the blackness. Feeling Duke's enormous head at the end of his mattress, the dog's breath on his toes. And then hearing Hannah's breath from across the room: sweet and soft and *alive*.

He hadn't once thought about his gun or painting the walls with his brain matter. Instead, he'd given himself over to thoughts of Julie. Thoughts about her killer. This was the last gift he could give his daughter: the concentrated attention he hadn't spared her in life.

He could solve this. He could look into this bastard's face before he put a bullet between his eyes. Or into his balls— probably the balls. He wondered how long it would take the fucker to bleed to death through a hole in his nut sack.

Then…padded footsteps, the clank of pots and pans. Make that one pan and a plate. Petrosky snapped his eyes open, feeling around on the mattress for the gun. *Gone.*

He jerked himself to seated, gaze darting this way and that for the weapon, and in the kitchen, Hannah startled and dropped the pan onto the counter, staring at him. Did she have the gun? Was she going to pull it on him? The morning light shone white and hot outside. A car horn honked somewhere below the window.

Hannah put a hand over her heart. "I'm sorry about the pan, I just… You scared me. Want eggs?"

Petrosky shoved his hand under his pillow, felt the cool metal of the barrel, and relaxed back against the bed. *Goddamn McCallum.* That bastard had gotten him all twitchy. "I don't have any eggs."

"You had a few." She glanced at the fridge as if trying to convince herself that she'd actually found them there.

Petrosky couldn't remember the last time he'd bought eggs; he was more of a toaster pastry and canned soup guy. *Shannon.* Had to be Shannon before she left for Atlanta. Either that or they were both about to die from food poisoning. He sighed. Shannon had really tried to take care of him. He could see her in her new kitchen, patiently unpacking the last of her plates, making the kids breakfast as the dogs circled her feet. He rubbed the tender spot on his chest. The thought of hearing Shannon's voice, the kids' voices, filled him with something that was not immediately familiar but not altogether unpleasant. Not joy, exactly—he couldn't even recall that feeling—but something warm, sedate was taking root inside his chest, where the pain usually sat. He'd call her later. After—

"They smell okay." Hannah was talking about food, about eggs. Just another Saturday morning—Hannah moving around the kitchen, Duke snoring in the sun as though they had always lived there. Like they belonged. Like Julie would have belonged.

But Hannah didn't belong here. He couldn't forget that. He was housing a woman who had admitted to killing a man, who had fled to the town where her father was brutally murdered. Though looking at her now, he saw no murderous rage, only anxiety. The bags under her eyes were more pronounced today than they had been yesterday, deep purple stains that didn't look like they'd go away with a nap. Julie used to look that way when she was worried about a big test. Or when he and his ex had been fighting.

Hannah pulled a glass from the cupboard and set it beside her plate. He should have brought Hannah to the precinct, made her tell her story, and either arrested her or let her go home. She'd broken down on the way back to the apartment last night, sobbing and shaking—the anticipation had to be making her crazy. Why was he even doing this? His apartment was a place to die, not a hotel. He searched Hannah's face, looking for a sign that she didn't mind being here so much, or maybe a signal that she minded a lot, so he would feel less guilty about bringing her to the station, but she dropped her gaze and turned her back on him, fiddling with something on the far counter. The coffeepot, the one he didn't use—the one he'd never purchased beans for, because he was supposed to suffer. But he didn't want Hannah to suffer.

The rich scent of Columbian grounds permeated the air above the smell of stale cigarette smoke. *Coffee.* Shannon had definitely left food.

Would Hannah bolt if he left her alone at the apartment? He couldn't keep taking her to work; Jackson would surely get suspicious, and that guy in the UP yesterday had recognized her too. Hannah was heavier and more worn-down, but someone would eventually realize who she was. And then she'd be behind bars along with any insight she might have about Julie.

Through the pillow, he felt the hard edges of the gun and then the bottle against his temple as he rolled to face the window. Feigning sleepiness. *Don't drink it, Petrosky.* He snaked his hand under the pillow and wrapped his fingers around the neck of the bottle, wishing he was alone. She'd seen him take that last shot before bed, and the sadness in her eyes had made the soft place in his gut tear open again, enveloping his heart in something hot and thick and vile. He could write off last night's drinks as a reward at the end of a long day, a relaxation exercise before bed. But if he tipped the bottle up now, before breakfast, he was just an alcoholic. Julie would have hated who he'd become. He released the bottle and pushed himself to seated again.

Hannah had told him about Julie. She'd made the connection. But she couldn't know any more about Julie's killer than Robin did. He was deluding himself, giving himself an excuse to keep her here. And for what? The tightness in her eyes spoke volumes—she didn't feel safe. Not just here, where no one would look for her. She didn't feel safe with *him*. She didn't trust him.

But trust was a two-way street, wasn't it? That's what his ex-wife used to say. What they used to tell Julie.

"What will you do today?" he asked Hannah.

Her eyes widened. "I…I'm not going with you?"

"You can stay here if you want. Or you can come to the station, give your statement." *Get it over with. Make all of this go away.* Let her move on, just like Shannon.

A shudder ran through her, so violent that the eggs almost shook from the plate in her hands. "No, I'm…I'm not ready yet. Just… I need a few days. To settle in."

Petrosky's chest lightened as if his organs had suddenly ceased to have weight. "If I leave, are you going to run?"

"I won't go anywhere."

"Okay. I trust you." Was that enough to make her stay? She hadn't run from the medical examiner's office yesterday, or from the Escalade during any of the three stops they'd made to verify facts on the latest homicide. Which had all led to a big fat nothing, just as the UP dicks had warned them it would.

She was looking at him so softly, eyes round with... shock? Amazement? She wasn't a stranger to being trusted at home alone—she was alone when he'd found her at Crandall's. But this was different. His trust, whether as a cop or as a stranger, meant something different to her than Crandall's blind faith. His phone rang, and Hannah startled, jerking her head toward the sound. The soft look in her eyes disappeared.

"You okay?"

She nodded and stared at the eggs as if that rubbery pile was the most interesting thing in the world.

The cell rang again. He tore his gaze from her and grabbed his phone from the window ledge. "Petrosky."

"Hey." *Scott.* The rookie was probably calling to bitch Petrosky out for stealing his case—and god knew Petrosky deserved it.

"Listen, I'm reading through the full confession from Melinda Charles."

Charles? "Mm-hmm." Petrosky stood, stretched. Hannah blinked at her meal.

"She said she used a scalpel, just like in the Ash Park murders."

The bile in his gut went rancid. *A scalpel.* He turned toward the corner and lowered his voice so Hannah couldn't overhear. "A scalpel? That's what she said?"

"Exactly." Scott's voice was strange, tinged with excitement, and Petrosky knew why: the weapon used on Montgomery was a paring knife or some longer, duller blade. Not a scalpel—and no way she'd get that wrong, even if Hannah's birthday had been a coincidence. Which it wasn't.

"I don't think Melinda Charles did it, Petrosky."

You need to watch out for these women, both of them, no matter how vulnerable you think Hannah is. It wouldn't be the first time someone you decided was innocent ended up being a murderer.

The Vermont PD might have convinced Charles that they could help her if she confessed. That her daughter would be better off if her husband had been killed in a moment of temporary insanity after years of abuse—self-protection, even if self-defense wouldn't fly. Who knew what they'd end up charging her with, or whether she'd even do jail time; she could get probation and a domestic violence program. Unlikely, maybe, but no one would give Charles any kind of break if she'd conspired with someone else to kill her husband. Confessing to abuse and a moment of insanity would make sense if she thought she was about to be busted for hiring a hit man or some shit.

Scott said, "We have the wrong person, but no one believes me. Again."

Petrosky believed him. But he didn't want to. If Charles hadn't killed her husband, someone else had done it for her—and Hannah would be their prime suspect. She had suffered severe abuse at the hands of her father, murdered her boyfriend, and then sneaked back into her hometown under an assumed name. A year later, Hannah's father had turned up dead. On her birthday. That was all too much coincidence.

"We'll figure it out, Scott. Just keep your mouth shut and let me take care of it." Letting other people take care of things had led them here—if he'd never walked away from Julie's case, from the *Looking Glass* case, maybe none of this would have happened. Then again, it was Scott's continued digging, not his, that had unearthed the inconsistency with the murder weapon—information Petrosky had overlooked accidentally, distracted as he was by Julie's case. Or maybe he just hadn't wanted to acknowledge that Charles might be innocent because, no matter what had happened, the thought of locking Hannah away pained him more than the prospect of her getting away with murder.

Hannah was at the stove, cracking more eggs into a pan when he said goodbye to Scott.

"I have to do some poking around on Robin's case," he told her. "Just call if you need anything." A tiny part of him hoped she'd be gone when he returned, that she would leave before he had to take her in for murdering two men. Because though she claimed she'd been home with her boyfriend the night of Montgomery's murder, he couldn't verify that Crandall's ass hadn't fallen asleep any more than Melinda Charles could verify she was out taking a walk. For all he knew, they were in it together.

Hannah dropped her gaze and nodded. "Okay." Her forehead wrinkles had disappeared—she could have passed for eighteen.

"How old are you now, Hannah?"

"Almost twenty-eight."

Almost, eh? Maybe he'd grab ice cream and cake sometime this week, in case she was gone by the time the date rolled around. "Why didn't Melinda Charles know about your birthday?"

"What? I've never met—"

"Then why did she kill your father on your birthday?"

Hannah stared at him.

"Melinda confessed. What I can't figure out is why your birthday would matter so much to her that she'd choose that day to murder your father."

"She confessed." It was a whisper.

"Hannah."

She didn't move.

"Hannah, the eggs."

"Oh!" She grabbed the skillet from the stove, smoke drifting from the pan's surface in black ribbons until she tossed it into the sink. "Sorry, I… She confessed?" She turned back to him. "I kinda thought that was a rumor."

"She did. But I'm not convinced she did it, Hannah." Petrosky rolled his neck, absentmindedly scratching his gut under the T-shirt he'd worn to bed, until she glanced at him. He dropped his hand and snatched clothes from the closet to take with him into the bathroom, his only outlet for privacy. "You really didn't know her, Hannah?"

She picked up her glass with a shaking hand. "No. I didn't."

But Petrosky knew if he found the scalpel Hannah had used on Dominic Harwick, he'd also find the knife from Montgomery's murder—he felt that certainty like a stone in his belly. But he'd never look for the knife. He couldn't find out he was right.

"So, um…did you want eggs?" she asked his back.

"I'll get something on my way in. You eat them."

"Oh. Okay." She sounded disappointed. Wow, he really sucked at this family shit. *She isn't family—she's a killer.* But he didn't care. Not because he didn't value his own life, but because there was no part of him that feared this girl.

She was innocent. Vulnerable. A victim, like his daughter. But unlike his daughter, Hannah was a survivor—she was who Julie might have been if she'd managed to escape her murderer. If she had known to lock her chin against her chest to staunch the flow of blood.

He didn't blame Hannah one bit for what she'd done. For either of the murders.

He paused with his hand on the bathroom doorknob. "I'm glad he's dead."

Not a sound from behind him until she finally squeaked: "Who?"

"Your father. I would have killed him too."

Behind him came the bright clang of shattering glass. That should do it; she wouldn't leave the house now, not after he'd essentially told her that he didn't care about her crimes. She was safer here than elsewhere, where she might run into someone less sympathetic. And she knew it.

He stepped into the bathroom and closed the door.

27

———

THE COMPOSITE of Julie's killer, Robin's attacker, would go out on the evening news, with a notice that this man was wanted for questioning in connection with a robbery—as a possible witness. That way, his friends might turn him in without question. Of course, the killer himself would probably be suspicious, but the drawing was unfortunately bland: a run-of-the-mill white guy, narrow jaw stippled with five-o'clock shadow, wrinkles around light-colored eyes, glasses too big for his face. Large, straight teeth, thin lips, hair sandy brown or maybe salt and pepper—she hadn't been able to tell in the glow of the streetlamp. And the man had thrown Robin down before she could get a read on his height. Her attacker could have been any of a thousand men in the metro Detroit area.

And the composite was six years old, making a current identification even harder. But the picture and the bracelet were their only leads—the bastard was careful. The bracelet could have been made a number of places, and though the internet wasn't as popular a dozen years ago, there were enough online stores that their killer could have procured it without ever appearing in person. He could also have

243

purchased it a decade ago from a now-defunct seller. The few sales records they'd been able to get their hands on were all people who had lost beloved pets, and almost all the customers were women, many of them geriatric. None reported their jewelry—if you could call it that—stolen. There were three local males who had purchased such a bracelet, and he and Jackson visited them in person. One was a black man with a furrowed brow who said he'd given the bracelet to his daughter after her dog died. The second was a man older than Crandall, back stooped so low he might as well have been bending at the waist. Their third dead-dog-hair-wearing suspect might have fit the description—thin lips, light eyes—but his fingers were so calloused from working construction that there was no way he was the soft-handed man Robin had described.

They'd hit a brick wall. The killer'd probably bought the bracelet at a garage sale. Or with his sadistic hair burning obsession, maybe the bastard had made that creepy-ass bracelet himself from his own pets. So who might know how to braid a bracelet? A hairstylist, maybe. But these days, anyone could watch a video and learn the craft if they were motivated enough.

They were down to baby-soft fingers. "Want to hit some salons? Manicure places? It's Saturday, so they should all be open."

Jackson raised an eyebrow. "You're more metrosexual than I gave you credit for."

"Not for—"

"I know, I know, my little fruit bat."

The nail salons gave them nothing besides a bunch of Asians and the occasional skinny dude with gelled hair looking at the composite photo like they were insane for asking. And there were probably a thousand manicurists around the city. With so much ground to cover, Petrosky and Jackson resorted to faxing or emailing the photos and calling each location a few minutes later. None of the nail techs recognized the guy. Another dead end, and really, all this guy needed was a nail file and some lotion of his own. He could be a pianist. A doctor. Though Petrosky had thought the *Looking Glass* killer was a doctor too, and he'd just been a businessman who enjoyed tearing out his victim's insides. Still, this case had none of the hallmarks of medical training; anyone could learn to destroy DNA evidence or think to wear gloves. It required common sense, not surgical skill.

Petrosky's brain throbbed a steady, painful rhythm against his temple as he headed for home, wondering if Hannah would still be there when he arrived. Wondering if he'd have the balls to call Shannon. Wondering if Hannah would pick tonight to kill him in his sleep.

Not like he'd be her first casualty. He rubbed his aching head. Maybe he'd sic Hannah on Julie's killer; these days, she was more badass than he was.

WHEN HE ARRIVED at the apartment, Duke ran to him from the corner and plopped his butt on the floor, tail wagging, surely smelling the takeout Petrosky'd brought in with him. He reached into his pocket, tossed a dog treat into the back corner, and watched Duke scamper after it. Then Petrosky turned to Hannah, who was sitting at his little bistro table with Morrison's old laptop open in front of her. She straightened, then put her hand on the top as if to close it.

He waved her back down. "Don't stop what you're doing on my account." He walked past her without glancing at the screen.

She hesitated. Looked at the bag in his hand.

"You like Chinese?" he asked.

She nodded.

"Good." He grabbed two plates from the counter, where they lay clean and drying on a towel.

"Oh…uh…"

He turned to her. She bit her lip.

"What?"

"It's just that if you unfold the takeout carton, you don't even have to use plates. But we totally can."

What sorcery is this? "Forget plates." He stacked the dishes back on the counter and set the bag down in front of her. "Work your magic."

Hannah took the first box, tentatively, as if suddenly worried that she was wrong about this, and used a fingernail to pull one side tab then another. Pork fried rice steamed atop the flat, waxed cardboard, the room filling with the scent of salt and herbs.

"I'll be damned. My life might be complete."

She smiled—actually smiled—at him, her teeth whiter, dimples deeper, eyes brighter than he remembered, though he wasn't entirely sure he'd ever seen her smile. He grinned back—shocked his lips actually remembered how—and she seemed just as surprised to see his teeth. In fairness, he probably looked like he was about to bite someone.

They ate in silence, the scraping of their forks against the now flattened cartons a quiet backdrop to their breathing and chewing and the occasional begging whine from Duke, which should have been annoying but was rather…pleasant. Normal. Peaceful. Not the charged, frustrated silence of a husband and wife at wits' end or the indifferent quiet of family members who simply had nothing left to say.

Every now and then, Hannah looked at him as though she had something critical to tell him, and he paused in his eating, waiting for some essential piece of information to come pouring out. But each time, she turned away, the purple under her eyes deeper than it had been this morning —looked like she had concerns that were too worrisome to verbalize. Did she know more about Julie? Did she want to confess? Was she thinking about Dominic, about her father, about that fuckboy Neil Crandall with his wrinkly, palsied ass, a man Hannah wasn't even willing to trust with her dog? He wanted to know. He wanted to take it out of her brain and look at it with her and conquer it so she'd smile at him again. And though the cop in him was desperate to interrogate her until she spilled whatever secrets she had, something in him whispered that if he did, he'd lose her forever.

No, not lose *her*. Lose the *information*.

Jesus, Petrosky. You dick.

But considering what her secrets might be ate at him. He cleared the table and headed for the bathroom to clean up before bed, the water only half drowning the parade of images in his brain: the Montgomery crime scene, the gore soaking into the carpet. And the Harwick crime scene, with the millionaire's intestines ripped from his gut like she'd grabbed them out of his belly and sprinted across the room with them. And Robin: throat slashed, voice box destroyed.

Julie. Dead and bloody and burned and so…small.

But Hannah. Breathing. Smiling. Alive and eating Chinese food at his table. He should have eaten more takeout with Shannon and the kids. Such a simple thing, and he'd missed it. He glanced at the oven clock—past bedtime in Atlanta, and he knew better than to risk waking the children.

Hannah was already asleep when he returned to the main room. He sat on the edge of his mattress, watching her eyelids flutter in rest, noting the way her dark hair stuck to her cheek and to the corner of her mouth. He was staring the way he used to do with Julie when she was small. Back when he thought he could protect her from the perils of the world.

He reached beneath the pillow. The gun was cold and hard in his hand, but comforting like a blanket on a blustery winter day. He glanced at the safety, thumbed it off, clicked it back on again. Slid the weapon under his pillow. Just because he wanted to help her didn't mean he trusted her. But he didn't have to trust her to care.

He sighed. Petrosky got up and returned to the kitchen. He wiped the counters, found coffee in the cupboard, and set the grounds out for the morning. He poured food in the dog's dish in case the animal got hungry overnight, but Duke kept snoring. The dog ignored him even when he dropped a bone beside the water bowl. When Petrosky finally lay down himself, it was Hannah's steady breath that lulled him to sleep.

28

———————

I'm TEARING *through the streets, running for the house I grew up in, the world around me flying by as if I'm in some interstellar void where the laws of physics have broken down, and nothing else exists but him and me.*

I don't want to believe the message. I don't. But she's never struck me as a liar.

I make it to the maple tree, taller and thicker than I recall, though everything is different now. I'm different now—I can almost reach the leafy branches I had to climb for as a child. But I don't care to reach or climb. I'm not a child anymore.

And then I see them.

I head for the side of the house, where the shadows are heaviest, the whole area steeped in dimness beneath the boughs. From here, the world looks a little tattered and worn around the edges. Rays of waning sun pierce the living room window like knives, illuminating the dust motes that languish in the still air. Sunlight beams through a fracture in the windowpane, splattering rainbows onto the opposite wall. Onto him.

His face is still in shadow, but I can see it just fine, those lines I memorized a long time ago: the crooked nose, the square, rugged jaw always covered with scratchy bristles of stubble. His white T-

shirt is irreparably slashed and stained, the button on his pants hidden under the sheen of slimy, red filth, blood pooling around his belly. Not dead—through the open windows, I can still hear him wheezing, his weak exhales as deafening as a scream. But he's beyond help. I can see it—I can smell the stink of his shit. And it didn't come out the normal way.

Why am I here? Maybe I'd expected him to apologize. For what he did to me. For what he made me do to the only other man I've ever loved.

Dominic. My heart speeds up, races around in my chest like a cracked-out rat. Dominic took me and made me shiny and perfect, held me, showed me that everything was okay, that I didn't have to run any longer. Then he severed the rope that he'd used to tie me together—but that was just as much my fault as his. I shouldn't have said anything. I should have kept my mouth shut. But a lifetime of pain had poured out of me that night. Pain my father had put there.

I can't breathe. That fucking rat, the one that's controlling my heart, he's brought his friends, and now they're using my lungs like a trampoline, forcing my exhales out of me, my breath mingling with the horrid stink of sweat and excrement and iron. I clench my fists at my sides. Tense my legs to keep from kicking the wall. This man—it's his fault. All of it. He turned me into this. And then he turned her, too.

I should call out to him, maybe, see if he remembers what he did to deserve this. His breath has softened to a low crackle against my eardrums. I inch my face closer to the screen, almost retching when I see the gore seeping into the carpet. I did this.

No...he did.

Then suddenly I'm inside the house, grinding my teeth so hard my jaw feels like it might snap, and I lower my face to his, gazing into his green eyes that are so much like mine, trying to recognize what I once adored, what sent me racing home to his arms after school each night. Trying to see the madness that sparkled there when he said: "Hello, Hannah banana." Trying to understand what once made me think that this was love. But now there is no spark, only the glaze of impending death. No fear either, just helpless acceptance. Giving up. The way I gave up when he took me that last time, me screaming and crying all the way to his bedroom, knowing I was carrying his child. The same helplessness I felt the night I ran away, to another city, another town, to anyplace that wasn't with him.

"You did this." I'm saying it aloud, but he doesn't respond, just... stops. No more breath. No more life. And something in me unravels, the little sanity I've had unspooling like yarn in a cat's claws. I stand, and I'm back outside again. My lip quivers, and I bite it until I taste blood. I wonder if he saw it coming the way Dominic did.

But I'm different than I was then. I'm stronger now.

Dominic made it so.

And there's no better place to start ridding the world of awful than a town like Willowshire, where denial is rampant, where no one would believe their neighbor is a rapist, because they barbecue together, for god's sake. Theodore can't be fucking his daughter, can he?

But he was then. And he is now.

I squint, straining my eyes for one final look at my father's body. And there she stands, purse still against her hip, the knife I gave her for protection shiny in her fist, my father's blood soaking her school uniform. And her mother, stumbling in behind her and grabbing the blade. They don't even look my way. And from my position in front of the window, still hidden in the shadow of the enormous maple tree, I feel a sudden sense of...peace. I wanted her to kill him. No, I wanted her to be safe. I thought she'd use the weapon to scare him. But maybe, on some level, I knew. I let a little girl stab my father because I was too much of a coward to do it myself.

But I could make sure she didn't go to jail for my mistakes. I was his first. His daughter. His Hannah banana, and he'd not forget that. In some ways, it made what he did to her worse than what he did to me. He never even loved her at all.

I jerked to sitting, almost toppling off the air mattress like a beached whale on a moon bounce. I panted around the knot in my throat while the amorphous shapes around me solidified. *It's okay, Hannah.* A streetlamp shone through the open window, spilling orange light on one of Duke's bones, on a discarded pair of pants on… A gun. Pointed at my face.

Petrosky was sitting bolt upright too, his weapon trained on me like he'd been holding it that way all night. The knot in my throat ballooned until it blocked my airway entirely. He wanted me dead, like Dominic had, like my father had. From his bed in the corner, Duke whined but made no effort to approach.

Petrosky lowered the weapon. The knot stayed.

"Hannah? What's wrong?"

I couldn't speak, just wheezed in odd little squeaks. *I'm not going to make it.* I was dying. I could feel it in the orange light spilling into the room from the streetlamp, crawling toward me over the filthy floor like claws ready to drag me out the window and fling me into oblivion.

Petrosky set the weapon aside, crossed the room, and sat on the floor beside the air mattress, so quickly it almost felt like one movement. "Hey, it's okay. I heard something, and at first, I didn't…I didn't know it was you." He was whispering. *Why is he whispering?* But I could already hear the click of something in the kitchen settling, the subtle arching moan of a floorboard somewhere in the building, and in this quiet, anything above a whisper would surely have sounded like screaming. The knot in my throat loosened, and I gasped in a full breath, grabbing Petrosky's beefy shoulder with both hands. My cheeks were suddenly wet—*am I crying?*—and all I could hear was my own labored breathing. And then him. Humming something familiar though I couldn't place it—not like I had much experience with lullabies. My father hadn't put me to bed in a normal way.

I lowered my forehead between my fists against Petrosky's shoulder, and he put his hand on my hair and rocked us back and forth, back and forth. The claws on the floor relaxed into tendrils of orange and black branches, just branches, and I let my breath match his movements.

Back and forth. In and out.

Breathe, Hannah, breathe.

His tuneless humming reverberated in my eardrums. It was the loveliest thing I'd ever heard.

"Did you sing that song to your daughter?" I whispered into the dusk of the room.

"I never sang her lullabies. I should have. But I didn't." The regret in his voice was so palpable I felt it in my own heart, filling my chest with a deep, terrible ache. I had regrets too, none bigger than the fact that I'd never had the chance to be normal. And that might have been my fault; I'd been a willing participant in most of those early games with my father before I knew what we were doing. Before I knew it was wrong. Maybe if I'd been different...maybe he'd have sung to me instead of fucking me.

"Why didn't you sing to your daughter? Was she bad?"

"Julie was never bad." His voice was so low it was difficult to hear over the whoosh of blood in my ears.

"My father didn't sing me songs. I always wanted him to, but I thought that maybe I just wasn't...you know." *Good enough.* I couldn't breathe. I clung tighter to his shoulder, my nails digging into his skin. His hand against my hair was immobile. Warm. Steady.

"He hurt you." Not a question. "You didn't deserve that, you know. What he did to you."

But Petrosky was wrong. I'd asked for it. I'd begged. Fantasized about being with my father forever, about running away so I could marry him. "I sure didn't try very hard to make it…different."

"Abuse isn't something you ask for," he said. "And a father's love isn't something you earn. It's something that is. You deserved better, just like my daughter did. I ignored the things that mattered. I let her slip away from me, little by little, until we barely knew each other. The day she died, I didn't even know she was missing until they stumbled upon her body. I should have known. I should have been the one driving her to her friend's house. Maybe if I'd known she was missing, someone would have found her before she bled to death." He coughed like he was choking.

Robin had told me that she herself would have bled to death in minutes if she hadn't kept her chin clamped over the wound—so surely finding Julie in time to save her was a pipe dream. But the guilt, the sorrow in his voice… Petrosky believed he'd played a part in his daughter's death. A dam burst in my chest, and the ache spilled through my abdomen like hot oil.

I slid from the mattress onto the floor beside him, hip to hip, and let him wrap me up in his arms, the simple act of sitting with him natural and almost wonderful. I'd say it felt like love was supposed to feel, but I didn't know anything about that, and there was none of the burning passion I'd had for either my father or for Dominic, just this weird… warmth. Silent and calm.

And then my mouth was moving, and I was pressing my lips against his ear, seeking his lips, his tongue, but he pulled back from me as fast as if I'd bitten him and leapt to his feet.

"That's not how this works." He stood silhouetted against the window, the orange light clawing again, this time at his shadow. "Whatever you need…you don't have to pay for it with *that*. And you don't need to give it to that guy back in Vermont either."

Shock and hurt and shame slammed through me. *That*

was all I had. I didn't know how else to love him. And cowering on the floor, with the warmth of his arm removed from me, I felt more alone than I had when I'd awoken.

"I'm sorry," I whispered, but I wasn't. I was already pretending he was mine, that Detective Petrosky was my father. Pretending he loved me.

"Don't be sorry. You didn't have anyone to teach you better. Dads don't always do their job." And when his voice cracked on the last word, I got the impression that he wasn't talking to me at all.

29

———

THE FOG WRAPPED him in gray so thick Petrosky couldn't see his own hand in front of his face. But still he ran, blindly seeking his daughter, her voice screaming to him from somewhere in the mist. *I'm coming, honey.* Then the screaming stopped, abruptly, like a radio someone had clicked off. The cloud parted like a curtain. There she was, throat slashed, the rest of her body obscured by a sheet. He collapsed beside her, rocking her, sobbing with his face buried in her hair, and she was warm, how was she so—

No…not Julie's hair. *Hannah.*

Petrosky pulled his face from the back of her head, shaking her hair from the stubble on his chin. Her breath was low and even like she was still asleep, but a twitch in her ankle made him think she was probably awake. When had she climbed into bed with him? Was he delirious? He tried to ease his arm from under her, but his elbow stuck fast. Or maybe he was just weak. He pulled harder.

"I have to tell you something."

He jumped half a mile in the air, and she jolted with him, almost toppling off the edge of the mattress.

"Tell me what?" He glanced into the corner at the dog—still fast asleep. *Lazy asshole.*

She pushed herself to seated. "I talked to Robin yesterday."

Had another precinct found her attacker? His head was swimming. Here's where he'd discover that he wouldn't get to nail the guy himself, or that Robin's case wasn't connected to Julie's at all, and he'd have to start over and—

"Might be nothing, but..."

He fumbled his cigarettes off the box beside his mattress as she retrieved his—*Morrison's*—laptop from the bistro table and flipped it on. She settled back beside him on the mattress, tapping keys.

"I think the guy who killed Julie might be a dentist."

He turned his head away from her and exhaled a plume of smoke at the wall. "Come again?" He watched the smoke curl toward the ceiling, taking with it the last remnants of sleepiness.

It might be nothing. *But it might be something.* And as she filled him in on Robin's flashback and her suspicion that Julie's attacker was in dentistry, the hope in Petrosky's chest welled up, spilled over, and expanded down through his lungs. He inhaled cigarette smoke, sharply, determined to quell the unnerving lightness of illogical hope.

Hannah pointed to the screen at what looked like a list of dental professionals. "I started looking at dentists themselves, but the killer might be a hygienist or something, too. That fluoride smell sticks around, even if it's subtle. My mom used to come home smelling like that, just this weird kinda medicinal scent under her perfume." She met his gaze, searching his eyes as though she were a child waiting for him to tell her she was wrong and stupid and ridiculous. Had he ever made Julie feel that way?

"So do you think it's dumb, or..."

He put a hand on her shoulder. "Thank you. It's wonderful." He stood so quickly that she was thrown off balance, and when he reached out a hand to steady her, she held his hand a moment longer. Then she let go.

"I'm going to run to the precinct, get started on this." Her smile was all the reason he needed to chase this the whole day, whether it came to fruition or not. And if she was helping him...she wasn't going anywhere. The atmosphere in the apartment had changed since last night, too: less tense, more friendly, less cop-prisoner, and more...what? He glanced down at his clothes. He had slept in his jeans. Petrosky clamped the cigarette between his teeth and pulled a button-down shirt over his tank top.

"I'm glad I helped."

"You did. Maybe you even saved a few people if we can find this killer sooner." From the look on Hannah's face, that meant more to her than anything else he could have said—for any life she'd taken, Hannah was giving more back. The air thickened with emotion, and he drew on his cigarette one more time to snuff out all the flowery bullshit with nicotine, then crushed it in the sink. "Try not to kill anyone while I'm gone," he said, and winked, but her eyes clouded. *Nice job, asshole.* If she left now, it would be his fault, but at least she'd probably fare better out there than she would here, just waiting for the day he'd be forced to drag her off to the precinct. He grabbed his shoulder holster and put his hand on the doorknob. Turned away.

"Would you still...um...like me if I did?" she asked his back.

He swiveled to face her. "If you did..."

"Kill someone." Her voice was so low he almost couldn't hear her, but there was a defiance in her eyes that made gooseflesh prickle on his arms. She was going to confess.

But she'd already given him a confession on Harwick—which meant this was about killing her father. He had no idea what he'd do with that information, but he desperately needed to know, even if he never told a living soul.

"Nothing you can do will make me not like you."

The relief in her eyes was so strong, so genuine, that he could almost feel it reaching across the room for him, wrapping itself around his heart and soothing the tired muscle behind his pacemaker. He waited for her to respond, but the moment had passed—there was a tightness in her eyes that said if he asked again now, he'd push her further from him. She'd closed down again, at least for the time being. If they could joke about it, would she be more likely to trust him? To tell him? He reached for the door again. "Even though I'll still like you…maybe try to keep the murder to a minimum," he said over his shoulder.

"Ok, Ed." She said it so quietly that he couldn't tell whether she'd called him "Ed" or "Dad." Maybe he didn't want to know. Maybe he'd rather guess.

Maybe they both needed to pretend.

30

———————

Jackson did not ask about Hannah, and Petrosky was glad of it. She didn't even bat an eye when he told her he'd done a little follow-up with Robin and gleaned the dentist information himself. It was a lie, but a little one, and he didn't feel one bit of guilt over it, especially after Jackson took off without a word, leaving him with a massive amount of research.

There were hundreds of dental websites, even after he'd narrowed it down to the ones who'd been in business six years ago. If Robin's attacker had smelled like fluoride, he had to be practicing then, unless he was at home, slathering the stuff on his naked body. Petrosky knew better than to put creepy shit like that past anyone, but… He shuddered at the image of a pasty nude guy covered in blue gel. If only they made bleach for your brain.

The dentists on the websites were a spindly bunch—thin, with intelligent eyes covered with glasses from squinting into people's mouths, consistent with Robin's composite. But none fit the profile. The set of their jaw or their eyes weren't quite right, and many of them were too young now to have been practicing back when Julie died… Then again, he couldn't be sure whoever killed Julie had been in practice at the time. The killer could have crafted his MO before he got his dentistry license. And though Robin had described the man as fortyish, with laugh lines around his eyes, it had been dark when she was attacked; a sixty-year-old might have been able to pass with some hair dye or a toupee or even a little plastic surgery. Did dentists make a lot of money? How much was a face-lift? He fingered his own fleshy chin and frowned at the screen. Where the hell was Jackson? Morrison had always been more reliable than that—more reliable than Shannon, too.

He drummed his fingers on the desk. He was mildly upset that Shannon hadn't called him back; he'd left her a message on his way to the precinct this morning. But hey, new place, new job. New life. And it had taken him a lot longer than a few hours to call her back after she'd texted him. He deserved to wait. He shoved the phone deeper into his pocket, telling himself he wasn't willing it to ring.

"Lunch has arrived!"

Petrosky looked up as Jackson dropped a bag on his desk. He could smell the soy sauce without opening it, and one side of the bag was already spotted with grease. "You trying to kill me, Jackson?"

"Like you need any help with that."

He peeled open the sack and breathed in the aroma of chicken fried rice and egg rolls. "If you want to off me, this is definitely the way I prefer you do it." He pulled an egg roll from the container. "So, where'd you go?"

"Nowhere."

He raised an eyebrow.

She pursed her lips. "Don't ask, don't tell, right? I'm sure you want your business close to the vest too. Just be happy you got food out of it, you crotchety old fart."

She plopped into the seat beside him and took out one of the containers, peeked inside, and then pulled out the other. "So, what'd you find? Anything yet?" She glanced at her watch.

"These guys all look the same, but so far, none of them are close enough to the composite."

"I'll help you look."

Fortified with greasy egg rolls and oilier coffee, Petrosky and Jackson combed through site after site, but none of the photos jumped out as being a good match for their composite, and with each new webpage, Petrosky's jaw clenched harder. At six o'clock exactly, Jackson patted him on the shoulder.

"I finally got a list back from the dental board, and we'll start early tomorrow matching driver's licenses since half these guys don't have websites. Maybe we'll get lucky there instead."

"Where are you—"

"Gotta run."

She always had to run. But he had no motivation to chase her, no fucks to give about where she disappeared to all the time. Nor did he give a flying shit about either of them cutting the day short.

Maybe he should stay and look. Maybe he should be more motivated to find Julie's killer. Maybe he was just as shitty of a father now as he'd always been. When Jackson disappeared down the stairs, Petrosky shut his computer down too. This killer spaced his crimes out—he wasn't going after anyone else tonight.

And if Petrosky was being honest with himself, he just wanted to get back to Hannah. The thought of sitting at his tiny bistro table with some takeout, watching something on the computer, or playing with the dog or just chatting with Hannah about his day…it almost felt like he was going home.

He opened his desk drawer. Julie stared back at him, face flushed with sun, dark hair flying, eyes bright. Just like always. Frozen in time.

Sorry, honey. All I ever wanted to do was protect you.

Now all he wanted to do was avenge her. And he would.

31

———————

THOUSANDS OF DENTISTS were currently licensed to practice, many more than they'd found online alone. Together, Jackson and Petrosky removed the ones they'd looked at the day before, then narrowed the remaining list to males, then further to those who were listed with the DMV as having a visual impairment, i.e., wearing glasses—though he could have just worn glasses to throw them off the trail. Just under six hundred matches.

It was a long shot, but a long shot was all they had right now, and cases had been solved with more ridiculous theories. Petrosky'd do what it took—he'd knock on every dentist's door in the entire United States if it meant coming face-to-face with the bastard who'd taken his daughter's life, tore away her future with a swipe of his blade. Petrosky would give him a blade. Petrosky would show him what that felt like to fight for one final, blood-soaked breath.

The thought made him feel *alive*.

Meticulously he pulled each name, each picture. Some were easy to eliminate, men of color, men with dark eyes not matching the description Robin gave, men who just didn't have the right build or the right face. Too thick in the jaw, too wide in the nose, too strong across the forehead.

Petrosky had just flipped to the second page of names when he became aware that Jackson was speaking to someone, and when he turned to look at her, she had her desk phone pressed against the side of her head. Then she was standing, grabbing her cell from the desktop. Then her keys.

Again? "Jackson?" Where the hell was she off to?

"Be back. Getting lunch. I'll bring you something." She didn't look over at him, didn't even give him her usual noncommittal shrug that said: "Hey, can't help being hungry."

He glanced at the clock. Not even eleven.

Irritation blossomed in his gut, the prickly heat of anger lurking just beneath it. He was being a hypocrite—he'd left yesterday too. But now? In the middle of the day? He watched her fly down the stairs. He would find Julie's killer with or without Jackson's help, but eventually, she'd find out about Hannah, and then…

Petrosky stood. He could use some dirt on this "up-and-up" woman in case he needed to keep her from telling the chief about his houseguest. He'd be damned if Hannah was going to jail just for protecting herself and her stepsister, or because Jackson couldn't keep her mouth shut.

When the door at the bottom of the stairs closed, Petrosky descended the staircase too, then peered through the cracked door for Jackson before flinging the door wide. Her Escalade was already at the street, poised to merge with the traffic. By the time he got into his Caprice, she had turned right, tires shrieking.

He squealed from his parking space, feeling vital, energized, as he hit the main road in time to see her whipping around the corner just ahead. He accelerated behind her, swerving around an old man in a Volkswagen Beetle who yelled something at him through the open window. *Idiot.* As if whatever he said could possibly excuse a grown-ass man for driving a car named after an insect. The damn thing looked like a turtle humping the street every time he hit the brakes.

Petrosky caught up with Jackson on her next right, her taillights bouncing over an exceptionally large pothole, and he couldn't tell if she was speeding because she'd spotted him or because she was late for some secret meeting. The backside of the park flew by his left window, then the abandoned school, and then they were hitting the freeway, heading north out of the city. Definitely not getting food, though he'd already known that. *Sherlock Holmes, over here.*

He almost smiled into his rearview as he reduced his speed, putting a respectable distance between himself and Jackson's Escalade. Her ride wasn't made to be covert; the top of it was visible over the line of Toyotas and Volvos and some douche in a Smart Car.

Jackson gunned her car up the off-ramp as they approached Southfield and honked angrily at some motorcycle-riding fuckhead who was weaving between the other motorists like a stunt driver. Guy must have had a death wish. When Petrosky passed the biker, he honked too and gave him the finger for good measure, waiting until the guy mouthed a curse before lowering his hand. He didn't have to worry his honking would attract Jackson's attention. She'd already turned right off the ramp.

Here the streets were quieter, and once the freeway traffic died down behind them, the road widened, and grassy lawns spread out on either side. Petrosky closed the distance between them, but slowly, and pulled his foot off the gas when she screeched into a parking lot.

A school? The word "Academy" on the front sign made it seem so, but it was small: a red-brick square that might have held eighty to a hundred kids, tops. He parked in the back of the lot, slouched down, and squinted at the rearview where he could see Jackson running up the walk and into the building.

His cigarette pack crinkled as he pulled out the last smoke and lit it up. What was she doing here? If it was about her kid, all she'd needed to do was tell him; not like he was going to say no after he'd left the state to pick up a lead without even...*oh*. No wonder she hadn't felt the need to run it by him. He couldn't demand she give him all the space he wanted while he monitored her every move—she'd slap him into October. If she were Morrison, he'd know what to say. If she were Morrison—

The front door opened, and Jackson emerged with a boy, his head down, though he was taller than she was by several inches, and...was he limping? No, he was *jerking*. Having a seizure? But his leg movements were far more controlled, and if he'd been having a seizure, the school would have called an ambulance and not his mother.

The kid stopped. Jackson stopped. Suddenly, the child brought his knee up toward his face, once, twice, three times, bloodying his own nose and splitting his lip. Jackson tried to cushion the blows by putting her hand between his knee and his head.

Petrosky was out of his car before he registered that he was moving. He tossed the cigarette onto the ground as he ran across the lot. "Jackson?"

Her eyes widened when she saw him, but she ignored his approach, just rubbed the kid's back like she'd been through this a thousand times before. The boy raised his knee once more, but this time the impact was softer, and the next time he jerked his knee up toward his face, the blow didn't land.

Poor kid. Some kind of disability, but determining what kind was outside his realm of expertise. "What can I do?" Petrosky asked.

"Back up." Jackson said it softly, with the measured calm of a kindergarten teacher, but her eyes were furious. Petrosky stepped off the curb and headed toward the rear of her car, where he waited, watching the parking lot with his back against her trunk. She murmured to the boy. He didn't respond. Eventually, she opened the car door and eased him inside, talking quietly all the while. Calm. Gentle. A far cry from her demeanor at work.

The door clicked shut. Petrosky straightened, and when he turned to go around the side of the car, he almost ran directly into her.

"What are you doing here?" she snapped.

"I was hungry. Wanted to make sure you got enough food."

She glared. Morrison would have smiled. "My son…has trouble. With people. Sometimes he gets stressed."

Petrosky nodded, watching her fists clench and unclench and clench again.

"I don't need this shit, Petrosky."

"Understood. Just let me know next time."

She crossed her arms. "The way you let me know when you're leaving the state?"

He'd been right about that one.

"You get what you give, Petrosky. And I ain't giving you shit unless—"

"I'll give better too." God knows he needed to. God knows everyone around him deserved better. Shannon had called on his way home the night before and told him about her first week at work, like nothing had ever happened, like he hadn't ignored her for days. "We're partners, right?"

Her eyes tightened like she thought it was a trick. "Yeah," she said slowly. "We're partners. So maybe we should act like it."

"You already bring food. That's a start."

"And the trust thing?" She crossed her arms. "Because you sure don't trust me."

"What's that supposed to mean?" She was right, but—

"I know she's not your niece, Petrosky."

The world stopped spinning. "She's helping me on a case."

"On a case." She scowled at him. "After that Howdie Doodie joker in the UP said she looked familiar, I looked up your cases, the highly publicized ones since he wouldn't have known about some random rape vic. Hannah Montgomery? Here? You know this isn't right. She's still listed as missing, and she obviously wasn't being held somewhere against her will since you just waltzed in wherever and picked her up. She ran. And hid. A girl that desperate has something to—"

"She isn't desperate, just scared. She's been through something horrible." He had to give Jackson some reason for his actions before she went digging around herself and found out Hannah was a murderer. Jackson would take Hannah away from him. *Morrison would have understood.* "She's the reason I know about Julie's killer."

"Say what now?"

"She called me." *Liar.* "Told me about Robin and her connection to Julie's case."

Jackson leaned so close he could smell the rancid coffee she'd had at the precinct. "I understand wanting to get justice for your child, but this girl would say anything to get you on her side, Petrosky. She disappeared. That's suspicious. Now she shows up and just happens to know who murdered your daughter?"

"But she does know, Jackson. She gave us this lead. It's going to help us find the—"

"You're a motherfucking detective." Jackson leveled a hard gaze at him. "Act like it." She walked past him and headed for the driver's side door, then glanced at him over her shoulder. "Anyone asks about this, I had no idea, you understand? I'll throw your ass under the bus."

"Shit hits the fan, I'll crawl under the bus myself, Jackson. You can count on that."

MEXICAN FOOD SETTLED Petrosky's lurching stomach as he pored through page after page of driver's license photos. His list of dentists had dwindled by the time dinner rolled around, but he had enough chips and salsa to stay sitting at his desk for a few more hours. By the time the sun set, he only had ten more names to check. Then none, just a list of thirty possibles, all the right age, the right physical features, the right coloring. *Goddammit.* He was ready to go out and punch every single one of them in the head when Jackson tossed a stack of papers on his desk. "Got him."

Petrosky grabbed the file, expecting to see a steely-eyed psycho staring back at him, but it was just another list. Dental conferences. He scanned the pages: Massachusetts, California, Texas, Nevada. Each attack had coincided with a conference, though it looked like they held conferences frequently enough. He'd probably be able to connect a dental conference or continuing education class to half the killings on his caseload.

"If we can get ahold of the conference organizers, find out who was registered…" She smiled. "Like I said…got him. Maybe, anyway."

Petrosky pushed the bag of chips toward her, and she pulled one from the top. "Watch the salt, Jackson."

"Screw off."

He almost smiled.

PETROSKY GRABBED MORE Mexican for Hannah on his way home. And that night, full of burritos and chips and something Hannah called baklava that she'd gotten from the bakery down the road, Petrosky again fell asleep listening to Hannah's breath. He almost wanted to ask her where she'd found the courage to leave the apartment to get the dessert. But he didn't really care.

He was just glad she had found it.

32

———————

THE KILLER REACHED for the cigarettes on the console and sucked in a delicious lungful of nicotine. Glorious. Just one more pleasure you could no longer enjoy. You had to cover it up. Chew gum. Use mouthwash like it was *shameful*. He watched the smoke drift from his lips as if he were watching his own lungs burning.

When the last of the smoke had dissipated, he donned his gloves, pressing the space between each finger to ensure the fit was correct. He straightened his glasses. Secured his tie. Every day, more of the same. Monotony.

He tapped his wrist. Buddy's hair was twisted into his bracelet now, a reminder of the amusement he'd felt as the animal's body finally gave out. His daughter had tried to be strong—oh, but that poor girl never made it more than a few minutes without a trembling lip. She was so predictable. She'd probably just cry if she found out what he did when she wasn't around; if she knew the interesting things that went on inside his head. But he would not test that theory by saying too much—he was not a man of risk. He didn't even take reminders from the women he killed.

But *this* was interesting.

He'd been following Petrosky since the detective had gotten back from Vermont, and today, the killer's lunches in the precinct parking lot had paid off. This morning, he'd seen Petrosky with his new partner and her child, a child who had been flailing about in front of the school. His own daughter was boring. But this kid of Jackson's…you could never know exactly what he'd do.

Fascinating. Maybe he would take the boy when mommy wasn't looking.

And she wasn't looking right now. Petrosky and Jackson were inside the precinct, searching for him, completely oblivious. How many times had they looked right at him and never suspected? How many times had Petrosky been an asshole to him, never considering what he was capable of?

Because Petrosky's daughter was the one time he'd made an exception to his rule about not taking souvenirs—her hair was wound in with that from his dogs. That was where she deserved to be, along with her bastard of a father. Maybe he'd kill Petrosky soon and add his hair to the bracelet. Petrosky wouldn't even think it strange if he approached. The detective might even smile.

He could take Petrosky's partner first, but that was boring. Predictable like the fact that he was late for dinner, predictable like the fact that his wife had probably made pot roast or some other watery shit in the Crock-Pot. Again.

He didn't like predictable. But sometimes it was prudent to predict, to plan.

They were searching for him. And he had too many unanswered questions to make this amusing. Who was the girl who'd come back from Vermont with Petrosky? A witness? It was an unusual development and not the enjoyable sort of unpredictability he experienced when stalking a victim, wondering whether she would fight, wondering at what point he'd need to cut her throat. This wasn't trying to guess what road she'd turn down so he could shroud himself in shadows and lie in wait. This was threatening—it felt like a risk, and risk got you into trouble. The last time he'd taken a real risk was with Julie.

He could go to Petrosky's apartment building, maybe, grab the girl himself. He wanted to know who she was. Why she was staying with him. Maybe she was just another of Petrosky's pet projects, one of his whores. She'd seemed so chagrined yesterday at the precinct, but he imagined she had a nice smile.

She'd give that smile to him. Then he'd watch the flames consume her. His zipper dug into him as heat burgeoned below his belt.

No…at Petrosky's apartment, someone might see him. Nor was he a fan of that dog she had with her—though if it ended up being docile, he'd take pleasure in bringing it home, and in a few months, adding its hair to his bracelet while his daughter cried about yet another animal she didn't really care about. He'd found it interesting the way Petrosky's guest talked to the dog, stroked its head with a reverence that suggested the animal was the most precious thing in the world to her. Such an intense adoration, far more profound than the lame scratches Layla bestowed upon their dogs. But if the animal wasn't as gentle as it seemed…

He'd have a much easier time at Jackson's house. Perhaps the boy would flail as he had in the parking lot. Hopefully, he'd do something unique as he died.

But even that wasn't terribly appealing. Killing the children of your enemies? Been there, done that, ten years before, very *Game of Thrones* and all, but…he needed something new. Exciting. *Interesting.*

Layla. He imagined her, his naïve and trusting little daughter, tears in her eyes, screaming through the flames, and a tingle ignited deep in his gut.

Not tonight, but it would happen, and soon. *When* would depend on Petrosky and Jackson. When would they figure out who he really was? And when they did, would they come for him at work? At home? Would they seek him out by warrant, squad cars flashing their lights up the road for his neighbors to gossip about? Maybe they'd come quietly in the night, no flashers just darkened shadows steeped in practiced suspicion. Would they send the FBI? That would be interesting, though he couldn't see Petrosky calling in the feds—as far as he could tell, the man had always hated them.

His latexed fingers squeaked as he gripped the steering wheel harder and sighed. He could almost taste the fat in the air, almost smell the acrid stink of blistering meat. He could almost hear them screaming.

But this time, he wouldn't be the only one to experience the salty reek of burning human flesh. They'd inhale the smoke from their own charring bodies, see their blackening skin give way to fat and muscle and tendon. Exposing them, and in their naked pain, letting them live once before they died, no longer wet blankets, but torches. There was no death like fire.

He inhaled deeply, the smoke in his lungs hot and caustic as scorched hair. He blew it out and watched the tendrils disappear into the breeze.

Fire to smoke, life to death.

Ashes to ashes.

Soon, they'd all go up in flames.

33

———————

The conference organizers were dicks. Maybe they didn't like being called at dinnertime. Maybe Petrosky didn't give a fuck, because the more irritated they sounded, the more he promised to hound them until he had every single name on their lists. Within two hours, he and Jackson were scouring the names of those registered for each event.

Half a dozen men matched two of the conferences. Five men matched three. But only one matched conferences in all four other states.

But this couldn't be right. They'd pulled males only and this person…wasn't that.

Eleanor Randolph wore a cross on a chain around her throat and had short brown hair with the sparest hint of white at her temples. The wrinkled but not yet sagging skin around her neck gave her a quiet, matronly look that kids probably loved; pediatric dentistry was her specialty according to her bio on one of the conference ads.

"What the hell is this?" Petrosky snapped.

"She's listed as male with the licensing board," Jackson said.

Had to be a mistake. Their victims had been raped, and while no DNA meant rape with an object was possible, Robin would surely have remembered that. Petrosky's heart felt like it was sighing the frustration straight into his bloodstream, each erratic thump in his chest moving anger from his gut and into his muscles, tightening every inch of his body. He threw the folder on the desk. "Goddammit."

"Wait, Petrosky." Jackson was still typing, every click of the keyboard driving a spike of pain into his head. "Here. This Eleanor woman…isn't…wasn't… Here, take a look."

Petrosky leaned over her shoulder and peered at the screen: name changes from the state of Michigan. Eleanor Randolph had been born…Earl Randolph? The sketch artist had done a shitty job, maybe, but in a dark alley… "Maybe she never got rid of the frank and beans." He stood. "Let's go ask her if she still has a cock."

"Hang on, hang on." Jackson scrolled through the information on the screen. "No, this isn't right. She changed her name here, and she's licensed here, which is why she's on our list. And she went to the conferences. But her practice isn't here any longer—she's based in Oregon now."

"Needed more than lopping off her dick to give her a fresh start?" But the words felt crass, even to him. It made sense that she'd need a new place to reinvent her practice, especially in pediatric dentistry. Parents were weird about that transgender shit, and it didn't matter that transgender folks were almost always the victims of abuse, rather than the perpetrators. People didn't like pesky facts ruining their stereotypes, and the stigma would have been a lot to bear.

Jackson's fingers clacked against the keyboard. "The dates in question in Michigan… She was a keynote at these conferences, which is why she attended them all, but there was no way she traveled here for all the Michigan killings." She stopped typing and sat back in her chair. "Possibly the very earliest two because she lived here then. But before the third murder, she'd already opened her practice in Portland, and last week, when someone was murdering our latest vic"—she gestured to the screen—"she was in Oregon speaking at a conference there."

It's not her. Petrosky massaged the center of his chest, the nodule of his pacemaker harder than before, or maybe his heart was finally turning to stone. Their most promising lead had been nothing but a wild goose chase. "What if we… There has to be another explanation." Something had triggered Robin at the dentist. The gloves? Latex had a distinct smell, and that would widen their suspect pool. He sighed. "I just figured it was the fluoride that made Robin freak because it's so strong." *No, you didn't—Hannah thought that.* And he'd believed it. He had wanted to believe Hannah so badly that he'd wasted days trying to track down a tooth jockey when he should have been searching for other leads. Not that he knew where else to start.

"Let's assume that the dentist thing was incorrect."

"Well, no shit."

"Petrosky, it still could be a dentist. Not like the conference schedule is the be all end all of murderous dentist identification." She tapped her fingers against his desk. "But let's say, for the sake of argument, it's not the fluoride. And let's say it's not the lights or the tools or the latex, because, with her surgeries, she would have been exposed to things like that a hell of a lot over the years." She narrowed her eyes. "What were they doing to her?"

"What?"

"At the dentist."

"I…" He wasn't sure. "Routine checkup? Couple of fillings, maybe?"

"What do they use for that? For the fillings?"

Petrosky grabbed his cell and dialed his home number.

He'd thought Hannah would be happy, finding out that her lead was moving them forward in their case—that she'd helped. But her voice was strained like she had hoped he was calling for something else, and it cut him to the quick. How many times had he called home and told Julie to put her mother on instead of asking her about her day?

Tonight…he'd go home and tell Hannah all about it. They'd eat dinner. He'd say it was all going to be fine now that the world was a safer place for women everywhere—a safer place for her. Then he would set her up an appointment with Dr. McCallum. Petrosky could keep her out of jail for killing Harwick—it was self-defense. And if Charles wanted to go to jail for her husband's murder, who was he to stop her? One day he'd figure out a way to make it right.

"Are you there?" Hannah asked.

"I'm here." He glanced at Jackson, who was examining him like she thought he might be ready to lose his mind. "I need to talk to Robin."

A FEW EMAILS and faxes later, and they had permission to access Robin's medical records. Turned out, they had done a root canal treatment the day she'd visited along with fluoride treatments and x-rays. The dentist's secretary was unable to tell them what chemicals might have been used in the process, but the office would fax it over. And then they'd… Maybe he'd call Scott, see what he knew about the chemicals, whether other professions used something similar in their work. The kid knew his shit, and Petrosky really didn't feel like dealing with their techs. Plus, it was probably only fair to throw Scott a bone after what had happened in Vermont. He'd been a real dick, especially since the kid was actually useful—he'd seen connections other people had missed.

Maybe he should pick Scott's brain about Julie's case—would the rookie notice some subtle difference and connect dots that would actually lead them to a break? But Petrosky already knew Julie's case was different. Hannah's was too.

The *Looking Glass* killer had tortured his victims, then murdered them in very short order. Hannah was an anomaly —Harwick had groomed her, for months, in his own home. And though Petrosky did his best to silence the thought each time it arose, Julie's case was an anomaly, too. McCallum had tried to protect him, claiming that the burns were "inconclusive," but Petrosky knew the truth because Thompson had told him. Julie had burned before death—and that was a deviation from pattern.

Anomalies didn't just happen, not with these killers, not without very good reason. Here, the pattern of rape and murder was so specific that to deviate at all was suspicious. So why was Julie different for this killer? Why would he want her to suffer more than his other victims? Was it because she was his first?

As Jackson headed for the stairwell, Petrosky opened his drawer and stared at his daughter's picture, letting it sear into his brain, hoping that this photo would steel him against what he knew had to come.

No matter what else Julie's case was, it was a clue.

HE COULDN'T DO IT. All this time and he still couldn't do it.

But he had no choice. The files were heavy in his arms as he made his way to the conference room.

Empty, thank sweet baby Jay-sus. He set Julie's file at the head of the table and laid out the others. One after another. So many girls, reduced to reports and crime scene photos and hidden in shitty manila folders.

He had Jackson's notes and his own, two pads filled with

scribbles about possible connections. Similarities. Differences. But only one case was inconclusive. Only one was different. Only one was his baby girl.

Jackson had noted no inconsistencies, no glaring anomalies, but they had to be there. Or perhaps he only wanted there to be something to find. Maybe he wanted his daughter to be special, even in death. But that was bullshit. He could feel it like maggots writhing in his gut, trying to eat their way out. There was something in this file, something he wasn't supposed to see. Julie *was* special.

He sat at the head of the table. Stared at the folder.

Opened it.

He could almost smell Julie's blood from the corner of the photos that peeked behind white and yellow papers. He started with the notes about the scene. Dog hair, paw prints, isolated location in a field behind a building, blocked from the roads on either side. Similar to the other cases in that there was protection from prying eyes. Below the specifics on location, Jackson had written: *Likely that perp knows the Ash Park/Michigan area better than others, as out-of-state locations were more clearly abandoned.*

True enough, but not a novel deduction. The UP vic had been attacked in the woods. California, another state park. Texas had been a movie theater, but the isolated nature of the building was common knowledge; Jackson had paper-clipped a photo of the theater taken from a website called "Houston's Abandoned Places." In Boston, Robin had been snatched off the street, on a road where almost all the homes were in various stages of demolition, ensuring there were no residents to see. And it had happened on a Sunday when no workers would be present to witness the brutality.

But in the Michigan cases, the locations were not as clearly abandoned—someone who didn't know the area would've had to spend a great deal of time on research. Julie's body was left in a field behind a recently closed plant, a place that showed no signs of decay at the time of her death. The other bodies were found in similar locations: a children's park, not abandoned but quiet, on a dead-end street where anyone could have happened by. The only reason teenagers avoided that particular park was the increased police presence, though patrols rarely ran down there after eight o'clock. Residents might know that. Or...those who did the patrols.

But he doubted the killer was a cop. Cops didn't travel for work, and not a one of them could take off a couple times a year to travel unless he was independently wealthy. And the soft hands...no way one of his brothers in blue was going home to do paraffin wax hand dips. Except maybe Decantor.

Petrosky turned the page. Lots of technical bullshit, the sizes of the paw prints, fruitless interviews with those nearby, nothing of relevance now. Then came the photos of Julie in life, and his heart seized. Her dark hair cascaded over her tie-dyed T-shirt, the pink and orange and purple not nearly as bright as her smile. His wife had told her she needed to put on a dress for school picture day instead of that shirt, but it was Julie's favorite. She'd worn that same shirt the day Petrosky had found a snake by the garage and gone to chop its fool head off. Julie had cried, begging him not to kill it, and he'd finally scooped it up and hurled it over the fence, though he still didn't know why murdering a snake by launching it through space was any better than smashing it. He traced his finger down the picture, over Julie's cheek. Petrosky had shoved the T-shirt into her backpack when she'd gone to change—he'd rather have had a picture of Julie smiling in her tie-dye than scowling in a dress.

Maybe he had done it to spite his wife, too. Maybe he had been an asshole long before Julie died.

But that mattered little now because when he looked up, he could see Julie at the other end of the conference table, tie-dyed shirt electric against the white walls, her grin radiant like someone had brushed it onto her face with sunshine. He blinked, and she was gone, but he could still feel her, her presence living in his gut, aching with the dull pain of helpless sorrow. *I'm so sorry, honey.*

He set her photo aside as if it were a thin sheet of glass, one wrong move, and it'd shatter into a thousand pieces along with his heart. The reports. On the body. On *her* body.

Much of the report was technical, so he scanned it with the practiced eye of one who's seen it all before, trying to pretend it was just another case. Trying to ignore the slithering sensation in his belly.

Severed jugular, bled out in minutes. *At least it was quick.* But he had to choke back the bile before he turned the page.

Antemortem—before death—tearing in the vaginal region. She'd been alive when her killer had raped her. But she'd not made a sound, because the killer had covered her mouth—antemortem bruising around her lips. There were also tears in her vagina that had occurred after death, so he'd probably put a hand over her mouth and slit her throat while he raped her, or slit her throat first and then raped her as she bled out. Or he'd raped her twice, once before she died, once after. Either way, her murderer's face was the last thing his daughter had seen.

Petrosky would make sure his own face was the last thing Julie's killer saw.

He read on, feeling Julie's breath on his neck, panting with him, as if she too were frightened about what was coming. The iron tang in the air gave way to char and to the acrid stench of burning flesh as he read about the lighter fluid, the accelerant that the killer had spread over the skin of her pelvis. That he'd put inside her. Then...the fire. Petrosky scanned for descriptions of the burns. Had Julie been hanging on, gritting her teeth, trying to pretend she was dead, as Robin had? And if she had been alive as Robin was...

that meant Petrosky hadn't gotten to her fast enough. He'd let her suffer.

And there it was. But instead of the word "inconclusive" as McCallum had told him, "antemortem burns" stared back at him, the words themselves glaring and sharp. Confirmation. He'd known, somewhere inside him that it was true, but he hadn't realized just how badly he'd wanted to be wrong until his breath caught, and he had to stifle a sob. She'd been burned before death. The pain would have been unbearable. Either McCallum was a liar, or he'd misunderstood. Only Thompson had told him the truth.

Petrosky scanned the rest of the report but paused at the signatures on the bottom. Brian Thompson was listed first. Then... That couldn't be right.

Alfred Woolverton? Thompson had taken care of this case, Petrosky knew that for a fact. But here... Woolverton had consulted? That rat bastard wouldn't sugarcoat anything to protect Petrosky's feelings. So why would Woolverton tell McCallum something different from what was in the case file? What the hell was happening here? He couldn't trust any of them. Everyone here had some agenda he wasn't seeing.

Petrosky needed fresh eyes.

He yanked out his cell and punched in Scott's number. The kid answered on the first ring.

"Hey, Scott, you got a few days to come down to Ash Park?"

"Well..."

"Scott, I need you."

"I have my father, he's ill and—"

"Bring him."

Scott paused, and for a moment, Petrosky thought he'd refuse. "I'll get someone to help here," Scott said finally. "I'll leave today." The kid was eager—maybe he was taking advantage. But it didn't matter, nothing mattered except the file in front of him. "You find something else on the Theodore Montgomery case?" Scott asked.

Fuck Theodore Montgomery. "I..." Heat bloomed in Petrosky's chest, the pain so white-hot he was half-certain he'd look down and see his own skin blistering. "This isn't about Montgomery. I need you..." He sucked in a breath, the air stabbing at his shuddering lungs. "I need you to dig up my daughter."

34

———

"No one's going to give you an exhumation order, Petrosky."

"This isn't some *Pet Sematary* style bullshit, Carroll. I just want a second opinion."

"You're not getting one. You have absolutely no evidence that the tests were done incorrectly." The chief planted her palms on the desk and pushed herself to standing. "I had hoped that Jackson's presence would be good for you, pull you back from the brink a little bit." She shook her head. "You're obviously going to seek the edge no matter what I do."

"This has nothing to do with—"

"Find another way to confirm your suspicions. You are not going to dig up your child. Because, *Pet Sematary* or not, you're trying like hell to bring your daughter back from the dead, and it's not happening on my watch. You've got another day, and you're off this case. I'll need that long to find a replacement."

"You can't take this case from—"

"I can, and I did. You're too close to this one. You had to know you'd lose it the moment I found out you were on it."

"But—"

"We're done here."

Petrosky stalked from the chief's office, his chest on fire. He'd been so hell-bent on finding out what lay beneath the lid of Julie's coffin that he hadn't considered Carroll yanking the case away from him completely. Now Scott would be here in a matter of hours, and he had nothing to give the kid.

Jackson intercepted him, shoving a file against his chest. "Where've you been?"

"Chief's office."

She cocked an eyebrow. "Looks like it went splendidly. There's food on your desk. And this"—she gestured to the folder—"is from Robin's dentist."

He collapsed into his chair with Jackson beside him and flipped the folder open. Maybe he'd feel better if he threw it across the room.

Jackson gestured to a few lines on the top sheet. "Most of these chemicals aren't relevant. But this one might be." She jabbed at one word near the bottom.

Formaldehyde?

"It's not as bad as it sounds—formaldehyde is present naturally in the body, and they apparently use it in root canals to clean out the hole before they fill it. It's one of those weird scents that hang around every dentist's office." She shrugged. "I wasn't sold that Robin could have picked up on it so strongly that she'd have a flashback during her dental work, but your friend McCallum said it's possible."

McCallum, huh? He rubbed at his chest. "Maybe our killer fancies himself a taxidermist. Got that dog hair bracelet and all."

"Maybe," Jackson said, but her frown told him she wasn't convinced. Formaldehyde was used in any number of professions. Dentists. Doctors. Embalmers. Funeral home directors. Or were they dealing with someone like…

He pulled out the composite. *Alfred Woolverton.* Their on-again-off-again medical examiner who'd somehow managed to report Petrosky to Chief Carroll during five of their oh-so-brief interactions. Rounder than the composite sketch, jaw too wide, but he had the glasses. And the fine lines around his eyes. Thin mouth. When Petrosky squinted, he could almost see Woolverton staring back at him from Robin's sketch of her attacker.

And if it was Woolverton…that was why he'd tortured Julie more than the other victims. Because he hated Petrosky. The air thinned.

This is all my fault.

"Petrosky?"

"Hang on." He slid the computer closer, hurriedly calling up lists of conferences for medical examiners, trying to ignore the walls as they tightened around him. But classes could have been held anywhere, and California and Texas boasted no conferences near the killings the week before or after the murders.

And Woolverton could have gone out of town for any reason at all. Petrosky sure as shit wasn't going back to Chief Carroll for the ME's attendance records.

He slapped the folder shut and stood. "I'm going to talk to the ME. See if he has some insight." He ignored Jackson's narrowed eyes and headed for the stairs, trigger finger itching to blast Woolverton into oblivion.

Dr. Woolverton's beady eyes radiated hatred. "I told the chief to send someone else."

You killed my daughter. No wonder the bastard didn't want to deal with him. "I'm not here about this, Woolverton." Petrosky gestured to the corpse on the table: large man, gray skin, gunshot wound to the chest. Nothing like the savagery he'd seen in Julie's file. *Antemortem burns.* His stomach heaved.

Woolverton's nostrils flared. "What do you want, Detective? I have things to do." He turned his hand palm up and swept it over the body on the slab like this poor dead guy was some kind of magic trick.

And maybe he was. Maybe Woolverton had killed him too. But no, that wasn't his MO. Shooting someone in the heart was closer to Petrosky's—and he'd make that shit work for him today.

Just give me a reason. Just tell me you did it. The file under his arm was practically alive. "You know why I'm here." *You prick.*

Woolverton crossed his arms. "Because you want to harass me?"

"Because you know more about a case I'm working on than you care to admit."

"Like I have time to keep up on everyone else's cases."

"Why don't you tell me about Camille Urban."

"Who?" Woolverton dropped his arms again.

"The girl who died last week in the UP," Petrosky said. "The girl someone burned to remove trace evidence." He stepped closer to the table, to Woolverton, dropping his voice. "You know about Camille Urban." He put his hand on the metal. "You were there when Jackson and Thompson were discussing her case, weren't you?"

Woolverton scoffed. "I can hardly be expected to recall the name of every person I consult on."

"Why would anyone consult—"

"I consult all the time. Unlike you, other people actually care what I have to say." He stood straighter. He might as well have dusted off his shoulders. Little prickly bastard, trying to make up for all the wrongs done to him. Just like half these cowardly rapist fucks he saw every goddamn day, getting their rocks off by hurting someone smaller. By reducing those around them to nothing because it was the only way they could feel superior. It was always about power.

"Bet that makes you feel pretty special."

"Special has nothing to do with it." Woolverton glared. "I happen to be very good at my job."

"Then why couldn't you tell Julie's body was burned before she died?" As soon as the words left his lips, the air in the room dropped ten degrees. Petrosky might have been encrusted in ice for the chill that shuddered over his skin.

Woolverton did not appear cold—his cheeks reddened, his eyes blazing fire. "Is this why you've always hated me? You thought *I* was the one who fucked up her case?"

"Fucked up her case?"

"Well, I mean…you never found the killer, right?"

"What makes you say that, Woolverton?"

Woolverton balked. "Everyone knows. It's hardly a secret."

Keep him talking. Let him slip up. Then Petrosky could shoot him in the face and stuff him in a metal drawer, hidden away forever like all the women he'd murdered. *You sorry sonofabitch.* "Know anything about taxidermy?"

Woolverton stepped back, face less pink and more maroon as the blood pumped into his cheeks. "What?"

"Taxidermy." He peered at Woolverton's wrist, knowing the asshole wouldn't wear a dog hair bracelet to work, but hoping he'd be dumb enough anyway. He was dumb enough to sign his name on the forms, dumb enough to act like a jackass—he hadn't even tried to conceal his contempt for Petrosky. "You have a dog, Woolverton?"

"I… No."

"Not anymore?"

"Listen, I don't know what the hell you're talking about, but I don't have time for your stupid games."

Petrosky's knuckles were white on the edge of the table as he leaned over the body toward the doctor. "Stupid games?"

His voice ricocheted off the metal drawers. "Someone killed my daughter, Woolverton. And I'm trying to figure out why you'd manipulate evidence."

"I never manipulated—"

"You told Dr. McCallum that the tests on Julie's body were inconclusive."

Woolverton nodded, and his shoulders actually relaxed, that psycho prick. "Yes, I did."

"But they aren't inconclusive in the file: it very clearly says that the burns were antemortem. And you signed off on that. Do you often sign off on things without reading them?"

"I did no such thing," he spat back. "I'm not a hack, no matter what you may think."

Petrosky pulled the folder from under his arm and removed the form he'd left on top. "Care to explain this?"

Woolverton glanced at it, and his eyes widened. "I…I mean, it was a long time ago, but I remember signing off on this one."

"Why?" *Because Julie was different?*

"Because it was you."

Because you were her killer. He reached for the gun at his back, the metal cool on his fingertips.

"Listen, this was one of the very first cases the department ever consulted me on, and it was a cop's kid." He paused long enough to suck in a breath as if preparing to launch into a tirade. *Bring it, fucker.* "And I knew about you, okay? We'd met a few times, and you had a reputation as being a bit of a…"

"Prick."

"I was going to say 'bully.'" Woolverton glanced at the body on the slab, then back up at Petrosky as if worried he'd attack. "I know where you're going with this, but no matter how much I may despise you, I wouldn't alter your child's file just to get back at you."

"I'm not worried about you altering the case file. I'm

worried about you fucking with my daughter." Petrosky thumbed the safety off the weapon but kept it hidden in the holster. *I've got you now, asshole, just admit it.* "I hear you're all over these cases. That you're asking questions. That you barged into Thompson's office while my partner was there the other day and stuck around while they were going over the specifics. Why are you so interested? So concerned? Think we're onto you?"

"I'm... No. I was there on something else. And later, Thompson asked for a professional opinion about Urban because he knew I'd worked on some of the other victims. I gave it to him." He shrugged but kept wary eyes on Petrosky. "Happens all the time."

"And why would he ask you about the Camille Urban case? That wasn't one of—"

"Said the original ME was having a hard time with it."

Petrosky's gun hand twitched. Smith hadn't needed a consult. Smith had examined the body and given them the answers they needed. Even if the UP doc did have a question, he wasn't going to call down to some piddly part of Detroit for an answer.

"What exactly did Thompson ask you, Woolverton?"

"He asked if I thought Urban was dead before she was...lit on fire." He looked at the ceiling and back at Petrosky. Anxious, but not in the agitated way of a criminal about to get caught. Worried. About something he'd said or something he hadn't?

Petrosky released his gun. "Spit it out, Woolverton."

"Thompson knew the answer already." The doctor sighed. "Any competent medical examiner would have known right away."

"Don't the burns make it harder to tell?"

"Not if you test the skin. There's a multitude of ways to figure that out. Just like there were in Julie's case."

But Julie's case had been different. Different because she'd been burned first. "You told McCallum that Julie's burns were inconclusive. If things were inconclusive, surely you could have rerun the tests if there are so many ways to tell." He'd catch this bastard in a lie, and the doctor would have no choice but to confess.

"I offered to rerun them, but Thompson got irritated that I wanted to check his work. And like I said, I was the new guy, so I did what I could and bowed out gracefully. I took a few extra photos, though." He flipped through the file. "They aren't here, but I keep a copy of all my consultations."

Woolverton headed to the far side of the morgue, where a steel door admitted him into an office. For a moment, Petrosky thought the man might try to run, but he reappeared carrying a thin manila folder, his shoulders square.

"Here's what I have. You can't keep it," he amended when Petrosky reached for the file. "I'm not letting my photos disappear, just in case you decide to keep accusing me of things that are utterly ridiculous." He passed the folder over the table, reluctantly, and Petrosky took it just as tentatively and flipped it open before he could consider what was inside.

Petrosky looked. Saw the mutilated flesh that had once been his daughter's thigh, the ruined skin of her belly. Yellowed patches that might have been flesh or fat. *Oh god.* He coughed, tried not to retch. At least it wasn't her face, but...

"You don't know what you're looking at."

"I'm looking at my daughter's—"

"You're looking at dead skin. Skin that was burned after the heart stopped pumping. Thompson didn't agree, so I told McCallum it was inconclusive, though, in my professional opinion, it doesn't get any clearer than this. If the burns occurred before death, there would be lines or redness, blistering, inflammation, increases in enzyme reactions, any number of things. After death, the vesicles are empty, just air —no inflammation markers like mast cells." He pointed to the file. "I'm not sure what Thompson was fighting so hard for, but he was convinced she was burned prior to death. I'd like to say that he rushed it, or that he was having some emotional issues because he knew you, but even then, the fact that she burned after death should have been of some comfort."

Thompson was a lot of things, but sloppy was not one of them. Petrosky looked into Woolverton's eyes—steely, but they'd lost their hateful edge.

Was this a trick? Was it possible that Julie hadn't suffered the burns before she died? Or did he just want to believe that? But looking at the photographic evidence…Woolverton had done it correctly. The burns had occurred postmortem. He had spent years forcing the images from his brain, images of his baby girl writhing in agony, her skin blistering beneath a blanket of flame. And those images…had been wrong. She'd died, but not like that.

How had Thompson screwed up that badly? Could Petrosky have misunderstood? But no, the weeks before and after Julie's death stood out in stark contrast to the rest of his life, like he'd recorded every moment of his loss on a video that had been playing on a continuous loop ever since. Even without the file, he knew exactly what Thompson had said: that Julie had been burned alive. He hadn't misheard shit. But Thompson had been wrong.

Julie's case wasn't special. Julie's body…

Was the same as the others. And Thompson should have known.

Thompson did know. And there was only one reason for lying about this: to make Petrosky suffer. Because Thompson hated him? Petrosky was a dick, and Thompson had been brusque at times, but they were as close to friendly as it got around here.

Petrosky's heart was trying to hammer its way through his breastbone. This killer had a pattern that meant something to him, an MO he fantasized about—he hadn't once deviated in his brutality, not even with Julie. But though Julie had not been burned alive, Thompson had made sure Petrosky suffered like she had.

Thompson had never tolerated Petrosky at all. Thompson had smiled to his face and punished Petrosky in the most horrible way he could—by killing his little girl.

The fury rolled over him like a wave of molten glass, so hot and sharp that his breath caught. Thompson probably jacked off to it every night, to the sounds of those women, of their last breaths gurgling through their severed throats. Thompson probably closed his eyes and came in his tube socks while memories of fire flashed in his brain, the smell of his victims' burning skin still lingering in his nostrils. Thompson surely remembered raping Julie as the dirt beneath them soaked up her blood.

And Thompson had been digging for information, bringing up the UP case to Jackson. He probably wanted to know how much they'd figured out. Or maybe Thompson wanted to relive his cruelty.

"Detective?" Woolverton's mouth had softened, eyes narrowed in worry.

Petrosky couldn't breathe, couldn't move, could only stare at Woolverton as if looking through a tunnel.

He'd been ready to shoot Woolverton in the temple—and he'd been wrong. Petrosky inhaled deeply and the heat receded from his chest, though his gut stayed tight. What was he even thinking? Brian Thompson? A hunch was one thing, but when he found the fucker who'd killed Julie… He didn't want to kill the wrong man. He'd never get justice for his daughter if he was locked away—or if he was dead. Petrosky needed verification. He needed proof, or something close to it. Motive was bullshit in cases like this, but opportunity… that he could find.

"Thompson around today?" But of course Woolverton

wouldn't know—the men worked at different hospitals. *Think, asshole.* Petrosky wasn't going to the chief; she'd call Internal Affairs, and Carroll had already told him to stay away from this.

"No idea," Woolverton said.

But there was one chatty bastard who always had the goods on J-Lo and Gwen Stefani and everyone else. Decantor wouldn't know Thompson's schedule for Julie's murder—he wasn't around back then—but he'd know whether Thompson was here when Camille Urban was killed. Decantor consulted Thompson every couple days about his own homicide cases.

Petrosky headed for the door.

"Detective!"

Petrosky whirled around, and Woolverton gestured impatiently at the file under Petrosky's arm. Petrosky walked back to the table, handed it to Woolverton, and met his eyes. Somewhere deep behind the defensive iciness in Woolverton's gaze, he just looked sorry.

———

DECANTOR RAISED AN EYEBROW, probably wondering why Petrosky was approaching his desk after months of hostility. Maybe Petrosky should have brought flowers or some shit, but Decantor was the reason he'd been alive to suffer these past six months. Yet his anger at that slight seemed to be simmering on some back burner now—subdued, dimmed by the fury over Julie that was threatening to explode from his chest and engulf the world in flames.

"Petrosky." The big man nodded. "How are things? You talk to Shan—"

"Working on a case. Trying to find Thompson."

"He's out. Why don't you call Woolverton?"

"I'd rather find Thompson."

"Of course you would." Decantor shook his head. "I never did see how that guy puts up with you."

"He's a medical examiner, Decantor. You know those guys aren't right."

Decantor's laugh was the most obscene thing he'd ever heard. "Fair enough, Petrosky." His smile faltered. "Listen, are you going to go to Atlanta? I know Shannon's really hoping—"

"You trying to piss me off, or are you trying to get rid of me?"

"Both?" Decantor shrugged, nonchalant, and the action was so much like Morrison's surfer-boy shrug that Petrosky's rib cage shrank three sizes, squeezed his heart painfully, and then released. He stared at Decantor without speaking, half because he was trying to be intimidating and half because he didn't trust his voice.

Finally, Decantor sighed. "I had to drive all the way out to see Woolverton on a case earlier because Thompson took the day off."

"What about last week?"

"I had to go see Woolverton then too because Thompson was out. Some travel-team soccer thing."

Soccer? Thompson had a kid? Was he married? The fact that he had no idea suddenly felt significant.

"Last time this happened, I told Thompson he should sign his kid up for hockey instead, but he didn't look amused."

"You're not very funny."

Decantor laughed again, and Petrosky resisted the urge to punch his bitch ass in the face. How could Decantor not see the bombshell he had just dropped? *Atlanta. Hockey. Soccer tournaments.* Petrosky's thoughts were racing a million miles a second. Thompson had been with his kid, watching soccer games by day and going out at night and…

Woolverton had been here while Camille Urban was being murdered. But Thompson hadn't. Thompson spent all day in the morgue, relishing the cold flesh of dead bodies. Then he went out at night to light living people on fire.

And Jackson had talked to Thompson this week—he knew they were looking into these cases again. Knew they were coming for him.

And that fucker wouldn't go down without a fight.

35

According to his license, Brian Thompson lived in Farmington Hills. *Hoity-toity bastard.* No legal problems, save one complaint filed against him for some insurance issue, but the charges had been dropped when he'd paid a fine. Married. One daughter, Layla. Petrosky couldn't keep his family together, couldn't keep his daughter alive, but this stone-cold murdering fuck could?

"Think they're in trouble?" Jackson asked.

"Let's hope he kept his crazy outside the house." But Petrosky knew better. And from the worry lines on her forehead, his partner did, too.

"Fucking white boys," she muttered.

Petrosky flinched, but he couldn't disagree—statistics, and the composite, didn't lie. Yet they still didn't know for certain that *this* was their white boy. They could haul Thompson in for questioning, but with no DNA evidence to hold him, all they had was a lot of circumstantial bullshit. Robin had already told them she wasn't going to testify, and she hadn't identified her attacker as reeking of formaldehyde either; she'd just had a panic attack at the dentist. They might be able to secure a warrant, but while they were screwing around with paperwork, Thompson could get wind of it and take off. Not like he was going to stick around here just to make another bracelet—he'd already proven that he could kill anywhere.

Petrosky had lost him before, or he might as well have—he had overlooked evidence right in front of his nose while more women lost their lives. Petrosky had spoken to him, smiled at him, while Julie had been in the ground. Every night, Petrosky had wanted to die while this asshole went on living like nothing had ever happened.

But, again...*if it was him.* The gun at his back was cold and hard, and it practically called to him: *Just shoot the fucker.* Maybe he'd haul off and blow Thompson away before he even opened his mouth to deny his crimes. He was almost certain Thompson was the killer—but he'd thought Woolverton guilty, too.

How to be sure? Thompson'd had opportunity, at least, and some shady dealings with the case files—that much they knew. And Robin might be able to confirm Thompson's identity even if she wasn't willing to travel to Ash Park. He'd contact Hannah to get Robin online for him and go from there. It might not stand up in court, but sometimes the court of public opinion—of a father's opinion—was all that mattered.

Julie's ghost was heavy at his back, breathing down his neck, infusing every cell in his body with the restless, purposeful energy he used to feel while on the job. An energy he hadn't felt in nearly a decade. He was a motherfucking detective, and he was her daddy.

He was back. He was alive. He was furious. And tonight, he was going to make Julie proud.

CONFIRMATION. Robin was certain.

This man had destroyed his entire life. This man had taken his only child.

Thompson was going to die.

Thompson's street was already washed in dusk, the disappearing sun stealing daylight from the horizon and blanketing the spacious backyards in a fuzzy haze, enveloping swing sets and fire pits and gazebos. Jackson parked her Escalade in the drive, and for once, her pretentious car was oddly perfect—every house on the block either had, or was about to have, a Hummer or an Escalade or a Suburban parked in the driveway as mothers and fathers returned from work.

Thompson's Tudor-style home had a pair of stone lions standing sentinel on either side of the front steps, and windows flanking a heavy wooden front door. A section of the upstairs jutted out to cover the porch, the roof angling sharply away on either side. Inside, the house was as black as Thompson's goddamned soul. And those lions. Petrosky would have liked to believe the guy was a football fan, but he suspected that Thompson fancied himself a lion of sorts: a king and a predator, a beast to be both feared and respected. It fit with the way he'd so brazenly attacked his victims, stalking them through the streets, biding his time, then striking, his blade as effective as any lion's bite. *Jesus.*

He was focusing on lions. Because every single cell in his body was alight with the knowledge that he was about to confront a man he'd trusted, a man he'd worked with for the better part of a decade. A man who had taken the most vital piece of Petrosky's soul and torn her into a million pieces while smiling to his face. As he rang the bell, Petrosky could almost see Julie's dark hair in his peripheral vision, swirling around her head as she spun until she was giggling and dizzy and happy. Had she been happy back then, at the park, in the backyard? He'd like to think it was so, but now the feeling of joy was so foreign to him that he might not recognize it if it bit him in the ass. But purpose…purpose he had in spades.

Petrosky dropped the door knocker—heavy, brass—and the sound rumbled through his marrow, a shuddering reminder that he was human, that he could falter, that any mistake he made here would impact him until the day they buried him. Perhaps he'd catch this guy and implode. Maybe his heart would finally stop beating once he'd taken Thompson's life—with the searing heat stabbing through his chest, he didn't doubt that death was possible. But later. It would be ironic to find Julie's killer and have a heart attack before murdering the bastard himself.

The thought of doing to Thompson what the fucker had done to Julie—the slicing, the burning—swelled Petrosky's chest with such an odd mix of fury and righteous indignation and almost pleasure that he knew…

I'll kill him. And he'd love every moment of it. Thompson wasn't going to make it to jail. Petrosky peeked through the darkened windows—saw only black. No sound came from inside the house. He should break in through the back door, wait for Thompson at his own dining room table.

But something wasn't right. The hairs on the back of his neck tingled, every nerve alight with a wary, primal energy like Petrosky could sense the death that waited somewhere in the shadows, crouched and ready to spring.

"Petrosky."

He turned to the lawn.

Jackson was halfway down the steps already. "Let's go." He stared at her for a beat—he'd nearly forgotten she was there. "If he sees us when he pulls up, he'll keep driving, and we're screwed."

But the tingle at the nape of his neck would not relent. Petrosky raised his fist and pounded on the door, every beat reverberating through his palm, past his elbow, into his shoulder until his chest ached. Still no answering sound from within.

"Come on, Petrosky. Trust me."

Reluctantly, he returned with Jackson to her pretentious car, and she drove farther down the street, tucking the vehicle under the bough of a tree near the intersection where it might be seen but wouldn't seem out of place. Unless Thompson was looking for it—would he know what to look for?

He glanced in the back seat at some kind of harness, probably for the boy he'd seen at the school. Trust? His ass. He really didn't know anything about her. Maybe she'd protect Thompson, or just let that murdering bastard hang out in jail with his chalky skin and his watery eyes. Let him go on playing chess and eating free food and *living* when Julie was dead.

He rummaged in his pocket for a smoke, but the fabric was too tight to open the pack—he dropped his cell into the console and finally freed a cigarette. "Do you need to get home, Jackson? I'll just take a walk around, and you can go take care of—"

"Like I'd be fool enough to leave you here, Petrosky." She snatched the cigarette from his hand and tossed it out the window. "We're not supposed to be here at all."

Oh shit. She knew about the chief reassigning the case. And yet...she'd come. But he glowered at her across the fuzzy dark inside the car. "All the more reason for you to head home."

"I'm not leaving you here so you can break into his house and screw up our case." She frowned again at his pack of smokes, and he shoved them back into his pocket.

"Nothing is going to screw up our—"

"Can it, would you?" The panes of her face were suddenly illuminated in stark white shapes, crossing from right to left like she'd stuck her head in a copy machine instead of sitting on it like any respectable person. Petrosky turned to see headlights streaking up the road, cutting a path of light from end to end with beams like lasers. Petrosky tensed, hand on his gun, waiting for Thompson to stop, to get out of the car —he'd run that fucker down and put a bullet in his nuts, and then… *Goddammit.* The car passed Thompson's house, the next driveway, and then Jackson's car, and then he could only see taillights in the rearview as it retreated into the night behind them.

Not Thompson. But the red stayed, reflected in the glass of the windshield even as the last vestiges of the passing car vanished around the corner. What the hell?

That's not a reflection.

Petrosky drew his focus back to the house. Through the upstairs window—black and dead a few moments before— shimmered the tiniest hint of orange. Glittering. Flickering. *Flames.*

Petrosky pictured the charred skin of Thompson's victims. Pictured Thompson's little girl in her soccer jersey. And as he and Jackson tore their car doors open, he could feel it, the prickling pain, intense and all-consuming, spreading through every nerve as surely as if someone had already taken a match to his skin.

Thompson had planned for this. Like Julie's, Petrosky's world would end in fire.

36

———

THERE HE IS. Thompson was only a silhouette from here, a thin, unassuming fraction of a man, peering down from the window above the door, haloed by firelight. But the mere sight of him emerging from the ashes like a psychotic phoenix, alive when Julie was dead, smug with omnipotence... *She's dead, you killed her, and you will pay for it with your fucking balls.*

The lower windows glowed as orange as the upper ones by the time Petrosky set foot on the front lawn. Perhaps Thompson had drawn a trail of lighter fluid from the upper floors and down the stairs to the living room and kitchen, then engaged it with a single match. But with the way the upper floors glowed so much hotter, Petrosky knew Thompson had reverently set the fire in each individual room, as meticulous and controlled as the fires he'd set in the flesh of innocent women.

He had surely seen Petrosky running up the road—and he'd be waiting. Petrosky ran to the window beside the door. Inside, the house had an open floor plan: living room in front, kitchen behind, dining room to the left, the flames there already licking at the table and walls, teasing and lascivious, like a vampire getting ready to devour a victim's flesh. The rugs were already engulfed. Thompson had definitely used an accelerant. But—

In the middle of the blaze lay a woman, facedown on the floor, already blanketed in flames, her body unmoving as if she herself were a pile of kindling. By the light of the fire, he could tell the dark halo surrounding her head was not oil or charred fluids, but the crimson tide of blood from a severed jugular. Even under pressure, Thompson was a creature of habit.

But this time, Thompson had not disappeared. The medical examiner stood behind the downed woman on a patch of wood floor just outside the range of the burning rug. He was smoking a cigarette, white teeth reflecting the flames as if the fire were being born from within his soul instead of flickering from the body at his feet. They locked eyes, no more than a second, but it was enough for Petrosky to glimpse the void inside the man—no ferocity, no anger or concern, only a dark, blank, remorselessness.

Thompson ran for the stairs and up, out of Petrosky's sight.

"Petrosky!" Jackson called from behind him. She was on the walk, gesturing wildly to the window where he'd originally seen Thompson. With one final glance at the now empty downstairs, Petrosky shot away from the glass to join her on the lawn, expecting to see Thompson there already, peeking out from above. But he wasn't. Upstairs, the window where they'd first seen the flames burned brighter, hotter, yet still not as fiercely as those downstairs—either Thompson hadn't used accelerant on the top floor, or he'd controlled the flames some other way to make these rooms burn more slowly.

And Petrosky knew why.

There was movement behind the panes that was not the orange glow of burning timber. Not Thompson. *Oh shit.* A figure with blond hair hit the glass, fire at her back, mouth open in a silent wail, fingers scrabbling at the locking mechanism. Had Thompson disabled the window lock? Of course he had; the man had always been a meticulous motherfucker. He wanted the girl to die there. But he hadn't slit her throat as he had his wife's, as he had with his other victims— because he didn't want her to die quickly. He wanted her alive so she could suffer. Maybe he wanted to watch her burn.

"Break it! Break it and fucking jump!" Petrosky was screaming, but either the girl in the window couldn't hear him, or she was too panicked to understand. On one side of her, the curtain went up in a blaze of yellow, and she jumped back from it, her terrified eyes reflecting the fire.

"The fire department will be here soon—"

"Not soon enough," Petrosky snapped. Jackson hadn't seen Thompson in the living room, the way he'd leapt for the stairs. That maniac would make sure his own daughter was dead, and if she died, if Petrosky lost her too…

"This way, Boss." Petrosky jolted at the sound of Morrison's voice and turned, frantically searching the lawn for him, but he saw only the glitter of orange on the grass.

"This way." This time he knew Morrison's voice was in his head, but he heeded it all the same and ran for the side of the house, peering into the gloom, trying to find—

There. A spigot. He cranked the nozzle and snatched the hose from its bearings, holding it above his head. Cold water soaked his hair as it poured over him like an icy waterfall, but the water did nothing to calm the heat in his gut, in his face, in his brain. He could not let this girl die. Not one more girl. When his shoes were sopping, he tore off along the walk again, soles squishing against the concrete as he raced up the front steps, grabbed the knob—

He jerked his hand back, the skin of his palm singeing with heat, perhaps blistering, but he didn't care.

"Petrosky!" Jackson grabbed his arm. "You can't, you'll never make it, the smoke will—"

He shook her off him, wrapped his hand in his wet shirt, and opened the door. It hadn't been locked—Thompson had left it open on purpose.

He'd planned for this.

Petrosky ducked inside.

37

THE SMOKE STRUCK HIM FIRST, a sweltering wave of heat that felt as if it would melt the flesh from his bones. He ran for the stairs, or where he thought the stairs were, but in the time it had taken him to douse himself in water, the smoke had thickened to a deep fog that engulfed his senses: his eyes burned, his mouth was full of ash.

He coughed and yanked his wet shirt over his nose and mouth, knowing he should crawl, but also understanding he'd never make it to the girl if he did. His shoes made sick squelching sounds that he could feel more than hear—every other noise had been sucked into the vortex of roaring heat. The stench, probably from chemicals in the furniture and floors, was acrid and nasty even through the shirt, and the wetness on his face sizzled, scalding his skin. Not that blisters would make him any uglier than he already was.

He took one more step forward and slammed his knee against the railing. "Fuck!" He was sure he'd yelled it, but the word, too, was swallowed by the flames. He grabbed the railing, ignoring the heat in his palm, and hauled himself up, one step, another, peering through the smog to the open upper floor where a waist-high banister formed a square around the top of the stairway. He was open on all sides. If Thompson had a gun, he could pick Petrosky off from anywhere on the landing—but if that was part of the plan, Thompson would have shot him when he barged in. At least the smoke offered some disguise. He hauled himself up, stair after stair, trying to locate Thompson through the oppressive screen of gray. Had he already killed the girl? No, he'd waited until Petrosky arrived to set the girl's room ablaze—he'd wanted Petrosky to see her. But that didn't mean he would keep her alive much longer.

Petrosky's legs were heavy, the air too thick to breathe. Smoke poured from beneath the steps and through the carpet, and though the stairs were not yet on fire, the bottoms of Petrosky's feet felt blistered as if the leather soles of his shoes were melting to his flesh.

Feet were for suckers anyway.

As he came eye level with the second story, the smoke thinned briefly, and he noticed that no flames had ravaged the carpet on the upper floor. Thompson must have lit the girl's room on fire, then gone downstairs to take care of his wife, knowing Layla couldn't escape—even if she managed to flee her room, she'd never get through the blaze below.

He tripped, righted himself on the landing, and then dropped to his knees, crawling, squinting through the smog at the open hallways that surrounded the staircase. Then... *there.* Thompson stood at the far end of the hall, watching him, and Petrosky could just make out a mask over his mouth and nose, bright white through the smoky haze. Petrosky knew the girl's door by the smoke leaking from beneath it and from the way Thompson stood in front: protective, arms crossed. But he had no oxygen tank that Petrosky could see, nothing that would keep him breathing once the smoke thickened on the upper floor. Maybe he had it hidden in another of the bedrooms. Or maybe he didn't plan on leaving here at all.

Thompson didn't move, though his daughter must have been screaming, still struggling with the latch—she had to be alive if he was standing in front of her room, right? Had she tried to escape? Had Thompson thrown her back inside, into the fire?

Thompson had wanted her to suffer. He was drawing it out, savoring her panic, lighting everything around her, but not the girl herself—this girl, his daughter, was Thompson's most significant anomaly. His biggest deviation from pattern. Daughters were special—they were always special.

But no child deserved this. No matter how many times Petrosky had let Julie down, no matter how unavailable he'd been…he'd been a good father, goddammit.

Petrosky shot to his feet and bulldozed down the hall, wheezing through his damp T-shirt. Though he couldn't see Thompson's mouth, he knew the bastard was smiling from the way the corners of his eyes crinkled. *Fucking cock sucking goat fucker.* Petrosky went for his gun, the pop of burning wood from somewhere in the house making him hesitate, thinking he'd already discharged the weapon.

Then someone screamed—the girl, had to be the girl, or was it in his head? For outside of Layla's shriek, all he could hear was the snap-crackle-roar of the fire eating through wood like a ravenous, flaming beast. Petrosky raised his hand, weapon trained on Thompson, but Thompson took off, three steps to his right, down the back hallway, swallowed up by smoke as if he'd never existed. Petrosky's finger tightened on the trigger.

He's getting away.

But he'd be firing in the dark. Petrosky squinted into the smoke. Surely the man had a plan for escape—he'd have ducked into another room. And if Petrosky fired blindly down the hallway after Thompson, he'd risk shooting an innocent girl. He wanted to give chase, but that took time, and if he waited…

Petrosky looked at the door beside him, at the smoke pouring from the crack beneath, far heavier than it had been just moments before. That's why Thompson had been standing there—he'd added fuel, done something to accelerate the process. This was endgame. *Out of time now, old man.* He barreled for the door, slamming into it with the thick shoulder that bore a tattoo of Julie's face, feeling the pins that had repaired his old gunshot wound snapping in bright agony.

But there was nothing as bright as the fire when the door gave way. It rolled over the mattress, engulfed the rug, licked at the ceiling, crackling and popping all around him. Minutes, if that. Mere minutes it had taken him to get here, and the room was an inferno.

Thompson's getting away.

Not one more girl. Was she already dead? Petrosky dropped to his knees and crawled again, the smoke too thick in this room to see, the air too hot and acrid to breathe anywhere but close to the ground. His shirt, almost dry now, slid from his nose, and he inhaled a full gulp of charred air and soot. His eyes watered, his nose ran, his tongue tasted like charcoal. The smoke was trying to invade him, to break him. The fire wanted to reduce him to ash.

"Layla!" He tried to yell, but it came out a wheeze. He groped along the still intact wood floor, shoulder vibrant with pain, the smoky shapes around him obscured in a haze of gray and sickly orange. His knuckles hit the leg of a table. He reached with the other hand, felt something hard—*bed?*— the wood as hot as the devil's taint.

The edges of his vision were black, and dark spots danced in front of his eyes, but he couldn't tell if that was due to the smoke around him or if his brain was shutting down incrementally as his body lost oxygen. He had to find the girl.

"Layla!"

His hand bumped into something else—softer, less

wooden. Flesh. Bone. An ankle? She wasn't moving. Layla couldn't have been the one who screamed—he had finally lost his mind.

Not that it mattered anymore.

He heaved himself closer, hovering over her still form, and when he felt her throat—whole, uncut—his heart leapt. Pulse thready, but there. He heaved himself upright, choking on the fumes, feeling for the wall and the front window. The curtains had fallen into a burning puddle on the floor, but the window was still intact, smoke rising from the frame, threatening to ignite.

He scrambled up the wall and grabbed for the ledge. Paint bubbled from the sill, and the smoke was so thick it was like trying to see through a towel. Petrosky yanked out his weapon and shattered the window with the butt of the gun, clearing the shards as best he could as he leaned through the opening and hacked on the cool breeze—it was like his body had forgotten how to process oxygen.

In the distance, red and blue lights flickered their way up the street, but the trucks would never get to the window in time. The walls on either side of him were already engulfed in flame. He wheezed, the pain in his chest fierce—more acute than it had been just moments before. He peered down at the roofline, at a small section like a shingled awning just below the center of the window. Angled roofs slanted away from him on either side. He couldn't toss the girl onto the roof—the flames inside the house had surely weakened the structure, and there was no way of knowing whether she'd fall through the shingles to be burned to death below. And if he set her on the awning and she rolled off the roof, she'd land on the concrete walk, possibly on her head. The other option was to dangle her feetfirst past the edge of the awning and drop her straight down onto the walking path, but she'd surely injure herself even there. Where the hell was Jackson?

He had no choice. Pain screamed through his arm as he

scooped her body from the ground—*still, she's so still*—her head lolling against his injured shoulder. His pants were no longer damp, but dry and crackling, and every nerve in his legs sang with heat and exquisite pain. His jeans were on fire. Petrosky ignored the flames and hefted her body out the window, every muscle shivering with exertion and terror— was it too late? *Wake up, girl.*

"Layla!" He shook her. No response. Petrosky held her arms, dropping her body outside the window and past the ledge, the air cloying with the sweet stink of his own burning flesh, like a pig on a spit. Blackness encroached, and the roofline wavered, casting him into darkness for a moment. *Layla.* When his vision returned, she was all he could see. He adjusted his grip, sliding one of his palms down to grab her left hand, then the right, his arms trembling as he lowered her as far as he could. Might not be enough. But if she landed on her feet...

"Wake up, honey. Wake up. You need to jump."

She groaned. Opened her eyes. And as the fire lit at his calf and fanned across his thighs, Petrosky let her go.

38

—————

Petrosky thought he heard a snap when she landed, but it might have come from behind him or even within him. Though he felt little pain now. Everything had stalled, time creeping around him in lazy circles like the universe was sucking him, slowly, down a drain. He peered behind him, into the room, but it was consumed by flames—even if he wanted to go after Thompson, he wasn't getting through that way.

He'd failed. Again.

I'm sorry, honey.

He turned back to the window in slow motion, the sky beyond the wall of smoke as deep as a black hole and heavy with sorrow. Maybe he'd just stay here. Maybe it'd be easier to lie down and go to sleep.

Then, from outside the window: "Daddy, come on, let's go. You still have time."

He raised his half-numb fingers to his chest, expecting to feel only blistered flesh, but…no, his shirt was still there. The flames had caught the sill below him, but the damp shirt had managed to keep his chest from going up. For now.

But his legs. His pants were definitely on fire, and it was

315

creeping steadily upward, singeing his ball hair and after that… Shit, he didn't even want to consider it. Roasted like a goddamn cocktail weenie was not what he wanted in his obituary.

And now he couldn't feel his legs at all.

"Daddy, come on."

Fuck this shit.

He gasped in another breath, trying to clear his vision, trying to see the ground through the smoke that was belching upward from the first floor.

They'd already taken Layla from the walk. Was she okay? Petrosky leaned out over the burning sill and tried to swing his legs beneath him. He was going to fall and bounce like a goddamn beach ball. It'd break every bone in his body.

"Come on, Daddy. It's okay, Daddy."

She was sitting on the roofline to his left, on a gutter that shouldn't have been able to bear her weight, and yet it was. He was hallucinating. Lack of oxygen. But he didn't give a shit when Julie smiled at him and motioned him forward. One leg, lungs burning, hair singed, chest hot, two legs—*oh fucking hell*—the fire was scraping at his nerves with a vegetable peeler, every single cell splitting open in a burst of voltaic agony.

One foot on the awning. The second. Julie was still on the roof. He turned his face to his daughter and shuffled left toward the incline where she sat. If he tumbled through the roof, he'd burn to death, but he deserved it, right? He'd been a dick to Thompson, and that bastard had murdered Julie because Thompson was too much of a coward to man up and tell Petrosky what he thought of him. Smiling to his face the whole time.

The rage burned hotter. He took another step toward Julie., one hand still on the windowsill—he was on the corner of the roofline above the living room now. He'd have to let go to move farther out. He had to let go to follow Julie to the edge.

"Go, Daddy! Jump!" She wasn't smiling now. Her face was tight with worry, cheeks streaked with tears, the way she'd looked the day she'd broken up with her first boyfriend. The day she'd had a fight with her mother. The day he'd missed her talent show. On the ground below, firefighters were surely readying ladders, and Petrosky could feel the heat coming through the shingles where he stood, the subtle give that already felt more spongey than it had mere seconds ago.

"Jump, Daddy!"

He could no longer see the ground through the billowing smoke. Behind him, something popped, loud and final. Petrosky let go of the sill. The roof below him cracked, gave way, and he threw himself to his right, off the roof, into the gray abyss of smog and ash.

39

———————

HE LANDED hard on his left side, his hip lighting up in agony, the world fading into nothing and then blaring back in a tidal wave of pain. The fire crackled and snapped somewhere behind him, but his eyes wouldn't focus—all he could see was a wide swath of undulating orange and yellow and black.

Then there were people, picking him up, trying to load him onto a stretcher, and he fought and kicked at them. "Get your fucking hands off me." His legs were numb. Was his whole body giving out?

"Sir, we need to get you to the—"

"You need to get off me is what you need to do." No way was he leaving. Not until he saw Thompson's charred remains. Not until he was sure the bastard was dead.

"There's risk of infection, sir. You could die."

Petrosky pushed himself off the stretcher, choking on the fresh air. He looked for Julie. She wasn't here—he'd been hallucinating, he knew that—but her face…he wanted to see her face again. Maybe he'd go back inside, seek out Thompson's body himself. Maybe his smoke-infested brain would give him one more image of Julie before the lights went out for good.

He staggered over to Jackson, where she stood in the middle of the lawn, staring at the house. She squinted at him. "You going to the hospital?"

"Fuck that noise."

"I thought as much. Because he's still in there." Not a question. "I keep circling the back, but no one's come out. When the next truck gets here, the backyard will be crawling with firefighters anyway, but until then, it's just us."

Just us. Maybe she would give him a moment alone with that fire-fucking twat. "He was upstairs when I went to find Layla." Petrosky licked his lips—blistered, though they didn't hurt. Yet. They surely would if he made it through the night. "Is Layla—"

"She's got some burns and smoke inhalation, but she was conscious when they whisked her out of here." She glanced at his legs. "Better looking than you."

He kept his eyes on the house as Jackson looked back at an officer near the curb. Only two cops so far, trying to keep people away from the yard, though more would be here soon. He was afraid to look down at himself; he didn't want to know if he was wearing fire-induced daisy dukes. Flesh could heal, but his pride might not. And more than pride, he didn't want to see the extent of his injuries. He knew something was wrong with his charred skin, the way it was cold and burning all at once, but he was more concerned about the places it didn't hurt, where the nerves were too badly damaged to even register pain. "The locals know we're here for Thompson yet?"

"Nope. But they will. Soon as they find out this is Thompson's place, they'll wonder who we are. Probably want to know already."

But he wasn't ready to tell them. Wasn't ready to go to the hospital even if it meant his life. Because the tingle he'd felt on the back of his neck when he'd first knocked on the door was still there, spreading across his scorched back and down his spine. Thompson was alive. He hadn't left yet. And neither would Petrosky.

Where had he gone after Petrosky had barreled into Layla's room? "Let's take a walk," he said to Jackson. He didn't need a witness to shoot Thompson in the dick, but he needed a partner if he wanted to catch Thompson at all; there was no way he could chase the man down if it came to it. He limped toward the backyard, watching the house, hoping he'd see Thompson peering from behind a veil of smoke. Hoping he'd get to see the fucker burn. No one would deserve it more.

But Petrosky knew he'd not get that lucky. Thompson might be a flame-humping psycho, but he was no fool. He'd had a mask. He'd prepared for every contingency, even stoked the fire in Layla's room at just the right moment—otherwise, she'd have been dead when Petrosky got to her. But plan or no, Thompson was intrigued by fire, and that might help Petrosky catch him if the asshole was distracted by his own flaming creation. He was probably jacking it right now, letting the heat of the flame warm his skin while his daughter fought for breath in the back of an ambulance.

They passed the spigot where Petrosky had doused his clothing earlier, though the memory felt detached from him now as if it had occurred in a different place, or maybe in a different life entirely. Yet the coldness of the water stuck with him—every now and then a series of icy jabs, like taking a shower in sleet, prickled down over his head, down his back, over his legs. He reached up. Some of his hair was present, but in the back, there was none of the usual fuzz, just skin.

He'd almost been burned alive. Without his sopping wet clothes, he'd have burns covering his back too, not just the back of his legs. He had been so close to letting that bastard kill him. The rage inside him burned more ferociously than the pain of any injury he'd sustained.

Jackson stopped suddenly, hand on her weapon, and Petrosky stopped beside her. His vision was still blurry enough to be a hindrance to both of them—he couldn't see much of anything in the shadowy yard. But he could see the house. And below one back window hung a metal safety ladder, glinting with the dull orange reflection of fire.

Thompson had gotten out. *Goddammit.* He'd run, he had to have run, but Petrosky could still feel those hateful eyes boring into his chest as he and Jackson skirted the flowerbeds. A crack rang through the house, and from the front came the wail of ambulance sirens. The shadows deepened before his eyes and the stench of burning wood assailed him as he took another step back into the yard—

Thompson. He was near the house, stock-still behind a bush in a corner flowerbed, close enough to feel the heat. Half of his face was still covered by the mask. Maybe Thompson'd had trouble getting out. Maybe he'd wanted to stay inside and enjoy the flames for as long as he could. Either way, he'd waited too long.

Thompson met Petrosky's eyes, the bastard's muscles rigid and coiled like the lions on his stoop. Jackson yelled something, probably "Stop" or "Freeze," but Petrosky didn't hear which—he ran, his scorched legs throbbing, his lungs shuddering, his heart hammering so vigorously he feared it would explode from his chest. But Thompson was faster. He was going to get away.

Fuck that. Petrosky pulled his gun as Thompson sped toward the back of the yard, flying over a boxwood like he had wings on his shoes. Petrosky got one shot off, but he missed, and Thompson ducked out of sight behind the brush. From his right, Jackson streaked by Petrosky, screaming something, but all he heard was the rush of his heaving lungs and the thunder of his heart.

They were going to lose him. After all this, he was going to fail his little girl.

Jackson disappeared over the boxwood, where Thompson had been just moments before, and she, too, vanished into the gloom.

Petrosky followed, his knees shrieking with pain at every step, but it wasn't just his knees, it was his legs, his feet, his skin. The sound of his labored breath in his ears agitated him, and the fact that he'd let himself get here, let himself become a person who couldn't catch his daughter's killer… Julie would have been ashamed. She was probably watching now, looking down, wondering why she'd been stuck with a dad like—

Pop. Pop.

Gunshots? He peered into the darkness around him, but the nighttime shadows were too deep to see anything past the reach of the flames. No other sounds to tell him where the shots had come from, just the low, heavy whoosh of the burning house. Then…a thin squeal of pain from the back corner of the neighbor's yard.

Had Jackson been hurt? Someone moaned, louder this time, and he ran toward the cry, trying desperately to rid himself of the image of Morrison's body: throat slashed, lips red with blood. But he couldn't stop seeing it, and in the darkness, he saw Julie too, dead, burned, her face grotesquely contorted in a silent scream—

"Petrosky, get your lazy ass over here!"

Jackson. She was fine, hidden somewhere among the nebulous shapes beyond the bushes. The bloody images faded.

"Did we lose—"

"I've got him. This way, you old codger."

From the front of the house, more sirens approached: fire trucks. And cops. Someone had figured out whose house this was.

Petrosky was out of time.

He ran harder, faster, almost tripping over Jackson as he

passed the neighbor's swing set, and then the world came into focus, thick and hazy as if it was made from the black smoke of his nightmares. *Thompson.* On his belly, Jackson's knee on his back, his arms pinned behind him, his face pressed against what felt like sand under Petrosky's tattered shoes. He hoped some cat had shit in it recently.

"Want to do the honors?" Jackson asked him.

He'd been wrong about her. She knew what it was like to lose. She probably wanted to kill him herself. "Yeah, I do." Petrosky shoved the barrel of his gun into the back of Thompson's head. Thompson lay perfectly still, waiting for death—for Petrosky to end him. Waiting like he was happy about it.

"Petrosky!" Jackson yelled. "I meant your cuffs!"

Petrosky pressed the barrel of the weapon harder into the back of Thompson's head and twisted until a sharp inhale of breath told him he'd hurt the bastard. *Good.* "He killed my baby."

"You shoot him now, you'll take me down with you. Besides, do you really think the boys in prison will let him slide?"

Kill him. Kill him. Petrosky could barely hear her now. Julie, his baby girl—Thompson had destroyed her, cut her down like she was nothing. The house behind them faded into the background, and instead of ash and the acrid stench of burning brick, he smelled Julie, her shampoo, the Free and Clear detergent his wife had laundered Julie's clothes in when she was little. He could hear her breathing somewhere in the dark nearby. But she couldn't be there. His oxygen-deprived brain was playing tricks on him again. *Kill him. Kill him. Kill him.*

"Daddy."

He jerked back from Thompson's prone form, staggering as if someone had grabbed him from behind and heaved him backward, though he managed to right himself before crashing to the earth. He shook himself. Retrained his gun on Thompson's head.

And then she was there, Julie's face, her shining eyes, emerging from the dark like a beacon. Fourteen, but with an expression mature beyond her years, all of her illuminated in the dim light, though he could see no other shapes around her. She stretched out her hands and opened them, revealing a single golden firefly perched in her palm. She smiled, and the firefly took flight, and the moment it lifted from her skin, its glow expanded outward like the radiance from an atomic blast, and the sky disappeared in the cloud of white. The gun grew heavy in his hand.

"Fly away, fly," she whispered.

She wanted him to let her go. But he would never let her go, not now, not ever. He'd regret every missed talent show. Every missed opportunity to tell her that he loved her.

"Fly away, fly."

The world went dark again. She was gone. But he could still feel her, and in the back of his head, something warm and liquid spread like syrup over the surface of his brain and down into his chest like a soothing balm that calmed his heart. Everything he'd done, he'd done out of love.

His gun hand wavered.

Julie, saver of snakes, protector of insects, would have wanted him to save Layla. To help others. She wouldn't want him to take life away.

He pressed the gun back into its holster and approached Thompson again, noticing Jackson's eyes were now slitted with concern, or maybe she was trying to ascertain whether he still planned to kill the bastard. The handcuffs almost glittered as he slammed the first onto Thompson's wrist so hard the fucker choked out a sound that was half cry, half moan. Petrosky fastened the other cuff even tighter.

The shouts of firefighters and the whoosh of hoses greeted them as they walked back around the house. Emergency vehicles cast red and blue over the grass, overshadowing the dull orange reflection of the flames. Jackson strode ahead with her badge held high. Petrosky followed her into the pulsing lights, Thompson cuffed in front of him, Morrison laughing in his head, *Nice job, Boss,* and then only Jackson's voice was bellowing over the chaos, telling everyone not to shoot, that they had things under control.

I got him, honey. I got him for you.

Jackson waved him to one of the patrol cars, her fingers bisecting the light in a way that made it appear she was holding the sun in her palm.

And maybe she was. Maybe she had a dead child at her side as well, a child only she could see.

As he ducked Thompson into the car, Petrosky shoved a little too hard, and Thompson's head slammed against the door. He didn't bother saying oops, just shoved Thompson's protesting frame harder, clipping the door once more before Thompson disappeared inside the vehicle. Petrosky slammed the car door and stepped aside, disappointed he hadn't caught the guy's leg. He didn't think Julie would have minded that one. She also might not be sorry that Thompson was surely going to get his ass handed to him in prison—but he hoped Julie didn't know anything about that. She'd stay innocent forever, and he alone would imagine the carnage once Thompson's bunkmates found out what he'd done.

And Petrosky would make sure they found out. Death might be the most absolute form of retribution, but it wasn't always the most painful. He took a deep breath, and the air felt lighter, cleaner.

"You going?" Jackson motioned to the passenger side of a patrol car.

He bent and peered inside—Decantor was in the driver's seat. Petrosky lifted his hand and waved. Decantor raised an eyebrow, mouth dropping for a moment before he smiled and waved back.

Petrosky straightened. "You go." Riding to the station, listening to Thompson breathing… He hadn't killed the bastard yet, but he wasn't a saint.

"Hospital?" Jackson asked.

He shook his head, the skin on the back of his neck, itching against his collar like sunburn. "I'll get the EMS guys to wrap me up."

But the world was wavering, and his lungs felt tight. He might still be in shock, though that wouldn't last much longer now that his adrenaline levels were falling. "I'll have them drive me over to the hospital. Just have to make a phone call. My cell's in your ride."

Jackson nodded and handed him the keys. "Your life, Petrosky. But don't be a dumbass." She hopped inside next to Decantor. "And Petrosky?" she called before closing the door.

"Yeah?"

"Thanks for the book. I enjoyed it." She slammed the door, and Decantor drove away without another word.

'Bout time I got a little appreciation.

Petrosky stood on the sidewalk, watching the other officers securing the scene and speaking to the families that had lined up along the opposite side of the street. He wondered who among them had been friends with Thompson. Not that it mattered—they'd all be safer without a killer around.

Finally, he turned and limped toward Jackson's vehicle, the road growing progressively darker until the glow from the red and blue lights disappeared beneath his useless shoes. He clicked unlock and paused at the driver's door. Then he pulled his cell from the console and dialed the only person he could think to call, the only other person who would find this moment as monumental as he did. He hoped some new boyfriend wouldn't answer. He hoped she wouldn't ask how he'd gotten the number.

Even after all this time, his ex-wife's voice stirred something in his chest that he'd thought was dead, that probably would be dead again the moment they met—if they ever met again. He collapsed against the car, the soot in his lungs thick and heavy, his heart buoyant.

"I got him, Linda." Tears stung his eyes, and he didn't give a rat's ass. He let them fall. "I fucking got him."

EPILOGUE

"I love it, Evie."

"I worked very, very hard."

"I know you did." Petrosky stuck the picture she'd given him onto the stainless steel fridge with a piece of tape. Duke sniffed the paper then wandered his lazy ass away. Since when were refrigerators not magnetic? *Bullshit.* He never should have let Shannon talk him into a new fridge, but it did go better with his new house in the heart of Ash Park: cozy, but with two extra bedrooms for when Shannon and the kids came to visit. And not a single liquor bottle. He had put Julie's night-light in one of the bedrooms, but left her boy band posters in the closet—he'd imagined plastering his brains over those smarmy bastards far too many times. But Julie's night-light made the place feel like home.

He didn't want to admit to himself that he hoped Hannah might come back one day. The night he'd arrested Thompson, he had come home to find her things gone, and a piece of paper on the kitchen table with a barely legible note: *Thank you. And I'm sorry.* She'd known they had gotten their guy when he called her to have Robin verify Thompson's identity. She must have panicked—either that or she'd thought her story here was finished, her contribution complete. It had been a few moments before he'd realized that Duke was still there, sitting on his bed. A dog she wouldn't even leave with her boyfriend in Vermont. The animal was a gift, not in an "I got a puppy for Christmas" kind of way—she trusted him. Maybe he was worthy of trust after all.

But she'd left him with more than that because on Morrison's computer—the laptop he'd used for ridiculous memes and silly names—was her social media account, open to the message screen. Someone named SugarBaby with an avatar that looked like a pile of shit had written Hannah a message.

Poop: "I think he's dead."

Hannah: "What happened?"

Poop: "I'm sorry."

As he read on, he'd understood. Hannah had told her stepsister what had happened to her—probably to warn the girl—and had even given Stacey a blade for protection, left in the mailbox for the girl to retrieve. Melinda Charles and Stacey hadn't lied about never meeting Hannah. And Theodore Montgomery had indeed assaulted Stacey, particularly viciously the evening of Hannah's birthday as if the man had chosen that night to take out his aggression over his missing daughter. That evening, her body still bleeding in the aftermath of the assault, Stacey had killed her stepfather while he slept.

Petrosky had been wrong about Hannah, and yet his guilt over thinking she'd killed her father didn't burn quite so hot as it seemed it should have. For even when he thought she was guilty, he had accepted her, hadn't he? He hadn't been perfect, but he had always been on her side. Maybe she'd even felt safe, if only for a moment in the early morning hours when he'd held her and told her it would be okay. He'd just wanted to protect her. No one else ever had.

And Hannah had kept Stacey's secret because she'd wanted to protect another girl her father had hurt. Now she was trusting Petrosky to protect them both, and rightfully so. The *Looking Glass* killer was no more. A pedophile was dead, and a woman had been arrested—might be the wrong woman, but there was nothing a parent wouldn't do for their child. Plus, it sounded like Charles would get off light. If she didn't, he might have to take a trip up there, but until then, he wasn't going to deny her the ability to protect her kid. If he had it to do over again, he'd give the rest of his life so that Julie could have hers. As it was, he would spend his remaining days making his daughter proud.

Petrosky had turned Hannah's written confession to killing Dominic Harwick over to the chief and closed the *Looking Glass* case—self-defense, open-and-shut—hoping that Hannah would be smart enough to delete her social media accounts before someone else went poking around. Because now that Hannah's work in Ash Park was done, she had a life to live. And though his heart still ached when he thought of her, it was only because he wanted to help her. Now she'd have to make it on her own. Something told him she'd do just fine.

Fly away, fly.

"Do you really like it, Papa Ed?"

He stepped back and admired the rainbow, beneath which she'd scrawled "Love You Papa Ed" in little kid writing. "You know I do."

Shannon beamed at him, but Evie beamed brighter, her little girl innocence unmarred and amazing. They'd come back to visit for the trial of Julie's killer. Petrosky suspected it was because Shannon wanted to hold his hand as each case was picked apart, as each photo of Thompson's victims was plastered on the poster board at the front of the courtroom. When they'd brought out photos of Julie's body, Petrosky had squeezed Shannon's hand so tight he worried he'd hurt her. But he hadn't grabbed her when Thompson's lawyer filed for protective custody after Thompson got fifteen stitches in his ass.

That exchange had made Petrosky smile. He smiled more lately than he had in a long time, maybe because the ache in his chest had lessened. The loss of Morrison and Julie would always be there, but as he watched Brian Thompson sit down with a wince, Petrosky thought maybe there was room for justice in this world after all. Though if that were fully true, he'd be able to eat more pizza and donuts. The oatmeal he'd been eating might actually kill him, though the doc seemed to believe the opposite. The long walks he took with Duke in the evenings probably weren't hurting him either. But no running. He wasn't that guy. At least his shirts were fitting better, so he didn't have to go shopping like some *Queer Eye for the Straight Guy* wannabe.

His phone rang with the "Bad Boys" ringtone, and Evie grabbed it off the counter. "Here you go, Papa!"

He put it to his ear. "Got one, Beeker and Fifth," Jackson said, far louder than was necessary. "Whoo, Petrosky, this shit is crazy. Gotta be a white boy."

Petrosky snorted, and Duke appeared in the doorway, head cocked. "Wasn't last time."

"This time, for sure. Ten-to-one odds."

"Loser buys dinner all week. And call Scott too, would ya?"

After a few apologies and explanations to the chief—and an agreement to go see McCallum—Petrosky had wasted no time telling Carroll about Scott's persistence, his tenacity, and as Scott called it, his "mad computer and forensic skills," though why skills would make someone mad, Petrosky had no clue. But having a high-profile crime like the *Looking*

Glass case under your belt sure made it easy to get hired. And though Petrosky had ended up giving the interviews to the ten o'clock news, he'd made sure Scott got his due—and a new job with the Ash Park PD. He owed the kid that much.

Besides, it was always good to have a forensics guy in your pocket. Scott was a good kid, and he deserved some goddamn respect—though Petrosky wasn't above buying the kid lunch, then asking for favors. He wasn't a fucking idiot.

Petrosky rather liked the kid's father too, which had shocked Petrosky as much as anyone else. George Scott was a Vietnam vet, recovering from bowel cancer with his son's help. Now that Scott had moved George here, Petrosky actually had lunch with him a couple times a week—even let George call him Ed, though he'd be damned if he let the kid get away with it.

"Scott's already here, you crotchety old bastard. Now hurry up." The line clicked.

"Sounds like you're getting along with your new partner after all." Shannon scratched behind Duke's ears, and the dog licked her hand.

Petrosky pocketed the cell. "I don't need a new partner." But he had one all the same. Jackson had frowned at him the other morning, though, when he'd brought her a granola bar. She'd even had the audacity to call him a hippie.

"Do you have to go?" Shannon asked.

"In a few minutes. I want to squeeze Evie one more time."

Evie leapt into his arms. "Ten times!"

"Twelve." He tickled her armpits, and she collapsed into a fit of giggles. He had time. Ten minutes, thirty minutes, he'd get there. And when he did, they'd find their suspect.

He was a motherfucking detective.

Detective Petrosky's not done yet! Read on for a sneak peek at *Recall*, the next book in the Ash Park series! *When a*

councilman's son is murdered, Detective Petrosky suspects there may be more to the death—which looks like a professional hit— than meets the eye. Can Petrosky discover the truth in this dark and immersive crime novel?

RECALL
CHAPTER 1

"How'd you hear about this place?" Eden stepped through the half-cocked gate, squinting at the halo of orange around the single streetlamp in the center of the cemetery—brilliant compared to the olive-black under the giant willows that hung recklessly over the entrance. The headstones glowed as if they were hot. Dangerously hot.

"Don't worry about that." Sammy smiled, that quiet, almost shy smile she'd fallen in love with in ninth grade, though she knew he was neither quiet nor shy. He cocked his head—he looked just like Kevin Hart when he did that—and she finally forced a grin, though the night felt like it was pressing against her back. Behind her, the dark was thicker still.

"Come on," he said.

Eden skirted a broken beer bottle and followed him past the rows of placards proclaiming everlasting love, each plot more overgrown and neglected than the last. Dead tulips lay on their side on top of one headstone, the petals flattened with rot. The night had fallen silent despite the charged bustle just a few streets over, the girls in the three-inch heels —"Hey, baby, looking for a date?"—the hushed desperation of the sleeping homeless, the night-shift workers pushing through the masses to get home with bags of take-out tucked under their arms, steadfastly pretending to be blind.

"You sure this is safe?" A chill crept up her spine despite the warm late-summer air. Here, even the wind seemed muted.

"Of course. Not like the killer is still here." Sammy laughed. "You ready?"

She raised her eyes. The mausoleum, stones of smoky gray that had probably once been white, stood in silent vigil, the door splintered along the side from long-ago vandals. Her breath hissed through her teeth—too loud. Loud enough to wake the dead. "So this is where..."

He smiled, that smile again, and edged his way through the shattered doorframe. "This is it," he called over his shoulder. "You look hard enough, and you can still see Meredith Lawrence's blood."

Meredith Lawrence was the most famous person to die here, the first victim of the notorious *Looking Glass* killer, but she was far from the only victim. Eden swallowed hard and ducked inside the building after Sammy, suddenly far more keen to step over the threshold than stand alone in the open air.

She blinked. Dark in here, damp, tinged with iron and mildew so thick she could feel it—heavy, almost meaty on her tongue. Something skittered in the back corner, a harsh scratch-rattle, too loud to be an insect, but she couldn't see beyond the orange-yellow rectangle from the streetlight outside the open doorway. A rat? She hated rats. *Please be a rat.*

Sammy turned to her in the dim and pulled something from his pocket...his cell. She squinted in the sudden glare of his phone's flashlight, directed at the enormous stone slab that ran along the back wall like an altar.

"See?" Sammy stepped closer to the altar stone, his voice high with an almost childlike excitement. "Right here!" He ran one slender finger—a piano player's finger—along the edge of the stone slab, the place where the *Looking Glass* killer had tied his victim. But blood? The slab, like the walls, was gray and rotten looking as a dead tooth—no bloody remnants of the words the killer had scrawled on the back wall, no poems. Nothing of interest that she could see.

"I heard they never found him. The *Looking Glass* killer." Sammy whirled on her, his eyes bright, hand still resting on the stone slab.

"I think they did," she said. Hadn't she read that?

Sammy shook his head and turned back to the wall. "That was a ruse. They want us to think they got him, so everyone feels safe, but..."

She rolled her eyes. She knew better than to argue with him about his obsession, and maybe he was right, anyway. Most of what she knew about the *Looking Glass* killer was probably more urban legend than anything else.

"Can we go now?" she asked, and though she tried to keep her voice even, it came out a little tight, a little strangled. This was the third crime scene or "haunted house" they'd been to in the last two months; their last excursion had taken them to an abandoned property no one had bothered to clean, the scene of a particularly nasty murder-suicide— blood on the walls, blood soaking the floors, and the flies... *god.*

He turned on her, cheeks hollow and ghoulish in the flashlight's harsh shadows. "Are you kidding? I've been looking forward to this for weeks!"

"I know, but..." The hairs on the back of her neck prickled in the warm breeze from the open door. And was that the rat again, scratching from the corner? "I just don't want to get hacked to pieces."

Sammy sighed and ran his hand along the back wall—the wall that had once been streaked with Meredith Lawrence's blood. Caressing it the same way he caressed her back or ran his fingers through her hair. "Not like the killer's here now, Eden, just his...essence."

"Killer essence? You're so weird," she said jokingly, but she shuddered anyway. And beneath the anxious vibration of her heart, her stomach turned—guilt. He was right. He had been waiting a long time.

Snap!

Not from the back corner like she'd thought, but Sammy didn't appear to notice, busy as he was examining the wall. She whirled on the broken door, listening hard—her breathing, Sammy's breathing, hissed through the air, her heart thrumming through the veins in her throat. Nothing more, no other sounds, but her rib cage had become a vise. "Seriously, let's go, okay?" She tried to keep her voice from shaking. "I'm tired, and we have, like, an hour to drive."

"Fiiiine." Sammy grunted and clicked off the flashlight, plunging the room into darkness. She blinked hard, trying desperately to force her eyes to adjust to the hazy orange film from the streetlamp that had lit the room earlier, but the dark seemed thicker now, more domineering—she could see nothing but the black.

"Sammy! Where are—"

A hand grabbed her waist and she shrieked.

Sammy laughed. "Just me, just me." He pulled her into his arms and pressed his lips to hers, and the damp mildew smell vanished as the scent of his soap filled her nostrils—spicy, almost flowery. She relaxed against him...but only a little. Why was it still so dark in here? But her eyes were slowly adjusting; already, she could see the outline of his form, feel the heat of his skin—warm. Safe.

"Come on," he said. "Come sit on the slab."

"On the...are you fucking kidding?"

"No one's here."

"I'm not worried about that." But she was, a little. That snap could have been a murderer coming to kill them like poor Meredith Lawrence. *No, that's the horror movies talking.* If there was one thing Sammy loved more than true crime research, it was movies about serial killers, the more gruesome the better. Perhaps she should mind that they spent so much time on his pursuits, but if she was really honest, there was something about the pounding in her temples even now, the jitter of nerves in her belly, that made their dates more interesting than pizza with some idiot jock. And certainly better than the clichéd dinner and a movie her parents thought they were enjoying. He was the most interesting boy she'd ever known.

"I guess I can take you home…" Sammy ran the tops of his fingers under the hem of her shirt, skirting along her backbone and sending little ripples of excitement through her nerve endings, melting the ice that had stiffened her spine since they'd arrived.

She stood on her tiptoes to whisper in his ear: "Maybe we should go back to the car."

He edged his fingers into the front waistband of her shorts and undid the button. She stepped back toward the stone. Maybe it was just an urban legend—maybe nothing had ever happened here at all, and, even if it had, it was so long ago. And the cemetery owners had surely cleaned it up, right? That's what they did with public property, after the police took all the gross stuff into evidence. And heck, she and Sammy'd had sex in the gooey mud beside the boathouse upstate, same spot in the dirt where three people had been shot to death. No way the police had cleaned that up completely.

Eden backed against the slab—thank god her eyes were working again—and hopped onto the stone. Orange light seeped through the broken door. She closed her eyes and leaned into Sammy, listening to the heavy thud of her heart and the soft whisper of his breath against her ear.

Snap!

She froze. "Sammy, did you—"

Sammy toppled backward—no, not toppled, *flew*, ripped from her grasp, the pads of her fingers burning, pain radiating from her twisted wrist. Her limbs felt disconnected from her brain, because someone else was there now, a man, a huge man, the subtle glow of the streetlamp hidden behind his bulk, and he had Sammy in the middle of the tiny room—had Sammy on his knees on the cold mausoleum floor, holding her boyfriend by the...face? Yes, hands on either side of his head. And the stranger was muttering in a low whispery growl, some other language, one she'd never heard before, but it was like in the old horror movies Sammy watched—was he summoning a demon? *Are we sacrifices?*

Oh god, all the horror movies were right, and Sammy was right, too, about the black guy dying first, because Sammy was the one on his knees. But the big-breasted blonde never lasted long either. Eden was next.

Her mouth went dry. Ribbons of panic sliced through her throat, cutting off her airway.

She wanted to cry out, to tell him not to hurt Sammy, to say that they'd do anything, anything at all if he'd just let them go, but her tongue was a weight, cold and dead against her bottom teeth.

The stranger was silent; no more strange words. Not even breathing hard. Maybe not breathing at all.

Then Sammy screamed once, kicked his legs; a quick jerk of the intruder's hands—*crack!*—and Sammy's head twisted, too far, too far, his screams degenerating into thin wails, like a mewling kitten. Weak. And then Sammy wasn't moving at all.

The giant man straightened and stepped closer. "*'Ana last aleadui.*" She strained her ears, trying to decipher the words. Was he mumbling? Or was it coming from someone else, someone she couldn't see?

"I—I...don't know what you want." Her voice echoed against the walls, her heart a frantic animal trapped beneath her ribs.

"*'Ana last aleadui.*" It hit her ears like a growl of thunder—

hushed, threatening, but somehow distant. The man stepped nearer still.

Eden skittered away on top of the slab until she felt the back edge—nowhere to go, just this little space between the slab and the wall where once poems had been scrawled in blood.

"'*Ana last aleadui.*" This time the voice seemed to come from somewhere behind the man, hitting her ears oddly, harshly. Too low.

"Please don't kill me," she whispered. Sammy mewled. *Alive, he's alive!*

The stranger's breath hissed, too close. "You'll live for now," he said in a voice like silk, and she jumped at the loudness of it—not at all like the growly rumble she'd heard before. "You'll live for now, if you run." He moved away suddenly, his back against the side wall, deeper into the shadows, and the square of orange light returned, flooding in behind him, so bright now, revealing the concrete floor— *Sammy, he's not moving, and his neck,* fuck, *his neck.* The man raised one thick arm. Pointed to the door.

Eden clambered off the stone slab and pressed herself against the wall opposite where he stood. Ten feet away. One step forward and—

She edged closer to the door, eyes on the stranger, stepped over—*oh fuck, oh fuck*—Sammy's body and she thought she heard him wheeze her name, but the crazy man was there and he was closer—he was almost touching her.

"Run," the man whispered.

She did. She left Sammy there, the only boy she'd ever loved, jumped over his legs like he was a bundle of old clothes, and burst through the splintered mausoleum door into the muggy night air.

The streetlamps glittered sickly orange against the dew-soaked grass like bloody tears.

GET *RECALL*
on https://meghanoflynn.com

Love psychological thrillers? Try the Mind Games series! Start the series with *The Dead Don't Dream*. *A psychologist must decide whether her sleepwalking patient is a victim or a brutal serial killer in this unpredictable psychological thriller.*

THE DEAD DON'T DREAM
CHAPTER 1

MOONLIGHT FELL in harsh blades of white against the hardwood floors. It bleached the oak, but it made the filth on his hands appear black, inky and shiny and somehow heavy —tacky against his flesh. It was caked around his wrist, too, pressed into the tiny crevices of his jewelry, smashed into the circular gilded edge, smeared over the leather band. The piece was old as the dirt itself, as reliable as the ground beneath his feet, but it felt... compromised. Soiled.

He stilled, held his breath and strained his ears, but he could not hear the steady *tick, tick, tick* that usually echoed through the room like a second heartbeat—the antique clock from the night table was on the floor. Ticking away for a century, and now it was dead.

Dead. The word ate at the soft spot between his shoulder blades for reasons he could not immediately place. Though he was unable to feel his own heart throbbing in his chest, *he* wasn't dead. He was in his bedroom. A dream—just a dream. But the expanse between the area rug and the floor-to-ceiling window was covered in scattered bits of grass and pebbles. He could smell damp earth, the musk of worms. His feet were bare, cold against the rug. His toes were... wet.

Mud.

He closed his eyes, trying to force his brain to understand, but slivers of memory slipped by without offering explanation. And though he was quite sure that he was alone, he could hear the wet hiss of breath against his ear, less like air and more like the rush of some unidentifiable pent-up emotion. He could still feel the sultry damp of her lips against his earlobe, her teeth like knives, the canines of a hungry animal, tearing his throat as if she intended to sever his windpipe. His wrists hurt as if he'd been tied.

Was it really just a dream? Some of it was. The woman, her long blonde hair, her blade-sharp teeth—those couldn't possibly be real. No injuries marred his neck; no bloody ribbons of skin hung beneath his hairline. Though his wrists were sore, he could not make out any abrasions that might indicate he'd been the victim of some attack. But there were parts that felt more vital—details that stuck out in sharp contrast. He could see the moon in his mind's eye, the outdoor world gray beneath its glare. He could hear the heavy weight of silence broken only by the crackling whisper of skittering leaves. He could feel the rocks, sharp beneath the knees of his sweatpants—he could feel those abrasions even now, the enduring sting from road-rashed skin. And the dirt…

The mud was real. That was definitely real.

He opened his eyes. The dirt… it wasn't only on him, nor was it merely on the floor as if he'd tracked it inside. It was *everywhere*. A swipe of grime marred the window, obscuring the night beyond. The bedspread was crusted in fine streaks of thick black and wider smears of filthy gray.

He touched his face, his fingertips gritty and sticky—mud in his facial hair. The top edge of his cheekbone felt sharper than usual, but the dirt there was dry.

The blood was not. And though the world was a black-and-white movie in the silver gleam of the moon, he knew now that it was blood. He could smell it, woven through with the damp musk of petrichor, the metallic tang of congealing life… or recent death.

Bile rose in his throat. He gagged, his heart thundering to life, pumping furiously as if his body had only now realized that he was being pursued by some predator, his meat snared in a frenzied dance of ichor and panic. Then he was running, wobbling and lopsided, off the rug, over the dirty floor to the marble tile of the bathroom—frigid against his feet. Goose-flesh shivered along his spine. He threw himself onto his injured knees in front of the toilet.

Bile and the bitter remnants of vodka tonic poured over his tongue and dripped past his lips. But the dirt… oh, the dirt. That was far worse.

This was supposed to be over.

He retched again, again, then slumped back against the wall. He inhaled deeply, trying to steady the frantic throb in his temples, trying to ease the pulse that was turning his vision into a strobe, but he only succeeded in lodging dirt deep in his sinuses. He gagged and snorted, staring in horror at the earth still crusted beneath his fingernails and the slippery weeping chasm along the pad of his thumb. He had tried so hard to stop, but perhaps he'd only been lying to himself. The proof was here, everything he needed to know.

He'd done something terrible.

Again.

GET *THE DEAD DON'T DREAM*
on https://meghanoflynn.com

For fans of Stephen King. Distressed by her fiancé's sudden disappearance, Chloe Anderson seeks answers at an old plantation steeped in dreadful history—even as her horrifying nightmares begin to appear during her waking hours…

THE JILTED
CHAPTER 1
Abram Shepherd, present day

THE MAN WRITHES, his body twisting against the mattress, fists clenched, face shadowed beneath the low-hanging beams of the roofline. His olive-skinned chest seeps blood from wounds I cannot heal. He licks his lips like a nervous animal, and then cries out, high and piercing, as if someone were running him through with a blade, such a guttural incantation it sounds almost inhuman. And it may be, for who's to say what is mortal and what is not? From the moment humans emerged from Earth's womb, we have carried a thread of sharpness within us, a fury that expands when we allow even the slightest hint of that agitation to catch our gaze. Because we focus there, you know, fascinated by the wickedness we see laid bare like the flesh of a lover.

That madness becomes our own. And soon it is all we see.

I clench my pipe harder between my teeth, the smoke circling my head like an herbal fog.

The man's eyes snap open and focus—for an instant only —but in that moment I see his humanity concentrated there, fixed in that tiny glint of light around the iris. "Please, Father …" he croaks in a strong Spanish accent, and his head snaps back, his spine contorts—"Father, save me, help me"—and then his words degenerate into glottal, hopeless blubbering. "Perdóname, Padre, perdóname."

Forgive me, Father, forgive me.

I cough once, trying to clear the putrid, meaty stench from the back of my throat, but it remains despite the smoke from my pipe, the air heavy as the cross around my neck. Perhaps if I truly wore the Roman collar as I'd once intended, I would be better equipped to fight this. But even if I were a priest, no one is remarkable enough to be granted forgiveness; my deeds here are but a physical prayer of repentance.

The man moans, froth forming at his lips and dripping down his cheek to the bed like the ooze of raw egg white. I have seen this surrender before, oh so many times, but they do not all go so easily; the skin on my left leg still burns with my most recent wound. *Helen.* She fought harder than most, crying out in prayer as she fled over the lawn, red scarf flying behind her like blood spurting from a neck wound. Afterward, I could almost feel the quivering nerves beneath her flesh as if they were mine, the sharp agony as The Dark bound her in coils of hate that tore her soul from her body and dragged it to a place I cannot begin to name. It was over quickly, as endings so often are, and though I hurled my prayers into the night, I was soon alone, my only response the bitter howl of the wind.

The man bucks off the mattress now, spraying spittle against the pillow, wetting the stained green blanket. It will not be long. He has gone so much faster than the others, perhaps because the evil is thicker since Helen was taken; I can feel the violence in the air, seeping from The Dark like pollutants into a water supply.

I can practically hear the good doctor, my only friend, whispering, "You're obsessed, Mr. Shepherd. Delusional." The doctor would tell me I should stop this madness. "Go back to your wife," he'd say. But I've spent far too much of my life ignoring my calling—the past looms full of abandoned things, wasted moments I could have used more wisely.

The man's arms and legs still, though his chest heaves with the rapid inhales of a panting dog—much too fast. Then he screams again, loud and long, and this time it is wholly and poignantly human, and my own humanity responds with a painful tightening of my rib cage. Staring at the glitter in his wild eyes, watching him go from madness, to horror, and back, my heart vibrates with such savage intensity I think it might stop altogether; I fight against this, for I am not ready to be tossed into the fiery pits with my ancestors. I know what they did—I found the journals in this old house, hidden beneath a floorboard, the pages tattered and worn. How I wish I had not read them. Because now I see fully the wickedness I am up against—see The Dark for what he is. He's been tormenting these grounds for eons, spreading malevolence like a virus, and far more will be sacrificed unless I find another strong enough to help me, someone who can lure The Dark out, so I might expel him from this place. And if I cannot weaken his hold here, I will not have the slightest chance of salvation.

The doctor may believe he can ease my burden, soften the pain of the cancer, but he cannot ease the suffering of my soul—he does not believe there is anything to fear. But he will believe. Soon he will see it too.

I can feel The Dark even now in the coldness whirling around me, though there is no open window, no earthly source for such a breeze. The man in the bed shudders then stills, his breath a thin wheeze, his shirt covered in crimson, so steeped in his own pain he cannot not see beyond the tip of his nose. So many exorcisms, and every one ends in defeat. I still hear those lost souls crying sometimes—or the wails of angels, admonishing me for my failures. Or perhaps that is my own soul, crying out in the night, reminding me that my faith is not strong enough to heal anyone.

Yet healing is not the goal. Expelling The Dark requires far more unusual methods than exorcism or mere summoning; and something far more dangerous. The demons here must be allowed to roam free and all those near will feel their presence even if they are not perceptive enough to identify that barbarous clawing at the base of their spine. I do not know what it will do to those who are able to see the evil. Perhaps they'll go mad with it, too.

I sit on the edge of the bed, and the man's eyes snap open, the fear reflected there deeper and more harrowing than the malignancy that tightens the air around us, the breeze suddenly hot as campfire smoke. The Dark is messing with us, trying to confuse me. It will not work.

"The Light or The Dark?" I ask him.

"The Light, The Light …" Blood bubbles between his lips. I press a rosary into his hand—his mother's, his most prized possession, and it is the last bit of comfort I can offer. "Go now, my son."

"No, no, Padre, no … help … help …"

I lean close to his ear, whispering, the stink of his sweat ripe in my nostrils. "I cast thee out." He coughs, and his eyes flutter closed, still and silent as if in death. Then his back arches and he shrieks—even the walls vibrate with the intensity of his screams.

I spread my hands in the air above his forehead, his fevered skin already writhing, like a nest of snakes is wriggling beneath his flesh, and though my rings do not touch him, the skin sizzles—the smell of burning fat seeps into my sinuses. My wedding band, and Justine's band on my pinky, warm, the engraved crosses inside them brighter, hotter, than the rest. It does not matter that Justine no longer recognizes me—evil remains, but love lingers too, even if it is harder to spread.

I close my eyes, feeling the room shrink and expand, the entire house breathing with me. "I cast thee out," I whisper again. "Into The Light." I lean closer and whisper the final words, once, twice, thrice.

The man shudders. I lower my hands, the flesh on the young man's head still sizzling, burning, then extinguishing itself with a staccato sucking sound. My rings are still warm against my palm. And as the breath leaks from him in one final exhale, I feel it, the thread of insanity, the demon beneath his flesh, squirming at my nearness, gnashing its horrible teeth. I know precisely how to recognize it—I brought it here. And I will send it back.

The room seems to waver, contracting once as if birthing the evil from the atmosphere. Then it is over, the vestiges of spirit vanishing like the dew evaporating from the grass in the rays of dawn.

I push myself to standing, bones aching, and hobble to the window, to that pane of glass as perfectly round as the moon outside, and I am struck with a coldness in the gut, as if I've stepped into someone else's shoes. Is this what my ancestors saw looking out this window? Tonight I peer out at another world from the one I strode through this afternoon—the front yard is empty, the grass a dusky greenish-gray beneath the towering oak, and the earth is no longer sodden with spilled blood. But my heart hammers against my breastbone, and I see Helen's red scarf in my mind's eye, hear her screams in my ears, and the *snap* of her spine, see the way it appeared as though every bone in her body was being crunched to dust, blood spurting from the ruptured shell of her chest.

Then the scene returns to normal—quiet, gray-green, empty.

But it isn't really empty. I feel the energy there, lingering in the shadow of the porch, waiting for the next soul to be lured by the force that emanates from this place.

For every slight, there must come a balancing blow. Every dark deed done must be repaid in blood.

The girl, that unfortunate girl, red scarf billowing behind her, screaming, screaming … Helen saw the madness of this world, the evil that must be quelled. Everyone does.

But never soon enough.

GET *THE JILTED*
on https://meghanoflynn.com

O'Flynn takes you on a twisted journey through the deepest and darkest corners of the human mind." ~*Bestselling Author Mary Widdicks*

"With unbearable tension and gripping, thought-provoking storytelling, O'Flynn explores fear in all the best—and creepiest—ways. Masterful psychological thrillers replete with staggering, unpredictable twists." ~*Bestselling Author Wendy Heard*

**LEARN MORE ON
https://meghanoflynn.com**

WANT MORE FROM MEGHAN?
There are many more books to choose from!

Learn more about Meghan's novels on https://meghanoflynn.com

ABOUT THE AUTHOR

With books deemed "visceral, haunting, and fully immersive" (*New York Times bestseller, Andra Watkins*), Meghan O'Flynn has made her mark on the thriller genre. Meghan is a clinical therapist who draws her character inspiration from her knowledge of the human psyche. She is the bestselling author of gritty crime novels and serial killer thrillers, all of which take readers on the dark, gripping, and unputdownable journey for which Meghan is notorious. Learn more at https://meghanoflynn.com! While you're there, join Meghan's reader group, and get a **FREE SHORT STORY** just for signing up.

Want to connect with Meghan?
https://meghanoflynn.com

www.ingramcontent.com/pod-product-compliance
Lightning Source LLC
Chambersburg PA
CBHW021242190726
48289CB00005B/1455